RAT RACE

PRAISE FOR CALLUM McSORLEY

'An astonishingly good debut. Wonderfully rounded characters… A compelling story laced with humour and humanity'

Peter James, author of the Roy Grace series

'Twisting plots, grotesque lowlifes, black comedy, puns, over-the-top violence – and dialogue that bounces along to the rhythms of Glaswegian street slang'

The Times

'Callum McSorley is definitely a talent to watch. I knew within a page that I was in good hands'

Chris Brookmyre, author of the Jack Parlabane series

'Pitch-dark and yet dripping with warmth… Packed with brilliantly drawn characters, laugh-out-loud humour, and lots of blood'

Caz Frear, author of *Sweet Little Lies*

'Shattered from staying up until the daft hours finishing this. Loved it… A serious talent'

Kevin Bridges, author of *The Black Dog*

'Side-splittingly funny and fascinatingly brutal in equal measure'

Scottish Field

'A tartan noir comedy crime with a dash of hard-boiled grit'

Scotsman

'A grisly and darkly funny crime caper, written in Glasgow patter'

Sunday Mail

'Extremely funny, exciting and ultimately touching'

Literary Review

'Just when you're thinking *Squeaky Clean* is probably the perfect crime novel, along comes *Paperboy*. The biggest laughs, the seediest urban underbelly, the most irreparably flawed yet inexorably engaging cast'

Sofia Slater, author of *The Serpent Dance*

'There's nothing I didn't love about it… The most fun you can have with an industrial paper shredder'

Sam Holland, author of *The Puppet Master*

'A deliciously gruesome, darkly comic and twisty piece of work'

Tom Newlands, author of *Only Here, Only Now*

'A full-tilt sprint through the darkest edges of the Glaswegian criminal underground. A viscerally hilarious and sometimes brutal crime thriller, it made me laugh, wince and gasp in equal measure'

David Goodman, author of *A Reluctant Spy*

'A riotously funny roller-coaster ride through the seamier side of life with everyone's favourite detective… A darkly comic triumph'

Marion Todd, author of *Next in Line*

RAT RACE

CALLUM McSORLEY

PUSHKIN
VERTIGO

Pushkin Press
Somerset House, Strand
London WC2R 1LA

First published by Pushkin Press in 2026

ISBN 13: 978-1-80533-639-6

A CIP catalogue record for this title is available from the British Library

The authorised representative in the EEA is eucomply OÜ,
Pärnu mnt. 139b-14, 11317, Tallinn, Estonia,
hello@eucompliancepartner.com, +33757690241

Designed and typeset by Tetragon, London
Printed and bound in the United Kingdom by Clays Ltd, Elcograf S.p.A.

Pushkin Press is committed to a sustainable future for our business, our readers and our planet. This book is made from paper from forests that support responsible forestry.

FSC
www.fsc.org
MIX
Paper | Supporting responsible forestry
FSC® C018072

www.pushkinpress.com

1 3 5 7 9 8 6 4 2

For Elliot and Nina
(when you're old enough)

PROLOGUE

The birthday cake stopped him on his way out. Homemade, off-kilter, icing dribbling over the side like melting candle wax. There was a present next to it. Wrapped. The size and shape of a shoebox. She'd telt him he was getting fuck all.

She was already at work.

The card—a big sixteen, fitba themed—had no message in it but what was expected.

The trainers were beautiful. Nike Air Max 90. Virginal white. Expensive. Fran knew because he'd already bought himself a pair with the money he'd stashed away in his room. Days of labour for his maw. Only a few deals for him.

Something ached in his chest; he put his fist through the cake.

Fran was waiting at the bus stop licking sponge, jam and icing from his knuckles when Ferrari ripped up in his VW Leaf Blower, windows down, tunes pumping out into the sharp spring afternoon, hint of winter hangover still in the sky. "Haw, bawbag! Get in afore cunts hink am kerb-crawlin."

"Even the maist desperate, toothless auld hoor widnae be temptet intae this fuckin shanner." Fran slapped the roof of the motor.

"Cheeky wee cunt. They new gutties?" Ferrari craned his head out the window.

"Aye. Like em?"

"Belters. They comfy?"

"Aye."

"Good tae hear. Enjoy the walk!" The engine revved and Ferrari tore away with burning wheelspin, making Fran jump back up onto the kerb.

Twat. Fran did not give chase. He didn't shout. He just smiled. The buzz of the VW faded as Ferrari turned the corner and disappeared, heading back through the estate towards the main road, but hadn't fully gone before it started getting louder again. The VW reappeared, arriving the same way it had before.

"Wide-o!" Ferrari grinned. "Fuckin get in."

Fran went around the front of the motor to get to the passenger side, knowing if he went round the back Ferrari would drive forward a couple of metres as he reached for the door, making Fran look like a dick and Ferrari bray like the fucking donkey he was. Just as Fran was square in front of the car, it lunged forward, knocking him onto the bonnet.

"Fucksake!"

Ferrari howled like a moron.

Callaghan had decent digs in Dennistoun. He didn't live with his maw but his flat was well kept. Must have been in his forties, going by the greys and the crow's feet. Fran first became aware of him at house parties and was eventually introduced through Ferrari.

He wasn't scary the way gangsters were supposed to be scary. He had a foppish way of dressing—trendy if you were a bit alternative. And had this booming, musical voice like he was doing panto. Nah, no way Fran would be afraid of this bender.

That was a year ago; his opinion had been changed.

"Mr Callaghan." Fran beamed and held out his hand, gave the man a firm shake. He'd been watching IG reels about being a successful entrepreneur and making lasting business connections. He'd gathered that it didn't matter what you were trading.

Whether it was nutritional supplements or class As (world leaders sold bombs to each other, fucksake!), professionalism and a can-do attitude to problem-solving were the keys to success. And a firm handshake. Fran was still working on that—his palms were too sweaty.

"Mr Forbes!" Callaghan ate this shite up too. Probably watched the same videos. "Moan in. Can a get ye a tea or coaffee? Goat ma paws oan some lovely beans roastit right here in Glesga. Artisanal coffee made doon the Barras, who the fuck widae thoat it, eh?"

While Callaghan was going through this spiel, Fran was being patted down by a huge lump of a man, big as a house, no lights on inside. Even Ferrari, the bold eejit, kept his eyes on the floor and his mouth shut as the Big Show squeezed his meaty digits all over him, dipped in his pockets, cupped his crotch.

Satisfied, he led them into the living room, which was charity-shop chic yet somehow expensive-feeling though it was all old odds and ends. The patterned couch was comfy and smelt like a library. Poncy affectation, all this, Fran thought, though he secretly liked it. Not to his taste but it was a step up for sure. A step he wanted to go up himself. Which was why he'd asked for this meeting.

"That's a loat ae gear," Callaghan said after a long, stagy whistle. "A admire yer ambition. But that's a loat ae gear tae front..."

Fran's heart thumped. He clasped his fingers together to stop them wiggling from excess adrenaline with nowhere to go. Callaghan was tipping towards agreeing, Fran could feel it, could see the almost-smile on the man's face as he considered Fran's deal. "The last three months av geed ye a return oan investment ae nearly two hunner per cent. Av tapped intae a growin stream ae demand an a client base wae the money tae spend."

Callaghan gave a big smile, showing off yellowed eye teeth which sat proud of the set. "Listen tae him, the Wolf ae Welfare Street."

Fran forced himself to laugh. "Fair doos. But a willnae be there firever."

"A don't believe ye will." Callaghan held out his hand. Fran's was still too sweaty but he stuck it out there. Callaghan snatched him, crushed his knuckles. Fran squirmed, could feel bones shifting, painful and sickly. "A need tae know ye understawn the stakes here, son." His eyes were piercing Fran's; Fran forced himself to look back, even as his eyeballs prickled from the pain. *Good eye contact is paramount to broadcasting your own confidence but also shows that you are *listening*.*

The Thing That Happened to Gary McOwen flashed through Fran's mind. ("They hud tae use skin fae his arse cheek tae make a new nose," Ferrari had said. "A fuckin arse-nose!")

"A do," Fran said, keeping the strain from his voice as best he could. Callaghan released him.

"It's a double celebration then." Callaghan was all smiles again. "Heard it's yer birthday the day, wee man! Sweet sixteen an never bin kissed!" He winked at his flunky, who went to the kitchen and returned with a bottle of whisky. "This is fir you, son. Lagavulin, sixteen year auld. Bin brewin yer hale life." They filled tumblers. "Here's tae us an here's tae you. Happy Birthday."

Fran and Ferrari were giddy when they left, not just from the whisky. It was on. Fran was on. Up, up and away. Ten days later, he would take delivery of two kilos of coke to punt.

Ten days later…

MARCH 2020

LOCKDOWN

…FUCK.

"This is a fuckin disaster, man! Fuckin Chinese bat-eatin bastarts!" Ferrari was yelling up at the first-floor window of the flat where Fran was poking his head out. Ferrari was holding a pot and wooden spoon, in case anyone asked what he was doing out there on the doorstep. "A awready used up ma ootside oor this mornin, hud tae get some fuckin peace fae the Wummin." Fran had pointed out it was only two in the afternoon and the "Clap for Carers" wasn't till eight, but it didn't seem to ruffle him.

Fran's own maw was at work. She was on the front line down at the Tesco Metro. School was off, though Fran couldn't give a fuck about that. He was leaving anyway come June, no chance he'd be taking part in Zoom lessons on the laptop.

"Pricks couldnae just stick tae fuckin chow mein an prawn crackers like the fuckin rest ae us! Wit the fuck we gonnae dae?! Callaghan's gonnae huv oor bawsacks hangin fae his rear-view mirror like furry dice—"

"*Shhhhh!* Fuck up!" The question had been bothering Fran too. As had the visions of what Callaghan would do to him if he didn't deliver on his end of the deal. He did not want to end up like Arse-Nose McOwen. "Bothering" was an understatement. He'd been clawing at the walls in sweaty panic. Getting outside once a day, to the same drab streets he'd lived in all his life, suddenly felt like being released into the wild after captivity. The air itself seemed fresh and raw, the quiet and distance from people and cars an eerie novelty. Everyone suddenly being friendly bastards and playing let's-get-along, doffing their hats as they made space for each other on the pavement, do-si-do-ing like country dancing... Mental.

It was good to have people out your fucking way though, especially when you're a steaming cauldron of stress. Fran's one state-sanctioned outdoor sojourn each day was a soldierly quick-march from the flat in Fernhill to the Cathkin Braes, where he'd find a nice quiet hill with a good view to scream at, then come home. Back to his sock-smelling bedroom, where he'd scroll influencer reels and leaf through overdue library copies of *The Art of the Deal* and *The Art of War*. Too bad there wasn't *The Art of Punting Two Kilos of Colombian Sinus Seasoning When Everybody Is Locked Up in Their Hooses.*

Ferrari continued whingeing. "Every cunt else is pure huvin a magic time oan fuckin furlough while wur goin doon the fuckin tube."

Fran suddenly understood that thing in cartoons where a character has an idea and a little light bulb pings on above their head. It was exactly like that. "Yer right. Some cunts are huvin the best time ae their lives oan full pay. Fuck aw responsibilities, nae early starts, nae late finishes. An perties are still happenin, whether Nicola says we can or no. The market's still there—it's distribution that's the proablem."

"Can ye stoap talkin like a fuckin bellend?"

"Naw." Fran laughed. "We just need tae get the *hing* tae the people. That's aw."

"An how dae we dae that? Evryware's closed an naebdy's allowed oot."

"They're allowed oot wance a day. An indoor places are closed but there's the hale wurrold ootside that's still open."

Fran was already searching Amazon for a pair of good running shoes, some spandex and an armband holster for his phone—better look the part. He brought up a Google map of Greater Glasgow and all its many parks and walking routes and green spaces and began to cross-reference with his contacts list. He'd prepare a message. Fran was still in business. And due to "product scarcity" and "hazardous delivery conditions", prices had to go up.

Fran ran all over Glasgow. He met people in parks, on nature trails, hiking routes. He ran to every corner of the city. He delivered product and he collected capital. Right out in the open. His feet pounded concrete. Miles and miles of the stuff. He ran for hours at a time. His muscles toughened, his breathing went from ragged to steady. His body, after the initial shock and resistance, began to crave the movement, the adrenaline, the punishing exhaustion. The blisters and chafed nipples became bearable torture, worth the pain.

He made Callaghan's money back and then some. He was in the clear. But he didn't care about that any more. He'd discovered something else. Something which made him truly free.

(Also, his times were really fucking good.)

NOW

1

All good things come to an end. An athlete's life is an inevitable parabola. Unfairly though, the upward climb is sharp, the plateau short and the downward slide long. Even more unfairly for Fran, the beginning of his descent was premature.

"Fuckt knees," the doctor had said. At least, that's what Fran's da had understood from the consultation.

(As soon as Fran started doing well running at national level, his auld man came crawling out the woodwork, keen to do a bit of fathering and a bit of coaching for his now-good-for-something son. Even so, by that time, Fran and his maw weren't speaking, so he made the questionable move of going to live with the man.)

Fuckt Knees: major surgery and rehab required.

→ Money required.

And though Fran had made a decent wedge from marathons and sponsorship deals, the occasional magazine ad, it was a US clinic he wanted to go to for the surgery, and it was out of reach. "We could find somewhere nearer hame, eh? Much cheaper options in Europe. Turkey—"

"Am no gettin a fuckin hair transplant, Da, this is fuckin serious. This needs done right. A want that guy in LA—bone surgeon tae the stars." The Californian orthopod was a miracle worker, famous for putting pro skateboarders who'd exploded their legs and NFL kickers who'd reversed the bend of their career-making knee back in action, and he could do the same for Fran.

Fran needed to run. It couldn't be over yet. He wasn't ready for that and he damn well wasn't going to slow down and accept it.

He was twenty-two: he was a prime specimen. He was (nearly) six foot of skinny wire muscle and rock-hard endurance with more stored-up sperm than the Dalai Lama.

But saving was taking too long. As the months passed, he was missing races and placing poorly in the ones he did run. He needed to do something drastic. He needed someone to lend him a fortune on tick.

"Well, well, well, if it isnae the Mo Farah ae Fernhill." Callaghan still looked ageing-hipster-suave in silvering beard, double denim, cuffs of his trews turned up high showing thick wool climbing socks and thick-soled Chelsea boots. He still talked like he was on a stage, although the whole act was more tempered, the man more secure in himself. That's what success does to you. Fran knew it. And while he'd been clocking up the miles and the medals, Callaghan had been doing the same in his own vocation. Kingpin of Glasgow now.

So Fran heard from Ferrari, who in six years had aged ten but still called himself Ferrari and drove an Aldi knock-off *Fast & Furious* motor and hung around with school-aged kids. Ferrari was not pleased to see his old mucker, and Fran's request to be once again introduced to Ruaridh Callaghan was met with a waft of gleeful *schadenfreude*: "How the mighty huv fallen, eh?"

Callaghan's ribbing had the same tang to it but the envy that drove it was better-hidden, not openly pathetic.

They weren't meeting in Callaghan's home as they used to—Fran gathered he was no longer in Dennistoun and had moved somewhere more befitting his status at the top of the food chain—but in the security office of an old indoor shopping centre which was in the middle of refurbishment. Callaghan sat in a worn-out swivel chair in front of a bank of dead CRT screens and VCRs which were home to families of spiders. It was kitschy in the same way his old flat was. Suited him. Fran remembered his very first impression of Callaghan and reminded himself to be afraid.

"So wit brings Francesco Forbes back tae ma humble oaffice? Av bin keepin an eye oan ye, ye know. Readin aboot ye in the papers, seein ye oan the telly. Even put a few flutters oan ye, won us a wee bit ae dosh, thank ye very much."

"Yer welcome."

"Fuckin great tae see a workin class boay dae *gid* so it is." People said this but often didn't mean it. Callaghan's theatrical schtick made it even harder to tell if he was being genuine or not.

"Cheers, Mr Callaghan."

"It's no a lifelang career, but. Is it? Bein an athlete, a mean. Early retirement age." The way Callaghan said it, Fran could tell he'd heard the murmurs around his presumed injury. "Yev goat tae make plans fir the future an aw. Be a shrewd investor. Which a know ye are, Mr Forbes." He smiled, showing his wolfish eye teeth, which gave an edge to his otherwise Glasto-dad style. "When Ferrari says tae me ye were lookin fir a meetin it put me in mind ae that time just afore Covid. A wis so impressed. Here's a young lad wae his heed screwed oan, a thoat. An a wis right."

Fran shuffled in his seat, uncomfortable with the compliment. If it was indeed a compliment.

"Who knew it wid lead tae this hale other life, eh?"

"No me."

"But here we are again."

"Aye." Callaghan's eyes were penetrating, not at all connected to the polite smile he wore in the silence between them. Fran held his gaze despite the nerves needling away in his intestinal tract like some cactus-haired parasite had climbed up inside it.

To look away would be submissive, beta. And he was already on the bad foot because he was the one asking a favour.

"Right then, son, cerds oan the table."

Fran told his story of woe and, crucially, the amount of money he would need to put things right, along with a repayment plan he'd devised which would, of course, be favourable to Callaghan. (You could not flub the accounts during a pitch—you need to know your numbers off by heart.) He'd factored in that Callaghan would certainly push him up on the interest points, but hoped he'd guessed correctly where the ceiling would be. (Know your enemy.)

"A fine idea," Callaghan said when Fran had finished. "Well thoat oot, clearly planned an, cept fir the interest percentage, which ad haggle wae ye oan, a wid, in other circumstances, huv bin happy tae lend ye the dough..."

In other circumstances. Fran's stomach dropped.

"But..."

But. His heart rattled.

"This time it's a no."

Fran visibly sagged. The rage and frustration which had been building over the last year of DNFs and X-rays and HA injections was ready to burst out of him. And if not looking someone in the eye was a beta move, then crying in front of them was somewhere so low on the Greek alphabet Fran didn't even know the word for it but it corresponded to "Z".

"Moan, son. Nae need tae look sae blue. Mind, am a bright boay too. A shrewd investor an aw. How dye hink a goat here?" He lifted his arms in a mocking gesture to the grand surrounds of the old security room. "When Ferrari goat in touch tae say ye wantet tae meet, the bubbles in the auld loaf ae breed startet poppin. Serendipity, you comin here like this, so it is. See, av ma ain deal tae offer ye. Hows aboot this?"

2

A month after they shook hands, Fran returned to the shopping-centre construction site to take receipt of the "key". After it had been handed over, he would immediately head to the airport. His flight to Istanbul via London left that night, then it was on to Moscow, arriving Friday evening. Hand luggage only. Essentials inside: passport; visa; watch; water bottle; tit tape; trainers, shorts and vest; his number for the Moscow Marathon on Saturday.

His da had went ballistic when he told him he'd signed up for it: "Ye want yer legs tae fuckin faw aff?!"

"Says you. How many fags an tinnies has it bin the day?"

"Aw fuck aff wae that."

"Wis it Greggs fir breakfast, lunch an dinner again?"

"It wis lunch, an it wis a ham fuckin salad baguette!"

This went on until the Moscow Marathon had been forgotten.

"Easy way intae the country," Callaghan had explained. "Well above board, an you bein who ye are, totally plausible an aw. Cover as tight as a rubber johnny." The rest of the plan was also "simple". Fran was to go to Moscow, do his thing (if he could hack it), then that night he was to head out for a celebratory drink at a specific bar, where he would be approached by some specific men. They would take the "key" from him. Job done. "Huv a celebratory scoop fir real, get oan the plane hame the next mornin, fresh as a weed, an by the time the wheels hit tarmac, yel huv the necessary fees fir the knees." How could Fran say no? It was much preferable to owing the man a debt for the next decade.

So he'd thought until he approached the old shopping centre on the big night and sweat started to prickle cold on his back and the Fear rushed him. It wasn't that Fran was unused to risk—sketchy situations were par for the course when you were a drug dealer (though one of the reasons Fran was so successful at it was that he'd cultivated a middle-class client list, which lowered his chances of being mugged for his supply or asked for tick)—but it had been a while. He preferred runner's high to the adrenaline blitz of carrying out a job.

Smuggling. Into Russia. Russia, for fucksake! You could end up in the fucking Gulag. Locked up in the Kremlin dungeons with Vlad Putin in a gimp suit.

He took deep breaths to calm himself, the way he did before a race when his body was over-eager to get moving. It wasn't like he was waddling through passport control with a brick of pure ski mask up his hole. It was just a USB stick tucked into the front pouch of his backpack. Just a key which accessed a crypto wallet with a million dollars' worth of Douche-Coin or whatever to trade for something which Callaghan would not tell him about—not his problem, best not to know, don't even ask.

"Here he his." Callaghan's voice boomed in the stripped-out mall. He wore a hard hat over his swept-back hair. With him were his chief whipping boys: the Big Show, who Fran remembered from his dealing days; a short, older chap who looked like he kept a nice front garden; a gorgeous model of a man, only a little older than Fran, with the same hints at Italian heritage in his features, and in the style of his tailored suit; and, ratty and out of place, Ferrari, who'd offered to take Fran to the airport fir auld lang syne.

Except for Ferrari and Fran, they were all tooled up. A panic crashed through Fran's brain and body that he'd walked into an ambush. That they were about to kill him. He got hold of it—they had no reason to do that. They needed him. He needed them. There was mutual benefit at stake. A solid business deal.

"Sorry aboot the hit-skwad look," Callaghan said, reading his mind. "Ye cannae be too careful. Load ae readies wur dealin wae, aye?"

"Aye," Fran croaked.

"Run me through the plan again," Callaghan said.

Fran regurgitated the information he'd committed to memory. His flight times, the route to his hotel, the marathon start time and potential end time, his path back to his hotel, where he would eat dinner, then the metro station he would go to, where he'd change over, where he'd head back above ground. The street and the bar and the drink he would order. Crucially, these last details, said in front of the group, were false. Only he and Callaghan were to know the real meet-up point. Callaghan's eyes drilled him as he spouted the disinformation and his mouth curled into a smile.

"Good! Easy-peasy. Folly it tae the letter an ye cannae go wrang." Then his booming voice dropped to a stage whisper: "Fuck it up an al still get ye the surgery, son, nae worries." He mugged for his troops. "But it'll be done wae a hammer an a pair ae pliers, an there'll be nae anaesthetic, ye hear me?" They guffawed with stupid laughter.

"Yer next race'll be at the Paralympics!" Ferrari joined in, killing the laughter immediately. Everyone stared and he took a riddy. Heads shook. *What the fuck, man?*

"That wis fuckin unnecessary," Callaghan said before turning back to Fran. "Here we go then." He took it from the condom pocket of his Levis—a regular memory stick. A cheap one from Smith's. Fran took it from him like a hot coal. "Guard that wae yer life."

Then a big hole opened in Callaghan's face.

3

McCoist watched Amy Caruso tiptoe around the dead, hunkering down here and there for a closer look, like a child searching among rock pools, her disposable overalls a toddler's puddle suit. They'd set up stepping plates everywhere to avoid contaminating the swamp of intermingled blood with their own footprints, which only added to the beach-combing effect. *Too long without a holiday*, McCoist thought. She took herself from the shore and back to the scene: an old shopping centre currently undergoing a refit, walls painted and floor glazed with the blood of six men.

"Incredible variety here," Caruso said, muffled through her mask. "They've been shot, they've been cut, they've been beaten. A proper skirmish went on."

"You want to sign up some auld geezers for a re-enactment?" McCoist said. "Beers and burger van, make a day of it. Bring your own balaclava."

"Well, we only have one wearing a bally." She stood tall and pointed to the body furthest from her. "Body armour too." That one had been shot in the hip—painful, but not as bad as the new gill he'd been given.

"Assuming he was one of the ambush party, the rest are Callaghan's men?"

"Can't say until we have them all ID'd," Caruso replied.

"Ugh, scientists. What are you an expert in again? Arse-covering?"

Caruso laughed, used to the DCI's style of grumpy bantering. Her irritation was usually only half put on.

"I can safely say this one is Ruaridh Callaghan, but. I can vouch for that, if my word is good enough for you?" McCoist had recognised Ruaridh Callaghan's corpse, even with the crater in his face—half his nose gone, left cheekbone exploded, leaving a pit of bone shard and mulched flesh. They'd had a run-in a couple of years ago:

A bogeyman called Billy Jamieson was threatening the lives of her ex-husband and their two teenage children. Callaghan took him out. McCoist had been there, had watched Callaghan tear the old demon's throat open with a knife better suited to slicing bagels than sawing necks. Callaghan's expression said "What a pity", while McCoist struggled to stop her stomach from emptying onto her shoes. Then DCI McCoist thanked him by trying her best to lock him up these past years.

And now she no longer had to. McCoist only felt a little disappointed. She was too busy wondering who would have done something like this. Callaghan was top dog in Glesga, big cheesy cheese, and not someone you crossed lightly. Not only because he was a heedbanger but because he made a shitload of money, a pillar of the local black-market economy (and probably created plenty of growth for the regular economy too). Under the captainship of Ruaridh Callaghan, the pockets of Glesga's gangsters were fuller than ever.

But there was always someone who wasn't satisfied with their lot, who wanted more, and was willing to go to extremes to get it.

This one's done then, McCoist thought with grim apathy, staring at Callaghan's ruined features, stomach turning at the gore, the rancid smell of it. *On to the next.* She'd seen out Callaghan's predecessors too—the last that spry old-head on the comeback trail Billy Jamieson and, before him, a ruin-yer-Ys-scary thug called Paulo McGuinn. McCoist had put him down herself. Flashbacks of the gunpowder explosion and the bloody blowback as she fired a bullet into McGuinn's head point-blank still plagued her; but she was fine. On to the next. Onwards and downwards.

"This is what I imagine a Bernard Matthews factory smells like." Gaz Travis arrived on scene with his nose wrinkled. With hard hat on and iPad under his arm, he looked like a surveyor rather than a detective constable on the Major Investigation Team.

"Gads! Why have you got to try to ruin turkey dinosaurs for me?" With him was DS Suffia Khan—sharp and reliable, a load-bearing staple of McCoist's working life.

"I'm not. I love dinos. You need to learn how to compartmentalise, Suffy."

"That sounds healthy."

"Healthy as reconstituted turkey snoods."

"Turkey snoods?"

"The weird haemorrhoid thing that hangs off its beak—the snood."

This earned another groan from Khan.

"Enough, please," McCoist said. (Although Travis was joking, McCoist thought he was right. There was no coping mechanism for spending your life around murders better than compartmentalising. The alternative was drink or, God forbid, therapy.) "Get your fill of the bloodbath and let's get organised with next steps. CCTV, door duty—let's see if anything odd was spotted in the area. Let's talk to the workies who are doing the refurb. I'll inform Callaghan's next of kin. We'll hopefully have IDs for our other victims soon and can follow those leads when we get them."

"Yes, gaffer."

"CIs—shake the trees and see what falls out. Someone knows what happened here. Too many people involved for secrets to stay secret." McCoist looked at the surrounds, the dusty, urine-coloured strip lights, the scaffolding towers and tools, the bare concrete floor where the tiles had been broken up, blank shopfronts with soaped-up windows. The headachy vapour of solvents was peeking through the thick stench of dead meat. "This place is owned by Callaghan. The reopening is his pet project. Let's look into that."

"Follow the money," Travis said.

"Good boy." Travis was about to make a no doubt witty retort but McCoist's phone buzzed and she excused herself.

It was her personal phone. Text from a withheld number:

What will they think when they find out?

McCoist whipped around, paranoid eyes scrutinising every nook and cranny of the rubbed-raw shopping centre. Not really anywhere to hide. The SOCOs, faces hidden behind masks and hoods, took on a sinister aura.

Of course, a text can be sent from anywhere; the feeling of being watched—that she could sense their malign presence in close proximity, their breath on the back of her neck, raising the fine hairs of her skin—was a natural product of the fear the message was supposed to engender. This rational thought did nothing to slow McCoist's racing pulse. *What will they think when they find out?* "They" as in her colleagues? Her family? And find out what? That was a difficult question because the list of things McCoist did not want "them"—whoever it was, anybody at all—to find out had become very long indeed.

4

[CONFIDENTIAL]
OP THUNDERHEAD / Audio Log
Recorded by Device OPT012/Loc B02
Speaker 1 believed to be TARGET Detective Superintendent Roy Devlin, on speakerphone. Speaker 2 is TARGET Detective Chief Inspector Alison McCoist.

SPEAKER 1
What have you caught, Bear?

SPEAKER 2
The body of Ruaridh Callaghan.

...

SPEAKER 1
Guessing it wasn't natural causes.

SPEAKER 2
Only in the sense that it's natural to die if a bullet goes in the back of your head and out through the front.

SPEAKER 1
That's your area of expertise. [Laughs]

SPEAKER 2
Looks like he and his boys were in a serious scrap. Five of them dead including Callaghan. And body no. 6 seems like it might be one of the attackers. No ID on him

yet and no idea how many were in the hit squad. Along with Callaghan, I recognised three of the other victims, all close associates. Fourth one was unfamiliar.

SPEAKER 1
What were Callaghan and his brains trust doing there? Business meeting?

SPEAKER 2
Maybe, though all of them were armed with something or other. Scene looked like the Roman Colosseum after the big lights go on.

SPEAKER 1
Deal gone bad?

SPEAKER 2
Could be. But, despite being scum, Callaghan has always been solid in a business sense. Not the kind to rip someone off in the conventional way. And I just...

...

If Callaghan was the aggressor, I don't see his entire squad getting wiped out. And it wouldn't have gone down on his turf. He was taken by surprise. It was an ambush.

SPEAKER 1
Suspects?

SPEAKER 2
Working on it. There are plenty of rivals, but anyone crazy and capable enough?

...

SPEAKER 1

What about our new favourite firm?

SPEAKER 2

I'll speak to the Burds ae Prey. I'm off to Callaghan's next of kin first.

SPEAKER 1

Happy hunting.

5

McCoist slipped her "dodgy" phone back into the inside pocket of her jacket. It had one number saved in the contacts, and the only calls it received came from that one number. *What will they think when they find out?* If there was one person who knew all about the things McCoist had done that she didn't want to be found out, it was the man attached to those eleven digits: Detective Superintendent Roy Devlin.

When she shot Paulo McGuinn—albeit to save a man's life—Devlin helped her cover up her involvement. Indebted, she'd begun a shadow career, working for Devlin while carrying out her regular duties with the Major Investigation Team—the mits. It wasn't that Devlin's aims went against those of the institution they both served, more that his methods often didn't subscribe to the laws that institution was supposed to uphold. He looked at the world as if it were a terrarium, where all life was a struggle to find the perfect place, balance and harmony, and from outside the glass he would make his adjustments where he saw fit. He lacked moral clarity; he was bent. And now, so was McCoist. McGuinn was the first person she killed. He wasn't the last.

But why would Devlin, the itchy-bollocked bastard, want to blackmail her now? And if he did, he had no reason to hide behind withheld numbers and cryptic text messages. No, maybe it was just a prank. Plenty of people had her personal number. In fact, it was probably one of Cam or Tess's eejit wee pals, daring each other to send silly messages.

She pushed it from her head, told herself to focus up as she saw the headlights of Travis's car sweep past then pull up onto the kerb in front of hers. They were outside a narrow, terraced house in Hyndland. Box hedges shrouded the ground floor and an overburdened apple tree took up most of the small front garden.

"Gaffer." DC Travis held the black iron gate open for her.

The storm door was painted defiantly lilac against neighbourhood regulations. Travis stopped McCoist as she reached for the bell. "One sec, sorry." He took three sharp breaths, puffing his cheeks with each one as if getting ready to dive into freezing water. He rolled his shoulders in a warm-up exercise and cleared his throat into his hand. Still, his whole body seemed strained. McCoist too started to feel burbles of laughter in her belly, not helped by Travis's little routine. The urge to laugh was common when doing a Death Knock. The body rebelled against the absurd and awful situation, attempted to usurp the solemnity expected. "Ready."

Ding-dong.

They waited. Too long. Travis was starting to crumble.

McCoist reached for the button again, was about to press it when a light came on behind the door. Then it was another eternity—Travis trying to shake out the giggles—before the door was finally opened.

She looked like anyone's wee granny. "Wit's aw this? Bit late fir Betterware."

Travis lost it.

The detective constable sat red-faced and humbled on a settee so deep his knees were approaching his chin. His chances of clawing back some dignity were slim. McCoist perched awkwardly at the edge to try to remain straight-backed and authoritative. The news had been broken and the tea and Hobnobs were out.

Mammy Callaghan's other son had been called over, his wife—a severely pale and skinny Tim Burton caricature—in tow. ("Make the teas, Brie," he'd instructed her upon arrival.) This son, Euan, had none of his older brother's style, nor the veneer of youthful enthusiasm Ruaridh wore. He had a pus like a soor sweetie was permanently lodged behind his teeth. When McCoist said a family liaison officer would be appointed and they could be given counselling, he'd responded, "Ach, fuck aff wae that." *Charmer.* (Admittedly, the idea of someone grieving over a psycho who could slit someone's throat with zero emotional anguish seemed ridiculous, but maws were maws and Mrs Callaghan seemed so sweet.) But what wee bro did have going for him was that he was not—as far as McCoist could see on the PNC—a criminal of any kind. Bad for McCoist though, he'd have made a good suspect otherwise. She'd have liked him as a suspect, *blowhard wanker.*

"So wit are yeez daein then?" he demanded.

"*Euan,*" his maw chided.

"Forensic examination of the scene is ongoing. When that's complete we'll have a better understanding of what went on."

"Al tell yeez wit went oan—ma brur's up tae his neck in psychos an wee rockets an, fuckin inevitably, he's been done in by them."

"Euan!" the maw shrieked, fresh tears streaming. Brie nodded her agreement and disapproval.

"But it's true, Maw, it's the way these hings aw-ways end up. In the jail, or in the groond."

His mother slapped his shoulder. "Reel yer fuckin neck in, will ye?!"

McCoist had to admit Euan had hit the nail on the head—big picture-wise anyway. Which "psycho" or "wee rocket" had done the deed was McCoist's problem.

"Let's all take a minute to—"

"Fuck up, Rodney."

Travis took a beamer—it wasn't the first time he'd drawn comparisons to the taller Trotter brother. He tried to come on stern but it wasn't in the young detective's wheelhouse: "Mr Callaghan—"

"Zit a crime tae insult a polis noo, aye?"

"*Mister Callaghan.*" McCoist had a much better line in "stern". Years of practice, years of fighting to be heard, years of doing donkey work for unappreciative morons who needed a map to find their own arseholes. In that time she'd cultivated an air of being just one disagreeable comment away from gassing you with pepper spray and torching your car.

Euan's puffed-up anger deflated a little.

"You didn't approve of Ruaridh's… choice of career?"

More hot air escaped and Euan sank down on the couch next to his mother, put an arm round her shoulder. "Naw"—his voice quiet—"like a says… it wis aw-ways gonnae turn oot like this. He wis aw-ways gonna brek ma maw's hert." He was crying too now, a thin dribble down his cheek he swiped away with an aggressive brush of his hand.

"And what did you know of his operations?"

"Sweet fuck aw. A telt him tae keep that shite tae hisself. Don't go involvin me or Maw."

The cosy old house in Hyndland said they were involved though—the mother at least. No way she was paying the mortgage on this gaff herself. Grand and a half a month, easy. In the catchment area for Jordanhill School—yummy mummies were practically camped outside waiting for her to die. "But you knew he was involved in organised crime," she pushed.

"Aye, cause he's bin a cerdboard gangster since he wis fourteen year auld. Keep at it lang enough an ye eventually become the real hing. But, a don't know any specifics, wit he wis up tae an aw that. No bin speakin tae each other much these past…"—he sighed—"ten year." He wiped at his face and nose. "Fuck."

"Mrs Callaghan—"

"Dorothy, hen."

"How about you, Dorothy?"

"He wis a good boay." An image of Callaghan hacking Jamieson's throat open burst into McCoist's head like the sudden gush of blood from the wound. "A good son tae me."

Euan grunted and Dorothy reached for his hand. "So are you." She turned back to the detectives. "A know he wisnae a saint. But, he did try tae dae some good. Those shoaps he wis renovatin. There wis gonnae be joabs fir the locals, a social hub fir the weans, a real place fir the community tae come thegether."

"Ach, Maw."

"Wit?"

Euan was clearly sick of hearing it. "Where dye hink he wis gettin the money fir it aw? He's no fundin it fae his paper roond."

"At least he wis tryin tae dae somehin. Naebdy else dis. No the fuckin cooncil, that's fir sure."

"Maw, ye huvnae even fuckin lived there in—"

A shrill, violent screech broke the argument. Brie jumped to her feet, cup of tea dropped on the floor. "WIT THE FUCK IS THAT?!"

A thing like a fat, snub-faced mouse was sitting on the plate on the coffee table, nibbling away at the leftover biscuit crumbs. Bold as you like, casual swagger in the way its tail draped off the side of the plate.

Now Dorothy screamed, and Euan screamed, launching themselves back as the rodent scurried off the table towards their legs, forcing them all to clamber up on the settee. Euan's stricken wife had gone into a fit, howling and shaking.

"Where the fuck's it goan?!"

"There!"

Shadow firing out from under the sofa.

Sensing a chance to be heroic, DC Travis was on his hands and knees after the bastard thing. McCoist rubbed the creases in her forehead, shut her eyes.

"Wasn't a mouse, it was a vole," Travis beamed when the threat was over.

"A don't care wit the fuck it wis," Euan's wife whined. "Didye kill it?"

"Aw, poor wee beastie, no, I put him out in the garden."

"Wit?" Euan looked incredulous. The silly smile dropped from Travis's face. "It'll just fuckin come back in! Are you seriously a polis? They actually let ye go oot tae catch criminals?" He appealed to McCoist: "Is it fuckin work experience week?"

"I assure you DC Travis is much better at police work than he is at pest control."

"Aye right," Euan sneered. "It's the same hing, just bigger fuckin vermin."

Outside, Travis took a deep breath and slowly exhaled—a nip in the night air made a little steam visible. He looked like he'd actually lost a few inches from his height. Not that the lanky bastard would miss them. "Sorry, gaffer," he said.

Annoyingly, it pained McCoist to see him like this. She couldn't help but see her own son, Cam, now sixteen and recently joined the wonderful world of work with all its frustrations and let-downs and tedium and embarrassments and malcontent colleagues. She wasn't able to protect him there. But she could throw Gaz a lifeline: "Don't worry about it. I've had worse Death Knocks."

"Aye?"

"No. But almost as bad for sure. Chin up." She nudged his arm and got a smile out of him. A small, warm glow blossomed in her chest and she couldn't help but smile too. She thought of Cam again, and Tess, her daughter. Hadn't seen them in a while. Work had been busy. Would continue to be very busy.

"Thanks."

"What the maw said about the renovation—community centre and social hub and all that—let's dig into that tomorrow. I also want to be sure there really are no dealings going on between the brothers."

"You think he's lying?"

"I think his anger is genuine; I think he's really upset. But where money—lots of money—is involved, things get... People will do anything for money."

"Except Meat Loaf. He'll do anything for love."

"No he won't."

6

It was like taking a cumshot straight to the eye: blinding, stingy, gloopy and hard to wipe off. Only the jizz was red and had ejaculated from the middle of Callaghan's face. Gritty with bits of bone and gristle.

Callaghan tipped forward, headbutting Fran, knocking them both to the ground, the back of Fran's head taking the hit this time as he collided with the concrete floor.

Explosions roared like a monster truck backfiring. Louder than anything Fran had ever experienced. He was deaf, blind, in pain. And stuck under the dead weight of Ruaridh Callaghan's corpse. Because he was dead, wasn't he? (Some approaching-rational part of Fran's mind was rambling, trying to weather the storm of adrenaline and confusion that had turned the rest of his brain to mince.) Callaghan had been shot. That's what had happened. He'd been fucking shot. Those noises were gunshots. Above, all around, they popped like fireworks. Distant now, because Fran's hearing had taken too much, felt like his ears had closed themselves off, the little tubes swaddling around the piercing pain deep inside. He kept his eyes and mouth clamped shut, his whole body locked up rigid, except the muscles around his guts, which loosened in terror, his sphincter gaping in shock.

Fran's bowels weren't the only ones to void. Dead men emptied out all around. The smell was ripe.

Soon it was quiet except for the harsh breathing of those left standing. Fran risked opening one eye a crack, so he could see some floor and legs through the spidery hairs of his eyelashes.

There was movement and he closed it again. His heart thundered, he prayed Callaghan's body was hiding the movement of his chest. He could hear someone moaning.

"Where's it hurt, big man?" a man's voice said.

There was a scream then some murmuring. "Take me tae the hoaspital"—voice a breathless whine. "Just fuckin drap me at the door."

More discussion that Fran couldn't make out. He risked another peep but there was nothing to see from his spot on the floor under Callaghan, whose blood was still oozing out all over him. He could taste dirty pennies; thought he might gag. Willed himself not to choke, not to move. *Stay fuckin still.*

"Please!" the whiny voice squealed. "It fuckin hurts."

A woman's voice: "Sorry, pal. Yer contract disnae cover workplace accidents."

"NO!" The word turned to a scream then a squelching gargle.

Fran's muscles twitched with fear. *Don't move, don't fuckin move.*

"Fuckin hell"—male voice. "We couldnae huv just—"

"Naw"—the woman—"where there's blame there's a claim." Her laugh was high-pitched and hiccupy, like she had a Guinness widget bobbing up and down in her throat. It made Fran cringe, lighting up the fur on his skin like a cold draught.

"No seein any big suitcases ae roubles kickin aboot."

"Search thum," the woman answered. "Wan ae thum'll huv somehin."

Grumbling from the men. "These are ma good gloves an aw. Real leather. The missus geed me thum fir ma birthday."

"Stoap whingein."

Noises of shuffling, ruffling, heavy lifting and heaving. Kicking and rustling. Bodies manhandled; pockets dipped.

Fran's breathing was short and sharp, heart thrusting its way out his chest.

"Ye only goat those leather yins wae ye or ye goat some latex an aw?" The woman did that awful laugh again, finding herself hysterical.

"Aw, moan tae fuck."

"Just sayin. If it's no oan thum it's maybe in thum."

Through fronds of eyelash Fran saw feet approaching. *Nononowitthefuckwitthe*—He squeezed everything tight, felt the USB stick still in his hand. *Goattaemovegoattaecannae*—Pressure as the man started to manoeuvre Callaghan's body about. *Fuckcannaehuvtaego*—

Callaghan was flipped over onto his back, Fran exposed. He opened his eyes. Above him, the man in the balaclava jumped as if he'd received an electric shock. Lying there, caked in Callaghan's blood, in his shitty shants, Fran must have looked (and smelt) dead. No wonder the geezer got a fright.

Fran reacted instinctively, as if he'd heard the starting gun go off. He lifted a knee and hoofed the bloke in the bollocks. The man doubled over with a yelp and Fran rolled and sprang up onto his feet.

He ran like Tam o' Shanter's mare: devils behind him. He put his shoulder into an aluminium tower the builders were using, brought the whole thing crashing down behind him as gunshots pinged off the metal struts, puffed holes in the plaster of the walls, cracked the window of an empty shop.

He barrelled for the fire exit—the stairwell where he'd come in a lifetime/ten minutes ago. Feet behind him. A hand yanked the handle of his backpack. He went with it, throwing his head and shoulders back hard, painful contact of some cunt's nose with the back of his skull. He slipped out of the backpack and crashed through the door. Didn't notice a bullet miss his head by a baw-hair, only vaguely aware of the door splintering.

Stairs three at a time, then the last five in one jump with his hands on the banister to swing him round to the next set, slow the fall.

Outside. Narrow lane between the building and a high wall which separated it from the road. A gulley of pallets and broken bottles and mangled shopping trolleys. Pushed off the shopping-centre wall, leapt up to the other, scrambling over and down into hedges, nettles, dog shit. Ripped himself from the bush and out onto the pavement. The road. His natural habitat.

His feet pounded the tarmac and his heart pounded burning blood around his body.

The key was still in his hand.

7

His watch was in his backpack so he couldn't say for sure, but he was pretty certain he'd broken a 10k record getting the fuck away from that shopping centre. PB definitely, maybe a world record. On his bad knees too. He'd been paying for it since: his legs were two lengths of splintered two-by-four. The amount of Deep Heat he was going to need, those masked maniacs would be able to find him by scent alone. Not that they'd need to, since he'd already given them his name, mugshot, DOB and birthplace—his passport was also in the backpack.

He was nearly home, moving on autopilot, body aching, movement pushing everything out of his overloaded mind (images of exploded faces, slashing knives, that squelching, bladdery-wet-meat sound as they killed that man, their own man for fucksake), when it suddenly clicked: *how easy would it be to find out where he lived from the info they already had?* They could be at the flat already, waiting for him. He swerved abruptly down a street of houses, then through a close, taking turns wherever as he tried to rack his brain. He could pick a hostel or hotel or something, somewhere random. Then he remembered the blood all over his face. No go. (He snatched his hood up, hid it as best he could.) He ran some more until he had to face the inevitable and headed for his da's gaff.

Da had bought himself a tidy wee two-bedroom flat in Govanhill a couple of years ago from the money he made being Fran's manager and coach. (His qualifications for the job were that as a lad he'd nearly got a start with Rangers before he'd done his cruciate, and that was that. Fran agreed because he was his da and that must count for something.) It was a bit of a mission, but given that he probably wasn't doing the Moscow Marathon on Saturday, Fran reckoned he might as well get his run in now.

His da's voice was thick with sleep and Carlsberg over the intercom. "Fuckin time's this?"

"Let us in!"

"Fuck." He buzzed him up and continued his grumbling as he answered the door. "Nae text aforehand? Wit if av goat cumpny?"

"A don't need that fuckin mental image, av seen enough horrors the night."

"Cheeky wee prick. Ye widnae exist waeoot ma stallion-like libido. Wit dye mean 'horrors'? Hawd oan, are you no sposed to be aff—*the fuck's happened tae ye?!*" Finally woken enough to clock the state of Fran's beet-stained visage. "Ye fuckin stink ae shite an aw!"

Fran pushed past him and slammed the door behind, pressing his back against it and sliding down to the floor, exhaustion piling on top of him.

"Fran. *Fraaan.* Francesco. Frangipane." His da knelt to get a better look at him, shook his shoulder. His voice seemed far away. "Moan, son. Wit the fuck's goin oan?"

"Big trouble," Fran mumbled, tears prickling in his eyes.

Parenting mode activated, Neil Forbes steered his son to the bathroom and switched the shower on. "Al burn these, will a?" he cracked about Fran's soiled undies and jeans.

Scrubbed raw and wearing one of his da's many silken dressing gowns (*Don't hink aboot it*), Fran stepped out of the steaming bathroom to a cup of sweet tea and a stack of pale, heavily Lurpak'd toast. "Get that doon ye," Neil said.

The tea was a necessary tonic but he could only nibble the toast, his stomach too seasick to handle solids.

"So wit's goin oan? Dae a want tae hear it?"

"Naw. Ye really don't."

Fran told him everything.

Neil peered out his curtains. No way was he sleeping tonight. He chained his Lambert & Butlers, chained his mugs of tea.

Fran stretched out on the couch, bone-tired but twisting with nauseous terror like he had a fever. The telly was on, showing repeats of topical comedy panel shows well out of date; Fran stared at it but wasn't watching, the cracks about Brexit and Boris Johnson washing over him.

The room was turning grey with dawn sunlight when Neil sat his considerable arse down on the coffee table in front of Fran, legs wide, showing acres of hairy thigh where his robe was riding up, and said, "Right. The way a see it, there's three options: wan, go tae the polis, hawn the hing oer an hope ye don't end up in the jail fir too lang—"

"How lang?"

"Hawd oan, let us finish. Two, we get it where it's sposed tae go."

"Ma flight's awready goan, a don't even huv ma passport."

"Right. Which brings us tae three..."

"...Aye?"

Neil lit a fresh fag and took a draw like he was smoking a ceremonial peace pipe, leaning in close, smell of oily aftershave encroaching. "We keep it. We take the money, beetle aff tae the US ae fuckin A, get yer knees sortet by Surgeon tae the Stars or whoever, an never fuckin come back." A smile drew across his face like curtains being pulled open. "Fuckin mint."

Fran pushed himself upright. His face opened up in wonderment. "You… are… fuckin… MENTAL!"

"Wit?!"

"Dye understawn a word yer fuckin sayin?"

"Aye! Dae you?"

"Here's *ma* three fuckin bullet points: wan, Ruaridh Callaghan, actual fuckin gang boss ae the city Ruaridh Callaghan, wis just scalped fir this key. They took oot his toap guys an happily fuckin finished aff wan ae their ain crew so he widnae grass. Pure psychos. They will fuckin kill me. And you."

"Me?!"

"Cause ye know an aw noo."

Neil's shoulders slumped. "Shite."

"Two, the hing rightfully belangs tae Russian mobsters. Russian fuckin mobsters. Right? Dae a need tae say mare?"

"…Naw."

"Three, it's in cryptocurrency. Wuv goat the key that opens a digital wallet, wae digital cash in it. A dunno aboot you, but av nae fuckin idea wit tae go aboot daein wae that."

Neil's face was so long he was in danger of tripping over his chin. His cigarette smouldered away.

"Oh, an al chip in an extra: how the fuck can a get tae America when, like we awready says, a don't huv a passport?"

Neil scratched at the stubble on the fleshy sack under his chin. "Aw good points," he conceded.

Fran dragged himself up and through to the poky galley kitchen. Could do with a good scrub. The meagre counter space was covered in tea rings and crumbs and turmeric stains. He clicked the kettle and stood watching it. He ran the problems through his head.

Don't bring problems to the table. Bring solutions.

Old mantras, Insta-clarity. His brain started to bubble up with the water.

Life is full of problems. What makes us different from them is how we handle those problems.

Frothing now.

The entrepreneurial spirit looks at a problem and sees an opportunity.

He remembered lockdown, how six years ago he'd turned what at first seemed an insurmountable obstacle into the greatest success of his career, how it had changed his entire life.

To learn, to progress, to show people what you can do.

Steam raged from the spout, the water spat and hissed.

8

"Bruce! Maisie! Come on!"

The dugs were racing around the green, tumbling over each other, barking with pleasure. Pigeons were playing with them, swooping close and being chased away. Tails thrashed with excitement at all sorts of smells in the grass, the wonderful, loamy stinks of mud and shite and God knows what else. Both were up to their elbows/knees in dirt.

McCoist called again. Tried whistling. Maisie stopped and cocked her head, taking note but nothing further. Bruce was oblivious, lost to ecstasy. *Fuck*. She'd have to chase them down to get their leads on. The bastards allowed her no dignity.

Bruce left two big muddy prints on her jeans as she wrangled him—*great*—his snout trying to force its way into her pocket, where he could smell biscuits, lunch-meat tongue lapping away at his slavering chops, drool splattering her in thick, jizzumy threads. Maisie was calmer at least. Both were rescues, of a sort. McCoist had acquired Bruce as a pup; Maisie came along a year or so later, fully grown and (McCoist had to admit) better trained. She'd belonged to a colleague of McCoist's who had disappeared—he had few family attachments so McCoist took Maisie in rather than let her go to a shelter. That was two years ago now. The investigation into DS Si Slater's vanishing act was ongoing but the leads were exhausted and it was heading for the archive. McCoist would rest a bit easier when it was finally filed away.

She walked like a paper doll, one arm out front being dragged by Bruce, the other behind for Maisie's more sedate pace, taking the path towards the fountain, wanting to keep well clear of the skatepark. DC Travis, despite being an adult, was into that sort of thing (she and Si used to call him "DC Sk8er Boi" but the joke disappeared with Si) and though it was unlikely he'd be there at that particular park at that exact moment, she didn't want to run the risk.

Kelvingrove wasn't a regular dog-walking haunt for McCoist—it was too far away from her house for convenience—but she'd chosen it this morning for its proximity to a person she wanted to talk to, to question, to consult. Unofficially, for now. This was not a person McCoist wanted to be seen to be rubbing shoulders with. There were enough rumours swirling around about her already, especially when it came to this family. (To say they had "history" was like saying the Louvre had a few paintings.)

The McGuinn mansion had been a gaudy, glitzy, overstated bully of a place. The downsized West End penthouse was approaching tasteful to McCoist's eye. Lottie McGuinn was refining her style and there was no trace left of her husband besides a couple of family photos arranged in the dead space of a colour-coded bookshelf. McCoist felt an involuntary spasm of guilt at the man's face but that was all. She was in control. *Have a meltdown about it later, if you need to.*

"How are the girls?" McCoist ventured, finally allowed inside.

Across an expensive, gnarled, live-edge coffee table, Lottie drove stakes into McCoist with her eyes. "Fine, cheers," she said. "How're the twins?"

"*Thriving*," McCoist smiled.

It wasn't only McCoist's kids who had been threatened by the old ghoul Jamieson two years ago—Lottie's daughters had been on the line too. Trauma bonding had not happened. Instead,

McCoist and Lottie treated the incident like an STD they'd caught from the same source.

"So..." McCoist leant back into the rich brown leather of the sofa cushions—a branding mark artfully visible on the tanned hide—crossed her legs and folded her hands in her lap. "How's tricks?"

"Och, cannae complain. Goat a wee weekend tae Paree booked fir winter, need a new tyre oan the motor, it's goat a slow puncture, an ma period startet yesterday—Wit the fuck ye daein here? Wit dye want?"

McCoist gave another big, fake smile. She rubbed a hand against the leather of the couch. "This is nice." Cast an obvious eye around the living room, up to the enormous skylight above them, the autumnal sky beyond. "I really admire what you and Luce are doing. The beauty salons, the product line, the sales reps. Business must be going well."

"*Thriving*." Lottie's false smile winked and died.

"Glad to hear it. It's hard for women to make it in that field." She did not mean health and beauty. "I'm rooting for you both."

"Dye huv tae be so fuckin insufferable? Is that part ae the polisman's interview technique? Annoy cunts intae confessin."

"Hey, if you have something to confess I'm all ears." Being a wind-up merchant was not in fact a technique taught in detective training, it just came naturally to McCoist and she enjoyed it immensely. One thing McCoist had learnt over her years in Police Scotland was to take pleasure in your work where you could find it, because it was mostly a river of shite.

"Fuckin ask wit ye came tae ask, will ye? Geez peace."

Fair enough, McCoist stopped dicking about: "What d'you know about Ruaridh Callaghan?"

"Snappy dresser."

"What d'you know about the big hole through his head?" McCoist thought she saw Lottie flinch, or twitch, really. McCoist herself needed to stifle a cringe at the expression she'd used, which put her in mind of Lottie's husband again, and the night she put "the big hole" through *Paulo's* head. But nobody knew about that, she reassured herself. It had been buried. Devlin had seen to that.

"Nothin. Did ye change yer mind?"

Lottie was referring to the Jamieson fiasco, their shared nightmare, the night he'd almost killed both her children and McCoist's. They were there together, her and Lottie in a grotty old flat, watching on a video feed as Jamieson's masked henchmen lay in wait for their loved ones. Callaghan had arrived on the scene and put a stop to it, forced the old devil to call off his men then run a knife right through his throat for good measure. (Should have put a stake in his chest and all.)

McCoist had been grateful. Desperately so. But when Callaghan hinted that she now owed him one for his benevolence, something snapped inside. McCoist ended up sticking a gun in his face. So easily could have pulled the trigger. She wanted to. She was on the wild borderlands of hysteria: she really might have done it. There was certainly a world in which she did. Just like McGuinn—squeeze the trigger, oh-so gently, and put an end to him. But something stopped her. God or the devil. Fear. "You want a favour?" she'd said. "OK, I'll let you have your life."

Did ye change yer mind?

This was the first time they'd addressed that night directly. Part of McCoist wanted to bridge the gap between them, say something real about what they both went through. Fear won out again. "It wasn't me. Not unless I'm capping gangsters in my sleep."

"Soonds like a lead."

"My dugs can provide an alibi."

McCoist thought she saw a glimpse of a real smile, then Lottie replied: "The weans no available tae vouch fir yer whereaboots last night?"

Whether intended or not—*of course it was fucking intended, the bitch*—it dropped McCoist like a rounders bat to the gut. Heat steamed from her face. Her jaw seized up like she'd been infected with some awful mushroom poison. Her heart quickened; blood rushed to her muscles. *Smash her right in the fuckin beak. Cow wouldn't know what hit her.*

McCoist wrestled all the bits of herself together, took a firm grip, and instead of throwing the schemey tart to the floor and dropping on her knees first like James Brown, she replied, "Too busy with their heads in their phones. You know what teenagers are like, it would take a bomb to drop in the front garden for them to notice anything outside a screen." *Good cover, made yourself sound like a right old wanker into the bargain.* Back to business: "Lottie—"

"Alison."

"Who's being insufferable now?"

"Sorry, ye prefer 'Ally'?"

She ignored the obvious bait. "Callaghan and several of his men were murdered last night. Quite the wee battle, the Scenes of Crime Officers were delighted. Care to speculate who would want to do that?"

"Nope."

"Because you don't want to tell me or because you really don't know anything?"

Lottie shifted, uneasy, a little chip in the confident veneer (would require a wallpaper steamer and a scraper to take the whole thing off, she wore that much foundation).

"If someone's decided to take out Callaghan and place themselves on the throne, what's to stop them consolidating their power by turning their attention to the rest of the competition?"

Lottie squirmed again, not much, but enough for McCoist's trained eye to catch.

"Unless you're the one who's taken the hot seat?"

"That an accusation?"

McCoist forced a friendly smile. "This isn't Cluedo. You're not under caution and I'm not on the clock yet. I just wanted to pick your brain. Thought maybe you could help me, that it might be beneficial to you too."

Lottie returned the look. "Am no sure how me an ma beauty start-up could be ae any help tae ye. Less the Callaghans are wantin a viewin afore the funeral?"

The door shut behind her. Arsehole, McCoist thought.

9

Arsehole, Lottie thought. But the DCI's visit had unsettled her. She got Luce on the phone straight away and asked her to come over.

Of course, Hannah came with. She went everywhere with her, like a growth on Luce's back. She arrived with a magnetic-sweeping thingy to search for bugs and immediately began to wave it all over Lottie's living room like some techy feng shui guru trying to waft away bad chi or some shite. It wasn't that Lottie didn't like Luce's burd or anything, just that she couldn't fucking stand her or anything about her.

"Anyhin—"

Hannah cut Lottie off with an insistent finger over her lips. She started scanning the walls, poking around the bookshelf, the back of the telly. "Aw good," she said when she was finally satisfied.

"Cheers," Lottie grumbled. "Hows aboot me? Should a assume the position? The only wire oan me is underwire, but, promise ye."

Hannah approached with wand outstretched but Luce intervened: "That willnae be necessary, hen, much as we'd aw like tae coap a feel ae those gorgeous silicone puppies."

Hannah shrieked, then, at the sight of Lottie's rolling eyes, exclaimed: "You would *never* know."

"They will in the nursin hame when Lottie's the only eighty-year-auld wummin wae nips above her naval," Luce quipped to another shriek from Hannah.

It wasn't just Hannah's face, voice, laugh, sense of humour and personality that irritated the life out of Lottie, it was the effect she had on her business partner. Luce was so much peppier now. She dressed sharper, she had a fashionable short haircut dyed deep red, she wore a single pirate earring in her left lobe, dangling to her shoulder like she was fucking Adam Ant or something. Luce had been haggard since the first time Lottie ever met her—back when she worked for her husband—a by-product of the tough, dangerous, hypermasculine business she had lived and breathed since birth. This new flair of hers put Lottie's teeth on edge, its cause embarrassingly obvious:

It was an age-gap relationship. Luce was what could be grimly described as "middle-aged" (Lottie wasn't quite there yet herself, thank fuck—she was in her mid/mid-to-late forties and planned to keep going till at least a hundred) while Hannah was still in her twenties. Only a few years older than Lottie's eldest, Ari. That maybe had something to do with Lottie's resentment of the lassie but she couldn't be bothered to unpack it.

"The biggest pair ae tits in this room right noo are yous two; gee it a rest."

"Awright, awright," Luce chuckled. "Hannah-bo-bannah, will ye make us some coaffees, please? Hannah makes *great* coaffee."

"Am yer fuckin tea wench noo?" Hannah had her hands on her hips, faux outrage on her face.

"Widye prefer 'Horlicks slag'?"

Hannah shrieked again and punched Luce on the arm (playful but still looked sore to Lottie). Luce played hurt for a second then pulled Hannah in for a smooch on the cheek.

"Yeez gonnae be carryin oan like this the hale time?" Lottie pouted.

"Sorry, Maw!" Hannah grinned.

"Yel be sorry awright," Lottie hissed under breath.

"No seein any action lately then?" Luce teased. "Thoat that Phil lad seemed awright. Wae the big shooders oan him."

"How's this fir action: Ruaridh Callaghan shoat deed last night, alang wae a crew ae his goons."

"*Fuuuck.*" Luce's mouth yawned open.

A sudden thump made them both jump—Hannah bashing the spent espresso puck out of the filter. "Sorry."

"Who…?"

"Dunno. A just heard fae Super Ally—she wis roon here fishin."

Luce huffed. "You an this wummin."

"A didnae fuckin invite her oer."

"Naw, just summoned her wae aw the time ye spend hinkin aboot her."

"Fuck aff."

"Av telt ye, we should just—"

"An a telt ye naw. She's a polis. It wid be a fuckin shitemare. Al soart it ma way."

"Yer bein saft cause ae wit happened between yeez an Jamieson."

"There's fuck aw saft aboot wit happened," Lottie snapped.

Luce backed off, accepted a coffee from Hannah. "Ad fuckin love tae dae in a polis," Hannah said, voice girlish and dreamy.

Ad fuckin love fir you tae shut up—Lottie bit back the words. Last thing she needed was an argy-bargy with Luce, who would no doubt side with her sweet little piece. Instead, she made an appeal to common sense and shared interest. "It wid jeopardise everyhin wuv built thegether."

Everything they'd built together was a tight organised crime syndicate combining: Luce's contacts and expertise in the import/export of black-market goods; the fear and weight Lottie's surname still carried along with her shrewd reasoning and eye for detail; a female-friendly work environment in a typically male-dominated industry; and a host of money-laundering beauty parlours and their attendant beauty-product pyramid scheme. Not bad for a couple of years' work, with plenty of scope for expansion in those to come. A good earner. Not too much bloodshed. So far. That looked like it could change in the very near future.

"Plus, she could be handy."

"How?"

"Well, like wae this Callaghan hing. She's investigatin it. She wants tae know who did him. A hink we should want tae know an aw. Somehin's comin doon the road."

Luce considered it. "Wid she be willin tae share information?"

"Wan way tae find oot."

Luce looked to Hannah. That was another thing that really fucked Lottie off. Like she had to run everything past this gym bunny who they'd essentially hired as muscle but was now part of the inner circle because they were shagging. "Awright, let's put the feelers oot, see wit they feel."

Summoned her.

It wasn't like Lottie was lighting candles or chanting or anything. There was, however, something of a shrine. In her office, locked in a drawer. Materials she had collected pertaining to one Detective Chief Inspector Alison McCoist. The keystone of which (the piece she would put in the centre of the pentagram, if you will) was a document she'd received from the late William Jamieson. A confessional work, handwritten by a man who had witnessed Paulo's death—shot through the head. Shot through the head by…

Drum roll…

No. 9 with a bullet: the then DI Alison "Ally" McCoist.

McCoist had killed her husband. She'd taken her children's father from them. She thought she'd got away with it.

Revenge was a long time cooling but it was nearly ready to serve.

10

They called themselves the Pacino Squad. Pathetic, and not a single one of them was even approaching good-looking or charismatic enough for it. McCoist suggested renaming themselves "the Grey-Team" but it was not appreciated. They worked out of an office in the almost-spanking-new HQ at Clyde Gateway—a brick-shaped box, each face a grid of black metal and blueish glass like a colossal, empty sudoku puzzle.

They were assumed to serve some dry, esoteric function for the managerial apparatus of Police Scotland by those who shared the building with them, shared the canteen with them, shared meek nods of "hello" in the lifts. They did not. These men had taken down gang lords and government ministers alike. Killers, all of them, even if they didn't get their hands dirty themselves. Devlin had other people for that, but these were his top acolytes, his high priests. The Pacino Squad were Devlin's inner circle, his go-to officers for any ops that needed kept off the books. Their roots were in both worlds, criminal and polis, their special interest organised crime. McCoist was one of them now. She'd had little choice in the matter—the things she'd done would land her in the jail and, likely, at the wrong end of a shank. Devlin could protect her and, in turn, she would do his bidding. She wondered if the rest of them were here on a similar footing. They certainly didn't seem to serve out of love.

"Here she comes!" Mal called.

"How dooz, Morning Glory?" Chip tossed out, waving from behind his screen.

The other three members of the Pacino Squad—Alan, Kirky, Hugo—grunted at McCoist's entrance. Interest in her following her initial induction into Devlin's top-secret little gang of manipulators and fixers had quickly waned when it was confirmed she had absolutely no relation to the other Ally McCoist. The jokes continued for another six months. They were highly original.

"Open a window now and again, will yeez? Smells like a nursing home in here." McCoist did it herself, letting an inefficient breath of air into the fuggy atmosphere of old man, aftershave and cigarettes.

To be fair to Mal, he wasn't an old man at all, he just smelt like it—clothes not properly dried, which gave off a pishy hum. Didn't live with his maw and didn't have a girlfriend. "I can guess why you've graced us with your presence this morning," he said.

"The super filled you in?"

"Aye. Tickly Tomlinson was on the phone as soon as he heard." Said with such lightness, but McCoist knew Mal wouldn't dare call Devlin that when he was within earshot. A reference to the gaffer's tic of itching his scrotum every couple of minutes—an undercover op gone wrong (back in the Late Cretaceous) had seen Devlin have one of his testes removed and pickled for him by none other than that psycho William Jamieson. Devlin had taken the news of Jamieson's painful death stoically: his reserved parking space was suddenly filled with a vintage Jag.

"Tomlinson" had been Devlin's alias, never to be revived. Roy Devlin scraped through with one ball left but Roy Tomlinson didn't make it, his career as an undercover detective laid to rest. Devlin had told McCoist this story himself. She couldn't imagine him sharing it with these trolls, guessed their insider knowledge was further testament to their investigative skills.

They also called him "Half-sack" and "Wonderball".

"Was the scene messy?" Mal continued.

McCoist recalled bodies strewn about, reposing in frozen agony like some deranged religious painter's vision of hell. Red pools, slick and gungy, still bright and fresh, the whole thing approaching surreal. It was the smell that left the biggest impression. The sewage stink of torn insides. "It'll take more than a song from Mary Poppins to clear up."

"What's the word on your end?"

McCoist gave a rundown of the orders she'd made so far, listed what information she was still waiting on from forensics, etc. Door-to-door reports were coming in with bits and pieces of comings and goings to the shopping centre and the CCTV dredge of the surrounding area had come up with some vehicles which could have been used by the hit squad, the search ongoing.

Bodies had been ID'd from wallets, cars parked in the shopping centre matching with each of them: Ben Gregson, Trav Rowlands, Andrew McKinley, Ian "Ferrari" McKenzie. The first three were KAs, going back with Callaghan for years. The last, Ferrari, was a small fish in the same pool, which maybe meant something, maybe didn't. Families had been informed, next of kin were being questioned. Busy day.

"Went to see the Burds ae Prey yesterday morning too."

"You suspect them?"

"No, I don't think so. McGuinn is too…"

Mal gave her a look that said, *Oh, here we go.*

"What? She's not like her husband. She's not running things that way."

"I agree she's not out there torturing people like a psycho but violence underpins every criminal organisation. It has to."

"OK, sure. But I still don't see it. If anything, I think McGuinn and Branson are potential targets for whoever took out Callaghan."

"Aye?"

"It's an absolutely wild power grab. Fucking mental when you think about it. If someone's willing to cap the big man, they mean business. Nobody's safe."

Mal gave her that look again.

"It wasn't McGuinn. I'm telling you, she didn't know. I'm hoping she'll give us a steer."

"She's not a CI, Ally." Meaning, her information couldn't be trusted. An official Criminal Informant had reason to be honest—it was play ball with the polis or play ball in the exercise yard in Bar-L (and a grass like them would likely be the ball). Lottie McGuinn was in no such predicament.

"Not yet."

Mal huffed.

"What are you keyboard warriors doing—" McCoist's phone rang. One of her phones. She patted herself down, found the culprit. Mouthed "Sorry" at Mal and stepped away to the half-privacy of a cubicle.

A soon as she saw his name on the screen her stomach dropped. *Fuck.* "Hey, I'm—"

"Where are you?" Mark was raging. Properly furious. She could tell because his voice was not raised. It was flat. It seethed.

"I'm at work, I'm so sorry, I—"

"It's Saturday."

"I know, but—"

"The kids have been waiting for over an hour. Are you coming?"

"I can't."

His breath hissed.

"Something major happened. I'm sorry, I forgot to call but I can't have them today."

"Tomorrow?"

"Eh—"

"Fine."

"I'm sorry, it was crazy busy and I—"

"You said that last month too. That's two out of four weekends with them you're missing now."

"I can't control when a big case comes up. You know that."

"I've got plans too, Alison."

"Oh, so this isn't about the kids seeing *me*, this is about you—"

"Piss off." The line cut. McCoist pushed her phone down onto the desk, gritted her teeth and pinched the bridge of her nose. Fuck. *Fuck*. How could she have fucking forgotten she was supposed to have Tess and Cam? Going on the attack against Mark was a really fucking poor choice too. Really fucking helpful. *Piss off*. Mark wasn't a swearing guy. Must be apoplectic.

After their near miss two years ago—not that Mark, Tess or Cam knew anything about the danger they had been in—McCoist had sworn she would be there for them, that she would protect them, look after them, no matter what. But her renewed dedication—resolve forged in the life-affirming afterglow of being snatched from the jaws of death—had given way to the cold reality that it was McCoist herself who endangered them. Her career, her corruption. Maybe the best thing she could do to protect them was to distance herself. *That's a noble way of putting neglect*, she spat at herself. Before she had time to sink deeper into self-loathing, another one of her phones rang. Always did. Ringing phones forever. Work phone this time, other pocket.

An unrecognised number. "DCI McCoist speaking."

"It's Lottie McGuinn."

"Oh, hi—"

"A huv something fir ye. If it leads tae anyhin a want tae hear wit it is. Awright?"

"Deal." McCoist swallowed, throat dry.

"Francesco Forbes. The runner."

"Runner? As in—"

"Professional runner. Marathon runner."

"Never heard of him. What's he got to do—"

"Has some intrestin histry wae Callaghan. Look it up. Parrently, he's bin talkin tae his auld boss recently aboot somehin or other."

"What?"

"Dunno. That's as much as we goat."

"Anything concrete to—"

"Just goassip. Mare goassip goes oan atween these cerdboard gangsters than a church knit an natter, Paulo aw-ways said." A sigh ruffled from the speaker. "Take it or leave it."

"...Cheers, Lottie."

She hung up. *Cow.*

McCoist did a quick google of this Francesco Forbes. Images of him all over the world in vest and short shorts, number pinned to him. Tall and wiry, a hungry skinniness to his body, every tendon and muscle shown in sharp relief under his skin. Boyish face which perched oddly on his lean frame. McCoist didn't recognise him but then she wasn't into athletics. Maybe she'd ask Cam: he was into the gym and sports and everything. (Cringe of guilt, quickly compressed into the well of healthy repression.) Rows of stats, times, records, places. Speculation around injury that had seen him recently drop out during races or miss them altogether.

An old MailOnline article: "Rising Scottish Marathon Star's Shameful Violent Past". There was a thumbnail of Forbes, a familiar professional shot in his running gear, cut side by side with the close-up profile of a boy whose face was bloated and misshapen, covered in purple bruising and angry stitches.

Before she could click on it, her personal phone shuddered on the desk. She flipped it over. Text from a withheld number:

Would they still love you?

11

He'd have felt like a secret agent if he wasn't dressed in his da's vintage (scabby) Diadora tracksuit, which was both too big and too small. He had to tie the trousers at the waist as if he were lashing himself to the mast of a ship in a storm, and they ballooned out like Aladdin's Arabian breeks, but still showed off six inches of white sock below the ankle cuffs.

His mission was to reach Pontoon's flat in Toryglen without getting gunned down by those nutters who had killed Callaghan and his team. It wasn't far, certainly not for Fran, though his knees were giving him some serious jip after Thursday night's escapade. He also did a bit of circling round, trying to catch if there was anybody following him. Every car buzzing past was potentially the one to pull over and snatch him away. He cut through the park behind the big Asda, hoping that getting away from the roads would calm him, but now there were all sorts of trees and hedges for bogeymen to step out from behind like Michael Myers.

He focused on his breathing, the movements of his body. Listened to the aches of his knees, the protesting of the meaty architecture around the joints that were the bastard cause of all this trouble.

What is done is done. You can't change what has happened. Don't waste time regretting or wondering what would have happened if you'd done things differently. You must adapt to the new situation and find a way forward.

That was what he was doing. He felt focused again. Calm.

Then he felt Callaghan's blood spaff onto his face, the weight of his body tipping onto him, the final twitch of his muscles as the dying brain fired out desperate signals, sputtering its last. He lurched across the path, hugged a tree to stop himself falling over.

He squeezed his eyes tight, controlled his breathing as it whooped in and out. Slowed it down.

Footsteps on the path.

Panicked glance over his shoulder.

Just a man and his dog. Fran pretended to be taking a pish against the tree, heard a huff of judgement as the dog walker passed by.

Nobody is going to do this for you. You have to be the one to take control.

He made it to Pontoon's gaff in one piece. Pontoon's maw's gaff, really. He still lived in the flat where he grew up, his childhood bedroom now his dominion. Despite all the guff he was posting about crypto trading and NFTs online, the whole endeavour obviously wasn't taking off. But Fran had spent the day before rifling through all his old contacts—customers, school pals, the lot—and Pontoon was the best he could come up with.

There were a few more knowledgeable computer guys on the list for sure, but they were too straight, too middle class, too much to lose. Buying a bag for the weekend wasn't the same as being willing to get involved in a serious criminal endeavour—they'd grass as soon as there was a whiff of trouble. No, Pontoon was just the right mix of clued-up and clueless.

"Fran! Good tae see ye, man!" Pontoon held his hand flat and rigid, like a Ken doll's, and swooped it in from on high for a hard, tight shake.

"You too, Nicky! Bin an age!" They hadn't been hanging around each other closely or recently enough for Fran to call him Pontoon to his face—the story behind the nickname was that the first time he ever went to a casino, one of his pals was explaining blackjack to him and he remarked, "It's just like pontoon," causing fits of laughter from his drunk mates and creating a new nickname which had, unfortunately, stuck—especially not when Fran was trying to ingratiate himself so he could ask a favour. A heavy one at that.

Fran gave Pontoon a pat on the shoulder to remind him to let his hand go.

"Moan in."

It was pretty much as Fran remembered it—he'd been round the odd time when he was younger to have a scoop and smoke a bit of ganj—down to the dilapidated shoe cabinet stuffed with trainers, slippers, wellies, Timbies, roller skates and the rest which you needed to squeeze past to get to Pontoon's bedroom at one end of the hall. The smell in particular, of mince and tatties and Ambi Pur, zapped Fran back into his teenage years.

This continued into the bedroom, which was depressing. The same anime posters on the wall, the shelves still buckling under the weight of the same dusty *Lord of the Rings* and *Game of Thrones* books and box sets. Same carpet, thin and pocked with singed hot-rock holes. Hopefully he'd at least changed the bed sheets in the five or six years since Fran had visited.

"How ye daein?"

"Nae bad, mate. Yersel?"

"Survivin. Seen aw yer mad runnin stuff oer the years. Amazin, man. So fuckin cool."

"Cheers, man." They smiled at each other, awkwardness rising. Now would be the time for Fran to reciprocate but he wasn't really sure how to congratulate Pontoon on not leaving home and not having a job and being duped into "investing" in shitty wee cartoon pictures.

"That you rich then?"

Fran put on a laugh. "A widnae say that. The money's no bad, but…"

"Yer wantin tae diversify yer assets." He leant back on his fancy computer chair, a deluxe wanking throne. One thing that had changed was the new computer set-up on the desk behind him: two monitors; weirdly sculpted keyboard with myriad flashing lights; and a mouse that looked like it might be a Transformer.

Fran cringed, tried not to show it on his face. "Aye, somehin like that."

"It's smart, man, cannae be an athlete firever." That one hooked under Fran's guard. *We'll see, you fat fuck.* "Wit dye want tae know?"

Fran squeaked up off the bed, went to the window and looked down onto the street. Weans were playing kerby; a young couple were pushing a pram. They stopped to wait for the next throw before passing the kids, in case the ball went too high and bounced into them and their precious cargo. There was nobody skulking about behind the street lamps in balaclavas, no cars with darkened windows crawling past.

"Ye awright?"

"Aye, sorry." Fan pulled himself away from the view, produced the thumb drive from his pocket. "Av goat this hing tae open a… a wallet?"

"Right." Pontoon reached out to take it and Fran instinctively snatched it away, tight in his fist, close to his chest. Pontoon held up his hands, a bit surprised.

"Sorry, a… How dae a use it?"

Pontoon squinted at him. A question formed on his face but he didn't ask it. "Well, a crypto key is just, like, the password tae get intae a crypto wallet, right? It's like yer bankin app, needs the correct login details tae use it, tae make it secure. Crypto wallet's the same. Follyin me?"

"Aye."

"Noo, ye can put this key, this password, intae cold storage..."—he pointed at the USB stick still clamped in Fran's hand—"...tae make it mare secure fae, like, oanline hackers or whoever. So, aw ye dae is, like, bang it intae the computer an—"

"A can get intae the wallet." Fran stood, began pacing in the confined space, jittery, heart tap-dancing.

"Aye." Pontoon gave him a smile but that question was still hanging there in his beady wee eyes.

"An how dae a change the crypto intae real money?"

"It is real money." Pontoon looked offended. "Loads ae places are takin aw kinds ae crypto, ye can buy—"

"Sorry, naw, a mean like, if a wantet it in poonds or dollars or witever."

"*Ah,* ye mean ye want tae exchange it fir fiat."

"Wit?"

"Government money. Simple, man, ye can withdraw yer crypto tae a normal bank acoont usin an app."

"...Which a can then—wit?—take oot in cash?"

"Aye. Well, depends maybe oan the type ae crypto, but. Wit've ye goat?"

Here's the bit where Fran would have to answer the question *Is this yours?* Because he didn't know exactly what he'd got. Just that he'd got a lot of it. He decided to get out in front. "Nicky, how would ye like tae make a bit ae money?"

Pontoon pushed himself back in his chair, beady little eyes flashing, fear and excitement rising off him like sweaty steam. "How much is a bit?"

12

Forbes wasn't home so she parked her motor with a view of his flat in the New Gorbals—at a careful distance—and waited. She was following up the tip alone for now. She didn't want the headache of floating an "anonymous source" with the rest of the MIT. There were enough murmurs about her around the coffee urn already. If it actually went anywhere, she'd work out a way to post-rationalise her actions then.

She read all the media on him, then their own reports. She got the number of a social worker assigned to him before he got too old for all that. Remembered him well: "Smart wean, actually, wis glad tae see him daein well wae the runnin, gettin away fae aw that shite he wis wrapped up in as a boay."

"The drugs?"

"Aw aye. Sellin thum, no takin thum. Fancied himsel as a bit ae an Alan Sugar. A telt him wance: 'Drugs are an easy product tae sell. Aim higher, challenge yersel.' He liked that wee speech, as a remember. Thoat ad goat through tae him."

"Maybe you did."

"Nah, am no takin credit fir wit the lad's achieved. Else ad huv tae take the derry when hings go wrang an aw."

"What about the arrest for assault?"

"Right, this wis when a first goat involved wae him. Goat in a scrap, polis involved, folk are wantin tae know: wit's this kid's hame life like? Enter moi."

"Bit more than a scrap. The other lad went to hospital with multiple fractures in his cheekbone and eye socket, *and* a punctured lung. Francesco was lucky the charge wasn't attempted murder."

"He wis a bit ae a fly wan. Jammy. Hing's just go his way, ye know?"

"And what was the story?"

"Didnae really get it oot him. Said it wis just a fight, that's aw. The other boay wis nae saint either, so who knows wit happened atween thum? Somdy's cracked a joke the other took wrang, somdy's got aff wae the other's burd. Teenage stuff."

McCoist gave a sceptical hum. "It wasn't about drugs?"

"Mebbe, no sure. A hink his Escobar phase came eftir that. When he moved school."

"Did he move because of the fight?"

"Cannae mind. Could huv bin."

"And what *was* his home life like?"

"Honestly, av seen much worse. He didnae get oan wae his maw but it wisnae like the wummin wis beatin him or anyhin. She hud tae work a loat so the lad probly goat mare free rein than he shouldae done, that's aw. Ungrateful wee pillock, really."

"And the father?"

"Seperatet fae his maw. In an oot the picture. Waste ae space."

McCoist winced at the casually damning summation. Mark's *Piss off* needled her again. *In an oot the picture.* No, she wasn't in and out, she was just at the edge of the frame sometimes, that was all. And it wasn't like she was missing time with her kids to hang out down the pub with her pisshead pals or anything, she was trying to solve a fucking massacre here. Mark could go fuck himself. She had killers to catch and leads to follow.

She ended the call and started the engine.

. . .

The maw, Corrina Leoni, lived on Fernhill Road in a block of flats across the street from where the *King of the Castle* used to stand—the whitewashed statue of a cape-wearing boy looking towards Glasgow through a pair of binoculars had been moved on to schemes new.

The lock on the close door was broken, so McCoist let herself in and went up to the first floor. She knocked and waited. Knocked again. Waited. She peeked through the letter box, got a glimpse of not much through the stiff bristles.

"Ye uptae?"

McCoist jumped. The letter box slammed shut like a steel trap, the noise in the echoey close like a hammer hitting an anvil.

The woman—twenties, tiger hair, an unsettling combination of fake eyelashes behind large specs—was watching her from the door directly across the narrow hall. McCoist bit back the flustered apology that was trying to escape. "I'm looking for your neighbour, Corrina. Is she in?"

"Dis it look like she's in?"

It wasn't an apology McCoist had to stifle this time. "D'you know where she'd be?"

"How?"

"Cause I'm asking." McCoist pulled her warrant card from inside her jacket.

The eyelashes twitched like the legs of a dying insect when she blinked. "Ye don't look like a polis."

"I left my trench coat and deerstalker at home today."

"Wit's that sposed tae mean?"

"Nothing. However I look, that's me on the card and the card says 'Detective Chief Inspector'. OK?"

"The wummin detectives oan the telly are either, like, sexy or auld."

"If only it could be both." McCoist flapped her arms to her sides. "Where might I find Corrina just now?"

"She in trouble?"

"No."

"Aw." The woman turned to go back inside.

"Hold on. Just tell me where I could find her, will you?"

Big sigh, like everything was a huge effort, even blinking those big, insect eyelashes. "Look, am no a grass but, like, she's *sooo* fuckin moany. Aw-ways whingein aboot the noise an aw that. An wur no even makin any fuckin noise. Like, we only hud a couple ae people oer, just like oor pals Mickey an Gemma an Fangle an Fangle's burd an, like, *she* is bangin oan the door an aw that—pure harrassin us, man. Go an dae her fir harrassin us, will ye?"

"Fine. Where is she?"

She worked at the One-O-One next to the community centre. McCoist spotted the name badge at the till behind the protective glass. McCoist showed off her own. "Time for a break, Corrina?"

They went out the back so Corrina could vape—a bulky refillable thing like a spaceman's pipe which stated she was serious about nicotine and tutti-frutti.

"He moved in wae his da, wance the runnin startet tae take aff." There was still pride there, obscured by a bitterness McCoist felt in a strong empathic wave, as if carried into her on the second-hand vape steam. "Neil aw-ways had the nose fir a quick buck."

"And when's the last time you spoke to Francesco?"

(McCoist had struggled to assuage the mother's fears that her boy was in trouble again, assured her she was only needing to speak to him as part of a larger investigation, that he himself hadn't done anything wrong. This was true—only Lottie McGuinn's tip was against the boy, and the growing nag in McCoist's gut—but

Corrina kept drilling McCoist with a weather-eyed look which said she was not convinced.)

She sucked in, the mouth of the device smeared with lipstick. "Aboot a month ago. Oer the phone."

"What did you talk about?"

"Nothin really. A just asked him how he wis daein an that."

"And…?"

"He didnae say much."

"No? He didn't talk about his running or… I heard he's been injured…?"

"Aye, somehin tae dae wae aw ligaments an, an tissues, a dunno. A goat that fae Neil, but. Drug it oot him."

"Why…" McCoist braced herself. "Why doesn't Francesco talk to you?"

The vape dropped away from Corrina's lips. "Ye hink am fuckin stupit?" McCoist edged back from her. "Detective fuckin *chief*. Big cheese. Ye want tae talk tae Fran aboot somehin, why don't ye go dae that? Instead, yer talkin tae me. Wit's actually goin oan? Where is he?"

Fear beneath the aggro, not that it was all posture. She was a severe woman. McCoist could easily picture the rows blazing between her and her teenage son now. Mother driven daft by anxiety and exasperation, desperate to try and regain some kind of control over him before he hurt himself, son only hearing nagging and griping and shameful reproach.

McCoist had these arguments with her own kids. In the past, Tess in particular was always keen to push boundaries and scare the fucking life out her (the last time they stayed, McCoist had noticed the book she'd brought for her bedside table, which raised an eyebrow: *She's a virgin sorceress; he's a centaur with a literal horse dick. But they must come together to save the world of Görgõn-Zôlà*), but Cam had been up to his own tricks recently. Since he'd begun earning a bit of money he was Mr Independence, answers to no one, went and bought a fucking second-hand piece-of-shite car—a Golf wrapped in purple vinyl with a ridiculous body mod and an exhaust pipe like a blunderbuss—which he wasn't even old enough to drive yet, and was currently declared "off the road" and taking up Mark's driveway. ("I thought you were saving for lessons?!" "It was too good a deal to miss!") But it wasn't like they were out punting gear, no wonder this woman was so highly strung. McCoist could only imagine.

"Nothing's wrong, Corrina. He isn't at home just now and I'm looking around, that's all. Is there a gym he goes to? Or a particular place he goes to run?"

She took a resigned puff. "Yed be better askin his da."

13

Essence of bachelor greeted McCoist when he opened the door. Fags, stale beer, microwave meals, funk from a bin somewhere that must be overfull and needing taken out. Pleasantly overlaid by a melange of competing aftershaves and Febreze. He was fully dressed, so that was something, though he looked like he'd had an Easterhouse wash rather than the real thing. He had a voice like he was chewing on something, speaking through a mouthful: "Sorry, hen, a didnae catch wit ye were oan aboot oer the speaker. A heard 'polis' an somehin aboot Ally McCoist?"

McCoist couldn't tell if he was trying to take the pish or was genuinely befuddled. His eyes had the look of a late night or three about them. It wasn't her nature to give people the benefit of the doubt though. "Don't start, Mr Forbes, I've heard them all." She held out her warrant card and repeated her introduction. "Can I come in?"

He gestured in a way that said "Can you?", but turned and lumbered further inside. McCoist closed the door behind herself. The living room lacked any character but was surprisingly tidy. A peek across the hall showed a kitchen unit covered in crushed tinnies.

"I want to talk to you about Francesco."

"How?" He scowled.

"I'm looking for him."

His face remained stuck apart from the twitch of a large nostril, proudly showcasing its fur. The eyes didn't look so bleary now. "How?"

"Do you know where I might be able to find him just now?"

"Aye."

Macho bellend. Classic fucking middle-aged-man bullshit. "...Are you going to tell me where?"

"Are you gonnae tell me wit yer wantin wae him?"

I have a wee inkling he might be involved in the murder of a bunch of hardcore, certified-maniac gangsters, all of whom were shot to shit, battered to fuck, macheted and left like Peter Weller at the start of Robocop. "Just a quick word."

"Aboot?"

"Thighs and glutes." McCoist squeezed an invisible arse cheek. "Part of a wider investigation—Francesco is a potential witness—"

"Fran isnae a potential anyhin." McCoist was surprised at the vehemence Forbes Sr's voice had taken on. Not at all the dull, cow-like mumblings of before. "He widnae be involved in any shite in any way. No at aw. It's bin fuckin near a decade since he wis. That boay's turnt his life aroon. He's a fuckin role model. An yous vultures willnae gee him peace!"

"The police have been in contact recently?"

"Naw. Ah don't mean polis, a mean fuckin... *haters.*"

"Haters...?" McCoist felt ridiculous saying the word. In her mind, Cam and Tess squealed *Mum, stop!* in fits of "cringe" so hard they might perish from it.

"Aye. Oanline. Social media. An those fuckin journos—if ye can even caw thum that."

"Are you talking about the *Mail* article?"

"Them an evry other fuckin rag wit jumped oan it."

"What happened?"

"It wis fuckin years an years ago, he wis just a boay. Noo the boay's done good, here comes some fuckin loser fae back in the day tryin tae huv a go, get a few quid fir it intae the bargain."

"It was a serious assault—you don't remember what caused the fight?"

"Naw. He wis wae his maw at that point." The finger of blame obviously pointing. McCoist could use that.

"And it wasn't just that incident though, was it? Francesco was getting involved in serious crime."

"Widnae know."

"Drug dealing?"

"Look, when yev goat a lad who's smart, an driven, but he's no goat like an outlet, right? He can end up… A mean, me, a hud fitba. A wis oot leatherin that baw since a wis knee-high. By the time a wis in the secondry school, it wis evryhin tae me. Playin fir ma school, playin fir ma club. Kept us oot ae trouble. Fran didnae huv that, no at first anyway, no till he goat intae the runnin. Then it wis aw change. Then he hud *direction*, wis *dedicatet*. The way a wis. Goat a start wae Rangers so a did. Fuckt ma cruciate though, doactor said ma kneecap wis flappin loose. Two years recovery, missed ma shoat."

"Fran is having similar troubles, no?"

"Och, naw. Bit ae strain, bit ae physio needed—he's bin hard at it fir years oan the trot noo, it's normal. Nothin he cannae work through."

"I'm not from the sports desk, Mr Forbes. Is his career in trouble?"

"Naw. That's bullshit, jealous gossip goin aboot."

McCoist worried he might say "haters" again. "There's no reason for him to be back in touch with Ruaridh Callaghan?"

"Who's that?"

It came off all right, sounded fine, not so casual it wasn't casual at all, but he immediately started shuffling around with a packet of cigarettes. Didn't necessarily mean anything—McCoist could be reading her own biases, her foreknowledge, into it—but it added to the growing sense of something being off. Lottie McGuinn's tip was good, there was something here, and the further McCoist probed the more she was sure she was onto a winner. She pressed forward. "He's a businessman. Someone Francesco used to know, back before the running."

"A widnae know aboot that, like a says, he wis wae his maw when aw ae that wis happenin."

"Mr Callaghan was murdered on Thursday night."

"Murder? An yer sayin, wit, Fran's a witness?" Took a few sparks to get his lighter going, thumb sliding against the wheel ineffectually.

"I'm saying it's important that I speak to him."

He took a draw and snorted the smoke out through his nose in one sharp huff. "Yer pishin intae the wrang tree here, hen."

"DCI McCoist."

"Fond ae sayin yer name, aren't ye?"

"Look, where—"

"Try the Glesga Club in the Gorbals. He disnae hawd himsel oot as too fancy fir the auld cooncil gym hall. He's a good lad, an yer really fuckin aff the track here. Wastin yer time. Evrywan's time."

"I'd better let you get on with it then."

14

"Safe tae come oot!"

Fran pulled back the shower curtain. "She's no ootside watchin the windies?"

"Naw, saw her drive aff."

"Great, so ye were stawndin there at the curtain like a fuckin creep?"

"The fuck dye want me tae dae? Hawd oan while a use ma psychic powers tae see if she's still there or no. Ye hink am Uri Geller?"

"Who?"

The bathroom door opened and Neil popped his big head in. "Michael Jackson's pal, bends spoons and aw that."

"Yev fuckin made that up."

"No a huvnae, he—look, she's goan, an a wisnae bein a creep. A wis just *appreciatin* her, she'll be used tae it."

"Fucksake," Fran grumbled. His maw tipped them off and they'd gone into a tizzy. What to do, where to go. Fran's immediate reaction was to get out the door and lose himself for a bit, till the coast was clear, then he remembered the journeys to and from Pontoon's, fraught with the potential for being whacked, the anxiety needle banging hard against the red "panic attack" zone. The streets were not safe. The park was not safe. The local vegan cafes were not fucking safe. In the time they spent debating it—Neil in a frenzy of tidying up in the living room ("Yer maw says it's a wummin")—trying to form a plan, the buzzer went and Fran threw himself into the shower cubicle, huddled down and prayed she wouldn't ask to look around.

He'd heard his da's tones wah-wah-wahing through from the living room, then a lighter, thinner voice that didn't carry so well—this poliswoman, McCoist.

"Wit wis she sayin?"

"She wants tae speak tae ye aboot Callaghan."

"Fuck." They'd found him fast. Was he caught on camera fleeing the scene? Fran quelled the rising panic by reasoning that she probably wouldn't have come alone if that was the case. Six dead, gunshots—no, they'd have showed up in force, probably tooled up and itching to plug him. (This was not helping the panic. Fran started to feel the need to sit on the toilet.) His blurry image would be all over the MSM and socials—or would they be waiting to release that later?

So far, the only headlines were that an incident had taken place, people had died, and a major investigation was underway. All else was under wraps. For now. The comment sections were going wild though. Callaghan's name was being bandied about as one of the victims. Someone claimed Ferrari had been there too. Some people were driving at something close to the truth, though there was enough of "The police did it"/"The masons did it"/"The IRA did it" to muddy the waters.

"She wis goin oan aboot auld hings an aw. They stories wit were in the *Mail* an that. Liam, the wee grassin prick. Should set aboot him again."

Liam Young. Fran had battered the fuck out of him. Leathered him. He could remember the pain, then the numbness in his toes as he kicked and kicked at Liam's body, stomped down on his face. One of those memories that assault you when you're hungover and low. *Don't forget wit a piece ae shit you are.* "No helpful, Da."

Neil went to the window, looked down on the street. "Let's get oan the move, hit the banks oan Monday. We need tae pack."

15

The circus had come to London Road. McCoist's small fiefdom was the big top, overrun with detectives pulled in to work on the Callaghan hit: Operation Winton. She always let Travis name them, it gave him puppyish joy. "Get it? Winton. Dale Winton. Supermarket Sweep. Right?"

"Very good, Gaz," DC Khan commented.

The atmosphere was sweaty and excited, the male cohort posturing with loosened ties and rolled-up sleeves. DI Griffiths wrangled the troops, handed out jobs, collated and passed information to McCoist. McCoist formulated plans of action and relayed orders, worried about press and budget and overtime allowance. Worried that at any time something might be found out McCoist did not want to be found out.

Escaping to the Pacino Squad office was a blessed though smelly relief.

"What a pleasure!" Mal exclaimed, doffing an imaginary cap.

"Back so soon?" Alan chipped in.

"Coffee anyone?" McCoist asked.

"No," they chorused. The brew McCoist made was notorious. It could be used to unblock drains. She liked it that way, and it kept her from ever having to make a hot drink for anyone else.

She plonked herself down on a chair, wheeled herself up to Mal's elbow. He studiously ignored her, tapping at his keyboard, sliding glasses up a nose pocked with divots where blackheads had been squeezed out. "So?"

"A needle pulling thread."

McCoist took a Mars bar from her pocket and sat it on the desk, tapped it with a nail. "It's a duo."

"There's no extra chocolate in a duo," he said, prim, eyes never leaving the screen, "it's just so they can claim it as two servings and make the nutritional info look less deadly."

"Tinfoil doesn't suit you, Mal. D'you want it or not?"

He snatched it and secreted it away in a drawer of his desk. "Something interesting for you. CCTV drudges had flagged this bloke up—first seen not far from the shopping centre." He brought up a video of a man running, face not quite sharp enough to recognise, absolutely caning it down a residential street. "They spotted him again on a couple of different feeds but he disappears. So—"

"A needle pulling thread."

He looked at her now, no trace of humour in his expression.

"You can dish it out but you can't take it."

He turned back to the screen. "So I had a look around the addresses you gave me..."

"...And?"

"You're welcome."

"I gave you a Mars Duo. Talk."

Mal gave a fussy wee grump. "Look, this is near the Govanhill one." The hood was up now, but it was the same jumper, man the same build.

"The next day..." Same camera, a man going in the other direction from the night before. This man was wearing a ludicrous, minging highlighter-coloured tracksuit. His face was towards them and, in daylight, much easier to make out.

"Forbes."

"Tracked him from here to Glenmore Avenue in Toryglen,

where he disappears for a while, then reappears going back the other way."

"Back to his da's?"

"A fair assumption."

"What was he doing in Toryglen?"

"You know, Alison, the last time his phone pinged was on Thursday around teatime. It's been off since then, can't track him that way."

"Makes sense."

"No, what I mean is, it's a lot of work."

He fixed his eyes on her again. "For fuck..." She took another chocolate bar—a Double Decker this time—from her jacket pocket and slapped it onto the desk.

A homeopathic nod of appreciation and he went back to the screen. "I started with these two blocks of flats here, cross-referenced the names with his social media and..."

He brought up an Instagram profile of a man who could have been anywhere from twenty to forty. "Nicholas Stewart," McCoist read. "League of Legends and crypto trading. DMs open." The bio was completed with emojis of a dollar sign, a Saltire, a Union Jack and a poppy, and the phrase "Less we forget". "Isn't this a bot?"

"One who lives at flat 2/3, 9 Glenmore Avenue."

McCoist got the feeling it would be easy to catch this one at home and she was right.

"How do you know Francesco Forbes?"

He was sweating already, hands moulded to the arms of a huge video-game chair, making sticky swallowing noises and licking his flaky lips.

She'd had a quiver of nervy belly when she knocked—she'd gone out alone again (while Operation Winton could follow the hooded man around the cameras all they wanted, it was connecting him with McGuinn's tip which gave McCoist this address, and she still hadn't come up with a way to insert this golden nugget into the official case without looking dodgy)—but immediately knew he'd be no trouble.

She towered over him, unwilling to sit on the bed because the sheets looked so stiff they might shatter into bits beneath her.

"A knew him fae back in school." His voice squeezed out as if her hands were around his neck.

"Close?"

"Eh, no really, palled aboot wae some ae the same folk."

"Seen him recently?"

His mouth made a noise like a cartoon character tasting something delicious—*tup, tup, tup,* dry tongue against the roof of the mouth. His knees bounced. He took far too long to answer. "Eh, aye he wis here the other day, wantin tae, eh, borrow somehin."

"What?"

"Ehm…"

"You need to be quicker on your feet to get away with lying," McCoist said. Her poise and attitude were pure Demon Headmaster.

He shifted his arse around in the big chair. "Aw, a, eh, a wisnae—"

Some locks need to be picked, others you can just go hell for leather with the hammer and blowtorch. "Right now you're obstructing a police officer. Up to twelve months in prison. I know Francesco was here, you need to tell me why."

The boy's eyes ping-ponged about.

"It's a first offence, so maybe you'll get off light. Your pal, however, is wanted in connection to six deaths. If you're helping him, so are you. Six murders. No one gets off light from that."

"M-murders?" he squeaked. "He didnae say a-anyhin aboot—"

"Come on, out with it."

"L-look, when a agreed tae—a didnae know aboot aw that, he just says…" His breathing wheezed towards panic attack.

Maybe the whole hammer/blowtorch had been a bit much. "Calm down, Nicholas. Take a second. Slow it down. You'll be fine. You're talking to me now, so I can help you." Gear change to soft, syrupy, reassuring—*motherly*, she shuddered. "What did you agree to?"

He leant back into his chair, took a couple of yoga breaths. He wiped his palms on his jeans. "A hudnae seen him in firever, that's true. Then he sent me a DM—"

"When was this?"

"Eh, yesterday."

"OK."

"Um, aye, he sent us a message, bummin me up an aw that aboot ma crypto stuff."

"You're a crypto coin trader, aye?"

The lad managed a smile at that. *Eejit*. "Aye, it's… wit a dae. An he says he knows am intae aw that fae Insta an wants a word aboot it. A says, 'Aye, nae problem,' so he comes roon here—"

"The same day?"

"Aye, right away, he wis keen. He comes roon an he has this private key oan cold storage fir a wallet. Right?" Nicholas was warming to it, the burden lifting as he spoke. To keep him sweet and, frankly, because McCoist didn't understand, she had him spell it out, and he told her about the USB stick Forbes had with him, which could access digital assets.

"Did he say how he came by this 'key'?" It was McCoist having to keep her voice steady now, excitement coming up, a clean amphetamine.

Nicholas shook his head, fear naked in his face. This was it. Had to be. Something went down and this "key" was the trigger. McCoist's whole body was prickling and light. "He asked us if a could help him change the crypto money intae cash… An says that he'd pay me fir it. A-a didnae know, didnae know anyhin aboot anybdy bein… *hurt*. A swear a didnae know."

"I believe you. But you've been worried about this, haven't you? Waiting for the knock at the door."

His eyes flickered down. Swallowed and licked his lips. "It wis, it wis a loat ae money. A loat ae fuckin money in that wallet."

"How much?"

His miserable eyes met hers. "Roughly speakin… Millions."

The rush engulfed her. She couldn't keep still. She needed to get on the phone. She needed this kid found right now. If she could make the lead official somehow—Devlin and the squad could finesse something, surely. How long would that take though?

The melee in her brain was interrupted by the sound of sobbing. "Am a, am a gonnae get in trouble?"

"No, but no more dodgy internet trading, all right? And tidy your room."

16

Lottie drove a Mini Cooper. When Paulo was around, it was all enormous Range Rovers and souped-up two-seater sports cars. Blacked-out windows, gunmetal alloys, engine noise like a monster truck. Motors that screamed, "Ill-gotten gains! Check my road tax! I sell cocaine and I'm insecure about the size of my penis!" (Paulo's pinger was probably on the larger side of average, but that's the male psyche for you.) Now he was gone, Lottie had downgraded to a vehicle which was sporty in a running-shoe sort of way but not flashy or attention-grabbing. That was Paulo's downfall. Too much attention. Lottie and Luce went about their business as discreetly as possible. They'd earned a reputation—with the right people—for being smart, even-handed and solid. They had risen quickly but seemed, for the moment, to have reached a plateau. Income was steady but growth shrinking, something she and Luce had talked round and round for months. And now some bastard had made a play for the top seat, causing absolute chaos.

They'd tried to set up some meetings but nobody was keen to congregate in case they ended up getting Callaghan'd. No firm had claimed the ambush as their own work, so nobody could be trusted. The situation was fraught and bank balances would be hit—except for that of the prick who'd just made off with millions in crypto.

That's what McCoist had told her. "Hear anything about that?"

"Naw. Al keep an ear oot, but. Wis it this wee guy Forbes who did it then?"

Snuffling of breath over the line.

"Moan, it wis a good tip, aye? Wis it him then?" It was Luce who had uncovered the odd link between the marathon-running Insta-gimp and Callaghan. Forbes had been a minion of Callaghan's years ago, before the running, back when Callaghan was still up-and-coming, still something of a minion himself. He'd taken a quick route up though, Callaghan, a quick time at the top too. Burnt hot and fast like a fuse.

"He's part of it but I don't know what part."

"Bullshit. This is sposed tae be a two-way street. Ye want oor help, then ye huv tae gee us mare than that."

"Missing crypto is the hot lead, I've given enough. I'm sure Branson can do something with it."

"Sat sposed tae mean?"

"Nothing." *Fuckin cow.* Lottie'd have her fucking heed on a plate soon. "She's the more experienced one, that's all. Full Rolodex. She'll know someone who knows someone who knows something." That snidey tone. No wonder her ex did a runner and took the kids. What a fucking nightmare.

"Leave it wae me." Play nice, Lottie told herself. Be sweet.

She parked outside the Pure Gym in her Mini and waited.

He turned up on schedule. *No bad fir a forty-somehin oaffice boay*. Bit saggy around the middle in his too-new athleisure gear but was working on it. Nice face. He wore the greys creeping up around his temples well.

Lottie got out the car, snatching up her gym bag and hurried until she was behind him. She spoke as he was about to let the door drop. "Fancy seein you here again."

17

He tells them. Everything. All he can tell. It comes out of him before they've even finished binding him to his chair. Comes out as easy as the pish from his bladder and the watery shite hosing from his sphincter, his hole loose as if he'd huffed a snootful of Liquid Gold. The words gush from his mouth. Triply incontinent.

There's no need to go further.

"That's aw. A swear, that's aw!" His voice is high, almost a shriek. "Swear! Swear oan ma maw's life!"

She—the woman who's been asking most of the questions while the other two masks tear through his bedroom—asks again: "Where is he?"

"He-he didnae say! He didnae." His breath is starting to whoop between words, air struggling to fill his lungs. "A. Don't. Know."

"Nothin here," one of the men growls.

"He widnae huv left anyhin wae this shitebag tae keep planked," she says, and he can see the smirk through the mouth slit in her balaclava.

Rather than offending him, her words give him minor relief. She's understanding, she's getting him. He won't lie, he won't hide anything from her. He is too afraid. There is no need—

She lunges. Her head darting down to where his hand is tied.

Excruciating pain. He gives a death-metal scream—a throat-blistering, skin-shivering scream. It keeps on hurting. His thumb. Even if he opens his eyes, stops thrashing his head around, he won't see what's happening, the back of her head obscuring the sight. It goes on. The pain keeps getting worse. A sharp, digging pain, getting deeper. Worse than anything he's ever felt before. And it goes on. Not in waves, just a steadily increasing, agonising pressure. Sorer, sorer, sorer. Even when she stops, the pain doesn't.

She stands up and spits. Something lands in his lap. Through tears he can't make out what it is. Even when he looks at the ragged stump where his left thumb used to be, he still can't make sense of it.

He shakes with adrenaline. His vision swims. He whities. Add it to the body-fluid cocktail he is sitting in.

Her lips are dripping with blood. It fills the cracks between her teeth. It's soaking into the wool of her balaclava. "Nine chances left," she says. "Nae keysies fir ye noo, either." She laughs, an ugly duckling honk.

"Wit's that?" one of the men asks.

"Keysies! Ye no mind that?" She sticks two thumbs up. "Keysies! Am in den, ye cannae get me. When yer playin tig as a wean, mind?" She laughs again and the man joins in. The other is keeping his distance.

A noise is coming from his belly, gurgling and groaning out his throat. A cattle-like noise. He can't control it. He tries to speak. "A don't... a don't..."

She takes his index finger in her mouth. He feels the soft, wet inside of her cheek. Then the teeth.

18

Nothing like carrying a big ole sack of money to turn you into a feeble, tweaking wreck afraid of your own reflection following you down the street in the shop windows. He felt like people could see right through the gym bag to the bundles of cash inside. He held the strap with a dead man's grip. He'd thought the trip to Pontoon's gaff had been a fraught affair… This was nerve-shredding. He was like the Warriors trying to get back to Coney through enemy territory, every man around him about to reveal his colours and throw down, every woman about to attempt to seduce him then stab him while he was vulnerable. An auld dear pushing along her walker gave him a look that made him worry she might pull an AK from under her skirt.

It's aw in yer heed, ye dafty. Imagination running riot. He needed to be on guard for actual threats. If his mind was blowing everything in view up into a potential danger, he'd miss the real thing when he saw it.

This feeling was familiar. He'd been all over the city with baggies, blades and cash (at the time, unimaginably large amounts of it) in his pockets as a kid. Risking violence, arrest, death. Before lockdown in 2020, when Callaghan had delivered the big one, Fran had felt something similar to this. An acid paranoia that threatened to consume him. But he'd got a lid on it and done the job. This was worse, but he needed to do it again. He reached for a mantra, a reassurance:

No risk, no reward.

It landed flat. A banal bro-ism. He remembered reading an article about how King—then Prince—Charles had received fat bundles of cash for his charities from some sheik in a briefcase once. And in holdalls like Fran's, and even in fucking carrier bags. The would-be king just standing there casually with three mil in hard cashish in a poly bag, bold as you like. *Channel that energy. Monarchy energy.*

Fran had been making collections. He'd set up accounts with different banks and transferred various amounts from the crypto wallet to each, which he was now bundling together. Just enough for now, not the whole amount, of course. There was too much. When Pontoon had told him what all that crypto was worth he'd nearly keeched himself. Again. He was sweet sixteen years old, brick of cocaine wrapped in paper and packing tape—*a don't know wit the fuck am daein. Am in oer ma heed, a cannae see the surface.*

But if that wee guy could do it... Fran avoided causing a scene, kept his pants clean, and made Pontoon a generous offer for his time. Then he went back to his da to report. Neil was so fucking amazed he jumped—a full inch of air between his feet and the floor.

The plan was fully in action. Fran made his last collection of the day at the Credit Union on Shettleston Road just before they shut up shop. Then it was off to the nearby station where he'd ride the train to Edinburgh and rendezvous with his da. Neil had gone ahead and was charged with organising a car, a place to kip and an emergency meeting with the passport office. Perfect. The thing was set up like a teetering Rube Goldberg machine.

As he was making his way down the main street towards the junction with Old Shettleston Road, where the teams of blonde and red tenements faced off against each other, the austere castle keep and spire of the old church presiding over the traffic, something brought him to a standstill.

There was a man walking towards him. Not looking at him. Carefully not looking at him. He wore a puffa jacket and jeans, trendy gutties with spring suspension in the heels. His hair was shaved to the quick and greyish, his nose a raw, violent pink, as if he had a cold. He was wearing a black snood around his neck.

Fran's heart started to rumba. He turned carefully, not as if he was about to dash away, but as if he had forgotten something, maybe, and needed to head back where he'd come from. As he headed back the other way, another man came onto the street up ahead—stepping out from a dead end that led to the academy. *Maybe his wean goes there. Couldae bin in tae speak wae a teacher or somehin.* It was a bit late, back of five. *Maybe he* is *a teacher.* He was rough-looking. *It's Shettleston, but. Disnae mean anyhin.* He had a cap on. *Height ae fuckin fashion.*

Both men were coming towards him now, a pincer.

Fran snapped, sprinted out onto the road to his right, horns blaring. He pumped his arms and legs, felt good despite everything. Pace set for miracle-one-minute-mile past the church, up Old Shettleston Road, the big Tesco in sight. Train station was up this way—too early, couldn't wait on the platform. Cast a look back—nobody behind. Not yet. Could have been wrong. Best to keep running for a bit anyway. Took a blind turn.

Into some houses, dropped from a sprint to a jog, knees protesting already, so soon. He resettled the bag on his shoulder. Still nobody following. A long close divided blocks of houses and he scurried on in, passing between rows of high wooden fences topped with nails and glass. *Bad move, bad move. Get oot ae this. Fuckin trench. Go back, naw, go foarward.* He pushed on, he was closer to the end now, almost out onto the other street anyway. One last glance back.

He turned his head forward to the car bonnet shooting out over the mouth of the close. He jumped. Weighed down awkwardly on one side by the bag. Almost clear but clipped it, went sliding over the bonnet, crashing off the other side onto the ground in a heap.

His shoulder and hip took the worst of it but the wind was knocked out of him, made it hard to get up.

The car door opened and a woman stepped out. "That won't be good for the knees," she said.

19

Shit! Bit more pepper than intended. The lad went bouncing over the bonnet of her car, splatted onto the road.

The Pacino Squad had finally managed to get hold of the bank info (mention of missing crypto millions, on top of a bunch of dead gangsters, had only increased Devlin's interest in the case; the stench of burnt arse hairs from the fires he was lighting under the Squad could be smelt for miles) and McCoist had been fighting her way through traffic, playing cat and mouse with the boy, always a step behind. She'd arrived in Shettleston knowing he'd already made the withdrawal. Cruising the area in rush-hour traffic would have been a turgid nightmare, one she was about to live until she spotted a man absolutely haring over the road by the kirk, kicking up a fuss, a gym bag over his shoulder. She'd gone into pursuit, losing him as the traffic lights went against her but picking him up not far away. He slipped down a close and she hedged her bets, hoping to catch him at the other end.

Maybe she'd been a bit too successful, she thought, as she looked at him curled up on the ground. He'd dented her car. "That won't be good for the knees," she said. Couldn't resist. Adrenaline always clogged up her brain-to-mouth filter. She approached with her PAVA spray in one hand, warrant card in the other.

He sat himself upright.

"Stay on the ground."

With a grunt he moved to get to his feet.

"I don't want to hurt you, but—"

"Ye fuckin ran me oer!" he panted.

"Fine, I don't want to hurt you *further*." She waved the can of self-defence spray. "I'm a police officer." Waved the card this time. "Detective Chief Inspector McCoist. I'm guessing you know I've been looking for you. Why don't you get in the car? We can get you checked out while we have a talk."

"I'm fine," he wheezed, sucking air in through his teeth, hands putting pressure on his hip.

"OK then, let's head straight to the station." Handcuffs replaced the card. "Francesco Forbes, I am arresting you under the Criminal Justice—"

His eyes went wide. Not at her. Behind her. She turned—

He lunged at the gym bag, wrenched himself up, launching from hands and feet into a ragged sprint.

Hard soles slapped the pavement. Big boys. Balaclavas covering faces—two from one side of the street, one from the other. McCoist's brain was processing too slowly—*where the fuck had they come from?*—frozen as one caught up to Fran and tackled him to the ground. *They wouldn't fucking fire guns in a housing estate with the sun still up, would they?*

She took the chance.

She dived into the scramble, dousing the masked thug and Fran in a cloud of PAVA. They screamed and rolled apart. A flailing boot hit McCoist hard and she dropped to a knee. She gave the guy another dose, held the button till the can sputtered to an empty dribble.

Fran had scrambled upright again and was on the move but the other two had nearly caught up.

McCoist rocketed in low at one of them, shoulder into the belly, fist into the groin. He was a solid unit, but. Gave only an inch. McCoist was rewarded with a two-fisted hammer blow to her back. Pain lit up the nodes of her spinal column. She screamed and hit the deck, face on the damp pavement, eyes in line with the chunky sole of a black boot. Its partner stomped down on her head.

Exploding, screaming pain sharp and hard like a table edge in the back of her skull. Then another, driven into her side this time, forcing stomach acid upwards.

"Haw, leave it. Get eftir him." A woman's voice, floating above, a sense of someone stepping right over her. McCoist's eyes were closed to the pain, a galaxy of nauseating swirling lights in her eyelids. Her back was on fire, head splitting. She wanted to stay where she was. Everything would be sorer if she tried to move.

But she had to.

She lifted her face from the road and a blistering electric shock ran through all her wires. Getting up onto her arse needed a lot of yelling through clenched teeth and swearing. Nobody was around. No sign of Fran or the gang of attackers.

"Get the fuck up," she hissed. "Get the fuck up."

20

[CONFIDENTIAL]
OP THUNDERHEAD / Audio Log
Recorded by Device OPT012/Loc B02
Speaker 1 believed to be TARGET Detective Superintendent Roy Devlin, on speakerphone. Speaker 2 is TARGET Detective Chief Inspector Alison McCoist.

SPEAKER 1
What happened?

SPEAKER 2
Got jumped. Three of them, wearing ballies, two men and a woman, I think. Forbes escaped, others got away too. I'm combing the area. No sighting yet. Need some help.

SPEAKER 1
Escaped together?

SPEAKER 2
No, they were after him.

SPEAKER 1
After the money.

SPEAKER 2
We need to find him.

SPEAKER 1

A lot of questions if we make it official—a tip from McGuinn doesn't look good.

SPEAKER 2

I'm sure you can handle it.

SPEAKER 1

Don't test me, Bear.

...

Are you injured?

SPEAKER 2

Can you get someone on CCTV at least?

...

Sir?

SPEAKER 1

Already happening. I've got a car heading out to you too. I'll send people to Forbes's flat and get eyes on his parents' places too. Are you injured?

SPEAKER 2

I'm fine. We need to know how they found him. Is there some way they could have been tracing him through the banks too?

SPEAKER 1

Maybe. I can think of another way they might have traced him though.

...

SPEAKER 2

Shite. Shite. No. Fuck! [thudding noises, car horn beeps]

SPEAKER 1

You need to stand down for now. Head to London Road.

SPEAKER 2

No. I need to check something first.

21

No answer. The door was unlocked. Something primal inside McCoist's battered body screamed at her not to go in.

She opened the door.

The sound of the telly came out to meet her. Overloud, the way her maw watched it, volume cranked up into the fifties, polished studio voices turned brash with distortion, polite laugh of the studio audience becoming a hideous, carnival roar. The hairs on McCoist's skin vibrated with the blistering static hiss of it.

There was a large dent in the woodchip wall that faced her. A unit had been tipped over, blocking the narrow hall, shoes spilling over the carpet. McCoist clambered over it, her back and her bruised flank not liking it one bit. The bedroom door was ajar.

On her last visit, it had smelt of dirty clothes piling up, a dense, mouldy hum of weed, a sickly plug-in scent from the rest of the flat fighting to annex it. Now there was the rank odour of a backed-up toilet.

They'd bound him to his throne. The skin was already swollen and blackening around the cable ties cutting into his wrists. Splinters of bone stood proud of the stubs where his fingers used to be, like stripped wires. His chin was on his chest, black T-shirt sodden, a pool in his lap. It was a small room. The spray on the wall opposite was considerable, and so perfectly fresh and red it might have come from a can.

McCoist stumbled back, gorge rising. *You'll be fine. You're talking to me now, so I can help you.* Her own words stuck her like barbs.

Nicholas's maw was in the living room. They'd made a mess of her.

McCoist took refuge in the kitchen. It was poky and smelt of dirty old frying oil, which was not sitting well with the queasy churning in McCoist's belly. It wasn't just the foul sensory overload of the brutality she'd just seen either.

She'd led them right here. Right to Nicholas, and his mother. They must have been on her all day, maybe longer. Whoever they were. *These fucks. Sick fucking bastards. Monsters.* She railed at them for some quick respite then turned the anger back on herself. Blundering around on some solo crusade again… No, not solo. There was Devlin and the rest. His little squad, his network. They played their part too. She was simply the poor sod at the sharp end of it.

This wasn't the first time someone she'd personally offered her "help" to had ended up dead. The ghosts were mounting up. The unintentional victims of her carelessness, in her tunnel-visioned pursuit of… what? She might call it "justice" sometimes, when she could summon the righteousness and self-deceit required. Aching and sicky and miserable, hiding in the kitchen from what was in the rest of the home, she could not.

Finally, her phone rang.

"Update?" The calm, pleasant inflection of his voice right then was an indictment of the bastard. McCoist always thought of Devlin as having the look of a librarian—a kindly, lived-in face, hazel eyes under the sagging folds of his brows, glasses at the end his nose—and the soft, warm tones to match. All a deception. Beneath was something so cold it couldn't be touched without you getting burnt. Mark used to joke she had a "snow-ball for a heart" whenever she said something Grinchy around

Christmastime. It was something approaching the truth with Devlin.

"Nicholas Stewart and his mother are both dead."

Rustling sigh. "Not good."

"No. They tortured them."

"They wouldn't have much to tell."

"Didn't stop them. They cut his fingers off and slit his throat."

"Getting upset isn't going to help."

Wanker. "I am not upset. I just—this is too big. We should have finagled McGuinn's tip into something official earlier. Then maybe—"

"Well, we didn't. And we can't change the outcome of that."

"Let's do it now then."

"Bear, you are here to handle this shit. If I didn't think you could manage it, I would have left you at that car wash holding the gun over Paul McGuinn's fresh corpse."

Sometimes, she wished he had. But it was too late, and she'd come too far. There had maybe been a time, earlier, when she could have come clean and still maybe avoided a lifetime in prison, but her pact with Devlin had been sealed two years ago, with Si.

McCoist wrangled her despair. Pulled herself together but made sure there was absolutely no deference in her voice. "What's the plan?"

"Same as before. Stand down. Get to London Road, do some real work."

"And what about Nicholas and his mother?"

"What about them?"

"It's a double murder, sir. A crime, you know?"

"A crime you should not be aware of. And I'm going to ignore the histrionics because you've had a rough day." *Prick.*

"So I should just leave them?"

"It'll get picked up eventually. They live in a flat. A neighbour will complain about the noise or the smell. Then we can look into it officially. If you want to get the Forbes lead on the books, this could be the chance."

She couldn't... The room opened around her, walls receding, she felt off balance. Her eyes strained, tears stinging, felt acid in her chest, oozing up her throat, swallowed hard. The back of her head throbbed where she'd been stamped on. *Let them rot. That's what he's saying.* She couldn't... *You'll be fine... I can help you...* She saw Nicholas's terrified, flabby face, eyes pleading. *Am a gonnae get in trouble?* Whatever they'd used to take his fingers off hadn't been sharp enough to do the job cleanly.

Fucked it. She'd failed him in life, no way she could do it in death too...

She staggered to the front door, closed it softly on her way out.

She'd driven a good couple of miles away before she had to pull over. Head against the steering wheel, hands gripping it tight, shoulders shaking, face leaking tears and snot. How had it come to this? Sorrow for Nicholas had turned to sorrow for herself. What had she done? Done now... The list was getting long.

The answer came when the shaking stopped and the tears dried: *You have done what is necessary*. The voice wasn't quite her own—she recognised and despised Devlin's influence. But wasn't he right?

It was too late after a long day for all this. "I'm going to ignore the histrionics," her lips mimed. *See if you can ignore my foot right up yer fuckin shite pipe ye bony auld cunt.*

She googled phone booths and drove to the nearest one. Dialled 999, didn't leave her name.

22

He lost them before Carntyne and kept on going till he was halfway back to the city centre. Even with dodgy knees and after being hit by a car (then pepper-sprayed—that was the fucking worst of it, the sting was unreal, like his eyeballs had gonorrhoea) Fran was still faster than the average henchman and had the stamina to outlast anyone. *Let's see Paula fuckin Radcliffe dae that!* That said, squatting to take a deuce mid-race took a lot of sack, maybe Paula would have this running from gangsters shite locked down.

Moving, despite the creaking all over, was good for him, buoyed his mood and energised his mind, though the second-half fatigue hammered him after mere miles. No wonder, he'd been living in a vinegary soup of adrenaline and cortisol for days now. There was a comedown approaching, a time when his body and brain would both collapse and he would have to rest whether he had time for it or not. Best to be somewhere safe when it happened.

He hailed a hack, hoping it was dark enough that the driver wouldn't notice his eyes looked like he'd been hanging out with Snoop Dogg. He cursed the poliswoman McCoist again.

"Could ye take us tae Motherwell, please, mate?"

The driver started to huff.

Lazy bastart. Cunt's litrally sittin doon aw day. Fran slipped his hand into his gym bag and pulled out a fifty. "There's a good tip in it fir ye. Promise."

Still another huff. "Awright, awright. Where aboots in Motherwell?"

"Train station."

The driver pressed a button to start the meter—Fran baulked at the starting fare, *robbin bastart!*—then flicked his indicator on and did a burly in the middle of the road, flashing lights and horns honking in all directions, Fran grabbing hold of the handle above the door, his sore side slammed against it as they veered into the correct lane. *Get me oan a fuckin train, please, God. Get me tae fuckin Embra.*

He hoped his da had managed his end of the plan and wasn't busy being a useless cunt. Delegation was hard for Fran. Especially when the people he had to rely on were of such a low calibre.

Surround yourself with like-minded people. People who want to push themselves, improve themselves, who are serious about growth, both personal and professional.

If only.

23

"Coffee, gaffer?" Travis had it made already, presented it to her two-handed like a trophy. "How you like it." He spoke slow and gentle, as if addressing a child. She must look rough.

"Cheers, Gaz."

Khan slinked up beside him apologetically with the paperwork.

"Cheers, Suffy."

Then it was Griffiths, steering her into her own office. "Are you OK?"

"Fine, Kelly, thanks. Take a seat. What have I missed?"

The question of why she'd been absent hovered between them, reproach in the DI's eyes turning to curiosity, suspicion. Switch it off, McCoist thought, exhausted. Fucking polis. It went unasked and Griffiths busied herself with filling McCoist in on the latest.

"Forensic report is back." Griffiths spread paperwork over McCoist's desk, diagrams of bodies with injuries drawn on. "Callaghan, Rowlands and McKinley all died from gunshot wounds, although there were other injuries on McKinley too—blunt force. McKenzie's skull was caved in and Gregson, ultimately, bled out from multiple stab wounds, the worst one being in his heart.

"We now have an ID for body no. 6: Arthur 'Arty' Sutherland. As he was the only one wearing a balaclava and a vest, we were thinking he was with the other team, the hit squad. Powder residue on the sleeves of his jacket certainly confirms he was shooting a weapon, but no gun was found on him or near him.

"Sutherland had a bullet in his hip—not lethal—and his throat slit."

"Very lethal."

"Callaghan's team were strapped but it looks like they didn't manage to draw down on time. Rowlands was found holding a shotgun which had been fired once, looks like he was the only one to get a shot off. SOCOs were digging pellets from the scene but no sign he hit anybody."

"So who shot Sutherland? Friendly fire?"

"The calibre of the bullet matches those inside McKinley, which would suggest that. But the throat… I think they killed him too."

"They…? His own people?"

"Uh huh. The cut through the throat was very clean and very deep. I don't see it happening in the middle of the scrap. And looking at the weapons left at the scene, the report says none of them are a good match for that type of wound."

McCoist chewed it over, pushed gory scene photos around. Wanted to go home. Wanted to see Bruce and Maisie and smell their fur and feel their velvety ears. "Do we know anything about Sutherland? Are we sure he wasn't with Callaghan?"

"Maybe he was, and I'm just… I don't know. It seems off; I think we can be sure the ambush party killed him, but something tells me he was a member of the party himself. The mask, the armour, the missing gun."

McCoist *hmmm*ed it over.

"He's been around for a while. Done work for most of the big names over the years, got his start back with Billy Jamieson."

"Jamieson?" The name sparked through her nervous system. "Could this be to do with him? His throat was cut." Right in front of her. McCoist had to be careful here, not let anything slip that she should not know. Like the colour of the meat inside Jamieson's neck.

"A reprisal against Callaghan?"

"Was never proved to be him, but that was the conventional wisdom at the time."

"Interesting angle."

Indeed. McCoist's knackered brain shook up its fizzy dregs. What if it wasn't a power play? What if it was revenge? Who cared about Jamieson enough to do all this? And how did Fran and all those millions in crypto square with that? Didn't quite fit for McCoist.

"Recently though, Sutherland has been linked to the Russian mob."

"The Russian mob?" McCoist nearly lost a mouthful of coffee. Now *that* fit with a king's ransom of Dobber-coin. *Fuck, fuck, fuck.* She heaved a sigh. She needed to get Forbes. It was paramount. "Anything further on the guy in the hoody seen around the shopping centre?"

"Lost in blind spots. You think it's a good lead?"

"Definitely worth ruling it out. Let's get the images out there."

"Will do, gaffer."

"Let's speak to all the victims' families again. Friends and associates. Someone will know something. They always do."

"On it." *Already on it,* was what Griffiths wanted to say to her clueless boss—McCoist could hear it in the tone of her voice. Her ear was tuned to it because Tess used it on her so often. Oh well. One day you're the young upstart, the next you're the old fart everybody wishes would retire.

"And speaking of family, was anything interesting dug up about Euan Callaghan?"

"Squeaky clean."

"Keep looking."

Duh.

. . .

McCoist was drawing some side-eyes, heading out again already. *Where is she always going off to?* She was too frazzled to care how it looked. She needed her home. She needed painkillers and a bath. She needed to let the dugs out into the garden. Travis caught her eye, a worried look on his wee face. Sweet really.

She tweeted the locks open on the car from the halfway line, already dreaming about her bed. Took her till she was about to open the door before she noticed the bloke hovering there.

"DCI McCoist?"

Twinge of fright, but then she spotted the dress uniform peeking out through the open buttons of his grey overcoat. *Oh, what the fuck now?* "Superintendent Ralston." He held out his card. "You can call me Eddie." Clip of a smile. "We need to talk. I'm in the blue A3. Follow me."

24

Three words on the man's warrant card had turned McCoist into a puddle of goo like Alex Mack:

Anti-Corruption Unit

She followed his red lights as if they were magnetic, hands slick on the steering wheel. He drove them through Brigton, then turned into the Green, pulled up at the busy car park at the football centre.

The floodlights were on over the five-a-side pitches, games being played as a fine haze of rain started to fall. Voices cried hoarse in the air—"Man oan! Tae me! Tae me!"—the Weeknight World Cup, a bit of a laugh, a bit of exercise, a bit of break-some-cunt's-ankle-if-he-tries-to-put-it-past-me.

Ralston crawled a few rows in and slotted into a space. McCoist pulled in where she could see his motor. His hazards flashed an invitation.

Shitshitshit. Which one of the many fucking things McCoist had done could he possibly know about? She wasn't under arrest though. Not even under caution. No interview room, no federation rep at her shoulder. She thought of those threatening messages—*What will they think when they find out? Would they still love you?* She thought about calling Devlin quickly.

The hazards flashed again.

The drizzle was cool against her thumping headache, damp on her clothes, bruises below.

Ralston's car was so low-slung that it hurt her back getting in. Inside, it smelt of clean, polished pride. Ralston himself had the same fresh essence of care and attention. Clean-shaven, crisply ironed, hair slick, shiny and blocked-out black like he'd combed it with tyre shine. By comparison, McCoist looked and felt like roadkill.

"How's the investigation going? Big one. *Big* one." There was sympathy in the way he said it, the raise of his eyebrows that told her, *I know what that's like.*

"Aye, plenty of leads though."

"Four days in?"

"Including the weekend. I like to think of it as two business days in."

She saw his teeth in the light spilling over from the pitches. "It's really nice to finally meet you in person."

Water glugged in McCoist's belly like a blocked drain, a shiver from damp hair running down her neck. "What does that mean?"

He made a musical hum. "You can probably guess, but let's make it easy. We've had our eyes and ears on you for some time."

"Why?"

His laugh was good-natured, thoroughly decent. "There are no bugs in *my* car, Alison, we can talk freely, you don't need to pretend."

"I'm not." The feebleness in her voice sickened her.

"OK, OK. How about *I* talk freely then? We—that is, my team at the ACU—know all about Simon Slater."

McCoist focused on the raindrops running down the windscreen, chose one and followed its path.

"We know you were involved in his disappearance. Pulling that thread, well, we know you had a hand in Paulo McGuinn's death too. Simon is dead, isn't he?"

She tried to guess which path the raindrop would take.

The wipers chopped up—McCoist jumped—and cleared the window.

The last she'd seen of Si he was being dragged off into a van, never to be seen again. Set up by Devlin. Set up by her. "He remains a missing person."

"Sure. But as you and I know, no body doesn't mean no crime. And we have enough information to gum up the works for you. And that's..."—frowny-sounding hum this time—"...the best-case scenario. More likely you'll lose your job and might spend a good while in jail."

The heat inside the car was stifling.

"Probably in the protected wing," he added brightly, "with the, you know, mums who've killed their babies and whatnot. How does that sound?"

"You think you can intimidate me?" Her voice was small, even with all her remaining strength mustered into it.

"You? Oh no. Not you." He leant towards her, checked his reflection in the rear-view, smoothed a stray hair. "I feel like I've got to know you quite well, and, frankly, I don't think I'd manage to intimidate you. I mean, Paulo McGuinn—there was a scary motherfucker. And Billy Jamieson? Christ, the stories you heard! No, no, I'm just... a desk jockey really. I make sure nobody's nicking the office stationery. I wouldn't even dare—"

"I had nothing to do with either of them."

"Or Sheriff Cresswell?"

"He did himself in."

"That he did." Ralston did his tuneful, irritating hum again. "And maybe you didn't have anything to do with that, or any of it. Maybe it was all Roy Devlin."

McCoist almost flinched, the name dropped on her like a brick.

"Maybe he's the one who deserves to be put away for this. I certainly think so. Roy Devlin is a malignant tumour, a growth feeding on our institution. He talks a good game about fairness and justice and keeping the peace, I know he does. I know his mothy old schtick, his views on morality and law. You could say I'm a good student of his. But at his core, he's a crook. A dangerous one."

His eyes implored her, she could feel them. He waited until she lost the fight and turned to look at them.

"Help me take him down, Alison. Cooperate, and the investigation into you can go away."

"You want me to grass?"

He liked that—teeth glowing in the dark, a delighted "Ha!" "We're the police. Grassing is our whole thing." He checked his watch, then pulled the handle on his door, indicated McCoist should do the same. She came round the car and he popped the boot open. The smell of plastic-polish detailing was replaced by sweaty socks, emanating from a gym bag. Ralston shrugged his overcoat off, folded it in half and chucked it in.

"We know about his network of stooges in the force." His dress jacket with the silver on its shoulders came off next. "We know you're a part of it. What we want..."—he loosened his tie and pulled it over his head—"...is for you to keep doing what you're doing. But..."—he unbuttoned his regulation white shirt, revealing the blue and white stripes of an Argentina jersey underneath—"...you report everything to us. You're our insider." His trousers dropped—full kit on—and he sat on the lip of the boot to pull his polished wingtips off. "You look for opportunities, anything incriminating, pass it to us. We need to find something we can act on." From the gym bag he pulled some long socks and a pair of dog-chewed Predators. "We're building a solid case but he's a slick one. We need more, and we need it faster. You are the dynamite we need to blow his whole operation wide open. Bring the dark into the light, Alison."

Suited and booted, he started to jog on the spot, bring his knees up to hit his hands.

"I didn't agree to do anything."

"You didn't?" He was huffing and puffing away.

McCoist's need for home had become a desperate longing. It was all too much. Thoughts and fears clashed inside her. Too beaten down to strategise, to weigh up the options.

He stopped the high knees, planted his feet wide apart, put his hands on his hips and started to gyrate. "I can't promise you you'll still be a DCI after all this is over, or even a police officer, but we can keep you out the jail. And that's a helluva lot better than being inside it. It's all in motion anyway, Alison, be my catalyst and I'll help you."

McCoist had been on the other side of this conversation several times. Offering her help in return for information. *Trust me.* Every time it had ended badly, Nicholas only the most recent victim. (She choked down an image of ragged finger bone protruding from a raw, liver-purple stump of flesh.) Yet, she found herself desperate to believe Ralston could indeed put an end to the paranoid nightmare her life had become and bring her through to the other side safely. *Too good to be true.*

She agreed.

"Brilliant! Yes! Thank you!" He clapped her shoulder, harder than intended. "Sorry, speak soon!" He jogged off towards the pitches, "MESSI" on the back of his shirt.

It was an effort to get from the car to the front door. Still, she managed a wave (lifting her arm caused a twinge of pain in her back) towards her neighbour, Edith—a strip of light between the curtains next door, nosy old bat. In the hall, she heard the sound of the dogs jumping off the sofa in the living room, where they bundled up together between walks and meals. Bruce gave a couple of sonorous, wolfish barks, the sound capable of conjuring a primal fear from deep in the human core—until you actually saw his dopey face and clueless eyes, his gangling, clumsy body that had none of the grace or majesty or sleek, hungry purpose of his ancestors. Maisie was a lady and would never bark.

McCoist opened the living-room door and was swamped in fur and paws and wet tongues. "Hello, hello, hello." Bruce bounded away down the hall and back again, launching himself at her. McCoist caught him, nearly fell over, closed her eyes as he lapped at her mouth and nose. "Stop, I know where that thing's been." She gently pushed his muzzle away and clapped his side. Maisie flicked at McCoist's elbow with her snout. "Oh, you too, you too. I'm not forgetting you. No."

She stood and Bruce darted down the hall again. "Garden, come on." She let them out and they bounded around the grass and did their business, absolutely wrecking the joint. That was one thing about having two dugs. The amount of shite McCoist had to collect... She was forever walking through the park or down the street with bags full of juicy, tan logs. Glamour was not something McCoist had ever worried about, but lately this image of herself in her manky raincoat, old jeans and wellies, sacks of shit swinging from her hand, had begun to niggle at her, make her uncomfortable. Midlife crisis looming? Could she head it off by buying a motorbike or something already? Quitting her job?

If only.

Her work was like a trap from *Saw*. Trying to pull away would destroy her. The only way was through, which involved a slow flaying.

Would she really spy on Devlin for Ralston? She fucking hated Devlin sometimes. But they'd worked together for years now, done some good too, even. Sometimes. She couldn't help having a sense of loyalty, ill-placed though it might be. It was all just… she sighed… so *big*. Staggering. It was like grassing on Jesus to God. There was probably a better analogy with Greek deities—they were more suitably unhinged and amoral—but McCoist wasn't up on the Classics. If she fucked up, one or the other would turn her into a goat or something, that was the point to remember. There would be punishment. Prison. Mark, Tess, Cam—they'd know about everything she did. How would she explain it to them? Make them understand?

Would they still love you?

Again, she felt tears building up against the dam.

What a fucking day.

Duped by whoever killed Callaghan. Leathered by them, letting a key suspect slip away. Maybe they had Forbes. Maybe the next time she'd see him he would be a corpse. She hoped all that running had kept him free.

Then she'd discovered their latest victims, Nicholas and his mum. Pointlessly tortured. He would have told them whatever he knew. He'd spilt to McCoist at the mere threat of trouble with authority. No way a blade would have turned him silent and stoic. Nor should it. He didn't owe Forbes anything, or McCoist. They both used him, neither caring about the consequences he might face. Not that she'd foreseen… *Ragged, meaty stumps, bone poking out, French-trimmed…*

Wine. Wine now. Wine and painkillers.

She filled the dogs' bowls with water, her own with red.

Then, to top a brilliant shift, the corn that crowned the shite sundae, the AC-fucking-U had her bang to rights. Finally. Inevitably.

She collapsed on the sofa, glass in hand, dogs piling onto her, digging and padding about for comfort, little care for McCoist's. In a way, she thought ruefully, it was these animals that brought her down.

Bruce she'd stolen, in a moment of madness, from a puppy mill she was to shut down. A minor transgression that set her on the slope. And Maisie—

She saw Si in her mind, standing in front of her, face twisted in anger and confusion, wrestled away into a van, howling against the gloved hand slapped over his mouth.

Maisie was a furry telltale heart.

McCoist wondered if there was some third dog out there, waiting to finish her off for good. She bent her head towards the dugs, breathed in their fur, let it calm her. They would love her no matter what.

She felt pathetic and cried.

25

"A want thum tae look like av just gutted a man wae them," Lottie had told the girl, who nodded cheerfully at the request and painted her nails a luscious, almost-brown aubergine colour marbled with gristly pinks and a hint of fatty white, a crust of tiny ruby-red stones built up at the quick. "Smashin, doll."

"Awright, hen?" Luce tinkled through the salon door.

"Where's Hannah?"

Luce ignored the tone, the face. "Work tae dae, cannae aw sit aboot gettin pampered."

"That so? Yer eyebrows thread themsels this mornin?"

Luce's laugh was a loud and bright thing these days. It irked Lottie. *Yer becomin a bitter auld maid,* she chided herself. That's what it meant when other people's happiness started to make you sick. Or maybe she was jealous of them. Or maybe she was just needing a good pumping. It had, as Luce guessed, been a while, though she was working on a wee something-something. She'd had a vivid, disturbing and arousing dream about Noel Edmonds the other night. It was a bad sign—maybe her plans needed to be brought forward. *What's in your box?* She shuddered. "Tea?"

"Tea! Tea an fags."

They did just that, sitting in the office in the back, window open to the chill autumn air where Luce sat puffing, fag in one hand, a fork in the other, picking at a tin of pineapple chunks. This was another new thing since Hannah: fruit.

"Pineapple makes yer fud taste good, ye know?" she explained.

"Bullshit," Lottie snorted. "They say the same aboot it changein the flavour ae men's spunk, it's nonsense."

"Naw, it's true, a swear. A read it in a magazine. Makes ye sweet."

"An who's their source fir that, eh? The Man fae fuckin Del Monte?"

Luce laughed. "Ye accusin us ae bein taken in by Big Pineapple? Ye need tae get aff yer phone, hen."

"Would if a could, but it never stoaps ringin." Lottie gripped a Wagon Wheel carefully between the tips of her newly manicured claws. Luce filled her in on the comings and goings, the jobs and the take. The issues, always issues, man. Haggling and logistics and, the worst, little boys falling out. Plus there was a woman kicking up a fuss on Facebook about their MLM beauty-product company, calling it a pyramid scheme and warning people away from it.

"Hannah's keen tae go an sort her oot."

Hannah needs a muzzle an lead. "Naw, last hing we need is a civilian gettin put in hoaspital. Is she merried? Weans?"

"Baith."

"Catfish her, get some nice photies she widnae want hubby tae see. Stefan's aw-ways game."

"You'd know."

"Aye right. Fuckin a cactus wid gee ye less stingy pains in yer chuff. Guy should come wae a list ae side effects. Gee him some ae yer fuckin pineapples."

Luce grinned. "Hows aboot the wan fae the gym yev bin textin then? Is it deal or nae deal?" She roared.

"Fuck aff! Should never bloody tell ye anyhin!" Lottie blushed but couldn't keep herself from laughing too.

"Wit if she disnae go fir Syphy Stefan?" Luce asked when they'd calmed down.

Lottie sighed, ran the pad of her thumb over her long, bloody talons. "Send her some pics ae her weans fae the school gates."

"That's better than geein her a doin?"

Lottie felt a knot in her stomach.

"There's mare kinds ae violence than physical, hen. Mind that," Luce continued.

"It willnae come tae it." She hoped.

"Just sayin. A know ye hink Hannah can be a wee bit… oer the toap, when it comes tae, ye know." She raised her fist like a boxing glove. "But is that any worse than gettin some guy tae trick the wummin intae shaggin him so ye can blackmail her wae photies ae it? Or threatenin her weans?"

"We widnae actually dae anyhin tae thum, but."

"Ye cannae make empty threats in this business, hen."

Lottie remembered two years before, sitting on a chair in some empty squat, watching on a laptop screen a live feed showing the outside of Ari's flat. Gemma inside with her. Two masked men holding the camera, and worse things besides. What they would have done to them, if Callaghan hadn't shown up and…

She couldn't bear to finish the thought. Couldn't bear even the echo of the feeling of such helplessness, such deep fear and despair. She could, however, perfectly recall the way the heel of her shoe had popped Billy Jamieson's eyeball—the texture somewhere between a pickled onion and a soft-boiled egg. *Plourff.* He was already dead when she did it, but the power that had been ripped from her came flooding back, from the point of the heel on up.

"Could Hannah just speak tae her, waeoot takin hings too far?"

"Depends oan how the wummin responds. Nae empty threats."

Lottie wanted something stronger than the tea Luce had made, bitter as it was with the teabag left stewing in it. Society said it was still too early. "Any mare oan the Callaghan hit?"

"Aye. Thread's bin pullt oan that Forbes lad, heard he's oan the run."

"Fae McCoist?"

"And others."

"The wans who killt Callaghan?"

"Guess so. Speakin ae yer poliswummin, has she geed ye anyhin back fir oor tip?"

"Wit a wantet tae speak tae ye aboot."

"Waow." Luce put her *Friends* mug down, stabbed her fag out on the inside of the window frame and tossed it outside. "She really geed ye somehin back?"

"In her ain special way."

"Slap-faced coo."

"She geed us a phone earlier, wis askin aboot Russians."

"Russians?"

"Aye. Wan ae the hitters wis also killed, local boy, Arty Sutherland, ye know him? Knew him? Goes way back, apparently."

Lottie scrunched up her face. "Hmm, al hink oan it."

"Arty's bin workin wae Russians, so she hears, an she wantet tae know ma thoats."

"An wit are yer thoats?" Luce smiled.

"A telt her a know fuck aw aboot Russians. Good dancers. But if a hear anyhin…"

Luce chewed it in, grunted. "Ye need tae be careful, hen. Is she danglin oan your thread or are you danglin oan hers?"

"Al leave aw the danglin fae threads tae yersel an Hannah. A know wit am daein."

"Awright."

"Meantime, maybe we should—"

"Find oot aboot some Russians."

Lottie cheersed her tea mug (pictures of dogs). Her phone pinged. "Mark Gym" again. Something in her reaction made Luce smile.

"Dirty wee stoap-oot."

26

"No. Way."

"Come on, Cam, do yer auld maw a favour."

"So you can crash mine too?"

"It's only a wee dent!" McCoist rubbed a finger in the basin of the arse-sized divot on the bonnet where Forbes had hit her car. (Or where her car had hit him, whichever way you wanted to look at it.) "A toilet plunger could take it out."

"Then go get one."

His responses had begun teasing but were hardening into genuine resistance. McCoist found herself gritting her teeth, "Just do what I tell you" wanting to break out and clap him on the ear. There was a phase when he was about three when he'd constantly refuse to use the toilet. *I don't need, I don't need*—then the inevitable puddle and clean-up. It became a running argument. In a sense it never ended, even though he was no longer a chubby toddler and was now nearly six foot tall and had hair on his chin, and muscles starting to show from the weights and the protein. (One of the first things Mark decreed when Cam started working was that he had to pay for his own eggs now.) It was just the subject that changed.

"You're not even using it."

"So? It's mine. And I don't want it to end up looking like yours."

"It wasn't my fault. They reversed into me." (McCoist had put the blame on a white van.) "Come on, just till I get mine fixed. I can't be seen going about in a banjoed motor."

Cam looked between the purple pimpmobile he'd bought and the forced smile on his maw's face. "No."

"You can't just say no to me."

"How? It's my car, I paid for it."

Little shite. *Why was he being so—I don't need, I don't need. Fucksake.* McCoist didn't have the time. She needed a car that she was sure wasn't being bugged. Even if it was metallic purple and had a spoiler like a paper aeroplane. "Look, I'll pay the tax and insurance, and I'll pay it again next year when you pass your test."

His eyes shone; she could see the internal struggle behind them. "No black box."

Cheeky wee bastard! "Black box but I'll pay two years."

His jaw jutted, lip being chewed. "…I'll get the keys."

McCoist did not say thank you. Cam passed his dad—now the shorter of the two—in the doorway.

"How's tricks?"

"Keepin on, keepin on. Yourself?"

"Fine." Hint of a smile. The venom of their last little chat seemed to have dissipated.

"Yeah?"

"Tired." More truth came out in the word than she intended. It had taken a long time for McCoist to learn she could be vulnerable in front of Mark. Too long, really. Then they were over and it was a habit she had to keep in check.

"They work you too hard." That was one way to put it. When it was divorce time Mark had put the blame on McCoist herself, rather than her employers.

"It's a big case. When it's done, maybe I'll take some holidays."

"You should. Definitely… for sure."

There was a pause, the two of them shuffling their feet, eyes glancing over the Barney the Dinosaur Golf she'd acquired.

McCoist almost filled it by saying that maybe she could take the kids somewhere with her, during the October week. She kept it in: "Everything OK?"

"Eh… well, it's—no, you're really busy already, I don't want to—"

Bluster. He wanted to talk to her about something. This is why he stepped outside to greet her, why he was not still angry about her missing the kids at the weekend. "Mark, is everything OK?"

"You know what, it's probably nothing. Sorry, I should—"

"For the love of God, just tell me. Please."

"If you insist." Lovely smile.

"Mark."

"Sorry. OK. So… I've been getting some weird messages."

Another jolt to the already frayed nerves. McCoist would be lucky if she lived to retire: all this strain must be taking its toll, chipping the years off. "Weird how? What do they say?"

"The first one was, like, 'How… How well do you know the people in your life?' Something like that. I deleted it, thought it was spam, blocked the number. But then I got another one, again withheld, but must have come from a different phone? Cause I blocked the first one, right?"

"What did the next one say?" McCoist fought to keep her voice level and light.

"'She isn't who she says she is.'"

"'She' being?"

"I dunno, didn't say, I mean, I'm… I'm not…" He cleared his throat. "The 'she' in my life right now is my mother." He chuckled, trying to ease the bumbling awkwardness. McCoist's internal lie detector pinged towards bullshit, but it was fine. They didn't talk about this kind of thing. There had been nobody serious enough for either of them, so far.

"Sounds like nonsense." She thought back to her own initial reaction—kids messing about, sending prank messages. Couldn't cling to that any more. Devlin and Ralston had the information, but no motive to wind her up like this. They needed her. Maybe someone on their respective teams? Again, though, why? What would they gain by threatening her like this? Playing with her? Were they hoping she had money? Looking for favours?

"I know, it is. It is. I blocked it again but…"

"Another one?"

"Said: 'She's a killer.'"

What will they think when they find out? Would they still love you? The questions hit like railway spikes in her chest. "Your mother? I'd believe it."

"The Curling Stone Killer. Look, it's stupid, I know it's stupid, probably someone messing around, but I don't *like* it. There's something nasty about it. The spirit of it, even if it's just a prank. D'you think I should… I dunno, report it to the police or something?"

McCoist forced a laugh. "You are reporting it to the police."

"No, I mean, like—"

"I'll see what I can do."

"You don't have to."

"No, no, it's fine."

"Sure?"

"Sure."

27

She parked the purple monstrosity outside the HQ at Clyde Gateway.

(The motor was a violet violator of all senses—an eyesore reeking of smoke and smelly feet, engine like a chainsaw, exhaust making explosive pops that nearly tipped McCoist into a hallucinatory meltdown of car soap and bloody bullet holes—but, most of all, taste.)

She needed to go in; she could not get out of the car. Her knees trembled. Her stomach was a rattly old washing machine walking itself across the kitchen floor. McCoist had never done undercover training. It wasn't something she'd ever been keen to do. She felt like she had "MOLE" stamped on her forehead. Or worse.

A sleepless night had been spent weighing up each side, Devlin v Ralston. She was sceptical of the power Ralston had to protect her when or if they rumbled Devlin. There was nothing to back it up, just his word. But she knew first-hand the power Devlin wielded from his shady throne. He covered things up, made things disappear. Even people.

There were at least three men McCoist knew who were dead directly because of Devlin's interventions: a sheriff, guilty of multiple murders, who had hanged himself; a hitman, working on the sheriff's behalf, beaten to death inside the jail; and Si, taken in a park on a bright, fresh summer morning from three feet in front of her.

Si had deserved it though. She believed that. Didn't she? He'd sexually assaulted victims of abuse, using his position of trust, the power he held over vulnerable women. He was going to expose McCoist if she spoke up about it. Making him go away was best for everyone. In fact, all three of those men were monsters. Wasn't Devlin right? Wasn't his function important?

But the first two were work. Si was personal, deeply personal. He'd hurt her, betrayed her. And he'd told Billy Jamieson where to find her children. Si was only part justice. She couldn't hide from the fact the other, larger part was revenge.

She'd played with the idea of walking in there and telling Devlin all about Ralston and the mission she was tasked with. No doubt Devlin could handle it. But then what? More of the same? She saw Nicholas's head slumped on his chest. The blood. Devlin's order to leave them. *A neighbour will complain about the noise or the smell.* He was a monster too, one he'd exempted from his own judgement. McCoist didn't have to do that though. The thought gave her the energy to open the door.

There it was, almost immediately: the flick, index and ring fingers of the right hand just grazing the sack through black trousers. Mal and Chip said they'd counted once—how many times Devlin did it in ten minutes. It was a lot. He couldn't seem to help it. Like the healing scar had never stopped itching.

McCoist wondered if he'd opted for a prosthetic or not. A fake baw didn't seem to sit right with the general austerity of Devlin's being, like it would be a vanity too far for him.

"Take a seat." *Scratch.* He took his glasses off, let them dangle from the chain he kept them on. Not that Devlin was a man likely to lose his glasses if they weren't tied round his neck. Nor did he sport them that way for coolness. It was pure economy of movement. He did not waste a single joule, except—

Scratch.

"What can I do you for, DCI McCoist?" Full kindly-old-librarian mode.

Reveal something incriminating I can pass on to ACU so they can lock you up instead of me, please. Devlin's presence, despite its placid surface, usually caused a nervous quickening of McCoist's pulse, but now she was going all Judas on him her heart was pumping like a piston. What if his vampire eyes could see the throbbing in her jugular? She hoped her general appearance of wired/exhausted because of the case/coffee would cover any extra tension and explain any odd behaviour.

"I want access to the Shit List."

The Shit List was a bucketload of kompromat they'd "inherited" from the late Paulo McGuinn. It contained an extensive list of names—politicians, polis, lawyers, businessmen, councillors, every cunt—matched with evidence (digital and physical) of their wrongdoing. From taking drugs, gambling and having affairs to more extreme excesses. Murder. Rape. Some of them were paedos. This was how Paulo had controlled the levers of official power, how he always got his way, how he avoided charges and kept ahead of the Joneses and the polis and anyone else.

And now it was theirs. Or Devlin's, rather. He'd been perusing this criminal cornucopia at leisure over the past couple of years, setting out and cataloguing his shiny new tools so each thing was safe in its place. Bringing investigations where he saw fit, squirrelling away other names and details for a rainy day. To serve the greater good, of course. What that greater good was could be hard for McCoist to discern sometimes, and he lorded over the blackmail bonanza like a jealous husband, making his intentions seem less than pure. All requests to access the List went through him. It occurred to McCoist then that the List's very existence, and Devlin's sole ownership over it, could be something Ralston would want to know (if he didn't already).

"Who are you after?"

In a pretence of propriety—and method of control—Devlin only allowed McCoist and the others targeted use of the List. Unlike him, they were not free to scroll their way through it. "I'm looking for someone who may have ties to Russian gangsters."

"You think that's who Callaghan was dealing with?"

"The guy on the hit squad who was dead at the scene, Arty Sutherland—rumours are he'd been working with the Russian mob. Could we see if he's on there too?"

"Sound idea. The crypto, the amount of it… Fuck." Even Devlin's facade seemed to crack at the notion of tangling with Russian mobsters. Maybe he wasn't all powerful. McCoist was banking on it. "Fine. You may proceed with the search. Take Malcolm with you."

McCoist's new motor smelt as if the upholstery had been shampooed with Lynx Testosterone, so Mal's wintery damp-oilskin notes didn't really bother her. What she didn't appreciate was him fiddling with the AC and the radio and the chair controls, adjusting himself backwards and forwards by inches, up and down. "Comfy?"

"Not yet."

"It's a ten-minute drive."

"Ten minutes too long to put up with suboptimal conditions."

"Optimal conditions for me would be if you were strapped to the roof."

He put on his belt and they got underway. They headed north, up through the East End until they reached Dennistoun, the "up-and-coming" neighbourhood of Glesga that was always upping and coming and never getting there. If the Southside was the new

West End then Dennistoun was the new Southside—according to estate agents anyway, justifying the constantly rising prices. The encroachment of independent coffee shops had been slow, though. Rents were twice what they were five years ago yet you still had to travel some distance to the nearest fresh-baked sourdough.

They turned off Alexandra Parade into a place where rows of low, weather-worn flats edged around a large grey scab of industrial units, livened by the yellow of the JCB warehouse's cheerful rows of vans and diggers. High fences, barbed wire, brick perimeter walls and, over them, metal Toblerone roofs.

They parked by a unit with no signage next door to a place that sold bathroom suites. There was no way to see inside it, there were no windows. Only a door. The handle of the door had a thumb reader embedded in it. McCoist placed her thumb on the scanner and the door clicked open.

Back when the Shit List belonged to Paulo McGuinn, he'd kept it in a self-storage unit. Boxes of mouldering evidence on shelves and a computer with no outside connection which contained the information: the digital photographs, the copies of text messages and phone recordings.

Devlin had set up something slightly more organised. He'd got fridge-freezers to hopefully slow the degradation of the physical evidence, which included all sorts of paraphernalia: weapons, soiled clothing, swab samples and rape kits. He'd turned the many, many folders on the computer into a searchable database. Like McGuinn, though, he kept it offline, only usable on-site. And every key McCoist tapped would be logged. Her access was temporary. Her thumbprint would only allow her through the door when Devlin authorised it and access would be revoked when she'd completed her task. She could tell Ralston about the Shit List, but working out a way she could show it to him would take time. Devlin's officers were only allowed to use it in pairs so they were accountable to each other.

("Tickly Tomlinson's paranoid about someone stealing his Precious," Alan had once remarked, causing a deluge of shite impressions and *Lord of the Rings* quotes from the sad acts McCoist was surrounded by.)

There was a tomb-like stillness to the unit, the feeling you were in the presence of some ancient idol that deserved your reverence. The Pacino Squad called it the Vault. The place hummed of history and buzzed with potential energy.

This was the thing her family were nearly killed for two years before. And Lottie's. Her nerves crackled. "Right, let's get this done and get going. Russians, Russian gangs, Russian dolls, Fabergé eggs. Give us something."

28

It was like waiting to see the dentist but if they didn't believe you when you said you flossed every day they'd call the polis on you. Fran imagined the woman behind the desk in the waiting room was all Dalek below the table, like Davros. She had the personality.

Women given even a little bit of power wield it viciously. Tommy Tungsten said that—an entrepreneur and fitness influencer Fran followed. Less so recently. Though Fran's interests had aligned with the geezer, some of the stuff he was coming out with lately was a bit off. Tommy had gone from bragging about how many women he slept with on the regular to ordaining that a man should never defile himself by shagging a woman who is not a virgin, then it was storing up sperm makes you strong and focused and being with any woman at all showed weakness. Finally, he decreed that a man should have close male friends who can offer him sexual release if he needs it (hands only). He assured his followers this was not gay but Fran was pretty sure that it was.

Not that Fran had a problem with that, it's just that TT's mental gymnastics around it were weird and kind of embarrassing. Wouldn't it be more alpha to be honest about it, rather than whatever he was trying to do?

That aside, the way the crone lorded over the waiting room, keeping her domain icy and uncomfortable for those who came to disturb it, reminded Fran of this nugget of wisdom. That McCoist wummin wielded her power viciously too. Ran him over then gassed him with chilli essence. Unreal, man.

His maw and all. Living under her roof had been like living in East Berlin. *Where are ye goin? Who're ye goin wae? Wit time will ye be back? Ye cannae dae this, ye cannae dae that.* So it had seemed. Time had softened his opinion a little. He hadn't been easy to handle and he had to admit that. What mother would be happy with her teenage son going out at all hours selling drugs and hanging around with gangsters?

The nagging had been fucking incessant though. "Yer so clever," she would always say. *If ye studied, if ye focused, if ye, if ye*—it was too much. Infuriating. And she'd put herself and his da down at the same time too, saying how much better a life he could have than them because of his "smarts", how many more opportunities he could have if he applied his "big brain" to something worthy. All that bullshit. He hated it. Emotional manipulation, he knew now, thanks to the therapy he'd been getting online. She had been trying to live vicariously through him too, he recognised. All these things she wanted *for him* she really wanted for herself. So that his success could be her success. So she could feel like she was somebody after all, not just a fuck-up like everyone else—

Left school with barely a qualification to your name, job at the supermarket, another job at another supermarket, footballer boyfriend, pregnant at eighteen. WAG dreams sunk before they even really floated by ACL woes. Single maw with a two-year-old. An ex who'd pumped all your best pals.

Fran had been wondering how he could let her know he was leaving. Probably for good. Maybe he could use a payphone sometime before they headed to Newcastle airport tomorrow.

Anxiety gripped his chest at the thought of tomorrow. Not that he'd be doing anything far outside his comfort zone—he tried to rationalise, soothe the worry. He'd spent years of his life doing deals with dodgier people—these guys would not be carrying shanks or shooters, that was for sure. The last thing he had done had gone quite badly though (Callaghan's face exploded in his); his nerve had been shaken. Lying underneath a dead body, a freshly killed human no-longer-being, for any length of time could do that to you. But this was different. Totally. No chance something like that would happen again. None at all. He tugged at his collar, felt parched.

Having a plan is necessary but you can only take one step at a time. Focus on each one as it comes. Be in the present.

He recited the mantra. First problems first.

The desk witch called his name.

He was allowed into a blonde-wood office with a nice view of the square courtyard in the centre of the building. The guy at the desk was a serious suit-and-briefcase type, handsome with healthy living, looked like he modelled for Just for Men ten years ago, before he actually went grey. Smelt of expensive aftershave and a hint of a sneaky fag before he went home at night.

"Please have a seat, Mr Forbes."

Fran perched on the edge of the chair, body strung tight.

The man clicked his mouse a couple of times then turned to face him.

Sweat prickled on Fran's back.

The man smiled. Radiant—natural but straightened, taken care of. "Sorry, I just have to say I'm a fan."

Relief flooded Fran and he felt everything slacken, dry well of confidence refilling. "Oh, ta so much."

"I'm right into running myself, done a couple of marathons even—not like you, of course, but, yeah, went and did London and Barcelona."

"Amazin, well done!"

"No, no, well done you, well done you. Your achievements—waow." He smiled again and shook his head. "It's great to see a young Scot out there doing well, ken?"

"Cheers."

"You've been taking a bit of a break?"

A break. Very diplomatic, very classy, Fran thought. "Aye, well, you'll know how it is. Takes its toll. Sometimes ye need tae slow it doon a bit, take the time tae build yer strength up again."

"Aye, of course, of course." Clearly happy to be included in this. *I do know how it is,* he beamed.

"That's kindae why am here. Sposed tae be aff tae this trainin camp in Italy the morra an av only goan an loast ma bloody passport."

"Really? That sounds wonderful. Whereabouts?"

Fran's great-grandfather on his maw's side was Italian, moved to Glesga after the war and married a local burd. Several generations later, in the third decade of the twenty-first century, Fran was about as authentically Italian as the puppets from the Dolmio adverts. As a younger child he'd thought his maw's regular cooking of spag bol was unique to her "Italian upbringing" until he started going over to his pals' houses and every cunt else's maw cooked it too. But there was one thing he knew about his great-grandad—the little town in Tuscany where he came from.

"Pienza."

"Lovely. Well don't you worry, we'll get you there." He gave Fran a thumbs up.

"Yer a saint."

29

Anthony Belov was a Russian diplomat to the UK, based in the consulate in Edinburgh. He owned a holiday home in the Black Isle. He had a wife who stayed in Edinburgh with him, and he had two grown children who lived in London. He also had a predilection for prostitutes and had been photographed multiple times by Paulo McGuinn's stooges in the act of rodding them. McGuinn had also stored some DNA (don't ask) on ice and filed away the paternity-test results carefully.

Of course, he was very busy, too busy, but he would try to make some time for her (once she'd dropped her little hints)—where is convenient? "I'll come to you," she said, sweetly.

They sat outside a quiet cafe in Haymarket. Belov was not quite what she expected based on the pictures. He was wearing clothes, yes, but it wasn't just that. He seemed skinny, grey, like he was ill. Maybe the anxiety was eating him. Imagine hearing Paulo McGuinn was dead and your problems buried only for a polis to show up years later claiming to know the length of your tackle and that you have a big mole on your hairy arse. Or maybe the mood lighting in the photos had done him a favour and he always looked like shit.

"Do you mind if I smoke?" There was little trace of his original accent. His English came with an international inflection, proper and polite.

"Please. Do you mind if I ask some probing questions without the usual niceties up front?"

"Please," he grimaced.

"Russian gangs. What d'you know? Who d'you know?"

He sniggered, laugh caught somewhere between the back of his throat and his nose. "Nothing."

"You're familiar with the Scottish variant."

"No, no."

"Yes. You had a working relationship with Paulo McGuinn, no?"

He made that thing like a blocked laugh again, a lovely set of dentures to go with. "Not really. I didn't know anything about him until after."

"After?"

"You know how these things go."

"I don't, please enlighten me."

"You're out, you are looking for a fun night, you are introduced to someone who knows a place..." The hand holding the cigarette made a cycling motion. "Maybe you go back there a few times, on other fun nights out, and, one day, a man comes to you with... pictures. And you pay the man. Later, yeah, I heard the place was owned by Paulo McGuinn and I realised how foolish I had been but, at the time..." He shrugged.

"And that was it? They just wanted money?"

"Mmm," he answered through his cigarette. "Otherwise they give the pictures to your family."

"But it was just money. They didn't want your help with anything?"

"What could I help them with?"

"Surely you have access to all sorts of interesting people."

"I think you are overestimating my importance."

"I think you're spouting a lot of bullshit for someone who knows the police are in possession of these images now and have grounds to open an investigation into you."

"The police use blackmail materials now?" The laugh was the sound of tar crackling in his lungs and tubes. "I don't think so."

He was a fucking cool one, all right. McCoist kicked herself. Went in with a straight one to the beak: "Did you facilitate any meetings between Paul McGuinn and Russian OCGs?"

"OCGs? Sorry, I don't speak cop."

"Organised Crime Groups."

"Then it's a no."

"Does the name Ruaridh Callaghan mean anything to you?"

"I am not the man you seem to think, detective. I had a tangential contact with this man McGuinn, but that's all it was. This is not my world."

"Aw aye? Where are you going for your 'fun nights' now?"

He held up his hands, fair point. "That is not something I am interested in any more. I was put off, sure you understand." He stubbed his fag out. "I need to go, thank you for the coffee."

"My treat," she said to his back. Cool one, definitely a cool one, but she was sure his temperature spiked when she mentioned Callaghan. The name rushed the conversation to a close but it wasn't over for McCoist. A nice excuse for a jaunt back to the capital sooner rather than later.

30

Holy fuck, it was her!

Fran jumped off the street into the alcove of a shop entrance, tripped—*Fuck!*—over something and landed on his arse. A bundle of grumbling, silky sleeping bags shifted under his legs. Tins of dog food were rolling out onto the street. A Jack Russell's pointy, raging face poked up from the tangle of sheets and started yipping at him.

"*Shh, shhh,* sorry, am sorry."

A woman's face appeared next, bleary eyes wrapped in layers of wrinkly flesh with a whiskery chin. "Ye awright, son?"

"Aye—aye, am fine, sorry, are you?" He sneaked out onto the street and snatched up the tins he'd knocked over, ducked back in beside the homeless woman.

Got another glimpse. It was her, he was sure of it. Ally McCoist. Sitting outside a cafe, sipping a soup bowl of coffee. What the fuck was she doing in Haymarket? Christ, they must be getting close. What if—

He peeked out again, this time scanning the street in both directions, checking the traffic, scouting for familiar faces, familiar motors. He almost checked the homeless woman for an earpiece. Her dog was growling. "Sorry boay, sorry." He crouched and held out his hand, moving slowly, let the dog get his scent. "Wit's your name, eh?" The dog started to lick his fingers.

"This is Babs."

"Aw, sorry girrul." He clapped her head. She was grey around the muzzle and eyes, the eyes themselves blind. "She's a wee beauty."

The woman started to chat all about her dog: where she got her and how long they'd been together and her peculiarities, and her favourite foods… Fran half listened, watched the street over his shoulder. Not sure what he was looking for—a guy reading a newspaper with eyeholes cut in it, maybe, or a big, blacked-out van with a satellite dish on top.

He had his new passport in his pocket (just in time for that elite training camp in Pienza—if only) and had been strutting his way back to the bedsit he and his da were hiding out in, elation making his body light and springy, easing his aches and pains, when the apparition had sent him scurrying.

He peeped out. She was still there, scrolling on her phone, absorbed, face an at-rest scowl. Didn't look like she was about to spring a trap, but then she wouldn't, would she? Fran's heart picked up to running pace. The good feeling of minutes before gone, the sick, twisting anxiety that seemed to be his default setting returning. Now he was a bit older, bit more mature and secure—he liked to think—he could be honest about how much time he'd spent afraid in his teen years. How he'd felt just like this.

It was worth it for the rush of success.

"Wit's yer name?"

"Denise."

"Sorry fir knockin intae ye, Denise." He pulled a fifty from his pocket and folded it into her dirty hand. "Look eftir yersel, an ma wee pal here."

"You too, son."

He stepped out, heading away from the polis. He'd take a roundabout route, wind his way back to the room. Get Da and get going. They were ready to rock and roll anyway—one last job to do in Edinburgh before they could head down south to the airport. Then they were outta here—leave this one-horse town in the dust, so long suckaaaaas!

Neil was not ready to go. Neil was entertaining. Rocking and rolling in a different sense.

"Da, fir fucksake!"

He pulled on one of his robes. Unmercifully short and showing a lot of chest hair too—bought when he was a much trimmer man. The woman gave Fran a little wave after she'd pulled the sheets up to her chin. "Could a huv a fag, Neil?"

"Course, hen." He turned back to Fran. "Sorry, pal, thoat yed be goan a bit langer."

There was an empty bottle of red on the counter of the kitchen that ran along one wall. (The room also featured a couch and a bed which Fran and Neil had to share—only a hundred a night on Airbnb, bargain!)

"Wit the actual fuck?!" Fran hissed.

"Aw moan, son, wur aw adults noo, it's no like ye don't know wit—"

"Da!" He dragged him into the relative privacy of one corner of the room. He put his mouth right to his ear. "We are oan the run. Fae killers. Fae the polis."

"She willnae say anyhin, a geed her a good tip," he grinned.

"Aw fucksake, man." Fran covered his mouth.

"Moan, ye cannae be like that. Ye came oot the fuckin hing! Miracle ae life!" He clapped his son on the shoulder.

"Just stoap it. We need tae get the fuck oot ae here. A saw that poliswummin oan ma way back."

"Here?!" Panic slapped Neil's face straight. "Fuck. But the meet's no till the morra."

"A know."

Neil paced and scratched.

"Get away fae the fuckin windae!"

"Cannae see anybdy oot there."

"Wit ye lookin fir, a cunt wae a pair ae binoculars?" (Rich, coming from Fran.)

"Haw, don't get cheeky, wee man."

"Don't fuckin 'wee man' me. Am oot there stickin ma neck oan the line while you're in here stickin yer—"

"Awright, awright, calm doon!" Neil held his hands up. "Let's hink."

"Please do, coach."

Neil looked like he was about to say something about him being snidey again but managed to hold it in. "Al gee thum a caw, tell thum we need tae bring it foarword tae the night. Then wull head straight aff, sleep in the motor somewhere doon the road fore headin tae the airport in the mornin. Right?"

Fran rubbed his eye sockets with the heels of his hands, grinding them in there, feeling grit between his eyelashes. "Awright."

"Right. Fuck. Let's—" He threw his robe off ("Da!" Fran wished for another dose of pepper spray) and grabbed his clothes from the floor. "Ginger, darlin, help yersel tae another couple ae big notes fae ma wallet there. Ye can see yersel oot, right? Just stick the key in the boax ootside, aye?"

Ginger blew him a kiss.

31

McCoist was right. Belov, her crispy-cool Russian diplomat, did know Callaghan. Just not Ruaridh Callaghan—Euan.

If the Shit List had one downside, it was that its lack of integration with any other system, its necessarily hidden nature, meant it couldn't be easily used for cross-referencing. A bit of time on the legal and above-board surface of the internet, however, had shown one of Belov's many investments was in a small aggregates supplier called Stoney Mitchell. The owner of the company was listed as Brianna Mitchell. Euan Callaghan was a manager there. A hard-working nine-to-five stiff, so it seemed.

McCoist remembered his claim that he and his mother avoided anything to do with Ruaridh's business, and how she'd doubted it in the mother's case because of the very desirable West End house she lived in. But what if it was true? What if it wasn't big brother supporting his maw, but little brother? Even making good money as a manager, that would be a stretch, though. He had his own house, his own expenses, his wife. Brie. McCoist remembered her jumping up onto the couch, screaming at the vole nibbling the Hobnobs. And her husband bossing her about: "Make the teas, Brie." Brie—short for Gabriella. Or Brianna. That was an unusual name, old-fashioned-sounding. A name created by a man called Brian who'd had a daughter instead of the son he wanted, presumably.

Didn't take long to find out that the owner of Stoney Mitchell, Brianna Mitchell, happened to be married to one of the managers in her company, Euan Callaghan. Now, if you *owned* the company, then maybe multiple nice houses became doable.

The company's listed address was a warehouse in an industrial estate in Coatbridge (McCoist spent the joyous drive back from Edinburgh fielding calls from Griffiths and Travis and Khan and whoever all else). The sign above the unit was a huge chequerboard with bubbly yellow text:

STONEY MITCHELL
Pave Paradise!

A man in high-vis and hard hat pointed her to a prefab site office in the corner, large windows facing out across the grid of pallets and bags and shelves of materials, forklifts moving among the rows, orange lights flashing. The gaffer was at a desk, tapping away at a laptop. She knocked at the window. Euan Callaghan looked at her the same way he had the vole. *It'll just fuckin come back in!*

"Can I have a word?"

"That's a good few awready." He beckoned her in with his fingers.

Hot air was blasting from an electric heater. The close atmosphere smelt of damp jacket.

"Back at work so soon?"

"Somebdy's goat tae keep the lights oan."

"You don't have anyone else who could cover for a bit?"

"No if a want hings done properly."

"Surely they'd cope without you for—"

"This joab may seem poxy an unimportant tae the likes ae you, *Inspector*, but av goat hale teams ae guys dependin oan this, dependin oan me, fir a livin. Tae feed their weans, keep a roof oer their heeds, the heatin oan. A take that seriously."

"What about Brie? Couldn't she help out? It is her company, isn't it?"

He raised an eyebrow. "Brie hud the start-up money."

"It's not an attempt to hide the fact that it's really you who operates it?"

"Managers aw-ways *operate* a business. Owners swan in an oot makin daft suggestions an needin their arses kissed."

"They also make the profit. And if you're married to the owner, and you share a bank account, and property, and cars…"

Euan closed the laptop. "A dunno wit yer gettin at. Evryhin's above board. Ye can check aw the records ye like. An it soonds like ye awready huv."

"I have, and was interested in a particular investor of yours. Your wife's, sorry. Anthony Belov."

"Aye." He sat back in his chair, clasped his hands. It was an office wheely thing, standard but much comfier than the school-grade plastic one McCoist had been offered.

"How does a Russian diplomat come to invest in an aggregates supplier based in Coatbridge?"

"Diplomat? A just know him as a suit. Has loads ae investments. He hud money in wan ae the hauliers we use, goat in touch."

"He had no interest in your relationship with your brother?"

The look he gave her—Stoney Mitchell indeed. "Wit relationship? A awready telt ye we wurnae close. An speakin ae him, a assumed the next time ad be seein ye wis wae some news aboot his case? Some progress. No tryin tae dig us up aboot ma books or witever the fuck this is."

"Good one."

"Wit?"

"'Dig us up.'" She pointed a thumb out the window, at the stacked warehouse. "Roads and that. Thought you liked a good pun?"

"Look, missus, huv ye goat any news aboot Ruaridh or no?"

Reassuringly easy to wind this one up, she thought. Definitely useful. "One of the men who attacked him has been linked to Russian organised crime."

Euan flapped his hands. "A dunno wit ye want me tae say aboot that. A know fuck aw aboot these hings."

"That so?"

"It is. We done?"

"No, not nearly. But let's take a breather."

The stench of bullshit was lodged up one nostril, testosterone in the other. A hit of smelling salts might be an improvement; the cold air outside was not enough. God, all these fucking men she had to deal with. These latest had been older than her too, couldn't blame Andrew Tate or Jordan Peterson or whatever TikTok alpha-influencer wank rag was popular at the moment for them. Just chronic insecurity and the hereditary idea they were owed something.

From the moment the twins had been given their first phones, McCoist had been worried about pervs getting to them online. Then she realised she also had to worry about what they were actively choosing to watch themselves, choosing to engage with. Or she would worry about that if she didn't have so much else to worry about already. The very image of her children in her mind was scabbed with their near death from two years before. She couldn't bear to pick it. Couldn't bear to get too close to them in case something else happened.

Something else was already happening.

"Mum?" Tess, conjured by the spiral of self-loathing McCoist had slipped into.

(When was the last time she'd been with the kids? How many times had she seen them, in person, in the last few months? The last year? Cam didn't like to phone either—their relationship was a WhatsApp chat.)

"Hi honey, how're you?"

"Fine. Fine, but… I got this weird DM."

Her stomach plunged. McCoist knew this wasn't going to be some nonce sending her teen daughter a photo of his windsock.

"…Oh? What kind of DM?"

"It was on Instagram."

"Isn't your account private?"

"It is." McCoist had been too sharp with her response, she could hear Tess going on the defensive. "But, I got a request to follow me and I accepted it because… It was you."

"What?"

"Your name, your picture."

"You know I don't do—"

"*I know*, Mum, you 'don't do social media'. But I thought maybe you'd changed your mind or you wanted to, I don't know, see what I'm doing or whatever."

"You thought I wanted to spy on you?"

"Not *spy*. Just, like, keep up with me, my life—"

"I do keep up with you, I see you—"

"Look, anyway, I accepted and they sent me a message and right away I realised it was off, so I blocked and reported." Her voice was high and words coming quick. "But I wanted to tell you. Somebody's made a fake account and you should, I dunno…"

"Thank you. I'm glad you told me. Did you show it to your dad?"

"No, he's not in just now."

"It's probably some phishing scam. These things happen all the time. People create fake accounts using real people's names and images and then—"

"I know, I'm not an idiot."

"I never said—"

"The message was pure weird though. Like, it wasn't just, 'I've been kidnapped in Botswana, send me ransom money.'"

"What did it say?"

"'A mother's love can forgive anything, but what about a daughter's?' I screenshotted it, if you want me to send it. It creeped me out. Like, the whole thing is creepy."

"It'll be someone mucking about, hon. Don't stress about it. You've done the right thing blocking them and letting me know. I'll speak to one of the techie guys at work, see if I need to do anything on my end."

"...OK."

"And let me know if you notice anything else strange. Online or off."

"Mum, you're scaring me." Her voice was childish, vulnerable. McCoist saw them all—Mark, Tess, Cam—two years before, through the video feed, night-vision green, bad bad men watching from outside.

"No, honey, no, don't be silly. There's nothing to be afraid of. I just mean..." Fuck, what did she mean? "Take the usual precautions, you know? And talk to me. You can always talk to me about anything."

"I know." Her words were brittle, painful lack of confidence behind them.

"Do me a favour and don't tell your dad about this." McCoist winced, *what a scumbag*. "You know how he is."

"He'd probably switch the Wi-Fi off for a month."

McCoist forced a chuckle. "He be like that sometimes."

"*Muuum.*"

32

"Awright?"

"Fran?"

"Aye."

"Fran! Where the fuck huv ye bin?! Av bin callin ye noan-stoap fir fuckin days!"

"We telt ye no tae dae that, it'll look suspicious."

"Yer da telt me no tae dae that—al be in the cauld groond afore a listen tae anyhin that waster tells me. An wit's suspicious aboot a maw bein worried fir her son?"

"*Ma—*"

"Don't fuckin—"

"Ma!"

"Where are ye?"

"A cannae tell ye that, ye know a cannae."

"Fran… son…"

"Look, am gonnae be away, probly fir a while."

"How long?"

"Dunno. A while. A good while."

"A can tell when yer lyin. A aw-ways could."

"Maw, yer blowin this way oot… it's aw awright, awright?"

"A love you."

"…Bye."

33

McCoist braced herself, dove back into the hive of her London Road office, the hum of bodies operating beyond capacity fuelled only by caffeine, chocolate and Pot Noodles. She saw a familiar face up on the big board and almost danced she was so happy: marathon runner Francesco Forbes. The two tracks of her investigation had finally come together.

When Griffiths explained how they'd come to have him up there, the impulse to Charleston left her.

"Following up on the hoody man paid its dues," Griffiths said, the attitude from their last meeting gone. "Movements took him near another crime scene being worked by another team."

Christ, McCoist would have been clocked in that part of Toryglen twice as well—first to talk to Nicholas Stewart, next time to discover his tortured corpse. She knew there were no cameras with an eye on that particular block of flats, and they wouldn't have been looking for her in the surrounds, but still. Her arse cheeks clenched so tight you could use the crack to bend girders.

"They found fingerprints belonging to this man." She tapped Forbes's face on the board. It was the shot of him running McCoist had seen before. Next to it was an old mugshot from when he was a teenager, charged with assaulting Liam Young. "Bit of a minor celeb—with a juvenile record." She ran through all the things McCoist already knew about him; she faked interested noises. "They had him in the area and traced him back to Govanhill, where we..."—Griffiths interlaced her fingers—"...had traced hoody man to. We believe they are one and the same.

"Their scene also had hallmarks of OCG involvement. Lad named Nicholas Stewart, who went to the same school as our man"—she tapped Forbes's picture again—"and his mum both murdered. Nicholas had been tortured first, his fingers were removed, then his throat slit. Mum's throat slit too." (McCoist didn't need to see the crime-scene photos, the gory details were blown up big enough in her mind to mount in a gallery.) "We'll be getting a close examination of these wounds done so we can compare with Arthur Sutherland from our scene."

"Good." The word was a hairball caught in her throat.

"They're already going to pick him up."

"Good." She coughed it up. "Let's get sloppy seconds on him when they're done."

"On it, gaffer."

As she headed to her office, Travis caught her eye. He blushed, gave a quick wave and looked away, busied himself with his computer. Something Ralston had said came back to her—*I feel like I've got to know you quite well.* They'd been investigating her for some time. Listening to her, recording her. Collecting information until they had enough dirt to flip her. Someone in her team must have talked to them.

She closed the office door. Considered Gaz Travis through the slats of the blinds. Khan opposite him, back straight and diligent. Three years they'd worked together now. It had been hard when Si disappeared. Just gone, like a big hole had been punched where he used to sit and crack jokes and sing every now and then in a big faux-Johnny Cash baritone. A death is easier in some ways. The DCs had looked to her for some kind of reassurance but she couldn't give it to them. When had lack of faith turned to mistrust?

Couldn't blame them. No, you know what? She could. Those back-stabbing, ungrateful, turncoat bastards! Grassed her to the

ACU over what? An abuser. A fucking rapist. If they knew... but they didn't. Because she didn't tell them. Because instead of doing things properly and reporting Si, she'd done something extreme to save her own skin, and scratch a furious itch too.

She wanted to lay her forehead on the desk and scream. Instead, she rifled her drawers for some paracetamol. Back fucking killing her. Head fucking killing her. Side fucking killing her. Maybe someone else could take the kicking next time. She'd taken more than her fair share. She was a detective for fucksake. A detective chief inspector. She wasn't supposed to be out there wrasslin cunts. She was supposed to collate the info the minions brought to her, stick it together to solve the crime and reap the glory. All from the safety of the arse groove in her office chair.

Fat fucking chance.

The painkillers had barely kicked in, the pile of admin barely touched, when Griffiths popped her head in the door. "Forbes isn't at home. They're going to go to his dad's place. Apparently, his dad is also his coach and manager. They're very close."

"Who's SIO for the Stewart case?"

"DCI Simpson."

"Tell DCI Simpson we'll go and speak to his mother."

"Will he like that?"

"Forbes is our suspect too, so he'll just have to. If he gets snippy, tell him a problem shared is a problem halved."

"I'd think that would make him more snippy."

"It will. You then tell him DCI McCoist is willing to discuss it foot-to-face."

"Ma'am."

"Meet me outside."

As she stepped out her office, she swooped past Khan and Travis. They both looked to her. Question in their faces. She wanted to tell them it was all right, wanted to tell them to go fuck themselves. Didn't do either.

34

When you step into Waitrose, they should give you a little badge that says "Class Traitor" on it, Lottie thought, that way the other shoppers wouldn't have to give you that look instead. That look that said: no matter how much money you may have now, you are not our kind; you do not belong in the aisle with the ethically sourced, small-business, farmers-market cheeses; you do not deserve the elegant, grown-up range of pickles or the imported chocolates that are not made by Nestlé or Cadbury's; you do not know how to appreciate these fine things. Even though she'd been in the Waitrose-shopper price range for a long time now, she still felt it. *Or maybe yer mad an folk are just tryin tae buy thur messages, gettin stared doon by some crazy burd when aw they want is some fancy sangwidges.*

Whatever. The shop was near the flat. Ari and Gemma liked the Belgian waffles they had and Lottie liked the nice coffee in the nice waxy paper bags. She got both and picked up a bottle of Malbec too.

"Would you like a bag?" The girl behind the till had an outrageous West End accent that gave her an authority well beyond the age suggested by her pockmarked skin and braces. Hers wasn't even just the annoying Glasgow Uni-style inflections Lottie's own weans had picked up; this was the sound of the gentry. Lottie felt her hackles go up. Mind running wild again. *She's just a wee lassie.*

The truth was, Lottie had been strung up tight enough to snap the whole banjo in two since her conversation with Luce about sorting out the keyboard-warrior woman who was bad-mouthing their pyramid scheme online. There were all different kinds of violence—did Lottie find some more acceptable than others? Did that make her a hypocrite? Surely everyone was. She worried at something deeper. That maybe she was soft after all. In the core, where it mattered. She didn't have Paulo's predilection for violence and she didn't want it, but she needed to believe she had that same steel. She thought she did, but that wasn't good enough. Everybody else needed to think so too, or she was done. She worried about her scheme with McCoist. Luce didn't understand it. Just kill her, she'd say. Eye for an eye. But Lottie didn't just want the eye. She wanted to ruin McCoist. She wanted to make her suffer. Alone. Forever.

She could do it.

"Aye. Cheers, hen." Lottie even managed a smile for the girl.

Byres Road was stowed with traffic, petrol fumes, bicycle bells, horns honking at people crossing between bumpers. A relief to turn the corner and move away from it, into the tenement rows where the leaves were colouring and falling in drifts, the postcard picture (Lottie had always felt there was a Parisian air to the West End) disrupted by the sheer amount of dug shite peppering the pavements. Getting home clean was like playing *Frogger.*

Luce's car was kerbed a few doors down from Lottie's flat, fifty-quid ticket already tucked under a windscreen wiper. (She made the fines herself—kerbside camo—looked legit enough from a distance.) Lottie checked her phone but she hadn't missed any calls or messages. What the fuck now?

They'd made themselves at home. Gemma had brewed the teas—Ari was useless—and sat with their guests in the living room, telling Aunt Luce all about her course and the pals she was making. Luce listened in earnest; Hannah champed at the bit to get up and move around, her smile painful-looking.

"Gemma, doll, could a get wan ae those an aw?" Lottie said.

"Sure."

"Take this tae the kitchen wae ye." She handed over the shopping bag and watched her daughter go—tall and gangly, she had an unfortunate amount of Paulo DNA but not the bullish charisma to help her carry it. She was kind though, and had some brains. Solid in many ways. Her older sister, Ari, was a much more volatile combo of the parental constituents. One to worry about for sure.

Lottie turned to the women when Gemma was out of earshot. "Somehin wrang?"

"Quite the opposite," Luce grinned. "Sorry we didnae ring first, but opportunity knocks, aye?" Hannah did her horrible laugh and Lottie rolled her eyes. "Talk in the car."

So it was a security thing. No phones. Must be a big deal. Lottie felt a sick tingle in the pit of her stomach, pushing out the hunger that had been there before. She could still do with that glass of red though. "Let us huv a quick word wae Gemma."

Losing daylight, they looped up north and back down through Possilpark and into Port Dundas, parked with the canal on one side and a row of converted factories on the other—flats above offices, memories of grinding poverty, sweaty brows and missing fingers echoing under the minimalist, nouveau-riche aesthetic.

Narrowboats nestled in the water, moored in a row against the wharf, plugged in and charging. A good few of them could have done with a lick of paint, their roofs strewn with rope and tools, dead pot plants and kids' scooters, dinghies hanging off them, ramshackle tents lashed on like plastic limpets. Not the one Hannah pointed out:

The *Hettie*, name exquisitely hand-painted along her flank, gold characters on darkly shining bottle green. Her equally gilded portholes oozed warm, candlelit ambience from within. Like a superyacht, she expressed luxury and money but without the brash wee-dick insecurity that went with it. This long broad was classy, elegant. If she were a real woman and not a boat woman, she would be the kind your maw would be proud to see you with. Lottie felt a pang of intense envy and resentment. *Livin oan boats is fir fuckin gypos*, she told herself. Plus it was small inside. Narrow, of course. Pure shite.

They climbed down a ladder from the bank and onto the decking, Hannah first, holding her hand out to help Luce, leaving Lottie to help herself.

"Watch your step, ladies." A man had appeared from inside. His suit fit well over large shoulders, the drape cut to fit a swimmer's tapering body shape. He was middle-aged, with silvering hair, a handsome face with a hint of scar tissue around the eyebrows which told them his role here. "Come aboard one at a time." This was less to do with preventing them from slipping and more to do with him searching them before they could take the steps down into the cabin.

Inside was, to Lottie's sensibility, painfully tasteful (small though) and redolent with wood polish and musky aftershave.

Hannah had her bug wand out as soon as she stepped in.

"We're quite safe from eavesdropping in here." Their man was seated at ease on a leather banquette which ran along one side of the cabin. From his voice you couldn't tell he was Russian. Been in Glesga a long time, his vowels came from down in his throat along with the glottal stops. He too wore an expensive suit, though with his small stature, neat figure and round face, even the best tailor couldn't keep him from looking like a character from *Bugsy Malone*.

"A like tae be sure," Hannah replied. The muscle loomed behind her and she turned to him, chest to chest.

"That's fine. I want you to be comfortable," the Russian said with a smile. "Stanley, some drinks please."

Stanley nodded and left Hannah to it, squeezed past them all and busied himself with a drinks cabinet that folded out of the wall like a Japanese puzzle box.

"I'll have the Balvenie, thanks. Ladies?"

"Wit's good enough fir you is good enough fir me," Luce said.

"Any tinnies in there?" Hannah cackled, still waving and poking around the room with her wand. *Stupit cow.* Lottie cringed at the girl's amateur attempts at being provoking. It was like her own behaviour in the Waitrose. Acting the rough customer. But Hannah had read the situation all wrong. She couldn't feel what Lottie felt radiating from the Russian. If he was relaxed and at ease it was only because he knew he could squash them like ants if and when he wanted to. He could afford the politeness, the seeming lack of hard front. Really dangerous people didn't have to posture. He was a languid big cat, and they were in his enclosure.

Demyan Sigarev was an estate agent. He was also an agent for a Russian cybercrime gang called the Recluse. He might have been an agent for the Kremlin too, who the fuck knew? Details on him were hard to come by, Luce had told her in the car, but armed with McCoist's meagre info, she had dug in every crevice, stuck her hand between every couch cushion, probed her finger up every arsehole. He had agreed to meet.

Even Luce had seemed surprised. Her demeanour when explaining the situation to Lottie was almost breathless, maybe excited, probably nervous. Unlike her wee burd, she knew the stakes. She knew about these people, the things they did. They weren't crime *gangs* as much as crime *dynasties*. They thought in decades, endured through centuries, and ended bloodlines. A question had hovered between her and Lottie, unasked: are we out of our depth?

"A red wine, if ye huv any," Lottie said.

"Of course, make it a large, Stanley."

"My pleasure." There was a crack and hiss of a can. "Glass for your Tennent's, madam?" Stanley asked Hannah. The bug wand fell to her side.

"Better, aye. Rats pish oan the cans an that." She regained her composure. *Fuckin moron.* Hannah seemed to be under the assumption that "cybercriminal" meant "computer nerd" and thought throwing her weight around would impress. She was oblivious. A danger to herself, a fucking rocket.

"Sit, sit," Sigarev said.

Lottie and Luce squeezed onto the banquette with him, a fading view of the canal out of the porthole by their heads. The wine was too dry for the cottonmouth Lottie's nerves had given her, hard to swallow. It left bloody runnels on the inside of the glass after each sip.

"So what can I do you for? Stanley said you were very insistent, Miss Branson. I wouldn't be inclined to meet anybody in this *fraught* moment but I have to admit I ended up too intrigued not to." His boyish moon face was cheery—sugary and sickly. He sighed too deeply at the taste of his whisky, like a woman in a shampoo advert on the verge of citrusy, flake-free orgasm.

"Actually, Mr Sigarev..."—Luce butchered his name—"...it's aboot wit we can dae fir *you*."

The cheeriness took on the twist of a sneer. "And what might that be?"

"Yer missin a good whack ae money, an we can help ye find it."

He chuckled. His tongue poked into his cheek, as if feeling an ulcer. "I'm not missing anything. A deal was made and fell apart. Nothing lost on our end."

Our. From the way he presented himself, you'd think he was the top dog. He wasn't. He was just a middleman, an intermediary, but Lottie was scared enough. She dredged up her voice from the phlegm in the back of her throat. "Nothin ventured, nothin gained, maybe. But wit if ye could huv yer cake an eat it an aw?"

He appraised Lottie with a sharpness that belied his lounge-lizard facade. "How do you mean?"

"Yev still goat yer product—witever it wis, we don't need tae know—but if ye could get hawd ae the money an aw, yed be in pure profit. Happy payday for the wans upstairs."

His eyes hardened on her, bristling at the mention of his superiors.

"Callaghan's no gonnae miss it."

"Somebody went to extremes to take it from Callaghan. Do you think you can get it back without similar reprisals?"

"We'd gee thum wit they deserved," Luce growled.

"Ready for war, are you, ladies?" His eyes turned beady, lost in his plump cheeks and heavy lids as he smiled.

"We can hawndle it, *gentlemen,*" Hannah piped up.

"And what are you after in return? Commission?"

"Just the chance tae dae further business," Lottie answered. Truth—she couldn't think of anything worse than having further dealings with this man, but they'd been looking for a way to level up and this was it. "Consider it a demonstration."

"A demonstration?"

"An ten per cent," Luce added.

Sigarev laughed, loudly and with all the authenticity of the way he sipped his whisky. "What do you think, Stanley? They're great, aren't they?" The suited butler/bodyguard smiled and bowed his head in ascent. "Glesga's Burds ae Prey. To you!" He drank and jizzed out another big, tasty sigh. *Wit an absolute fandan.* Lottie's heart raced. "OK then. If—and that is *if*—you can get the money, I will arrange for a meeting to discuss future partnerships. And you will get five points of the take."

"Ninety pur cent is a good deal when ye could get none." The words were out Lottie's mouth before she could run them through the filter. She felt all eyes on her—even Luce and Hannah were staring a telepathic *What the fuck?*

The mirth was gone from Sigarev's baby-doll face, which turned it into something hard and stunted. "I met your husband once, Mrs McGuinn." Lottie tried not to wince at the mention of Paulo. "He was a tough one. And reckless. But even he wasn't foolhardy enough to try to dictate terms with the people I represent."

Lottie had jumped in with both feet, no getting out of it now. She dug in for the reserve that bubbled inside, searched for that steel. "It's no 'foolhardy' tae know yer ain worth; it's good business practice. Ten pur cent."

The lounge-lizard charm had been shed like a skin. His cheeks were red. "Take the five, and if you do find the money, you can try haggling with the Recluse. See if that's good business practice."

Lottie's whole body was pulsing, like she was high at a rave. "Deal."

"Deal. But the risk is yours, ladies. If things get messy…"

"Ye couldae hud him fir that ten points, hen, he wis oan the ropes, fucksake!"

"A didnae hear you jumpin in tae back us up!" Lottie snapped at Luce, shut her up. "Absolutely shitin yersel!"

Luce held her hands up, the cigarette in between her fingers burnt down to the filter in two draws—Lottie not the only one rattled. "Look, am no criticisin—"

"Ye fuckin are."

"Soarry. Ye did great, hen, an a wis shocked when ye went fir it, a really wis, but it wis fuckin brilliant, ye shouldnae huv pullt back at the last gasp."

"Well ye can take oan that advice fir yersel when we get this money an speak tae the high heed yins. The fuckin Recluse or witever the fuck they caw themsels."

Luce barked a laugh. "Like fuck am a barterin wae the Russian moab. A may huv cut ma teeth doon the Barras ae a Seturday mornin but am no up fir that. The five will dae us, an there'll be plenty mare tae come. Nae point bein greedy."

"If we can find the money. Can we find the money?"

"Course we fuckin can!"

"Hear, hear!" Hannah shouted from the driver's seat. "Drink tae celebrate?"

But the wine wasn't sitting well in Lottie's empty stomach and she wanted to go home.

35

You should really visit more often.

The text was accompanied by a picture of McCoist's da on his knees in the front garden, warring with the weeds, image sharp enough to make out the leather Levi's 501 badge on the back of his jeans. Maw was on the doorstep with a cup of tea in each hand. She was wearing a pinnie. When had she started wearing a pinnie? McCoist hoped it was just for the gardening. Christ, what if she started pulling about one of those wheely pensioner trolleys next? Death's tartan chariot.

If you won't, maybe I will. Parents love to hear all about the wonderful things their children get up to.

The temptation to text back FUCK OFF was strong but McCoist knew it was pointless. The messages kept coming from different numbers that seemed to be immediately abandoned. It would be screaming into the void. Might make her feel better though. The tension was crushing her, the constant dribbling of anxious adrenaline into her system creating an acidic sludge in her veins that was being pumped into all her organs, making her feel nauseous, her joints ache. She gubbed more painkillers—ibuprofen this time, going both barrels with the paracetamol from earlier.

"Gaffer?" Griffiths knocked the car window.

"Coming."

From one maw to another:

Corrina Leoni was home this time but it was a struggle getting through the front door. Her eyes looked crazed, like she hadn't slept in a while. McCoist also got the impression the woman had been expecting (and dreading) their visit. Her veiny, not-blinking-enough look rattled between the two polis and her jaw jutted out like a battering ram. She repelled them with the same blunt intensity.

"You need to tell us if you've been in contact with him, Corrina. He is wanted in connection to a serious crime. If it turns out you knew anything you could be charged with obstructing a police officer in—"

"A fuckin knew ye were lyin!" she shrieked.

Griffiths gave McCoist an odd look. *You know her?* Fuck, that wasn't good, how could she spin—

Corrina howled. "Wit's happened?! The fuck's happened?"

"The fuck's aw this noise?!" The bratty neighbour appeared opposite.

"You fuck aff!" Corrina screamed.

"Fuck ye sayin, ye mad coo?!" She stepped out of her doorway and Griffiths blocked her.

Jackpot. Feckless wee tramp was good for something. "Get *her* inside," McCoist commanded Griffiths. She took the opportunity to push a flailing Corrina inside her own flat and close the door. "Calm down, come on, come on." McCoist took a slack fist to her shoulder, absorbed the hit. "Stop that, come on."

"Wit's happened tae him?" The tears and snot were in full flow—McCoist pinned the woman's arms in a hug and absorbed those into her shoulder too. "Ye says..." Corrina breathed hard between words. "Ye says ye wur only wantin a word aboot—a fuckin knew... knew ye were lyin, a knew somehin... wis wrang."

"I wasn't lying. Things changed. And now you need to help me. To help Francesco."

"Yer gonnae loack him up. How's that helpin him?"

"Locked up is better than the alternative."

"Wit?!" Corrina started to hyperventilate.

Nice one, Alison, why don't you tell her about the lad with his fingers cut off and his throat slashed? And his maw too while you're at it. "You need to tell me if he's been in touch. For both your sakes. If you know where he is..."

Corrina started to pace up and down the tight hall.

"I'll do everything I can, I promise." *Promises, promises,* her withered conscience chided her. She recalled all those others she'd promised to help over the years: Davey Burnet, Tim Drummond, Chuck Gardner and, most recently, Nicholas Stewart. Half of them MIA, the other half chopped up. *Either you are doing everything you can and it's not good enough, or you've not been arsed to put in the proper effort and are calling it bad luck.* Neither was good. She pushed on. "The sooner I can get hold of him, the less chance there is of him being hurt. Come on, Corrina."

Her face was twisted downwards, mascara running, comically dramatic, like a clown with a sad face painted on, an emoji of grief. She pulled her phone out. "He called but it wisnae his number." She scrolled until she found what she was looking for, held it out for McCoist to see.

There was a tap at the door and Griffiths entered.

"We've got a number to trace," McCoist announced. *Let's get the fuck out of here.* "Let's go."

36

Fran's knee bobbed up and down under the table—pain twinging with every movement. Fucking late, why were people always fucking late? Fran had forever been hanging around waiting on people. Every passing second another opportunity to get busted. Couldn't they understand that? Selfish pricks. *Time is money, but it isn't just money. Time is all you've got, it's your life, ticking away. Don't let people waste your time, your life. People who do that don't respect you. Timewasters are wasters full stop. Don't work with them. Don't be friends with them.*

"Ye want another juice?" Neil asked. "It's free refills."

"A don't want another fuckin juice. A want tae get this done an get the fuck oot ae here. Gee them another text."

"Hen, hen!" There was a beat between the waitress acknowledging Neil and her smile switching on. "A Coke an a Diet Coke, please. Hawd oan. Ye sure ye don't want somehin tae eat?"

Fran glowered at his da.

"They wings look good." He poked a finger at a picture of oily red chicken wings on the massive threefold card menu.

"Am awright," Fran growled.

"How hot are the wings, doll?"

"Too hot fir me," she said.

"Aw a doubt that." Neil winked. "Al huv wan plate ae they wings then, please. Tell the chef tae go easy oan me."

She tapped the order into a tablet that was strapped round her shoulder and swished away with their empty glasses.

"Their oaffice is doon the fuckin street an thur still late," Fran muttered. "Chose this fuckin place fir *their* convenience." He gave the restaurant a dirty look—a mass-market chain place in the food court of the Gyle Centre, aimed at families and those terminal cases who spent their whole lives trawling about shopping malls and for whom strawberry margheritas by the jug, a monstrous portion size and an atmosphere of vague Americana were the height of fine dining.

"It's no oaffice oors, but. Just try tae chill oot. They'll be here. Be happy they could bring it foarward at aw."

"Yed hink they don't want the fuckin money."

Neil put a hand on his shoulder. Fran shrugged him off, hard. He knew it was supposed to be a comforting gesture, but he and his da weren't like that. Had never been like that.

The wings arrived and there was still no sign. Still empty space on the greasy pleather of the booth on the other side of the table. Fran sooked at his drink—a mammoth tankard of ice and watered-down mixer from the softy gun—for something to do. His bladder protested, already uncomfortably swollen, but it would be sod's law for them to show up when he was in the Dutchman's clogs, and he would *not* stand accused of making anyone wait. Not even these doss cunts.

The minutes ticked by on a glowing Dos Equis clock above the bar. Fran was on the verge of breaking and heading to the bathroom—his organs starting to float on a rising sea of fizzy pish—when they showed:

One guy in shorts who had the face, facial hair, body and gait of a man who wore shorts all the time and would be buried in his best fucking shorts, and another that looked like a sleazy, skinny-jeans, lines-off-the-toilet-cistern version of Brains from *Thunderbirds*.

"Awright, Neil?" Shorts said, holding out a hand.

Neil, up to his wrists in fiery sauce and chunks of chicken skin, shook. "Yeez want anyhin, boays?"

"I'm all right, cheers." Shorts picked up a napkin as he sat down.

"No thanks," Brains said with a tight smile.

"Nice to finally meet, Francesco." Shorts held out his degreased hand again.

"Aye. Sure it is." Fran grumbled. He shook the man's hand. "Happy payday."

37

Rendezvous was at the loading entrance round the back of the shopping centre. McCoist would be going no further—the ARVs from Fettes had arrived just ahead of her: two hulking four-by-fours—suitable for off-roading it up Ben Nevis or picking your weans up from the school gate—wrapped in blue-and-yellow chequerboard, cheerful compared to the all-black gimp suits of those inside, strapped with all their toys.

McCoist prickled with white-out static as she stepped from the warm safety of her car. She had her warrant card ready. Felt predator eyes on her from the ARVs as she approached. Felt herself appraised, judged, sniffed for hints of a threat.

The sodjers stepped out too, four of them, dressed to kill, armour warping the shapes of their bodies, silhouettes of the Ninja Turtles. A fifth was unarmed and wearing high-vis. If they were the TMNT then this must be Splinter, the Operational Firearms Commander. He gave her a lift of the chin by way of greeting. "Sergeant Morris."

"DCI McCoist." Another car pulled in. "This is DI Griffiths."

She'd lost Griffiths on the M8 somewhere. McCoist had never done the proper driving course but she was never shy about undertaking middle-lane drivers and she'd take the hit on the speeding ticket if necessary. Least of her worries. In fact, maybe getting papped out for some kind of petty misconduct would be the best thing for her. Save her the trouble of being Devlin's stooge and Ralston's stooly. Giddy thoughts assailed her with the grunt of the engine, the wild momentum, the acceleration in the pit of her belly.

“Edinburgh area code,” she’d said as soon as they left Corrina’s flat. “Call it in on the way, get it traced.” She’d made her own call to the Pacino Squad, see who could get the goods faster. The call had come from a payphone at the Gyle Shopping Centre in the West End. There were a couple of uniforms already on site, keeping the peace, putting off the shoplifters. They were sent the mugshots and told to scout the place, check the security feeds. And bingo, there he was-o. Stepping into Crockett’s with the auld man for a bit of BBQ.

The problem was that now the investigation into Forbes was official, he was wanted in connection with a grisly murder as well as a shoot-out. He was potentially very dangerous and maybe armed. McCoist felt he was unlikely to be either, but feelings were not compelling evidence, so they had to call in the troops. And Devlin was coming down from the mountain too. The situation was a nail bomb of potential fuck-ups.

“We’ve got authorisation,” Morris said, tapping his earpiece. “Let’s go.”

The skwad formed up and marched into the building. Leonardo in first.

Watching them disappear inside, McCoist had two thoughts:

One—Cam would love this.

Two—I hope they don’t fucking kill anyone.

38

The sports bag was under the table. Fran pushed it forwards with his foot. His knee protested, recoiling at the weight of it, sending a juddering shock up his leg. "Aw there," he said.

Shorts played footsie with him as he slid the bag closer to his side of the booth.

"That'll be it sortet?"

"No problem," Shorts smiled.

"Spend it wisely," Fran said, "cause it's the last wan."

A look passed between the two. Brains adjusted his glecks, rubbed at the red welts on the bridge of his nose where they dug in. "Well, eh, good for you. Really. But I think you're misunderstanding the situation."

"Wit?" Fran could have done with another sip of ginger for his dry throat but his bladder wouldn't have it.

"This isn't a zero-hours contract."

"Fuck ye tryin tae say?" Neil said, drawing a look from a nearby table.

"Voices down, please," said Shorts. *Condescending bellend.* "You're not just paying per job, you know? You're paying for our… ongoing silence. Yes?"

Aye, aw fuck aye, Fran would like to make this cunt's silence ongoing another way. Or at least put his glass through the boy's face. "Fuck ye oan aboot?" he hissed. But he knew.

"And the money's not just split between the two of us."

"No, no, no, no." Brains shook his head. "There are multiple people involved in this operation, all of whom need to be paid their fair share. But hey, you're good for the money."

"Naw. This ends noo," Fran seethed. "Am leavin the fuckin country, am no gonnae be back."

"Oh, not to worry." Shorts did that fucking smile again, the gooseflesh-thigh-tattoo wanker. "Athletics is international. We work with people from everywhere, all helping each other out. We can still look after you, wherever you go."

"Look after your reputation too," Brains chimed in. "Your legacy."

"Yer a couple ae greedy fuckin rats," Neil said, his face red to match his fingers.

"Us? Isn't cheating, at the end of the day, driven by greed?"

"Am no a fuckin cheat." Fran grabbed Shorts by two fistfuls of his collar and pulled him over the table. "Fuckin say that again." Words sprayed the man's face. Fury burned through Fran. He got that twentieth-mile tunnel vision. All he could see was this cunt's smug pus and the landscaping he wanted to give it.

Something about the way Shorts looked at him reminded him of Liam Young, that day in school when Fran attacked him. Fran had grabbed Liam out of nowhere, just like this, scruff of his school shirt in his fingers. Liam's face—once the shock had passed—said, *Are you mental?* Because Liam was tough as fuck. Liam was the hardest lad in the year. What could Fran possibly do to him? Shorts looked the same way. And Fran could fuck him up the same way he did Liam. Smash his nose with the hard bone of his skull, boot his baws, do the bouncy on his heed. Fuck aye. And this time, he actually wanted to do it. "Fuckin say that again."

The four at the table were so engrossed they didn't notice the Mexican wave of surprise and fear flowing towards them through the restaurant.

Didn't notice until the shadows were right over them.

Until someone shouted, "Armed police!"

And they looked up into the barrels of four serious-looking guns, held by four serious-looking figures dressed like something from an action film.

"Keysies!" Neil yelled, sticking his thumbs up and closing his eyes.

Fran's bladder could take no more.

39

The loading bay was swarming with polis now, uniforms and plain-clothes, Glesga and Embra, bigwigs and bit players. Excited shopping-centre sookies and stressed-as-fuck managers were in the throng as well. Old Firm atmosphere—festival fun with the edge of potential violence. Even Devlin, with his alligator's calm, seemed to have contracted some of the energy. "Here they come," he said, as the back door opened.

Leonardo and Raphael out first—the former carrying the sports bag McCoist had seen Forbes with before—followed by a string of four men with their hands bound behind them with flexicuffs. Donnie and Mikey brought up the rear. Each suspect was a different shade of shiteing it. Francesco Forbes's joggies were wet. An unfortunately light grey, McCoist thought. His da seemed to have soaked up some of the spill. The other two McCoist didn't recognise. More gangsters? Involved with the Callaghan hit? Maybe, maybe not. Certainly about to profit from it, by the look of things.

The four were pushed down onto their arses, backs against one of the ARVs. Leonardo was bellowing at them. Still buzzing from the operation, not hitting the downer yet, still itching for action. A dangerous phase. Devlin approached Morris, who was jabbering away to the ITFC on the other end of his earpiece while giving out orders to his team. DCI Simpson—with an arsey glare for McCoist as he passed by—had arrived and got stuck in too, plus some brass McCoist assumed to be local.

"Looks like it went well." Griffiths appeared at her shoulder.

"For us."

Simpson's face was as red as Clifford's massive lipstick tube, his jaw in a Neanderthal jut, finger wagging at Devlin as he spoke. Devlin looked back meekly through his glasses, seemingly placid but McCoist knew he was ready to snap that finger right off. Wouldn't come to it though. The silver on Devlin's shoulders gave him authority, and the way Simpson suddenly folded in on himself like a kicked mutt suggested there was something else too—something Devlin had over him, something to make him yield, make him do what he did not want to. McCoist knew that feeling. A snivelling, grotty helplessness.

Simpson stalked off and then the Edinburgh super jabbed a parting shot before leaving too, sizzling. Morris held up his hands, then directed something at his turtles.

Devlin was almost bouncing on the balls of his feet as he came back. "This you?" He pointed at the aubergine monstrosity. "This is trendy, isn't it?" He yanked a back door open. "Two in here!" he called to the FOs, who hauled Forbes and his da onto their feet and marched them over.

McCoist's nose wrinkled at their pishy trousers as they were bundled into her motor, black gloved hands on the tops of their heads. Not her motor, actually. Cam's. Fuck, she'd be throwing a deep clean into their deal too. Oh well, it would be good to have a chat with these two eejits on the way.

"Other two in mine!" Devlin said. He turned to McCoist and dropped his voice. "We're going for a wee tea party. Order Griffiths back to London Road."

"Tea party" was code. (Devlin loved a bit of code. McCoist wondered if he'd love the Pacino Squad's code for him—TT, Tickly Tomlinson—or McCoist's much more prosaic "Mr Itchy Baws".)

It meant Mad Hatter's, a closed-down dress-up and magic shop in a small industrial estate in Cambuslang. The unit had been acquired cheap for use as a temporary safe house to store suspects and witnesses for short periods of time. The mothy, gothy window display had been kept and, together with the rusty shutter and padlock over the door, gave the impression the place had been abandoned for some time. Anyone pressing their nose up against the greasy windowpane would get a glimpse—between one horrific, blonde-wigged, no-faced Alice mannequin and another done up (cross-wired) like Gene Wilder as Willy Wonka—of mouldy boxes and empty shelves, a poster of Keanu Reeves in *The Matrix* peeling off a wall, flyers for a circus that passed through twenty years ago on another. On the floor above was a sparsely appointed flat with some heavy-duty locks on a door which looked like an ordinary PVC number but was so strong it would take a tank or Vinnie Jones to pan it in.

Devlin used it for various things. Sometimes for keeping witnesses safe. Other times…

McCoist kept close behind his Jag as he belted it back down the M8 towards Glesga. Simpson was in her rear-view, framed by two very sorry-looking lads in her back seat reeking of pish. She cracked a window, let the motorway fumes in. "You've put us to a bit of trouble," she said.

"Don't say anyhin," Neil Forbes told his son, who glared at him for saying something.

"Bad advice. Would have been easier if you'd just said something a few days ago. Could have avoided the whole scene in Shettleston—"

"When ye ran us oer ye mean? An pepper-sprayed me."

"Those were both accidents. I was trying to protect you, really."

Fran snorted. "Will yer bosses agree wae that? Or the fuckin complaints people, whoever?"

"Could have avoided sending in the troops too, kept your undies dry."

He took a beamer, and McCoist could see real hatred in his eyes for her. Wee boys could not handle embarrassment. It was the easiest way to rile them, get a rise, get them shooting their mouths off, going against the "No comment" advice from their lawyers and the laughably flimsy *omertà* of the young teams. "Fuck you," he hissed.

"I know you don't mean that." She smiled into the mirror.

"Stoap talkin, baith ae yeez," Neil said. "Ye cannae talk tae us waeoot a lawyer, hen. Put the radio oan or somehin."

Now it was McCoist's turn to be riled, even though she knew better. "Detective Chief Inspector." She got a handle on it, aimed for sugary again. "But if it has to be an animal, at least make it a pig, keep things appropriate. And speaking of appropriate, you're right. I can't question you without a lawyer. But here's the thing, your lawyer will tell you not to say anything… At first. But once we get through the CCTV footage linking your boy here to a massacre that happened at the weekend, plus this money he's been collecting and was apparently about to offload, compound that with his DNA found at yet another crime scene—this one a double murder in Toryglen—"

"Wit?!" Fran's head snapped round from the window. "Who—Pontoon? Wit the fuck—"

"*Shhhh!* Stoap! Talkin!" Neil screamed.

"Well, at that point your lawyer is going to shift from 'play ignorant' to 'plea bargain'. They'll be saying, 'Admit you did it and get a third off the sentence.'"

"A didnae fuckin dae anyhin!" His voice was hoarse and high, sheen of tears in his eyes about to burst.

"FRAN!"

The boy turned away again, snuffling into the window. McCoist let the air cool, a mile whip past. "Are you a Radio 2 or a Radio 4 man, Neil?"

40

Double murder. Double fucking murder. In Toryglen. That's what she said. Pontoon. It must be. He'd been to see Pontoon, and the heedbangers that took Callaghan out must have followed him there. Fuck, oh fuck. Double—who was the second? Who else could it be? Doubt Pontoon had many visitors to his grotto. Could only be his maw, fucksake. Poor wummin. Fran had got them involved. Him and his da and this crazy fucking scheme they'd cooked up. And why? Why had Fran got involved in the first place? Because he could not accept the inevitable; he had peaked all too soon.

Fran shivered, trembled. Couldn't stop. His joggies had gone cold now, horrible against his skin. Reminded him of how he'd pished himself during the Bristol marathon a couple of years ago—stopping would have cost him too much time, imagine being off a PB by the length of a slash, unthinkable—and spent the last ten miles with his thighs chafing raw against his shorts.

Sobs caught in his throat and he tried to choke them down. *Pontoon didn't have to agree to help*, a weaselly wee part of him argued. *He wanted to get paid.* A braver part bit back: *But you never told him how you got hold of the crypto key in the first place, that a gang of psychos had butchered five men and even finished off one of their own to get it. It was hardly likely that they'd let it go.*

He tasted salt on his lips, blinked hard trying to stop the flow.

His da made a grunting, phlegmy snort beside him in the back of the motor.

They couldn't pin that on him though. Surely they knew he would never kill someone. He wouldn't. He—he remembered Liam again, the feel of the boy's cheekbone crunching under his shoe. His lawyer had to argue it down from attempted murder. He hadn't meant it. But he had—he'd made a plan and he'd followed it through. Perfect. Too perfect. But that wasn't him any more. That was a lifetime ago, maybe not in years but in personal growth. He had his running now. He *had* running.

His knee joints throbbed. Too much haring about without warming up. Too much sprinting, that wasn't his game.

It was all over. Whatever they charged him with, they had those two dickheads in custody with a bag of dirty cash as evidence. Shorts was right: Fran was a cheat.

They turned off a main street—traffic and shops and cafes and witnesses—and onto a narrow road looping through a leafy den and into a street of run-down flats on one side and a flat-roofed pub on the other promising Sky Sports, Carling and a Sunday roast for a fiver. Beyond both were factory units and garages, warehouses converted into wholesale shops and dance studios.

They took a right into one of the industrial estates, splashing through huge puddles in wrecked tarmac, past a couple of cars growing moss, roofs speckled black with tree sap, alloys touching the ground, a buckled Heras fence lying flat keeping nobody out of a weedy lot/dumping ground beyond.

Turned and stopped by a two-storey red-brick gable end that looked like it had been ripped off the end of a row. It had a dank shopfront window display of nightmarish mannequins and a faded sign above that read: The Mad Hatter's Trick Shop.

This was not the polis station.

Fran's eyes flickered to his da's. His fear was not reflected there, just bovine confusion complemented by a wrinkled brow. That made it worse. Fran's heart had been in fifth since the restaurant, the next step up was surely cardiac arrest.

The woman let them out of the now pish-scented car into the fresher atmosphere of damp wood and bins. The punchable, smug look on her face had gone and that worried Fran even more. "Where ye takin us?" The reedy warble of his voice was pathetic.

Shorts and Brains were being taken around the back of the building by one of the high heed yins he'd seen earlier, out the back of the shopping centre, when he was pressed up against a motor having been patted down and felt up all ways with the black-hole eye of a gun watching him for any twitch of resistance. (In his mind, he'd seen the blood spirk from Callaghan's face again, felt a nauseous dread imagining the feeling of that terrible, instant penetration.) The big yin was wearing a uniform—fancy uniform, with spangly epaulettes—and a pair of glasses hung around his neck on a chain—not fancy, VL attire. He had a meek, almost kind face. Somebody's granda, pouring tumblers of ginger beer for the weans, letting them raid the Celebrations tin. Fran's heart didn't know what to make of that and pogoed about in its cavity.

The back door was sealed with a code which the bloke at the front of the queue knew—weedy-looking geezer in a cardigan who might have been thirty or sixty or maybe just in a folk band.

It occurred to Fran that he might be able to batter all of these cunts even with his hands tied, but the soggy, cold cotton of his joggies pressing against his thigh reminded him again of facing the firing squad. He assumed the same thing was keeping Shorts and Brains in line too.

The door opened to a set of stairs—"Mind how you go," Mumford & Grandads said—and the stairs led to a small open-plan living room and kitchen with safety locks on the windows and the frigid air of student digs. Another two men were waiting inside. One a meaty polis type, civvies sitting on him like a wean's superhero costume; the other wouldn't have been out of place in Callaghan's firm—forties, heroin skinny in a tracksuit, chib marks on the chin, a mountain range of knuckles with a set of gold rings on each hand. What would they feel like crashing into your pus, eh? Probably wouldn't have to wait long to find out. *Don't let your mind get carried away with potential negative outcomes. Spiralling does you no good. Assess the situation calmly. Look at what is in front of you right now.* Fran tried to take some deep breaths without being too obvious about it, tried to dial in some of his teachings. What was in front of him?

He'd been arrested but he hadn't been taken to the polis station. Instead, they'd come to some faceless flat above a closed-down joke shop. Men were waiting for them. Apart from the one with the fancy silver, there were no uniforms on show. This was a snuff, right? The strength went from his legs.

"Woah! You all right there, son?" It was the fancy uniform who spoke, the look on his old face kind, concerned. "Help him up, Jules, please. Can someone get a chair?"

Jules was the rough-looking one. In Fran's short time as a cocaine cowboy, he had grown to recognise the difference between a bampot and somebody who was a real danger, and even with a bit of moss growing on the old instincts, this Jules boy was definitely the latter. The feel of his fingers on Fran's upper arm reminded him of when he was a wee boy and he would play with his maw's hair clip, clamping its teeth onto his lower lip. A dining chair was placed under him. "Steady oan," Jules said.

"Watch, he hus bad knees," Neil said.

Fran shot him a look. Hopefully they'd do him first. *Assess calmly. What is right in front of you?* There was no way they could kill all four of them here. No. It was carpeted, for Christ's sake. And what would be gained by doing it? What good would killing Fran do them? They had the money in the bag, they had the rest of it in the crypto wallet, the key taken off him when he was searched along with his wallet, phone and keys. If they wanted him to take the blame for killing Callaghan and Pontoon—

Fuck, was that it? They wanted a confession? Lucky his bladder was already empty, all the muscles in his lower abdomen loosened in tingling fear.

"Stick the kettle on, Kirky," Mumford said. He started taking orders, even asked Fran, who could only shake his head in reply.

"I'll make my own," the woman, McCoist, said.

"There's not a barista alive that can make a coffee as bad as Ally McCoist takes it," the cardigan grinned.

The DCI's smile was straight and bloodless like an old surgical scar. There was an uneasiness in the way she responded, her quippy demeanour fading now they were here, wherever "here" was. Fran was unsure whether to be buoyed by this or not.

When the brews were made, the suspects seated and cable ties cut, the chevron-shouldered uniform took off his cap and spoke: "OK, gentlemen, thank you all for being here today." Couple of smirks—*arseholes*—and a snort from the cardigan. "Let's make this as easy as possible. You tell us everything." He scratched his crotch before perching against the arm of a tatty but comfortable-looking settee.

"…And?" Shorts asked. His voice was hoarse.

"And what?"

"Well, we tell you everything and *you*…?"

"No," the man smiled. "No, no. You tell us everything. That's it. What you were doing in the restaurant. What the money is for. Where the money came from. All of it, start to finish, no track-skipping."

"Who are you?" Shorts puffed up.

"We're not saying a word without a lawyer," Brains said, getting bold too.

The man in black blew on his cup, sipped and winced. The word "hot" hissed from his lips. "Detective, get the phones, will you? Malcolm, get your kit ready."

McCoist laid out four evidence bags on the table, a smartphone in each—the ones taken from them at Crockett's. The cardigan—Malcolm—whipped out a laptop and opened it up.

"You were right," the man addressed Shorts. "There is more to it. But it isn't 'You tell us everything *and*', it's 'You tell us everything *or*'. You tell us everything or my tech witch Malcolm here, with his fancy tech cauldron, will ruin your lives. I mean, all of you in here are connected to gangland murders so things are already looking bad, but they can always get worse." Fran swore he could feel the change in the air pressure from the shock wave coming off Shorts and Brains. "How? you might ask. Well, what Malcolm will do is fill your phones with so much dark-web filth that you'll be locked up in the beast wing at Barlinnie for a long time to come."

"Wit?" The word squeaked from Fran's fist-tight pipes, his insides a morass of jellied horror.

"Oh yes. They say in showbiz that you should never work with children or animals but tell that to the people who make this stuff." There was a hint of a smile on the man's face, nothing changed from that kindly demeanour which seemed to be his default.

A large portion of not-too-spicy hot wings and three pints of Coke reversed out of Neil's digestive system in one hot surge down his front, pooling in his lap and gunging down to the floor. The acrid, zesty tang of it stung Fran's eyes and he fought to keep his own gorge down.

The polis all stepped back, expressing their disgust and covering their noses, except the main man, whose face wrinkled only slightly. "Keep quiet and take your chances with your lawyers if you want, but whatever then happens with all this business with the money, one day, down the line, sure as shortbread, you'll get the knock at the door and it'll be the SOPU there to take you away, break the sad news to your family, friends, colleagues and neighbours that a monster has been living among them."

Brains burst out in tears, big shaking wails like a wean.

Fran followed a guy online who was a self-styled paedo-hunter—his channel was called "Nonce Trap". He would go on forums pretending to be a prepubescent girl and lure would-be child molesters into meetings where he and his cronies would then spring out at them, threaten them and beat them and humiliate them, make them… do things. The pathetic specimens would be rolling on the floor, crying, begging him not to tell people, not to post the video he'd made, pishing themselves and snivelling and trying with feeble desperation to come up with excuses. The invective in the comments was like nuclear waste:

Beast. Monster. Cretin. Hang the bastard. Cut his dick off, take a meat hammer to his bollocks. Sodomise him with a rolling pin, no punishment too harsh for scum like him. They should be branded. Raped to death in prison.

Fran imagined this righteous, guilt-free hate aimed at him, felt the dirty shame of it, the primal fear deep in his bowels. A headline flashed through his mind: *Marathon monster—local running hero's sick kiddie-porn collection.* He couldn't hack that, no fucking way. Maybe he should confess to the murders. Better that than people thinking…

"You can't do that." Shorts sounded adamant.

"Well let's see." Kindly smile, the boss man pulled on a pair of blue nitrile gloves and checked the notes on the evidence bags, selecting one. He gave a nod to Jules and the big plod. The two snapped into action. Plod wrapped his beefy arms around Shorts's body from behind, pinning him. Jules grabbed his head, a hand over each ear.

Shorts cried out, tried to twist away.

Smiling boss approached with the phone, lock screen held out towards his face.

Shorts clamped his eyes shut, tried to turn his head.

Boss followed his movement with the phone. "Come on, son, it's this or we take your thumb."

"No, no, *aagh*, FUCK!" He gnashed his teeth and thrashed as much as the man-manacle would allow.

Fran couldn't watch. He turned away, saw McCoist's face—too pale, eyes alive with panic.

"That was a wee joke," the boss said with a chuckle. "Sorry. I can have Malcolm break into it, it's just it would be quicker if you stayed still and let us—hold on, there it is. Bingo!" He handed the unlocked phone to Malcolm, who had also donned a pair of rubber gloves.

"Stop," Shorts wheezed, Jules and the enforcer letting him go, the former giving him a tap on the head as he did.

"We don't know anything about any murders!" Brains cried out, tears running down his cheeks.

The nerd hooked the phone up to his laptop, started tapping on the keys.

"We're from UKAD! Anti-Doping!"

Anti-Doping. A pit opened up inside Fran's belly.

The boss held up a finger and Malcolm stopped typing.

Shorts and Brains exchanged a defeated, terrified look. "We're helping him beat the tests," Shorts continued, with a tip of the head towards Fran, who was trying to fold himself up small enough to drop into that black, bottomless pit inside.

"Helping him?"

"For m-money," Brains clarified.

The boss appraised them all. Fran felt singled out for judgement.

"Let's get you boys cleaned up."

41

He looked worse now than when McCoist had run him over. That lad had the determination to scrape himself up off the pavement and keep going; this one was done. A flat tyre. At least he didn't reek of pish any more—there were spare clothes in the cupboard in the bedroom that just about fit him.

Neil was a different story. They had nothing in his shape so he had to make do with chucking out his chilli-oil-infused, puke-stained top and wearing his jacket zipped over his bare bod. He'd been given a wet flannel for his trews and shoes. They opened the windows as far as the safety catches would allow.

McCoist put the hot drinks on the table, needing another one for herself after the first "interrogation". It had put the shites right up her. She knew Devlin was a ruthless bastard—she'd helped him kill people—but there was something about that particular threat (*children and animals*) that made her skin shift around as if it had come loose from her muscles. Sweat slicked down the small of her back. She was cold, breathless. In the sudden bout of dizziness she thought she could hear the echo of a gunshot, smell the exploded powder, the exploded brains. There was a touch on her shoulder—Devlin's hand. Nausea. She'd had to sit down on the sofa until the spell passed.

He would have done it too. No doubt. She saw again Mal's almost cheerful performance as he followed the orders, tapping away at his keys. That, as much as Devlin's threat, had coiled her guts. Maybe he knew he wouldn't have to go through with it, or maybe not. Either way, she couldn't look at him quite the same way now. Gravy stains in the old cardigan turned her stomach again.

It was just the three of them left now, with Fran and Neil. Kirky and Jules had been sent down to wait in the car with the crooked UKAD guys. It seemed being caught cheating had dampened Francesco Forbes's spirits more than being caught with stolen money and accused of multiple murder.

"You want to tell me about it then?" she asked.

Fran stared into his mug. Neil looked to him then up at her, face more jowly and saggy-looking than before. The eyes pleaded for something. "It wis aw ma idea," he said. He reached out, as if to squeeze his son's shoulder, then stopped short, hand falling limp by his side. "Ye can write that doon."

The words snapped Fran's head up, his mouth making a fly trap. "Da?"

"The dopin, stealin the crypto, it wis aw me."

"Da!" Fran grabbed at his father's shoulder, getting a handful of slick polyester.

"Leave Francesco oot ae it aw. Al take the derry."

"No!" The boy was stunned.

"This isn't a matter of simply apportioning blame, Mr Forbes," McCoist said. "I need to know everything that has gone on and why. Eight people are dead, including two civilians." *Civilians.* Devlin's language coming out of her mouth. "I need to know the truth. You already know the consequences of withholding it."

The lad still had a hold of his da's jersey. The big man put a hand over his son's, gently loosened his grip. "The dopin *wis* ma idea, but. When his knees went bust, the recovery wisnae... goin well."

"A wis slippin doon, no finishin races." Fran's voice was monotone, a buzz coming from his throat.

"An he wis deed against it, so he wis! A made him. Soze he could stay competitive, till we goat somehin proper sortet."

"A wis gonnae start losin sponsors."

Neil's brows dove towards his beetle eyes, his cheeks and chin waggling as he flinched, as if Fran had tried to hit him. "It wisnae aboot the sponsors. It wisnae the fuckin money. How could ye hink that? Dye hear a word a fuckin say?"

"Wit?"

"Twenty-two is nae age fir a lad tae retire fae the hing he loves. It wis ma fuckin knees an aw that did me."

"Here we go," Fran grumbled.

"Aw, yev heard this wan afore, huv ye?" Neil scoffed. "Cos it seems like ye werenae fuckin listnin at aw. A know exactly wit it's like tae lose the hing yer passionate aboot aw too soon. A know wit it does tae a young lad. A fuckin lived it. An a widnae be huvin that fir ma son an aw. No fuckin way. So…"

Fran was looking at his da as if Troll hair had suddenly sprouted from his baldy dome.

"It wis sposed tae be tempry. Till he goat the surgery."

"There's a specialist in the US, an expert in this stuff."

"Sounds expensive," McCoist said.

"Aye, an those bent dopin cunts were bleedin us dry an aw. Fuckin crooks," Neil spat.

"So a went tae Ruaridh Callaghan. Knew him fae back in the day." Fran told her how he'd accepted a job from Callaghan—to smuggle a crypto key out of Scotland and into Russia under the cover of running the Moscow Marathon. Once there, he'd deliver the crypto to persons unknown and Callaghan would cover the costs of his trip to the US clinic.

"But you never made it out of Glasgow."

Fran shook his head.

"Goat as far as Embra," Neil chimed in.

The theory that Fran and his da had orchestrated the hit on Callaghan and his crew to steal the money drifted up and McCoist dismissed it. Not these two eejits. "What happened?"

The story jerked out of Fran in fits and starts. McCoist knew well the terrors and psychic perils of reliving moments of extreme violence and let him take his time. He told her how Callaghan's face exploded inches in front of his own nose as a bullet passed through it, and for the second time in that dank wee flat she saw herself killing Paulo McGuinn in much the same way. He told her about being trapped under Callaghan's body, witnessing the vicious destruction of the others and how one of the gang—the woman with the ugly laugh—had even killed one of her own team. He told her how he had fled, the adrenaline overriding his damaged ligaments, how the crypto key was in his hand.

"And you thought, 'I'll just keep it for myself.'" McCoist failed to keep the judgement from her voice. Not judgement at him breaking the eighth commandment, judgement at him doing something so colossally fucking stupid.

"A never—a never meant fir Nicky tae get hurt." He closed his eyes, pinched the bridge of his nose, big bubbling sniff trying to keep the tears and snot inside.

"Nicky isn't hurt. He's dead." She put her phone on the table, a slide show of the scene photos making the men push their chairs back. Close-up of chewed flesh and snapped, proud bone. Harsh, but the boy needed to understand, the pressure needed to stay on, and McCoist even felt a flush of anger as she twisted the knife. At him, at herself. "The people who killed Callaghan and his boys tortured and murdered Nicholas. His maw too. If you'd come straight to the p—"

"That's enough," Neil said, trying to scrape back some kind of authority, as much as is possible when there are flecks of vomit drying on your shoes.

"If you'd come straight to the police, they would both—"

"What's done is done, DCI McCoist," Devlin interrupted, getting up from his perch with an itch of the ol' sack scar. McCoist knew that tone, that look of quiet cheerfulness on his face, and knew she was about to be made very unhappy.

"But, sir—"

"I don't see what the problem is. Neither of them killed anybody, we've gained serious intel about who did, we've recovered the money, and DCI Simpson is the one who'll be red-faced at having to let them go."

"They were involved in serious, organised criminality which *caused* the deaths of Nicholas Stewart and his mother."

"I would say 'led to' rather than 'caused'."

"How's that any better?" McCoist was danger-close to shouting at him now. The worst thing about losing her shit with him was that it never achieved anything, never fazed him. The most "rise" she could expect from Devlin was that the near-constant twist of a smile he wore would flatline for a moment.

"A chain of events is never as simple as it sounds. There are always multiple chains, branches. It's intricate. Links work on each other in ways you might not even perceive."

McCoist shouted anyway: "Utter bullshit!"

He chuckled. *He chuckled.* Maddening prick! "Maybe. But as it stands, they are cooperating. I do not want people who are cooperating with us to be in custody. OK?"

"So they're in witness protection now, are they? You gonna send them to Center Parcs? Fuck, send them to the US, a trip to Disney World, get the boy's knees fixed for him and all while you're at it."

She'd done it. The smile was gone. The volume of his voice dropped and he *e-nun-ci-a-ted* his words very clearly and carefully: "Engage your brain rather than your mouth for once, DCI McCoist. If we hurry up about this and stop fucking around here, they'll be back on the street before anybody knows they've been lifted and lost the key."

McCoist flushed with fresh rage. "Great! Great. So they're not protected witnesses now, they're bait."

"I would say they're 'a lure'."

I would say: Shut. The. Fuck. Up.

42

Neil whistled. "That wis a near fuckin miss, wis it? No a bad result, kid."

The new respect Fran had gained for his da because of his speech during the interview/interrogation/confession had quickly flushed away. *Fuckin spanner.* Still, he'd had a glimpse of something back in that room. A man who cared about him, a man with some kind of emotional insight and maturity, a man who was capable of actually being a father. Unfortunate that it took such extremes to coax him out. Fran idly wondered what the therapy influencers might think about that before crunching back into gear.

"Wuv no goat the money any mare, wur passports an bank cerds are frozen an there's still a gang ae heedbangers oot there eftir oor scalps. Near miss ma rusty ringpiece. Wur still in the fuckin blender here, waitin tae see which cunt pushes the button."

The poliswummin, McCoist, had dropped them off at a bus stop in Cambuslang, face sour as a sherbet Dip Dab and attitude acid enough to melt through the metalwork of her bonkers car. "See yous soon," she'd said, tearing off, tyres squealing, exhaust farting. He'd take her over that creepy, smiling bastart Devlin, but. Or the sleazy dark-web cardigan. Or the other two, the tough cunts—Clydesdale Horse and Scabby Donkey. *Fuckin cops, man. The real fuckin criminals. Hung us oot tae dry.*

"Where to?" Neil asked.

"They might be watchin baith oor gaffs. Dunno where's safe…"

. . .

She slapped them each across the face—a rigid, calloused whopper on the cheek that left a red stamp. Then she grabbed Fran into her, a desperate hug, digging bony fingers into his clothes, nails pinching through to his skin, her scream muffled by his shoulder.

"Maw! *Maw*—" He tried to ease her off him. Neil tried to help prise her away and was rewarded with another crack across the chops.

"Ye fuckin mental coo—"

"*YOU* fuck aff oot ae here!" she snarled, lifting her hand again. Neil flinched, threw his own hands up to protect his face.

Fran grabbed hold of his maw's wrist. "Maw, stoap it! Moan tae fuck!"

"Where huv ye bin?! Wit the fuck's been goin oan?! Av hud the fuckin *polis* roon here—"

"Inside, Maw, inside!"

They managed to hustle her in without being further skelped, Corrina falling into a fit of sobs, the tension holding her together gone. "A thoat somehin hud happened, somehin…"

"Am awrite, everyhin's fine." The words "Geez peace" champed to burst out through his teeth but he managed to hold back—that was the old Fran, the teenager, the wannabe Scarface. (Actually, he'd fancied himself more an Alan Sugar, really.) When his maw got like this—and she had on many occasions back then—it made him irrationally angry but he could see now it was really shame he was feeling, guilt at letting her down, and he'd been lashing out at her because he didn't know how to deal with it. But he was nothing if not self-improved these days—levelled-up, *evolved*—so he didn't snap back at her, didn't lose his temper. He drew in some slow breaths, let her do the same, waited for her breathing to calm, the shaking to stop.

"Put the kettle oan," he whispered to Neil, who understood

fuck aff fir a minute, then he sat down next his maw and let her lean against his shoulder.

"A swore ad never huv that man back inside ma hoose," she mumbled. "A telt him, an so far he's respected it. Must be serious."

"Willnae be fir lang."

"A never asked you tae leave, but. Never kicked ye oot, nae matter wit happened."

"A know."

"It wis your choice tae go wae him."

"That wis years ago, a live in ma ain place noo anyway. An it wisnae—a didnae…" He sighed. He thought about all those buff alpha entrepreneurs and gymfluencers he followed and wondered what they were like with their maws. They quoted that Brad Pitt line from *Fight Club* a lot: "We're a generation of men raised by women, blah blah"—that one, whatever it was. It was a bit… There was a fine line between alphas and incels, Fran had started to think. Fuck, he needed to get back to the running. Properly. All this time to think and stare at his phone and all that bollocks was melting his brain.

But he had no money to go get the operation now. And what if the doping stuff came out? He had no idea what would happen to the UKAD boys now. Had they just been let off too? *Don't forget the gun-toatin, throat-slashin, finger-coppin maniacs…* Fucking hell. He wanted to cry now too.

"That poliswummin telt me ye might get hurt an a just—"

"Who? McCoist?"

"That's the wan."

"Didye tell her ad geed ye a call?" Fran stood up so fast Corrina fell sideways onto the couch.

"Eh, a-a wis so worried, she—"

"*Fucksake!* Fuck!" Fran grabbed fistfuls of his hair. "Ye fuckin telt her—"

"A didnae, a didnae!" Tears were falling again. "She asked if yed bin in touch an a—"

"Fuckin grassed me in!" His voice was a teenage whinge.

Corrina swiped the tears from her face with the blade of her palm. "So wit!?" she screeched. "SO! FUCKIN! WIT! Ad rather see ye in the fuckin jail than the fuckin kirkyard!"

Fran puffed up, face red, knuckles white. He towered over her and she cowered, eyes wet and wide. He snatched a cushion off the settee in his fist, turned and launched it. *Smash* as it hit the trinket cabinet, taking the glass shelves down, laden with bits and bobs and bric-a-brac, framed photies of Fran as a wee lad, his cousins as babies, tourist tat from the beachfront shops at Troon and Tenerife, one fancy plate. All in a mess on the floor.

Neil appeared, kettle in hand. "Wit the fuck?" He took in Fran, who was shaking, shoulders rising and falling hard as if he'd just finished a run.

Corrina held her face in her hands, weeping.

Fran's eyes dribbled too. His chest and throat hurt trying to keep everything in. He wanted to kick and punch and smash his head against something. The sight of his maw cringing away from him, his da's face slack and shocked…

He pushed past and out the door. Slammed it behind him. Took the stairs down, two, three at a time, swinging himself round the corners at the landings. Out onto the street. Started running, twinges in his knees. Fuck it. Fuck it all. His arms pumped. Legs swung. Feet hit concrete, *slap, slap, slap*. Banging them down, tearing up the ground. His lungs burned. Eyes streamed. No pace, no control, just sheer bloody movement, revs in the red, gears crunching and spinning loose.

On fire, he ran and ran.

43

Ralston's hair was Vantablack in the bald light of the supermarket, his teeth iridescent (would make a Geiger counter twitch), his suit pressed by petrol plate compactor. A line from the Coldplay song playing over the speakers slipped through his lips as he chose between a Bombay Bad Boy or a classic Chicken & Mushroom.

"I thought you wanted a debrief," McCoist said.

"I do, but I also need to get a few bits while we're here." He pushed his trolley out of the dry aisle, fighting a squeaky back wheel as he *Tokyo Drift*-ed the corner into the next. "You have to make this job work for you, Alison, otherwise it takes over your life."

McCoist grimaced—her teeth trapping the "Fuck off" in her mouth—at the condescending platitude, the overfamiliar use of her first name. "Very wise, sir."

A laugh chirped out. "I'm sure that's not what you're thinking. You can be candid with me, I don't mind. We're old friends, sort of." He lowered his voice and added, "Drop the 'sir'," though stopped short of giving a paranoid glance up and down the aisle.

He rummaged the soft white loaves while he hummed to himself, looking for a good date, ignoring the tartan wax packets of the Mother's Pride along the top shelf which called to McCoist, the blackened crust and firm, savoury tang a staple of her childhood. Piece and butter and jam. Piece and crisps. Piece and tomato sauce. She was a fussy eater as a wean, only wanting things with no nutritional value. Maw didn't mind too much. Not the way McCoist did with her own kids when they were inevitably afflicted with the same issue. By the time she became a mother (and, undeniably, had climbed to a class bracket above), fussy eating was a sign of complete parental failure and giving your child a packet of Salt & Shake, well... you might as well have given them the solvent spray to go with it.

McCoist gave him a quick summing up of what happened at the Gyle Centre and everything after.

"D'you think any of the others at the safe house would go on record too, down the road?"

"Mal is smart, and I wouldn't say he's in thrall to Devlin either." (It was Mal who'd first coined the nickname "Tickly Tomlinson", and he did not use it with affection.) She recalled him tapping away at his laptop, apparently ready and willing to download a life-ruining neutron bomb of highest-category CSAM onto the suspects' phones. "Depends if he's there because Devlin has something on him or not."

"He always does. That's how he works."

McCoist thought of the Vault, the Shit List, her own indiscretions held against her. "Then it depends what he has on him, how serious." It made her ill to think it, but Mal certainly knew his way around the dark web, knew where to go to find that... stuff. "Kirky is getting close to his pension, could be a good angle." McCoist felt another pang of nausea—she'd been working with these guys for years now, and here she was selling them out. The unease around what had happened at Mad Hatter's placated her conscience for the moment. "I'd never met Jules before, looked like a UCO."

Ralston sucked air in through his teeth like he'd been jabbed with a needle. "Those guys... spider's webs inside spider's webs. How about the suspects?"

"Scared shitless. Unlikely to want to rock the boat."

"Maybe. I like the sound of these UKAD boys. Careers in the balance..."

"They'd take sacking and disgrace for the things they really have done over what Devlin would have them accused of."

"But if Devlin's discredited—"

"But if he isn't—"

"Ye of little faith!"

"They won't take the chance. Trust me."

"How about Messrs Forbes?" They were in the medicine aisle now. Ralston tipped in a couple of packets of paracetamol, a tube of Deep Heat, tube of Anusol, tub of stool softener, a bottle of multivitamins.

"They're gonna end up dead at this rate."

"Then we'll really have a case!" He put a wingtip shoe onto the bottom of the trolley and pushed with the other, sailing a couple of metres down the aisle. Skidded to a stop and a box of Kleenex was tossed into the trolley. He turned and smiled at McCoist's forehead-heavy expression. "Just a joke. That would be bad. You'll just have to make sure it doesn't happen then."

Just like an ACU cop to make it sound like the main, actual job of policing was nothing but a wee jolly, McCoist thought. *Glorified HR prick.* What was she doing here with this cunt? What a fucking mess. She wobbled, sweat prickling, heat rising through her, heart too fast, the exhaustion of the past few days dropping like an anchor and chain, pulling her down. The supermarket hum of produce and spilt milk carried a waft of blood to her nose.

The floor was cold on her cheek. She didn't remember falling.

A man in Sainsbury's maroon loomed overhead, edges of her vision still a sparkling fizz of shadow and colour. "Ye OK, hen?"

“Fine.” She sat up and immediately needed to lie down again, the dark in her brain trying to swallow everything once more. Staying down was better.

A spotty teenager appeared with a first-aid kit. Fingers dug under McCoist’s back and they rolled her onto her side. Better, much better. The rolling blackout in her brain subsided when she stayed still.

In the view from the floor, Ralston’s polished black wingtips were nowhere to be seen.

44

A twenty-year-old boy comfortable perusing the wine list and not just going for the house vinegar. Lottie didn't like it. Nor did she like the way he spoke. Not the words he used. He was polite, more than polite, eager to make a good impression on her. It was his voice, his accent. "Cut-glass" was the term people often used. It too was polite, what it meant was "posh cunt". It meant private school and nannies. Skiing lessons. Holidays abroad in every break. Your gran didn't have a caravan at Craig Tara, she had summer houses and city apartments. It wasn't middle-class pretensions to being posh, either, it was the real thing. You heard it in the voice.

"Could we have a bottle of the Château Pédesclaux, please?" he said.

Château Pédesclaux. A glass of the Château Pédesclaux, si'l vous plaîs. Un poisson rouge et un baguette, monsieur. J'habite dans le garre. Olivier Giroud. Haw, haw, haw. Wanker. Full French accent too. Lottie remembered back in the high school doing Standard Grade French, garbling out sentences about her nass-ee-on-a-lee-tay and what pets she had all in her native Possilpark accent—"Ji ma pell Charlotte"—the most authentically French-sounding part of it being her own name.

He looked up at her across the white cloth in the snug low light of the "Mitchell-in"-starred Cail Bruich on Great Western Road. "Is that OK with everyone?"

It was one hundred and eighty quid a bottle. For red wine. Rancid grapes touched by the manky bare feet of French peasants.

Sure, sure it was OK. All-fucking-all right. He pivoted to Ari, seated to their right, who replied, "That will be wonderful," in a voice imitating his—vowels stretching, tongue hitting the hard consonants like a pin hammer on tacks. There was a manic gleam in her eyes.

"Actually, a huv ma ain suggestion, if yeez don't mind?"

If the boy was taken aback, he didn't show it. Ari flashed a psychic warning to her mother.

Lottie took the menu back off the waiter and pointed to the bottle at the bottom of the list of Bordeaux reds, tapping it with her killer nails, equally red. "Excellent choice," the sommelier said and practically bowed as he left. *This hing wi the Russians better pan oot,* she thought, having just spunked nearly a grand and a half on a bottle of juice.

Ari didn't seem to know whether to be pleased or not about this move. Would it impress her rich boy? Was her mother trying to intimidate him? It crossed Lottie's mind this was the kind of thing Paulo would have done. He wouldn't have stopped there though, he'd have had the lad followed, checked out, strip-searched, maybe. Ari had never had any serious boyfriends while her da was still alive. This one should count himself lucky.

"Toby Armisten." He'd introduced himself with his full name, as if Lottie might reply, "Oh, of the Lanarkshire Armistens?" or some shite. He was handsome but had a too-big face. Lottie could imagine it in twenty more years, bloated red nose, jowly cheeks, foppish hair receded to monkhood, belly gone the opposite way, mushrooming over his belt, casting his preppy boat loafers into shade. For now though, his plain, tailored shirt sat well across a wide chest and broad shoulders, the open top two buttons showing the knotty kinks where his clavicles met and the dark curls between.

"Shall we do oysters?" he said, in the way most lads his age would suggest a round of shots.

"*Yeeess!*" Ari crowed, responding in kind, a clap of her hands.

Lottie cast her mind back to meeting Paulo—she'd never been so hopelessly, openly infatuated, had she? She didn't think so. She'd made him work for it, money or no money, and he certainly had plenty by the time they met. What he didn't have was a knowledge of fine wines and a taste for oysters. They never developed as the years went on either. It was Lottie who dragged them out to nice restaurants and swanky hotels. Her pretensions. Her aspirations of moving up the social ladder. Still, she baulked at Ari's performance. Ari was her mirror image, people always said. So alike. The colour and shape of the eyes, the cut of the chin, the movements of the facial muscles beneath the skin that stretched and knitted into eerily familiar forms when they smiled, frowned, smouldered.

"Al leave ye baith tae it."

"Not a fan, Lottie?"

Lottie. "A prefer ma fish cooked," she fake-smiled.

"Battered too," Ari chimed in.

Wee cow. Keep it up an yel be the wan battered. "Somehin aboot tryin tae swally doon salty white goop activates ma gag reflex."

Toby had a sudden coughing fit, cheeks flushing. Ari cringed and turned it into a scowl. Lottie pulled a "What did I say?" face.

"Why don't we skip them and go for the tasting menu?" Toby recovered.

The smart little portions kept on coming, their waiter delivering a spiel that was part sermon, part prose poem with each. They chatted about uni. Toby was in his third year of business studies, which was "a bore" but a good base for his career. What that would ultimately be he wasn't so certain of—the one point in the conversation where that self-assuredness that irked Lottie in someone so young had faltered. He played a bit of rugger. His parents were still together and lived down in the borders. His daddy was in finance, his mummy in fine art. Sideline in land and property, Lottie thought. Family fortune on one or both branches.

"Ari tells me you run beauty salons," he said, making Lottie realise how one-sided the conversation had been, that she had been grilling him, like dating her daughter was a job he'd been invited to interview for.

"Aye, goat a few wee shoaps oan the go. Hair, nails an that. No much tae interest ye."

"Not at all, I think it's really admirable, running your own businesses."

Lottie searched his simple smile. She wondered if he knew anything about the McGuinns, if he'd heard any rumours or if his life so far had been too removed from Glasgow, from the street.

Ari looked anxious, like she was thinking the same thing. How old had she been when she began to understand the kind of business her da had been involved in? Certainly before he was killed. Not that his death wasn't a shock to her, but she didn't question the manner of it. Shot in the head—executed—in a manky wee car wash on Bell Street. How long before? How young? Lottie had never sat her down for a talk about the life of crime they were all living but bits and pieces must have filtered through to her over the years. She was no eejit. Blood money was paying for her flat, her living expenses while she studied, her clothes and her nights out. To get close to someone, to bring them into this family, was to put a mark upon them. Lottie wondered whether her daughter, in love, had thought of that.

"...and it really is beeyootiful there, I keep saying to Ari that we should go on a trip sometime, head up into the hills and..."

Lottie's phone buzzed; Ari noticed the surreptitious screen check, made a face.

It was a WhatsApp message from Luce: a gif from *High School Musical,* Zac Efron's smiley wee fizzog prancing about in the gym with his teammates, red basketball jerseys, caption reading "Get'cha head in the game".

Hot blood flushed through her, her heart spiked, and it had nothing to do with Troy Bolton's baby good looks. "Am so sorry, doll, a huv tae go."

"What?"

"It's work, it's—"

"Mum."

"No problem, Lottie." Even Ari gave the boy an irritable look at this interjection.

"But, Mum—"

"Sorry, really, it cannae wait. Here." She slid Ari her Amex. "Go fir a drink eftir an aw."

She asked a girl to get her coat with a flash of impatience.

Ari grabbed hold of her sleeve once she was out on the street. "Mum! What the fuck?!"

"Look, doll, am sorry, a really am, but it's *work.*"

"You've been a bitch the whole evening."

Stung like a slap. Not least because Ari was right. Lottie had to grit her teeth not to respond with one of her own, a physical one.

"What is it? You don't want me to be happy? You're jealous?"

Lottie snorted, lips twisting into a grin. "It takes mare tae impress me than a wax jaiket an a toff accent—" On the list of wrong things to say at that moment, that one was right near the top and Lottie immediately regretted it.

“Fuck off!” Mascara running, Ari stomped back inside the restaurant.

“Ari!” Lottie huffed, could see her breath in the autumn air, turning crisp with the dark. “Fuck.” Her phone buzzed again—*No the time, Mark. No the fuckin time.*

45

It had been a hard shift. The past week had been a bastard. Brutalising. Ever since Fran had announced he was off to Moscow it had been one bloody misery after another. Neil needed a pint, some decent scran and a shag. Maybe a bath first.

After Fran had done the runner from the old flat, Neil didn't stick around for long himself. He left Corrina rattling and gurning on the settee, the glass and the ornaments in bits on the floor. He saw Fran standing there, towering over her—his maw—eyes, nostrils flaring. Neil knew the rage, but for him it was only ever something that came upon him on the pitch. The boy wouldn't have hurt her, he told himself. Wrecking the gaff was out of order, a childish tantrum, but he wouldn't go so far as to…

"You're lucky he's not being sent to a youth offender institution, Neil," the lawyer told him all those years ago. "This is a win, trust me." The other lad's face had looked like it had been sculpted from play dough by a toddler. They showed pictures in court. *Look at what this animal did.* A confusing mix of pride and shame had knotted in Neil's gut and never fully come undone. Over the following years the line of the pride/shame graph had nosedived as his son got further into the gangs, the drugs, then rebounded, soaring up exponentially as he found his way with the running. And who had helped with that? His auld da, that's who.

Silly cow shouldn't have grassed them up. Worried or no. You don't do that. Especially with Fran's old record, and everything he'd done to change it. Not to mention Neil nearly dropping a brick in his undies when the firing squad showed up. You don't fucking do that to somebody, do you? Then again, she couldn't have known things would go that far. Or what happened at that joke shop, what they'd been threatened with...

And now Fran had disappeared somewhere. Neil tried calling but it went straight to voicemail. Phone still off. Ach, fuck it, he'll show up eventually, he thought, when he cools doon. Boay's a survivor, a grafter. He'll be back. An he'll know wit tae dae. Because Neil's big problem at that point was that he didn't.

Fran had rubbished the idea that they were off the hook. There were still people in the shadows waiting for them, he'd intoned. So where should Neil go now? And what should he do?

In addition to the bath/beer/burger/blowjob which were high on his agenda, he also needed fresh clothes and a nap. He wanted to go home. Badly. He wanted his own bed. Craving it. Fran could be wrong. Paranoid. Neil recalled that story about the wee Japaneezy sodjer back in World War Two, who hid out in the jungle in the Philippines for decades thinking the fight was still on, didn't formally surrender until the seventies. Poor cunt. That could be him right now. Silly bugger.

He opened the door an inch. Peeked a slice of darkness. Sniffed the air—like home, with a whiff of the gym bag he always left in the hall. Nothing foreign detected. He opened a little wider. Listened. Ears twitched over the sound of traffic on the street, hairs on his body reaching out like antennae.

He pushed the door fully open through a drift of leaflets and takeaway menus on the doormat. Good sign. (Unless someone monkeyed up two storeys and in through a window.) Stepped in, walking on the balls of his feet, a peek behind the door. Nobody there. Hit the light switch. White spotlights, second one from the end of the hall out. Same old, same old. Gutties lined up under a narrow side table where he kept his key dish and a signed photo of himself and Walter Smith, Fran squeezed between them—about eight or nine years old he must have been then, giving the camera a smile that was all teeth and dead eyes, the way kids do when they're told to say cheese for a picture.

("Ye willnae mind me, Mr Smith, but a played fir the under-18s squad back when ye were wae us the first time aroon. Goat injured, but, else, ye know, maybe ad av...")

Nothing out of place, he didn't think. Wasn't sure he would notice if it was. Unless it was something really obvious. He thought of *Pulp Fiction*, Bruce Willis staring at the Pop Tarts in the toaster.

But nothing was going on in his kitchen. Or his bedroom or living room or bathroom. Nobody was hiding in the wardrobe or under the bed or behind the shower curtain. Nobody had contorted themselves into the cupboard under the sink, ready to spring out next time he went for the Fairy Liquid.

Well, fuck it then. He'd have a shower and a wank. If some balaclava'd, gimp-suited geezer wanted to witness that then God help him.

The water was hot, the bathroom filled with steam, Neil in the semi-buff when his phone rang and gave his heart a baw twang. He grabbed at his strides, tangled round his ankles, and fumbled in the pockets. *Must be Fran!*

But it wasn't.

Caller ID withheld. Usually Neil wouldn't answer these. It would be nonsense, spam or whatever. Some call centre in Skypark or fucking Utter Pradesh. Instant hang-up, don't even give them a second of your day or a second thought. Usually... But with everything that had gone on recently...

"Hello?"

"Hi, Neil." A woman's voice.

"A know you?"

"No yet. But a hink we're gonnae be best pals soon enough."

46

"He's heading out. I'm on it."

"Rather you than me," Khan replied over the radio. It had started to chuck it twenty minutes ago. Still, DC Gaz Travis knew it was a lie. Because they'd been sitting watching the flat for hours—Travis the front door, Khan the close that led to a communal garden and bin shed between the blocks—and she'd be as bone stiff and bored to fuck as he was. He'd have gladly stepped out the motor into a hurricane at this point. A bit of autumnal pitter-patter would be refreshing. He had his brolly and his waterproof jacket and a thrum of adrenaline inside him to anaesthetise the cold. This was the good shit. Not that he didn't like being in the office, sending emails, perusing reports, making calls—that was the meat and potatoes of the job—but these few action-movie moments were crack for the part of Travis that craved adventure, even danger. It spoke to some reckless, youthful part of him that still burned beneath the thirty-year-old man with responsibilities and bills he had slowly morphed into, the slide into respectability somehow unnoticed.

In the rain, his hood up, brolly low, he was a kid playing spies. He was Humphrey Bogart in a black-and-white film. He was Blade Runner.

The street was quiet—late hour, pishing rain—so he made sure to keep a fair distance from the target. Neil Forbes was in a hurry, though. Maybe because of the rain, but Travis's gut told him no. He wasn't popping out to the takeaway or something. He was a man on a mission.

They walked down Cathcart Road in tandem, Forbes doing the heavy pedalling, Travis coasting at the back. The railway tracks were over the wall on their right, dug down in a gulch. Forbes took the right, crossing over the lines onto Queen's Park Avenue—clean, pink tenements on one side, big fuck-off mansions on the other hidden by trees.

Travis hung back as they approached the end of the avenue and the entrance to the park itself, this area being somewhat open. *Where now?* Forbes crossed the empty road and into the QP Recreation Ground. Travis lingered a moment before doing the same.

This entrance had no gate, unlike the grand affair at the Vicky Road one. You walked straight into the small skatepark through a gap in the fence. Here, Travis's excitement peaked again. He was a skater himself. That one allowance to youth that had managed to survive unchecked.

His former sergeant, Si Slater, used to call him DC Sk8er Boi as a joke. It was the kind of thing his da would say. That was Si, though. A good one. And Travis had dealt with some absolute fannies in his time in the polis. Lazy cops, apathetic cops, hard-ons, baw-breakers, blowhards and self-important wanks. Most were decent people though, and Si thoroughly so, even if he did give Travis a bit of a ribbing.

Si disappeared one day, into the clear blue ether. Case still open. The gaffer couldn't or wouldn't get involved. It was unlike her. She did take his dog in, save it from going to the rescue home, but the whole thing never sat right with Travis. Then the ACU came calling and things started to make a twisted kind of sense.

She knew now. Ralston had given him a heads-up it was coming down the pipe. The way she looked at him... sour guilt curdled in him. Knowing he was in the right didn't help. But if she was involved in Si's disappearance, she deserved everything she got.

The rain danced, a soothing rhythm, on the fibreglass ramps. Queen's Park skatepark was proper shit. Locals called it "the Wrecks". Tiny, rough terrain of chewed-up tarmac, poorly thought-out obstacles, the whole thing decades overdue for a revamp, but it was home to one of Scotland's important cultural and historical landmarks: a freestanding vert ramp.

Nine feet of sheer terror. Not very wide across, not much flat bottom. Utterly liquefying. One day though, he promised the monolith, one day he would conquer...

His stomach lurched and he remembered what he was supposed to be doing. Like a nudge as he drifted off at the wheel, his heart pounded and he cast about, looking for—

There he was. Trudging up the path towards the brick block of the old changing rooms by the bowling and tennis club, reflective stripes of his tracksuit bottoms glinting under the fizzing street lights.

Travis risked a few words into the radio: "Inside the reccy grounds, heading towards Langside Road." Langside Road separated the Recreation Ground from the main body of the park. A left turn saw the window lights of the "New" Victoria Infirmary blazing through the rain, the facade of the old part of the hospital a darkened K'nex web of scaffold behind high chipboard walls shielding the almost finished (and definitely haunted) flats they were grafting onto bits of the original, 140-year-old building. A right turn circumnavigated outside the black iron fence of the park and ended at Pollokshaws Road—a very long cut for Forbes if that was where he intended going, which would indicate he was paranoid about being followed or already knew. *Fuck.*

No. Forbes crossed over and into the other side of the park.

Travis puffed a few hard breaths, a little relief, reminded himself to keep back before following. Anyone going through the park at night would have a heightened sense of the darkened world around them—prone to take a look over the shoulder or stop to listen to a noise they may have heard, maybe an animal, maybe a footstep that wasn't their own—and if Forbes was up to no good that would go doubly so. Travis tried to keep close to the trees that lined the path up to the hill—the flagpole and observation deck at the top, woodland beyond. Unfortunately that meant skirting close to the pools of light spilling from the lamp posts too.

They came to a crossing out in the open fields of grass. Forbes continued ahead towards the flagpole. As Travis came to it, he heard something. Soggy steps, huffing and puffing.

There, coming towards him from the left: a runner. A fucking runner out in the pishing rain, beanie hat and hoodie, short shorts and high socks, high-vis bondage straps on his upper body, hard breath pluming in the cold air.

For fucksake. Not now. These cunts, Travis cursed them. Why? Fucking masochists. Slaves to the Fitbit. *Slap, slap, slap*—trainers on wet tarmac. Meeting Travis at the crossing. Fuck, if Forbes turned round now, spooked by the sound of the runner… *Shite.* Should he turn the other way? Or, maybe—

47

Kssssshhh!

The windscreen shattered; Khan shat herself.

What in the actual fuck?! She threw the door open, pure reflex, adrenaline mainlined, nerves on fire.

Geezer hoofing it down the street. Khan after him.

He was slightly built, black puffa jacket, black tracky bottoms, black woolly hat, black snood. She'd made out the silhouette of him coming towards her car, difficult with the rain hitting the windscreen (would be even harder now, having been spammed with a brick or something—*Autoglass re-paaair, Autoglass re-place*). Loads of kids wearing that outfit these days, inspired by the self-styled "roadmen" down south. For most it was just fashion, for the others though it was their uniform. Her old sarge, Si, had lamented this. Said he missed the bright colours of the Berghaus mountain-climbing jackets all the wee guys used to wear back when he was on the beat. "Didn't know they had Gore-Tex in the eighteen hundreds," Gaz had joked.

At first, Khan tried to pretend Si had simply got fed up with the job and fucked off to a beach somewhere. But he would never have left Maisie behind. He loved that dug. The calendar on his desk had been one of those custom-printed ones, every month a picture of Maisie. She filled his phone too. As technophobic as Si claimed to be, he had no trouble taking and sharing a million pictures and videos of his dog sleeping, playing, running, licking herself, being a dog, etc.

She could not imagine Maisie's new owner doing the same thing. There was something cold about Alison McCoist. Khan couldn't decide if it had always been there or if she'd frosted over since Si vanished. McCoist had a wry sense of humour Khan used to like but she'd begun to notice an edge of nastiness to it. Again, had it always been there and she was only noticing since the ACU approached her last year, or was it new? Maybe Khan was just trying to assuage the guilt of going against the gaffer in secret while playing happy families to her face. But if she was what Ralston said she was...

Roadboy hung a left. Khan followed. He was quick, but so was she, even if a little stiff from being cramped in the car for hours, bladder getting uncomfortable and blood sugar low. She let the adrenaline buzz do its work, pumped her arms, reaction—flight-or-fuck-this-guy-up—tipping hard one way.

Gaining. Almost within an arm's length. Ready to spring.

Tunnel-visioned. Didn't hear the whine of the electric engine until the dirt bike was at the kerb, right alongside, and—

"*Aarrrgh!*" Sharp pain in the back of her head, legs gone, momentum carrying her forward through the air, face into the wet pavement.

48

Pain and stars.

Punch to the face—landed in the comfortable nook of the eye socket. Sparkled.

Hard dig in the ribs folded him, shoved him sideways onto the ground. Wet soaking into his jeans.

Then the kick in the belly. Winded.

Then the kick in the baws. Almost puked.

Slap, slap, slap. Sound of trainers on wet tarmac, fading. The fucking jogger.

Travis tried to get his head off the ground. Caught a glimpse of someone running. No high-vis straps now. Tried to stand up but his belly lurched and the pavement along with it, everything tilting like he was on the deck of a ship in a storm. Right enough. The rain was lashing him now. Sore and miserable.

"Suffy!" he wheezed into the radio. "Suffy! Been… fuckin… jumped. Need backup!"

He tried again, managing to sit this time. His face throbbed. He imagined some massive, pulsating sore around his eye like a cartoon character stung by a bee. No sign of the jogger. No sign of Forbes either. "Suffia! *Suffy!* You there?"

49

For the second time today, Neil was strung up in the back of a motor. This time was worse. This time he was alone. This time his head was covered by an itchy balaclava, worn backwards. The wool caught on his stubble, prickled at his eyelids, tickled his nose hairs. Nausea rose as he was flung around in darkness, his brain not able to comprehend or counterbalance the movements of the car as they drove to destination unknown. The motion sickness was nothing compared to the fear, but.

His own stupid fucking fault too. She'd sounded so convincing. As soon as she mentioned "doping rumours" his mind bounded off down the track they'd laid for him. *Aye, sure, al meet ye in the middle ae the night in the park where there's nae light or surveillance or witnesses tae discuss the issue.*

That's what she'd said she'd wanted to do: discuss.

"Am sympathetic tae the boay, ad no like tae see him ruint. A really widnae." What she meant was she wanted money in return for her silence. Neil didn't have much in the bank but he was sure if he met her in the park, in the woods (no light or surveillance or witnesses) he could make the problem go away with a little intimidation. If not, he could grovel, offer to set up some kind of payment plan.

She hadn't been alone; grovelling it was.

Two other lads all in black, faces covered. Guns, also black, boxy but still sleek in a minimalist sort of way that paired well with their trainers—the Adidas × Glock collab you didn't know you wanted. *The Brand with the 3 Stripes for Whacking Cunts.* Again, second time that day someone had pointed a gun at Neil. He wasn't getting used to it, felt like his body was sculpted from Angel Delight.

They put him on the back of a moped thing. It was electric. They hummed down the paths of Queen's Park like a formation of UFOs. A distant skelf of Neil's mind, floating numb and divorced from the terror, noted the absurdity.

What if he jumped off the thing? Tipped it, made a run for it? Hid in the bushes or up a tree till morning. It was hard to see how fast the pavement was moving under him in the dark. With no helmet, the rain lashed him. Took too long to decide, they were out the park and a car pulled up alongside the kerb and they were all screeching to a stop, tyres skidding on slick road.

Then it was the hood and the cable ties and being scalped by the roof of the motor as he was pushed inside. Snick of the door locks as the car took off and picked up speed. Then his own heavy breathing—too hot on his face—and the terrible itching. Guts churning, a puddle of toxic sludge weighing hard in his stomach, bubbling and frothing. Fire in his shoulders whenever the car turned, pushing his weight into the seat and his arms, tied behind him. (A one out of five for the Uber rating, and a re-evaluation, a reluctant star added, for DCI McCoist's earlier effort, to account for its relative level of comfort.)

"A cannae… breathe."

"Fuck up."

"Am gonnae be sick. Am gonnae be SICK!"

"Fucksake."

The wool was lifted off his mouth, the mask pulled up to nose level. The air in the car was fresh compared to his own stale breath. He could smell the leather of the seats, someone's aftershave. Something was pushed into his hand—crinkle of paper. It was pushed up towards his mouth. Unmistakable scent of Maccy D's under his nose. So often a nostalgic smell—transporting him to carefree days of childhood, then, later, treating his own son in the same way, creating the same memories for him—at the moment it gave him the boak. Stale grease and sharp pickle-vinegar aftertaste.

"Fill this up," a man's voice said.

"Better no get any puke oan ma fuckin seats, man," another came from the front.

"Probly tastier than wit wis in it afore," the first voice laughed.

"You're fuckin rank, man. Fuck aff."

"Am tellin ye, it wis disappointin as fuck. They nuggets huvnae bin the same since they hud tae start usin chickn breast an no witever tasty beast bits they wur made fae afore."

"Gads. Wit's wrang wae ye?"

"Same as the burgers. They used tae be, like, steroid-infused, hormone-enriched coo hoofs, an noo thur just dry mince ye could use as a fuckin frisbee."

"Please stoap talkin," Neil groaned, chunder touching his back teeth.

Something pressed against his temple, pushing into the soft gap between bone. "Who the fuck telt ye tae speak?" The man's voice had turned sharp and hard like an iron nail. A moment of silence, then he burst into screeching laughter, the driver joining in.

Under his mask, Neil clamped his eyes hard against the tears.

50

She'd managed to convince the manager at Sainsbo's not to call an ambulance and the over-eager teen with the first-aid kit not to fire up the defibrillator. "My hair's a state enough as it is without getting zapped." There was a message from Ralston waiting for her:

> Apologies for the French exit, you seemed to be well looked after. Wouldn't be good for me to be hanging around if ES were called. Let me know you're OK.

Her being "OK" was assumed. McCoist attempted to self-assess. The results weren't encouraging. She'd experienced some *problems* after killing McGuinn. Same after what happened to Si. Moments of breathless panic, sometimes her mind and body would freeze, she would hear, and even smell, these snapshots of the past, these pivotal moments of her life. Bad ones. Blood and brain matter featured heavily. But it would pass quickly. Always did. She'd never fainted during one of these "episodes" before. That was new.

It had been a stressful time, though, hadn't it? Even more so than usual. The pressure from Devlin, Ralston, everyone... Finding Nicholas Stewart and his maw... No wonder she needed a wee lie down. Her body had simply taken it upon itself to make her.

She ordered herself home. See Bruce and Maisie. Take them a walk, get something to eat, have an early night. That's all she needed. *Check in with the kids.* Fuck, and there was that too. Not just the guilt that always assailed her when thinking of Tess and Cam these days, but the reminder there was someone out there trying to blackmail her, threatening her family—you know, in addition to Ralston pretty much doing the same thing officially. Christ, life was like juggling turds at the moment, trying not to drop any on her shoes.

Bruce and Maisie were happy to see her though. She got the hero's welcome she always did, kneeling in the hall, swarmed in a melee of paws and fur and tongues and fishy dog breath. A taste of heaven. She announced it was time for walkies and the dugs' excitement ratcheted up even more, and if they could have lifted McCoist onto their shoulders and paraded her around as if she'd won them the World Cup they would have. The silly, lovely beasts.

She managed to get the leads and collars on after a bit of a tussle and hit the street, Bruce and Maisie charging in front of her, McCoist thinking it might be a good idea to strap some Rollerblades on one of these days. They did the familiar circuit of the neighbourhood, checking the lamp posts and postboxes, grit bins and fences. The dugs were sentries, marching the perimeter of their territory, making sure everything was right. "We'll get out on a proper walk somewhere else soon, I promise," she said. The last trip to any park had been Kelvingrove, when she'd stopped by Lottie McGuinn's gaff to sniff around for info about who had done Callaghan. Two more deaths, a good deal of running about, a scrap in the streets, rumours of Russian mob connections, a major operation involving the firearms team, a bit of psychological torture and blackmail and still no answer to that one.

She pondered her next move. They had teams watching the Forbeses, waiting for whoever it was to make their play. But maybe there was something proactive she could do with regard to Lottie McGuinn—see if she knew anything about Euan Callaghan and Anthony Belov, feed her something to work on. In return for what?

Maisie curled out a fat jobby and McCoist fumbled around in her jacket pockets, among various keys and phones, looking for a bag while trying to pull Bruce away from the poo, which was obviously giving out an enticing aroma. The rain started. A spattering of fat, chill drips which hit the ground with loud, ominous intention and quickly became a power-shower deluge. They ran the rest of the route, the dugs loving it, McCoist trying to keep hold of both leads with one hand while holding her hood in place with the other. She could feel the wet seeping through the seams of her coat and into the jumper below.

Towelling required all round.

The house stank of wet dug. McCoist lit some candles and took a scalding shower. Her belly was growling for something to eat but she made the error of lying down on the bed and it was very hard to get back up. Her muscles wouldn't even try, limbs beaten by the water and steam into jellyfish tendrils.

Her phone buzzed and a tentacle flopped out to drag it in. WhatsApp from Tess. Shite, she was going to phone—

She exploded up off the bed, a popcorn kernel touching a screaming hot frying pan. *What in the name of fuck?!* Tess had sent a picture, taken candidly. Caption: "He said he was going to the gym. Not sure if this counts as unusual. Maybe delete this. Sorry." The shock started an avalanche of understanding, building and battering down the hill towards full realisation. (*That cow, that fucking cow. But why?*) Fear came with it. If McCoist had got the right end of the stick then—

Her phone rang again. Other phone—work phone. DI Griffiths calling. "Yes?"

"Sorry, uh, we have a situation, gaffer."

. . .

The heavy bruise under Travis's eye pulled his lower eyelid down, showing some red, giving him the look of a sad basset hound. "You should see the other guy," he said, handing McCoist a note he'd scribbled down describing his attacker as best as he could remember, including a terrible, scratchy biro sketch of a man's face with a penis growing out the top of his head.

"Could you describe the length and girth?" McCoist deadpanned, getting a smile that seemed to cause him pain. Angry at him as she was, seeing the lad hurt like this reignited some latent protective instinct inside McCoist. Yes, he might have fucked her over, and he absolutely fucked this surveillance job he was on, but he was one of her team, her people. Her responsibility.

"Suffy is still at the hospital, waiting on getting her head scanned," Griffiths said. Griffiths had given McCoist the outline over the phone as she threw her clothes on and distracted the dogs with treats long enough to get out the door. "Says she feels fine though."

"Shouldn't you be there too, Gaz?" They were sitting in McCoist's office, Travis in soggy, damp-smelling clothes, pressing a can of Coke to his eye between sips.

He shook his head. "I'm OK. A few bruises, done myself worse injuries."

"Skateboarding?"

"Nah, after the pub." He grimaced again.

"We got someone on the CCTV hunt?" McCoist directed this at Griffiths, the bags under her eyes almost as bad as Travis's shiner.

"Aye, boss. Seeing what we can get around the exits to the park, and around Forbes's flat."

"Check the time before Suffy and Gaz were attacked too. They must have been watching them watching Forbes. Waiting for the right time to pull the distraction." Travis winced at the word "distraction". "Look out for kids on those bikes zooming about the neighbourhood in the lead-up."

"These are the ones that killed Callaghan, right?" Travis asked.

McCoist nodded. "Probably." She looked at Travis's face, its younger-than-its-years, healthy-diet-and-exercise, spring-water-and-oats-detox veneer ruined by the blistering in the white of his eye, the fat leech swelling below it. "The Stewarts too." Ragged bone from bloody stumps—forensics said teeth marks. "I'm… I'm really glad you're OK. Both of you. Could've been a lot worse."

Travis's cheeks flushed, the pain on his face not just physical. "Thanks, Alison."

"Go home and rest, son."

For her, though, it was coffee time. She heaped the granules in like she was making Bisto, poured it short, plenty of sugar, drank it while it was still lava from a white mug with the NYPD crest on the side that she'd bumped from somebody after her own World's Best Maw one had broken at the handle last year. Damn near ten years of police service that mug had given. Bloody shame.

They'd come for Neil Forbes faster than expected. And Francesco was off the radar—maybe snatched too? And then what? They didn't have the money. The bag of cash and the crypto key were locked in the productions room. So what then? Ragged bone; bloody stumps. Her conversation with Ralston echoed:

They're gonna end up dead at this rate / That would be bad. You'll just have to make sure it doesn't happen…

Fuck.

She woke Devlin to give him the good news.

"Bear?" voice groggy. Unbidden, an image came to her of him in his bed—silky PJs or bare chest?—and she scrunched her nose, forced it away.

"Neil Forbes has been taken. The officers tailing him were ambushed, lost him in Queen's Park."

A sigh crackled through the phone speaker. "That is a fucking pickle he's got himself in."

"Took the words out of my mouth."

McCoist thought she heard something in the background, a woman's voice maybe, followed by Devlin's, mouth away from the handset. She didn't know Devlin was married. Or if he had kids or pets or any attachments. Never asked, was never invited to ask, probably wouldn't answer anyway. Now the image was of Devlin with a woman lying next to him trying to sleep, grumbling at her husband who was always on call, waking them in the dead of night, slipping out the sheets at all hours. It was incongruous with the idea of him McCoist had built in her head all these years: a demigod of intellect whose interest was purely in strategy, in controlling the pieces, his corporeal form—the grey hair, the glasses, the librarian smile, the uniform—no more than a projection hiding a sentient gas cloud or some shit.

She remembered him telling the story of how he'd lost his testicle in his undercover days, the Roy Tomlinson days, and made it sound like he was simply trading a part of himself for something else, not having a bit of amateur, un-anaesthetised surgery done as a punishment.

Maybe it wasn't a person's voice, maybe it was the telly or something.

"We did think this might happen. They moved bloody quickly though, I'll give them that."

"Does that mean we have a plan then?"

"Indeed. The money is off the streets, there's no way these mystery movers and shakers can touch it and there's nothing either of the Forbes gentlemen can do about that. Nor can our

Russians or their agents get hold of it either. All *they* can do is take reparations from the people who botched the deal."

"So we should…"

"Keep an eye, see how it unfolds. We'll mop up any spillover, try to keep it discreet."

"What? But what about the Forbeses?!"

"Played with matches, blah blah blah, becomes a life lesson for everyone."

"Then why did we tail them?"

"It would be to our advantage to know who we're dealing with, who ambushed Callaghan's deal with the Russians. Tonight was a missed opportunity but I'm confident we'll find out once the bodies start turning up. You'll see."

Seething anger on top of the pharmaceutical-grade coffee almost snapped McCoist's phone in two. She took a deep breath. What did she think he'd say? Predictable really. Suddenly she couldn't wait for Ralston to take this cunt down. She didn't need the full thirty pieces of silver, she'd do it for free. Or half, maybe. Girl had to eat. "Understood."

"Goodnight, detective."

McCoist hung up, stuck her phone between her teeth and bit into the shockproof casing. *Mother. Fucker.* Right, she had to find Fran Forbes. Or at least establish if he had been taken too.

She also needed to speak to *her*.

51

"He disnae look like he runs much," Lottie said, surveying the lump sitting in the wheelie office chair. They didn't have to tie him to it, he wasn't going anywhere. Even Lottie's jibe about the man's age/weight/expanding island on the top of his head only elicited the slightest of reactions, a look of hurt darting in her direction.

"This is the boay's da," Hannah said. A pistol grip stuck conspicuously from her belt, muzzle tucked against pubic bone under black jeans. *No the kind ae bullet ye want near yer clit,* Lottie thought with a twist of unease.

"Also his coach an manager," Luce added. "Wuv goat blood an business mixed thegether here. Voalatile combo."

"An why dae we need him? Thoat we wur gonnae catch the lad an shake him doon? Simple."

"Nothin's ever simple, hen." There was an edge to Luce's voice that wasn't just the scratch of three decades of Mayfair King Size down her throat. Irritated by Lottie's attitude or worried things were off to a poor start? They'd pressed the deal with Sigarev, what if they couldn't deliver? A little research online suggested to Lottie that the Recluse were not into second chances. There was one story about a debtor in Moscow who'd snuffed out his own family—wife and three children under ten—by injecting them with morphine before doing himself just to avoid their retribution. Was it true? It was Reddit, but still, Lottie couldn't shake it from her mind. And if Luce was rattled too… "We couldnae find the boay, but wuv goat the next best hing: bait tae reel him in. Good leverage an aw."

Hannah squeezed the handle of the gun, shifting its position. "Geez the money or it's cheerio, daddy-o." She did a horrible, haunted-doll giggle.

Lottie walked round the desk to where their captive sat avoiding her gaze, perched her arse on the edge of it, folding one leg over the other, dinner dress riding up over dark tights. She clasped her hands around the knee, talons interlocking, the bloody teeth of some meat-hungry monster. "Dis yer son care enough aboot ye tae pay up?"

The man kept his eyes fixed to a calendar on the wall, pinned to a cork noticeboard with the rota and various scribbled memos torn from notepads. The office they were in was at the warehouse in Ibrox where they kept the stock for the not-pyramid scheme, House of Blusher. Their logo was on the calendar along with their mascot (the Doll of the House of Blusher), a tattoo-friendly rip-off of Betty Boop done in an art deco style. One of the warehouse jockeys had drawn a pair of minimalist tits on her—two Sharpie-thick *U*s with a dot inside each. A craft honed since school, no doubt.

"Am talkin tae ye." Lottie put the point of her heel against the man's shoulder, pushing so he and the chair turned towards her. "If yer life is in the balance, will yer wee boay pay up tae save ye?"

His face remained slack, eyes at her navel, but Lottie noticed the shine in them, the redness at the lower lid. This was taking him an effort, he wasn't catatonic with fright, he was forcing it.

"We'll find oot," Hannah said cheerfully. She whipped the gun from her belt and tapped the barrel—*dink*—off the top of his head. Not hard, but enough to make him hiss and grit his teeth, make a renegade tear roll free down his cheek.

"How lang will this take?" Lottie murmured, pulling Luce aside. "Cannae keep him here—"

"Wull put him in the loack-up, be fine fir a few days." Lipstick and face powder was not the only thing they stored there. A false wall at the back of the unit hid a cage where other goods could be kept safe before transportation. Another kind of pyramid scheme at work. One that was not in the grey area of legality but definitely in the prison-time-if-caught area.

"Wit if wan ae the guys sees or hears somehin?"

"Thur paid no tae."

"Merchandise is wan hing, but. A person is another."

"These cunts are the best-paid stoack boays in the fuckin country, an hawf ae thum wid be oot oan the street waeoot us. It'll be fine." There was a challenge in Luce's eyes. Lottie had been uncomfortable for a while about using the Blusher warehouse for extracurriculars. Luce knew it too. Her "passion project" Luce called it to tease her, making jokes about her wanting to be an influencer: "We could get aw the lads tae dae a wee dance routine wae ye." The MLM was a good money-spinner, Lottie pouted when she was on the defensive.

As she was now: "Fine. But let's get this done pronto."

"Hannah'll keep him fed an watered; she's bin sayin she wants a pet."

52

Fran had run until his legs were ready to fall off at the knee. His longest in a while, and no Apple watch to record it. He was moving without aim, came to when he collapsed into a tree at the side of the pavement, huffing and spitting, dizzy. The pain of long-distance running had always been cathartic to Fran. He would find himself almost out of body in a rush of chemicals to his brain, lifting him above the tomb of agony his flesh had become—could almost understand the druggies and the self-harmers, there was something in it, Fran just liked to do it in a more healthy, socially acceptable way. But this pain was different. It was like hot pokers in his knees, the wrenching sensation of damage under the immediate ache.

When he caught his breath, he stretched his legs out and rubbed them with firm, palpating movements. Sweat ran into his eyes and he blinked it away along with after-images of his maw cringing, bracing for impact. That one was going to haunt him. *Wit kind ae fuckin scumbag are ye?*

It wasn't the first time he'd scared her though. Back in his wannabe-hard-man days, there were a few occasions his rage had forced his maw from a room, made her hide behind her bedroom door. Stuff he hated to remind himself of, scenes he'd promised himself (but not her—he'd never brought it up with her) would not be repeated. Not now he was older, wiser, reconstructed, a real man. *A fuckin bullshitter an aw.*

He focused on his knees, felt his way around to the blistering cores of the pain. Moaned. A woman walking past with a wean in a buggy picked up a bit of speed, the squeak of a wheel pulling Fran's attention to his surroundings.

The tree he rested against was by a wall with a railing and a hedge growing up and over it. Above and beyond was a block of flats—famous ones. The building was like a modern castle with sandstone turrets and the ghoulish figure of a woman, cloaked and barefoot, suspended from the roof by a chain over an outdoor walkway between the two apartment blocks. Perched on a tall plinth in the centre of the walkway was a huge photograph of what looked like the girl from *The Ring*. Lovely thing to come back home to at night.

He was in the New Gorbals, not far from his flat—autopilot following the homing beacon. Must have come all the way down through Rutherglen, past the old dug track at Shawfield and the Southern Necropolis. Ten miles at least. Fuck. He wished again he knew the time. His brain couldn't fathom a guess. It seemed simultaneously like he'd been going forever but also like he'd clicked his fingers and teleported from his maw's front door to here.

He checked the time on his phone, see if that helped, but it didn't. He had a bunch of missed calls from his da he didn't intend on returning at the moment. Texts too.

No, he needed to—what? What was he going to do? What the fuck could he do? Where should he go? Panic wormed its way in and he fought back with some deep breaths. *One step at a time. Make a list and organise it. Triage. What takes top priority?*

Scraping himself up off the ground.

Right. He tried to heave himself up, screeched as knives slid behind his kneecaps, and sat back down again. Deep breaths. First attempt failed. Didn't matter. He could fucking crawl if he had to.

. . .

Second priority was to get off the street. His flat was a no-go, ditto his da's gaff, and he'd written off his maw's. For now, the pub was as good a place as any. Witnesses were his friends.

If Fran had indeed had to crawl on his hands and knees into this place, nobody would have raised an eyebrow.

Carnage.

Rod Stewart pounded from a jukebox. Middle-aged drunks swung off the fixtures, spilling pints of beer and cider, jugs of wine onto the ancient carpet, which was greasy and soft with a hundred years of absorbed fluids, pitted with fag burns and tarred with the memories of tens of thousands of heavy nights. The sound of the puggies—reels rattling through strawberries and lucky sevens—competed with Rod in a hellish cacophony. And the reek of vape smoke and snouts. And the dribble of pish down the trouser leg. And the bump of Splenda in the bogs, lines off the old Armitage Shanks. Dae Ye Hink Am Sexy? The condom machine working overtime, pumping out johnnies, Male Angels, chewable toothbrushes.

Fran sidled towards the bar, trying hard not to rub up against anybody, the likelihood of someone kicking off at the slightest brush of the shoulder high. The melange of stale beer run-off and Guinness guffs hung low over the revellers pressed against the scarred wood of the bar top. The men were red-faced, sweat lashing down large foreheads and soaking through rumpled, half-tucked goin-oot shirts. The women were gloriously overdone, bolshy in big heels and wearing enough foundation to plaster a house, the worst offenders looking—after a good few hours on the bevvy and the bag—like something made on *The Great Pottery Throw Down*. (Blindfold challenge.)

Fran got a pint and shuffled his way back out of the scrum, finding a nook beside a decommissioned cigarette machine (not removed, simply with a handwritten "OOT AE ORDER" slapped on it).

He wasn't a big drinker, training didn't allow it, but thought it would be too conspicuous if he ordered a softie. *Diet Coke, please. Wae wit?* As such, the warmth of the lager spreading out from his belly, down into his legs and making them rubbery, was noticeable. The ache in his knees began to subside with the second one. The third was bought for him by a man at the bar who was getting a round in for the lads. "Moan, son, get that doon ye!" There was a shot of voddie to chase it with.

Fran was soon dancing with the guys, doing the bouncy along to "Mr Brightside", screaming the lyrics at the top of their lungs, arms over each other's shoulders. Fuck the knees. Fuck the money. Fuck the polis and the fucking gangsters and all.

Couldn't trust the bathroom floor. Not only was it covered in water but it kept moving too. He made it into a cubicle but his whitey still ended up sprayed down the wall. Fell to his knees. Tried not to think about what was soaking through them from the floor. He heaved a second time, into the bowl, his liquid dinner frothing out much the same as it went down. Tears stung his eyes but the walls started to right themselves. His (face) cheek touched porcelain and a shiver ran through his bones.

A shadow crossed over him. He'd left the cubicle door open. A man stood in the frame. One of the boys he was drinking and dancing with. Couldn't remember his name. Lacoste polo shirt, face like a soap-opera beast-of-the-year, chubby but hard. Glazed eyes took Fran in, on his knees, wrapped around the toilet. "Zit awright if a huv a wee toot an aw?" The man winked one nostril.

Fran shook his head, motioned his hand towards the vom dripping down the wall. The guy started laughing, staggered off to the one free urinal. The other was overflowing with pish, a wee lad about eighteen in a barman's tight black tee bailing it out into a bucket with a pint glass.

Need tae get the fuck oot ae here. Need tae get…

Stepping out into the endless tundra of the Antarctic would not feel as fresh as hitting the wet Glesga street outside that oily fire-risk honky-tonk after the hours Fran had been cooped up inside it. He turned his face up to the black sky and drank the rain, let it cool his swelling head. He stumbled one direction, then the other. Where the fuck should he go? Where was he? He couldn't get his phone to unlock, thumb sliding across the wet screen.

He found a bus shelter and tried again. The missed messages assaulted him from the home screen. All from Da, by the looks of it. He opened WhatsApp. The most recent message was a video captioned "Acknowledge this please".

Wit the—?

Who wis—?

His da. Tied to a chair, tape round his mouth. Close-up, only his top half visible, not much background. Bright lighting washed out his face, threw his furrowed brows into sharp relief.

Fuck, oh fuck. Wit—

Camera panned to a gloved hand holding a-a gun? Fran was about to chunder again—heart maybe coming up with the beer this time. Or maybe—no, the barrel wasn't right. Was it? Too small. Shouldn't—

Fuck!

The gun went to Neil's head. Neil pulled away from it, as much as his bonds would allow. Tinny, his already muffled screams hissed from the phone speaker. A gloved hand pressed against the side of Neil's head, pushing it away too. *Why*—the gun moved from his temple towards his ear. His earlobe. Finger on the trigger. *No, no, oh—Click.* Neil trumpeted through the tape on his mouth and thrashed. The camera zoomed in on a shiny gold stud freshly punched into his fatty lobe.

Acknowledge this please

Fran's thumbs, numb, jabbed at the keyboard: *What you want*

Sent

His heart managed a good few 150bpm pumps before—

Seen

Typing…

…

You have two days to get the money. Then we will tell you when and where to meet.

They didn't have to state the consequences.

53

She didn't have to find him in the end; he came to her. "Says he'd only speak tae you, Chief Inspector, sorry."

Nor had she been waiting long. "I'm up anyway."

His words were slurred over the phone—when she pulled into the bus stop he'd dropped his pin at, he was pishing against the signpost with his arse crack to the road, confirming her suspicion he was bladdered—but the panic in his voice was genuine.

"You gonna wash your hands before you get in?"

He wiped them on his trackie bottoms. "Soarry. Ye gonnae geez a fine?"

"Least of your worries, by the sounds of it." *And mine.* He'd begged her to come alone. His reluctance to trust the wider police force was understandable after his recent experiences; he'd only called her because he was "desperate", and he'd "disappear" if she tried to lie or trick him. So she agreed, and kept her word. Seeing him now, she doubted he'd manage the promised vanishing act in his current state.

He got into the passenger seat, bringing the stink of booze and BO with him.

"Belt."

It took him a few tries to get plugged in. "Al just hawd it roon me, like ma granny use tae," he chuckled, words saggy and out of shape, as if formed round a swollen tongue.

"Let's get you a coffee."

. . .

The big twenty-four-hour Tesco on Dalmarnock Road had a Costa machine. Terrible middle-ground pish. Nowhere near as awful as McCoist needed it to be, nor was it the really bitter and powerful high end (possibly-should-be-a-class-C-substance) gear you got in the trendy cafes. Still, she loaded it with sugar and got one for herself too.

"Got you a yellow-sticker pasty and all, help soak it up."

"Aw, cheers." He turned over the Ginsters packet, squinting and struggling with the nutritional-information table.

"Whatever's in it can't be as bad as whatever you've clearly put in yourself already. Eat up." She let him horse his way through half of it before speaking again: "I take it you know your dad has gone missing?"

Nodded, made a noise, sprayed crumbs and pastry flakes onto his lap, brushed them onto her mats (Cam's mats—she needed to remember to get a mini-valet before she gave it back). He used two hands to wrestle his phone from his pocket, the pasty hanging from his teeth. He tapped away at it and handed it over.

A WhatsApp chat was open—"Neil" at the top next to a profile image of Fran's da in a Rangers jersey shaking hands with—*oh for fucksake, it had to be him!* She scrolled the messages, noting the times. All were from before Neil vanished into Queen's Park. Most on the same theme—asking Fran where he was, *geez a ring*, etc. "What am I supposed to be looking at?"

"Wit?! The fuckin—here." He snatched his phone back. His finger dithered, sliding up and down. "Wit?" The pasty dropped. "It's… goan."

"What's gone?"

"There wis, there was aw these messages, an then they sent us a video—ransom video, wae ma da, he wis, he wis—" His chest started to heave with too-quick breaths. Bad, especially with a mouthful of pastry flakes.

"Slow down, Francesco." McCoist started casting around for something he could potentially whitey into, otherwise that mini-valet was going to level up to a full detail and shampoo.

"He wis tied up an they hud a gun—"

"A gun?!"

"A stud gun."

"What?"

"Like an ear-piercin gun." He mimed the action. "They pierced his ear."

"I'm not… what?"

"They pierced his ear."

McCoist's face creased, a combo of confusion and exasperation fighting over her expressive muscles. "Is he being held at Claire's Accessories?"

"Aye, aye, very funny, very fuckin funny. They bastarts huv goat ma da an yer just—" He picked up what was left of the pasty and smashed it against the glovebox.

"Hey!"

He grabbed at the door handle but McCoist was quicker on the locks.

"Fuckin let us oot!"

"Fran—"

"If yer no gonnae fuckin help then—"

"I'm sorry. Francesco, I'm sorry. Calm down, please. Come on. Please." She risked a hand on his shoulder. He glared at her, fear and fury in his eyes—a wee boy's look. "Tell me everything again. Everything you remember. Start from the beginning. Where did you go?"

He told her about his run, and the dive he went into (explained his condition) and seeing all the missed messages, which had vanished. Then the video asking to be acknowledged, the short conversation that followed—all gone. ("They've set it tae 'disappearin messages', a didnae notice afore…")

"Two days tae get the money, then thul tell us where tae take it."

"They want the crypto key?"

He nodded.

"It's been logged into evidence… D'you think your dad will have told them that?"

"Maybe. Probly. Even if he did, it disnae change wit they want fae me. The fuck am a gonnae dae?"

Francesco started to tremble and snuffle. He started to grab at the door handle again—not to escape, McCoist realised, too late on the button, the window only a few inches down, not enough, when he hurled.

She regretted getting the pasty.

He was probably empty now but she put the basin—taken from the kitchen sink—on the floor by his head after throwing the bedcovers on his fully clothed carcass.

"Thanks," he grunted. In the light of the cheap bedside lamp, his face looked like that of a French mime, pools of deep black shadow on too-white skin. He hadn't been thrilled to be back at Mad Hatter's but McCoist couldn't think of anywhere else short notice—and not without going through official channels. She could remember the key code and guessed it would still be vacant. "Just for a couple of days, son."

Plus, there was no way she'd be taking him back to her gaff. Not with Edith twitching the venetians next door. Last thing she needed was gossip going round that she was keeping some toy boy locked up in her house, much as she was sure Bruce and Maisie would enjoy having him there. Absolute hoors for attention, the two of them.

"Just want this aw tae be oer," he whispered, pulling the duvet tight to his chin.

"It will be soon," McCoist replied. As if she knew. After weighing up some decidedly thin-on-the-ground options, she'd come up with a plan as straightforward as possible: give them what they want. It was the best chance of getting Neil Forbes back alive. Fuck it, they could have the crypto millies, it was cursed treasure anyway—as Devlin had pointed out, anyone carrying it was a walking target. Handing over the digital doubloons wouldn't fuck up the super's "leave the rats in the barrel and see which one eats all the others" plan—if it could even be called a plan. But it could save a (mostly innocent) man's life.

"A wish ad never done it."

"Me too."

"Naw, a mean the dopin. The cheatin. A wish…" Big sigh. "So many fuckin hings…"

"Can I ask something? The assault charge on your record—Liam Young. You put him in hospital and never said why."

Fran coughed and McCoist got the basin ready but he pushed it away. "Wis movin tae a new school. Rougher wan. Nae pals there, nae nothin. Thoat it wid be good tae go in wae a reputation, at least. Liam wis just… he wis a hard nut. People knew aboot him, outside oor school an aw. Made sense at the time."

"And now?"

"Any paracetamol? Ma heed's awready bangin."

54

Futz was on duty. He was a productions keeper. Ex-job, retired and returned.

(Mentalist, McCoist thought. When she was finished they'd never see her again. She'd be out the door so fast they'd all be choking on a cloud of dust.)

Futz was a big, hairy troll and the productions locker his cave. And like all trolls, he was in a bad fucking mood the majority of the time. "Cerd," he said, tapping a fat finger on the desk.

"Good morning," McCoist returned, chirpy as a cheerleader as she put down her warrant card and slid it over.

As he studied it, a change came over his face, even his thick grey moustache seeming to twitch upwards at the tips. McCoist doubted it was because of her rank—Futz couldn't give a fuck if you were a gofer or the chief constable, if you were here asking him for something you were a pain in his considerable arse. "McCoist. Yer no relatet tae—"

They'd had this conversation before. Several times. Futz had probably been a shitty polis. "Maybe. Who's your team?"

He glanced over his shoulder to the shelves of seized evidence, then over McCoist's to the door behind her, then began to undo the buttons on his shirt. Three down, he pulled it open to reveal a saggy chest covered in freckles and grey curlies, and the RFC crest tattooed on his tit above a turned-in nipple.

McCoist had been shown this before, expected it, hid her distaste behind a cringing smile. "Help me out with this and maybe the big man will send you a Christmas card this year."

Futz gave her a sharp salute and a rare smile, then buttoned himself up. "Wit can a dae ye fir?"

"Signing something out to take to the computer geeks."

"Number?"

"I don't know it."

He scowled.

"It's a USB stick, was logged in yesterday, from the action over at the Gyle Centre thing—will be part of the Ruaridh Callaghan murder inquiry, Operation Winton."

"Ye should really know the number."

McCoist smiled as sweetly as she was capable of—and hers was not a face used to, or suited to, doing so. "Sorry, it wasn't me who logged it in. I don't know it, but I do know where my *uncle* likes to drink on a Saturday night."

Futz squinted at her, drew his lips in until they vanished under the stache. "Al huv a look."

A thumb drive as nondescript as they come with a key ring on the end of it. That's what eight people (so far) had lost their lives over. As McGuffins went, it was no Maltese Falcon. It wasn't like it contained the nuclear codes or anything either. Just a password to a wallet. Just money. Sure, it was a lot of money, and people had certainly been killed for much smaller amounts of the stuff, but still, McCoist couldn't help but regard it with a kind of disappointment and distaste. Maybe she'd feel differently if it wasn't crypto, if it was physical—a briefcase loaded with bound hundreds. Maybe then she'd feel its One Ring to Rule Them All pull. As it was, she'd have no problem casting this silly thing into the fire.

She gave Mal a pair of nitrile gloves to wear before handing over the USB in its paper evidence bag.

There were only the two of them in the Pacino Squad office, the vommy smell of the old hoover the cleaners used still in the air, dust motes in the golden morning light. She'd asked him to meet early. If she had to, she'd tell Devlin what she was up to, but if she could keep it to herself until after… better to ask forgiveness and all that. She didn't want him stepping in at this point. Once Neil Forbes was safe, she'd be happy to hand over chasing the money to him.

"Need a copy of this."

"You got me out my scratcher for that?" Mal pulled off his glasses and wiped a greasy lens on the sleeve of his cardy. "I'm sure you'd be capable of doing it yourself."

"Aye, I would, but that's only the first step. Once it's copied over, I want you to load the new drive with goodies."

"As in?"

"*Spyware,*" McCoist said, with a jazz hand twinkling.

Mal looked past her to the locked door of Devlin's office.

"I want to know where it goes, where and what it gets plugged into, who accesses it—I want into their computer, I want into their accounts, I want into their fucking fridge if you can do it."

Mal licked dry lips, resettled his specs. "Anything's possible. But why?"

"The less you know…"

"Has *he* sanctioned this?"

"He will."

"That's not—"

"For you to worry about, constable."

Mal's nostrils twitched. His eyes, enlarged by the lenses, met her stare. Hierarchy was not so clear-cut in the Pacino Squad. They were a tight-knit gang, the central node of a network that operated outside the law, hidden within it, and as such, things were not so simple as who had the most shiny pebbles on their sleeve. Mal had been there longer and filled a role that was arguably more indispensable than DCI McCoist's.

"I'll square it up, it's on me. But, you know what? He won't be around forever." She'd suggested to Ralston that Mal might be a possible flip, time to test the water. "Every dog has its day."

The evidence bag crinkled, Mal's hands tightening on it. Something rippled across his features but whether it was worry or hope, McCoist couldn't tell. Without another word, he took out the USB and plugged it into his computer. McCoist resisted the urge to say "Good boy".

"Right, first part will only take a mo, but you'll have to give me some time to work on the—hold on. You sure that's the right stick?" He picked up the evidence bag and read the label.

"What d'you mean?"

"There's nothing on this. What is it you were wanting copied?"

Tingling blossomed in McCoist's belly. "Nothing? What? Show me."

He tapped the screen, an empty window. "Right there. Whole lot of nothing."

"There's supposed to be some kind of password. Maybe it's encrypted? Somehow? Or hidden?"

"No, no, there's literally nothing saved on this thumb drive. Empty. Blank. Whatever you want to call it."

What the… How? Francesco had used it before. He'd accessed the crypto wallet and withdrawn various sums into several bank accounts—then collected it as cash. Nowhere near all of it though. That's what he'd said and the money in the bag agreed. Had he drained it to some other account he hadn't told them about?

She thought back to Mad Hatter's, the look of abject terror and disgust on his face when the threat to infect his phone was made, then the crushing blow of the doping reveal which so quickly followed. That was his bottom of the barrel. He had nothing left to hide after that. She could feel it. And he wouldn't have needed to come to her if he had the money stashed away all along. No. Not Fran.

"You're making me dizzy," Mal said. "Can you sit down?"

"Who…" She checked the label on the productions bag again, the signature.

55

Ralston's socks had Daddy Pig on them. He helped the wee one—a pot-bellied, double-chinned toddler with blonde curls in a pair of denim dungarees—up into the soft-play frame ("Go find your brother") and padded over the utilitarian grey carpet back to McCoist, who was sitting at a table on the side of the play area. His suit had been swapped for beige chinos and a black turtle-neck—après-ski style went well with the dye job and teeth bleach. Maybe it was the environment too, seeing him there with his wee ones, but McCoist thought it took a few years off him.

"D'you miss this once they're older?" He hooked a thumb at the netted play frame covered in foam tubes and cable ties.

"What? Having to squeeze myself through tiny plastic tunnels and wade through ball pits? Or the inevitable D & V that comes from letting them loose in a plague pit?"

Ralston chuckled. "I know what you mean. I catch myself just chucking them in and sitting at the side having a coffee, and I worry that I'm, I dunno, missing out on something. Or not making the most of it." A scream came from somewhere up above. "Hold on." Ralston ran off, hauled himself up into the thing, clambered over a rope bridge, disappeared in a maze of primary-coloured, easy-wash vinyl.

He came back with a deep groan as he sat.

"Everything OK?"

"Ahh fine, there's this hump thing she can't get over and big brother abandoned her to it."

"The apple doesn't fall far from the tree."

Flash of too-white choppers. "I did say sorry about that. I got my excuse in there early too. Is everything OK with *you*?"

"Dandy. I think I might have something concrete for you."

The easy-charm smile vanished. A hunted look replaced it, a quick eye around, check if any of the other harried, unwashed parents mainlining extra-large cappuccinos were actually secret agents. Then it was back. "Something worth risking the D & V for?"

"Check Devlin's financials. I think he may have stolen money that was seized in the case we're working." The idea had galled her at first. Devlin was a lot of things, but a thief was not one she'd expected. Part of her thought she might be mistaken. Sure, he was the last one to have touched the USB key before it went into the productions locker, but someone else may have made the switch, or copied and deleted the code, before that. Maybe. Maybe she'd been blinded by all his proud talk of justice, balance and system stability, and look-at-how-clever-I-am. All that "For the Greater Good" bullshit he spouted any time she disagreed with his methods. "It's crypto—"

Ralston whistled. "Easy job for someone there."

"But maybe he'll have moved some into his regular accounts or—"

"They've been checked. His financials have been gone over with a midge's moustache brush. There's never been any hint of Devlin receiving money that can't be accounted for. We've been working on the basis that his interest is in power, not in making bank."

So had McCoist. "But aren't those two things *always* linked?"

"Daddy! Daddy!" A boy about six years old with Eddie Ralston's eyes came running over to the table. "Marsie's stuck at the top of the chute."

"OK, OK, I'm coming." He gave McCoist a *here-we-go-again* eye roll and got up.

"It's a lot of money. *A lot*. Look, he logged a USB drive with the key to a crypto wallet on it into evidence. I just checked the drive and the key is gone. Deleted. Or the memory stick itself has been swapped. Can you check his accounts again?"

Ralston sighed through his nose.

"Dad, come on!"

"I'll see," he said. "Keep plugging away."

56

The contact hurt his toes. Like kicking a waterlogged fitba. He did it again and again until the pain was a throbbing, sparkling sensation in his little piggies. Grip on his upper arms dragging him away. The boy on the floor, the hard man, fourteen years old, crying.

That wasn't last night though. His regrets about last night were only over showing off his dance moves. The Sprinkler, the Lawn Mower—all gardening-related; it was all he knew. In the discotheques of Europe, they called him Fly Moe. He could live with that shite.

He could also live with chucking up all over DCI McCoist's purple pimpmobile. *Ooft*, that memory returned with a bit of sweaty panic. But the video of his da, his ear being pierced—*two days*—crashed into him on a tidal wave of nausea. He couldn't rewatch the clip, it was gone. All he had was the blurry memory of it. It was an earring gun, right? But he was sure what it meant, wasn't he? Two days. The money.

If he failed—could he live with that?

He made it to the toilet to heave (pretty much all water now, thank fuck) and it settled him. Next best move was to get in the shower. A "re-evaluation shower", one where you brace yourself against the tiles, let the water cascade down your face, take deep sighs and ask yourself: "What the fuck are you doing with your life?" (Fran had first heard this term from Ferrari, who said he'd coined it after accidentally jizzing in his own face while having a delirious wank to some particularly mucky stuff while hungover. Ferrari was dead, full of holes.)

But it was hard to get up off the floor. His knees were in bits. The pain was like having a tiny iron maiden clamped round each leg, his kneecaps the baldy napper of Pinhead from *Hellraiser*. He dragged himself into the bath—fuck, he'd be needing one of those walk-in tubs for pensioners, with the door and the seat. He snorted a bitter laugh, turning to tears as he saw the undigested sweetcorn of truth in it. There would be no op now, not one way or the other. If he got the money back—and that was a big if—it was all going to pay the ransom. The best he could do was get on some waiting list, do the physio, take it easy, take break after break while his prime years whipped past, wins and sponsorships peeling away with it.

And then what? He had nothing to fall back on. No higher education, no work experience, no trade. His only job had been the best part of a decade ago and he couldn't stick "drug dealer" on his CV. *Responsibilities included delivering packages on time, cultivating customer relationships, managing cash flow, and evading the pigs*. Where did that leave him? A job at the till next to his maw?

A return to a life of crime was clearly out—this whole thing, the comeback, the "one last job before retirement" had been an unmitigated disaster. One problem after the other. *Don't bring me problems, bring me solutions*, went the mantra in his head. For the first time it did not help. It did not rally him. It sounded fucking stupid, actually. What did it even mean? He curled up in the bath with the water falling on him from a great height, going cold in a puddle underneath his body.

The creak of the front door pulled him upright. His heart went in the other direction, dropping towards his arse in a whoop of panic.

"Just me!" McCoist's voice. "Got breakfast and coffee."

"Minute!" he called back, his voice dry, mouth sticky and teeth furred like he'd been drinking full-fat Coke—another thing he usually avoided along with the booze. He dried and borrowed another outfit from the cupboard—the second from this flat, the first of which had replaced the clobber he'd got from his da. Couldn't remember the last time he'd had his own clothes on. Something that fitted and smelt normal.

"Painkillers," McCoist said, handing him a pack of paracetamol with the Starbies cup to wash it down.

Fran grunted his thanks. The coffee was better than the engine oil she'd fed him last night and even after one mouthful he felt like he was on the path to resurrection. He took a tentative bite of a floury bacon roll.

"While you've been having your beauty sleep, I've been working. We've got a problem."

"Another wan?" *Bring me solutions.* Surely, as a detective, McCoist was a solutions-oriented person too. She looked a far cry from the entrepreneurs Fran followed and read about and listened to on podcasts though. She was a woman, for a start. She was also over forty. Her business-casual outfit had come off the rack in Next or Markies. Her face was creased at the forehead and eyes, hair grey at the temples. That said, there was a leanness to her, and the way she'd entered the fray in Shettleston said she was no stranger to training.

"They come in threes."

"Aye?"

"Naw. Running off with a huge wedge of bleep-blorp-gold that belongs to gangsters just happens to create a lot of them."

"Sorry. Wit's the latest then?"

"Someone has run off with the money. Someone else."

. . .

He'd thought he was better but the ride to the West End proved him wrong. The suspension in McCoist's ridiculous aubergine go-kart was stiff as your granda on Viagra. Every bump in the road juddered up through Fran's spine and wobbled his brain in its murky fishbowl. McCoist's driving didn't help either—twitchy on the accelerator, the turbo kicking in and making them lurch forward after every stop, whipping Fran back and forth. "This hing isnae fae the pool is it?"

McCoist grimaced. "It's my son's, I'm borrowing it for a few days."

"Ye write aff yer ain motor mowin us doon?"

"I said sorry for that."

"Didye?"

"Can't remember. But if I did it was sincere."

They turned off Byres Road into a row of blonde sandstone tenements with regulation black and white window frames, a leafy, tree-lined verge splitting the street in half, cars parked nose to tail all the way along, their every corner scuffed and streaked with traded paint. Somebody got a little helmet-purple added to their bumper as McCoist wedged herself in.

From outside, the flats looked pricey but unassuming. You wouldn't look up at the top floor there and think it was the McGuinn stronghold. That's where they were going.

Fran knew the name, of course, from back in the day. Way above his level, but. He'd never shared the same air as the man. In Fran's time away from the game, Big Paulo had been killed and now the missus was making her own play. The Burds ae Prey—Callaghan had mentioned them. "Sisters daein it fir themsels! An good oan thum. It's the fuckin twenty-first century eftir aw." (Despite his lip service to "woke", which went nicely with his dandy suit, waxed beard and Doc Martens, he didn't seem to rate them.) McCoist said they might be able to help somehow.

"Why wid they dae that?"

"I've got something over Lottie McGuinn." She said her name like it tasted sour.

"Wit?"

"It's personal. May as well use it to our advantage. Pull every string we've got."

McCoist buzzed the door.

"Wit dae *you* want?" came the answer.

"A favour." She pulled Fran into the eye of the camera above the buttons; the door clicked open.

Lottie McGuinn was waiting for them three flights above with a look that made the jelly in Fran's bones wibble-wobble. Her forehead had been frozen and eyebrows carved into something severe. Along with eyelashes like a cheval de frise and a bold shade of pink on her lips, she cut a vicious figure against the old, patterned tiles and bare cement floor of the close. Fran might have labelled her a cougar at a distance, joking, not meaning it literally enough. Up close, danger radiated from her. "Am still daein ye the last wan ye asked, am a no?"

"That was a mutually beneficial exchange, not a favour."

"This cunt's goat Russians an fuck knows who else eftir him." Being the sole occupant of her gaze was like being exfoliated by a sandblaster. Fran wanted to cover his face. "Just goat the sash windies refurbed, don't want thum full ae holes."

"This will only take a minute."

The front door opened into magazine luxury, the kind of place a character in a film might live. The novelist's spacious New York apartment, the design student's penthouse. His maw's voice in his head said, *Don't touch anyhin!* And he didn't have to feel the leather of the sofa or the weave of the rug to know they cost more than a black-market organ. He could see the money, smell it. There was a spareness to the living room—not the macho minimalism of his own gaff (Fran had no fucking idea what to put in a room beyond a place to park your arse and another to park your telly) but a careful curation at work.

Despite her remark about Fran's wanted status, Lottie McGuinn didn't close the curtains but instead went to the open-plan kitchen and began to work a coffee machine that looked like a gleaming hot-rod engine. "A dae cappuccinos an that's it."

"Much obliged."

"Eh, cheers." Fran noticed Lottie's nails as she worked the knobs and steaming spouts: blood red and shaped like fangs. A tingle passed over him, as if their tips were tickling across his skin.

She handed them each a small cup with a few thimbles of coffee in it.

"Well?" Lottie stood over them, hands on hips.

McCoist licked foam off her lip. "Pretty decent, actually. I don't usually go for—"

"A meant the favour. Wit dye want?"

McCoist made a show of settling her Borrower cup on a leather-cushioned coaster on the live-edge coffee table before fixing Lottie straight down the barrel. "I want you to make a move against the bastards who killed Callaghan."

Fran's heart tripped; liquid nitrogen steamed in his stomach. *Slap of hot blood in his eyes, Callaghan's face opening like a carnation.* Was this a bluff? Must be a bluff. Crazy talk.

Lottie's expression, limited in its degree of motion as it was, asked the same questions. "Ye know who did it?" But her voice betrayed her interest.

"Not yet, but I know where they're going to be." McCoist's voice was perfectly level. Was she mental? Acting? "They have the lad's auld man..."—she jabbed a thumb at Fran—"...and want the stolen crypto in exchange for his safe return."

"So gee it tae thum."

Again, Lottie's eyes abraded Fran's face and he shielded it by studying the pattern of the rug beneath his feet, which he addressed his words to once he found them down the back of his boak-burnt throat: "A don't huv it."

"Wit?!" The intensity stepped up from medium grit to coarse. "Wit dye mean ye—"

"He doesn't have it," McCoist said.

"Naw, really."

"Really. He doesn't know where it is. It's in the ether." McCoist slurped the dregs of her coffee. "Always was, this crypto shite. None of it's real. Or if it is, it's only temporary, till people decide they like some other thing better. Gotta cash out quick, I guess."

Lottie's lower jaw was pushing forward—Fran thought he heard bones clicking. "So wit then? Yer wantin ma firm tae wipe thum oot fir ye instead?"

"Hmmm, not 'wipe out' per se, but you could neutralise them somehow?" McCoist's smile was almost sweet, as sweet as she could manage. Aspartame.

"Could a? An why wid a dae that fir ye? Just a wee favour ye says, an yer in here askin me tae go tae war. Fuckin kind ae polis are ye anyway?"

"Lottie, I just want to keep as many people safe as possible. This crew who did Callaghan are fucking lunatics. They murdered one of their own who got injured at the scene. Cut his throat from lug to lug."

Fran heard the echo of the man's scream, then the awful, wet burbling it became as his windpipe opened up and filled with blood. Then the laugh. The woman's laugh—ugly and hacking, reminiscent of the sound of the slit throat.

"So arrest thum."

"I'd love to, but I don't know who I can trust."

Lottie smirked. "An ye can trust me?"

"Not at all, but with you I know exactly where we both stand." McCoist took her phone from her pocket, started to unlock it when the front door opened and a voice interrupted her.

"That your wee purple motor oot there, Inspector?"

Two women in the doorway: one a bit older but alt-trendy—short, punky, coloured hair and flattering clothes taking a few years off—the other genuinely younger, closer to Fran's age, with spooky big eyes and the tips of cute buck teeth digging into her lower lip. It was the older one who had spoken. "Didnae huv ye pegged as a street racer. Fast an Furious Dennistoun Drift."

The younger woman laughed at the joke.

Fran's pulse stopped.

Squealy, breath-catching, donkey-bray laugh. Produced a horrible, cringing sensation in the listener, like rubbing your incisors together.

His heart kickstarted again, mainlining adrenaline. McCoist was saying something to them, he couldn't hear what, couldn't focus. "C-can a use the lavvy?" He might have shouted it or whispered it. All eyes on him.

"Doon the hall, second oan the right," Lottie said. "It's the wan wae the bath an sink an toilet in it, if that helps."

He tried not to run but didn't want to appear as if he were trying not to run. It was a long walk, those twenty paces down the hall. The fleece-lined zippy he had on did not breathe, he was boiling away inside like a ham wrapped in foil. An excruciating eternity later, he got the toilet door closed and locked.

Hands sweaty, fumbling the handset. McCoist the top of the chat list: *It was them who killt Callaghan!* Send. Sending. Still sending. Signal bad. Sending. Fucksake. Fuck. He ran the tap. Sending. Hand hovered over the flush of the toilet. *Come oan. Moan tae fuck!* Finally, two grey ticks.

He flushed, washed his hands. He took some deep breaths, counting, focusing on his heart beating, slowing it down. His hand trembled on the door handle. Still grey ticks, she hadn't seen his message yet. Fuck. *Moan ye fuckin blues.* He couldn't stay in there forever. Maybe he could go out there and nudge McCoist or something. Try to get her to look at her phone. Hope she could stay calm enough that they could make their excuses and walk out the door.

One issue at a time. Prioritise. What do you have to do first?

Open the door.

He opened it.

She was waiting outside. The young one—psycho eyes and rabbit teeth. The one with the horrible laugh. The one who had murdered Callaghan and Ferrari and the others. Had slit the throat of her own teammate.

She was smiling. "Bit ae air freshner eftir wouldnae go amiss, pal."

57

Lottie was scunnered. To put it mildly. Lightly. As an angel feather.

First, because Luce's stupid fucking plan to kidnap the boy's geezer and exchange him for the money had fallen apart so quickly. And second, because that fucking balloon—hydrogen balloon at that—Hannah was waving a fucking gun around in her home.

The lad returned from the loo with a face on like a lost wean. Hannah was right behind him, pistol at the small of his back, barrel digging between the vertebrae.

McCoist looked like she might start foaming at the mouth. Oh, and there was the third thing—they'd done all this with a polis sitting on her Darlings of Chelsea couch. At least it was this one, but. Bent. A murderer. "Good work, ladies," the inspector said through vice-tight teeth. "You got me. I thought it was the other firm who had taken him, our mystery assassins. Here I thought we were working together when all the time you were angling for a piece of the pie."

The boy opened his mouth but Hannah closed it with a dunt to the head from the butt of the pistol.

McCoist jumped up, found herself the target of Hannah's weapon and her awful laugh. "Haw!"

"Christ, Luce, tell her tae fuckin take it easy," Lottie huffed. *Mad bitch.*

"Am no a fuckin dug," Hannah said, bristling. Lottie's skin tingled with the threat of violence that radiated from the girl. *She widnae dare, widnae fuckin dare tae point that hing at me. She wants tae, but. She widnae?*

"Naw, dugs are better trained," Lottie needled, her voice low, calm, designed for maximum irritation.

Hannah's face scrunched, turned plum.

"A couldnae trust *you* no tae shite oan ma flair or hump ma pillows."

"Lottie! Enough!" Luce got between them. "We're here tae discuss business, no harp at each other like a bunch ae bloody menfolk."

"Fine, let's talk business." Lottie's voice was acid. "Let's see where yer wee plan is goin next. The sodjer here wis just tellin us the boay's no goat the money. Naebdy's goat it. Nae cunt knows where it is."

"I might have an idea," DCI McCoist butted in, sounding bold as brass but with a face on the pale side of "corpse". "Let me chase it down. Give me the original deadline. Meet same time, same place."

"An if ye cannae get hawd ae it?" Lottie asked, drilling into McCoist's mud-brown eyes.

"Why are you asking me?" McCoist fired back. "That's your decision to make."

There's mare kinds ae violence than physical—she knew what this kind would be though. Clean shot through each head, bam, bam, then chopped up and cut back and ground to dust and blown away on the wind. That was if Luce got her way. If the job was left to Hannah...

"Soonds fair," Luce said. The lad moved as if to say something again but just the threat of the pistol grip was enough to stop him this time. "First, but, let's huv a faimly reunion. Least we can dae is let thum spend their final oors thegether."

The da was a sad sight. Not because Hannah had laid hands on him again, but because he looked as crumpled as the empty bags of crisps scattered all over the floor of the makeshift prison. The family-size multipack of assorted Golden Wonder was supposed to last him the whole two days. He sat slumped on a wheelie office chair, mouth greasy, chest covered in crisp crumbs, wheezing like an asthmatic.

"Da!" The boy grabbed hold of the bars. The man looked up, saw his son, and blubbered.

"Naw, naw," Neil whined. "Ye werenae sposed tae—a didnae tell thum fuck aw. A swear, Fran. Swear oan ma life."

"A know, Da, a know." The boy was greeting too.

Lottie felt a lump in her digestive tract, like a snake who'd tried to swallow a horse. She wasn't the only one uncomfortable. McCoist's eyes were reading the cracks in the cement floor. Odd for someone who just twenty minutes before had put up the men's lives as collateral. Odd for someone who had shot Lottie's husband in cold blood then covered it up by sending Lottie's nephew to prison.

Lottie had sat in the passenger seat on the way over, the inspector squashing in the back with Hannah and the gun between her and Forbes. Lottie found herself trying to catch McCoist in the rear-view, read the expression on her face as they drove to the warehouse in loaded silence.

"Open up, Mitch," Lottie told the lackey guarding the pen.

The lad stumbled in, grabbing his da in a bear hug. The old man couldn't bring himself to stand and let his son collapse on him, as if he were still a small child, jumping into his lap in need of comfort. The wheelie chair threatened to tip them both over.

Lottie followed him in. "Look, a don't hink a should huv tae tie yeez up, but if there's any nonsense, Mitch right there'll be in here wae his taser an his slipper an yel huv tae spend the rest ae yer tempry porridge strung like a roast beef—"

The cage clanked shut behind her.

58

"Are yous huvin a fuckin giraffe?"

Hannah laughed; skin shrivelled from bones at the sound of her.

McCoist's heart nudged faster, already at a steady clip, needle of the beat-ometer into the red. *The fuck is going on?* Contrary to the wee mad lassie's response, Luce Branson's face did not seem to agree that shutting Lottie into the pen was a "fuckin giraffe". Lottie McGuinn knew it too, no matter the words that spilt from her mouth.

"This wis boond tae happen eventually, hen."

"Wit wis?" Lottie seethed.

Luce's shoulders slumped a degree. "Yer tae saft fir the gig. An we don't need yer name above the door any mare."

"The fuck? Luce! LUCE!" Lottie grabbed the bars, white knuckles, crimson nails. "This is fuckin—fuckin bullshit! If yer pushin us oot fir a bigger share at least just fuckin be honest aboot it ye greedy fuckin dyke!"

"Fuck ye sayin?!" Hannah shrieked, pulling her gun, striding to the cage, barrel through the bars.

Lottie grabbed Hannah's wrist, bent it back on itself, pressing against the metal of a bar. Hannah made a sound like she was retching up rusty screws.

McCoist made a dash for the gun—

The sensation was like licking a battery. Except instead of it just tingling across the tongue, she felt it through her whole body. And the battery was Zeus's massive, pulsating kidney-cracker. Her musculature seized, body turned to a plaster cast, rigid and brittle, and she piledrived herself into the floor. Nose burst against concrete; lips burst against teeth. Strobe of pain through her spine, celestial sparkles in her eyes.

Lottie screamed, somewhere beyond the sound of McCoist's own heart in her ears.

"Let's aw calm the fuck doon"—Luce's voice.

McCoist felt hands on her—the guard, Mitch, helping her sit up. He took off the snood around his neck and gave it to her to staunch the blood streaming from her coupon, then pulled the taser prongs from her back with a couple of sharp tugs. "Sorry aboot that, love."

"You fffuckin will be." She had to drag the words out of her throat and through the throbbing, tenderised ruins of her mouth, the pain raw and agonising.

"That's the spirit." Mitch clapped her shoulder.

Lottie was on her arse too, a hand covering her brow. Hannah retained possession of the gun. Luce shook her head at the whole bloody inconvenience.

"Why noo?" Lottie asked, catching her breath.

"Bin puttin it aff fir a while, really. Figured when ye foond oot wit wis really wit that'd be the natural time. The boay knows noo, so, best tae come clean an… Here we are."

"Who? Him?" Lottie turned to Francesco. "Knows wit? Wit the fuck ye oan aboot?"

"It wis her who did Callaghan," Francesco said, pointing to Hannah, and was rewarded with her signature Jimmy-Carr-swallowed-a-dog-toy laugh. "She wis the wan who ambushed him. She wis there. A recognised her. Back at the flat. She killt him. An Ferrari, an the others." The lad started to tremble, lip petting, tears dribbling. "Pontoon. Ye killt Pontoon, didn't ye? An-an his maw. His fuckin *maw*."

"Aw in a day's work, babe," Hannah said.

"The fuck wid yeez dae that fir? Wit's goin psycho oan Callaghan gonnae help us wae, Luce?"

Luce treated Lottie to a rare smile, a sad thing. "See, hen, this is wit am talkin aboot. Yer happy wae yer salons an yer wee make-up marketin scheme—that's where yer heart is. The shallow end. No in the proper business. Yev no goat the belly tae swally the real stuff.

"A heard aboot this big deal Callaghan hud set up wae some mad Russian gang through his campadre Arty Sutherland. The plan wis tae crash it, get rid ae Callaghan, an take oer the deal in wan big push. Put us where we belang—oan tap. Players oan an international scale.

"Didnae fuckin coont oan lang legs in there runnin aff wae the goods, but."

That's where Lottie's tip about Fran came from then, McCoist thought through the cotton wool in her brain, scarf in her mouth. Straight from Luce herself. Probably claiming she'd heard it off someone who knew someone who knew something, etc.

"So ye doubled doon oan yer fuck-up an went an promised they Russian cunts yed find the very hing yed tried tae bump fae thum?" Lottie scraped herself up onto her feet. "Ye were keen tae huv me take part in that—somebdy tae blame if ye couldnae pull it aff?"

"A can see yer hurt, hen. Like a telt ye, this hale hing isnae a good fit fir ye."

"Fuck up! A wantet this. A wis the wan who came tae *you*, mind? The wan who startet it. Waeoot me—"

"Look, a wis glad ae that, a really wis. Yer belief, yer… capital. The clout that comes wae bein a McGuinn. Much appreciatet. But we don't need ye any mare."

"We? Is this her?" Lottie spat. "Fuckin Lady TikTok Macbeth?"

Hannah bared her teeth.

"Cause ye know how that ends."

Luce shrugged. "Never did that wan in school. Oor class did *Romeo an Juliet*. The fillum." She turned to McCoist. "Right then, Ally Bally Bee. The crypto key by the morra night—let's caw it midnight—back here. Come alane. Fuck me aboot an al pile aw the nail-varnish remover in this warehouse intae that cage an light it. Right?" A sob racked through Neil's body, turning into a helpless, cattle gurning.

Lucky for McCoist's rapidly swelling mouth, her answer didn't require any consonants. "Aye."

59

The stench of man musk was making it hard to keep her head in the present place and time. Stale sweat covered up with a bushel of Jean Paul Gaultier, invading and suffocating her squashed nasal passages. Dragging her mind away, to another man with an overbearing presence and pheromone—his head opening up at the squeeze of a trigger, his blood spraying hot on her face, her clothes. The obscene, ear-puncturing noise of the bullet's sonic boom, its powder cartridge exploding within the echoing stone walls of the grotty wee car-wash unit where it all went down, where McCoist's life changed, irrevocably, forever.

That and the ache in her muscles from the fly-zapper and the burning throb of agony her face had become. A quick look in the mirror in the passenger-side sun visor had shown swelling around the eyes and nose coming up already, nostrils crusty, a ragged tear in her top lip still oozing, and her front teeth jagged where their biting edges had been smashed.

"Where tae?" Mitch, the prick, had asked.

"I need to clean up." More than clean up, she needed a dental surgeon and a trip to ED for some stitches. But that would eat up more time than she could afford. "Take me home."

"An where is hame?" He smiled a smarmy smile.

Cunt. McCoist baulked at the idea of this horrible bastard knowing where she lived. But there was a burning in her gut that couldn't be doused by a few Rennies, a burning that said, *The prick won't be out walking free for much longer anyway, I'll fuckin well see to that*. She gave him the address.

. . .

She had him pull up a good number of houses before her own. "We're better walking from here round to the back door. My neighbour Edith sees all. I doubt you want her clocking you. She forgets nothing. It's like living in the fucking panopticon round here."

Mitch shrugged. "A could just huv a wee word wae her." Face and tone pleasant enough. He didn't do a knowing smile or crack his knuckles for emphasis or anything so dastardly. He sounded like he meant exactly what he said. Just a word. Truth, it gave McCoist a shiver. *Aye, it'll be sweet putting this one away*. The bravado kept her going.

The creaky gate to her garden set Bruce off barking. McCoist could picture Maisie's disdainful stare at the silly mutt. Maybe she could set the dugs on dear old Mitch? Bruce had come to her defence before. Putting Mitch away would be nice, but an angry, painful part of her also thought seeing him get his bollocks ripped off might be even better.

But no, it wouldn't do her any good. Mitch had been assigned to shadow her every move. Limit the opportunity for scheming, for going beyond her remit of obtaining the crypto key and returning it to its non-rightful owner. If she had Bruce geld sweet Mitch, disembowel him, break his teeth, etc. and toss him into the Clyde, it wouldn't be long before Luce Branson missed him—assuming they would be in regular contact—and she would know something was up. And she might send more heedbangers after McCoist. Or she might shoot Francesco and Neil.

Maybe Lottie McGuinn too—whether that would be a bad thing the angel and devil on each shoulder could argue about for some time. Lottie had been blindsided, that was for sure. Much as she masked it behind attitude and Botox, the vulnerability was plain to see in that moment. She was not her husband. McCoist thought about what the scheming bitch had been up to, the photo Tess had sent her... What kind of danger did she really represent? But it was hard to be objective. The threat was there, a threat to McCoist's family, and McCoist had vowed no such threat would ever be made again.

She had to push Bruce away from licking her burst face. Not only because it would hurt but also because the boy spent an ungodly amount of time licking his own arsehole and his tongue was a Wuhan lab Petri dish. "Down, down, come on you silly beast." Her words were thick and lisping.

Maisie trotted over to see what the fuss was and Mitch set about clapping her. "She's gorgeous. Aw, yer a wee beauty so ye are. Wit a cracker."

I stole her off a man I arranged to have disappeared, McCoist wanted to say, the raging extremes of her emotions in the moment allowing her to confront hard thoughts she usually kept under lock and key. But she wanted him to know. Who he was dealing with. What she was capable of. A man—another man—had threatened her, put her family in danger of their lives, and now he was gone and she had his trophy dug. That was two men punched into McCoist's belt now. *Room for more, pal.*

She needed to get a handle on it. Not fantasies of violence; she needed a plan. "I need to wash up, get some painkillers. Could you put some food out for them?"

"Aye, nae problem!"

"Second cupboard there," she pointed. "Stick the kettle on if you want too."

"Cheers, doll. Wan fir yersel?"

"I'll make mine after. I drink it straight from the kettle, don't like it to sit."

"Fair dos."

She went up the stairs, could hear him shaking the bag of food and playing with Bruce and Maisie, the sound of clattering paws, the two of them dancing round him, tails thrashing. Wee slags.

She took some time washing her face with a cloth and soap, dabbing, wincing with every sting. The cut on her lip was up over the border and onto the skin—scar territory—and she did her best to contain the bleeding with some Steri-Strips. Worse to look at were the shards of her teeth, a rocky skyline she associated with the druggies she'd spent her formative policing years chasing down. She rinsed with mouthwash.

Maybe the screaming was the reason she didn't hear him on the stairs.

Maybe he was just that good at creeping.

Either way, his appearance right outside the bathroom door elicited a second scream almost as loud as the first. "The fuck are you doing?" She'd nearly belted him one and all—pure reflex and the MMA training she'd been doing for a few years.

"Sorry," Mitch said, sounding genuine, "but a cannae be lettin ye swan aff where ye can get up tae witever waeoot me hearin."

Let me put my fuckin hands around his throat. "What if I'm just taking a shite? D'you need to hear that too?"

"Orders is orders."

"That could make things difficult. There are people I need to speak to if I want to get hold of this thing, and they're not going to like a fucking wannabe James Bond henchman extra hanging out the back of me. It's suspicious, no?"

Mitch chuckled. Friendly, friendly. "Well yel just huv tae work it oot. Luce disnae want ye oot ae sight or earshot. Any caws, any texts, any meetins, huv tae be witnessed."

"Sake… We're at least taking my car then, it's—" A plan! McCoist had a plan. "It's… at my sister's."

. . .

McCoist was an only child. She'd left the dented Civic kerbside at Mark's after getting Cam's keys. No chance she'd be letting Mitchy Boy know this was where her kids lived most of the time. *Fuck.* Maybe she had been right after all. Maybe distance from her family was truly what was needed to keep them safe. That they needed to be safe from her...

She needed to work. Mind on the job. Lives to save. Fran and Neil needed her. She could not let them be two more names chalked up to the melee of gangland tragedy. There had been too many already. Collateral, Devlin would say. Like kids bombed because of geopolitical, economic feuds between state leaders. Or poor people burning to death in a tower block because the council wanted to save money. It happens.

Fuck that, McCoist would say.

She put her foot down and tore away from the kerb. "I need to call a senior detective who I think has information I need to get hold of the key. Is that all right with you, Blojob?"

"Wis that another James Bond joke?"

"I don't like telling people this but I'm actually a bit of a fan."

"Aw aye? Who's yer favourite Bond?"

"Roger Moore; daddy issues." (Now another reason to make sure this guy spent the rest of his life in a hole.)

She called Ralston on the car speakerphone. Throat dry; palms wet. Ralston's squad must have known she'd switched cars, but with a bit of luck they wouldn't have bothered recovering their listening devices, or whatever else they'd tagged the motor with.

"Hey, howsit going, Alison?" Bright and cheery.

"Aw-ight, hanks."

"Sure? You sound a bit..."

Her lips were still sticky, tender and swelling. She played it up for both Ralston and Mitch. "Am in the car, usin speakerphone, probly just the sound, dodgy microphone or transmission or somethin, not picking me up well."

"Aye? I mean, I can hear you fine, it's more you sound… I dunno."

"Jus a bit unner the weather. Maybe gettin a bug or somethin."

"Well, don't push it too hard. Remember what happened the other day."

She could feel Mitch giving her a look, kept her eyes on the road. "Thas rich comin from the source of all my stress."

"Oh come on." She could hear his smile. "I can't be the only one."

"Fair. But none of the rest of them are givin me the 'we care about your well-being/have a mental health day' bull at the moment. Nuffin to worry about. Listen, it's just a bug. A wee bug, that's all."

"If you say so. What's going on, anyway?"

"Listen, I'm in the car at the mo, have some time to check in, wanted to ask if you had another look at Devlin's financials?"

Long snort of air fuzzed the speakers. "I have put someone on it, going back over the most recent stuff but, like I said, he's been clean his entire career, I doubt—"

"Really? He's not so much as tapped a fag and not declared it? No recent wires to or from dodgy accounts? Secret accounts?"

"…No, eh—"

"Listen, while I've caught you on the car phone, I was thinking it's time to flip Mal Cuthbertson."

"Aye?"

"He's ready. He's also one of the best tech geeks I know, maybe he could help with the financial stuff."

"I can assure you my people are perfectly capable, Alison."

“I’m sure they are but Mal’s a wizard. And he’s incentivised. Give him the chance to get out from under Dev—” Old Tickly Tomlinson. Mal’s nickname for the gaffer. TT. Undercover alias Roy Tomlinson. *Those guys… spider’s webs inside spider’s webs.*

“Hello? You still there?”

“S-sorry. Can you hear me? Did you lose me there? All these fucking devices—technology, honestly. Load of sh—”

“I can hear you.”

“OK, I had a thought. Get Mal first though. He’ll be useful, you following me?”

“Following.”

“Tell him to meet at Mad Hatter’s—he’ll know what you’re talking about.”

“Good, cause I don’t.”

“I’ll drop you a pin.”

“What time?”

“Hmm say six, let him finish his shift. Don’t want him running out the office in case Devlin’s in.”

“See you there.”

60

[CONFIDENTIAL]
OP THUNDERHEAD / Audio Log
Recorded by Device OPT012/Loc B02
Speaker 1 is UNKNOWN. Speaker 2 is TARGET Detective Chief Inspector Alison McCoist.

SPEAKER 1
Is that some kind ae cafe?

SPEAKER 2
Joke shop.

SPEAKER 1
Whereaboots?

SPEAKER 2
An industrial estate in Cambuslang. It's not really a joke shop.

SPEAKER 1
A guessed. Pull oer, a want ye tae show us it oan the map.

...

Right. We're gonnae get there wae plenty ae time so a can huv a shooftie. Watch the others arrive.

SPEAKER 2
You don't trust me?

SPEAKER 1
...Who are we meetin there an why?

SPEAKER 2
Eddie Ralston, the guy on the phone, is anti-corruption. He's building a case against Detective Superintendent Roy Devlin and I'm helping him with it.

SPEAKER 1
Yer a grass?

SPEAKER 2
I'm a polis.

SPEAKER 1
Fair, a guess, but people who live in gless hooses an aw that. Wit's this goat tae dae wae oor hing?

SPEAKER 2
I think Devlin might have stolen the crypto—we caught the Forbeses with it but Devlin let them go and the USB stick that was checked into evidence is blank. He had the means. Motive—well, it's a shiteload of money, but from what we can see, Devlin's clean in that one, particular respect. So I need evidence. The other man we're meeting, Mal Cuthbertson, I think can help with that.

SPEAKER 1
An he's a grass an aw?

SPEAKER 2
Remains to be seen but let's hope.

...

You sending all that back to your gaffer?

SPEAKER 1
Your business is ma business but ma business isnae yours, right?

SPEAKER 2
If you say so, but that reminds me, we need to think of a reason for your presence in all this—if you're not planning on waiting outside. "Hey everyone, this is Mitch, he's my hostage-taker."

SPEAKER 1
Fuck up. A cannae just pretend tae be a polis? Quite fancy huvin a wee badge an that. "Haw you, put yer hawns up! Bend oer an spread yer cheeks!"

SPEAKER 2
Convincing as that was, let's keep thinking for now. We've got the time. Can we get coffee and food if we're going to be sitting about in here for hours?

61

"Take that yin there. Get close intae yer right."

"You want me to climb out through the boot?" Mitch had pointed her to a parking space hard up against the trolley shelter. "What would be the use in me doing a runner anyway?"

"People dae funny hings unner pressure. Av seen it aw." Believable, from the trenches around his eyes. "Or maybe ye just don't gee as much ae a fuck aboot those cunts back there as the wummin hinks."

"Your boss, you mean?"

"Don't twist it. Ad gee a man the same respect. Am aw fir equal rights. If a wis a sexist pig a widnae huv tased ye, wid a?"

McCoist squeezed out the gap between the door and the scratched, vandalised plastic of the shelter—PM loved JS 4eva, Gemma Smith had a saggy fanny, Tony Cartwright's da would arrange to give you a toothy BJ if you gave him a call on 077…

They hit the Morries bakery and the biscuit aisle, the crisps and sweets too—McCoist no stranger to the stake-out, and nor, disconcertingly, was the non-polis Mitch—then the Costa vending machine. Americano with ten of those long sachets of sugar stirred in. McCoist pointedly stuck the divider down on the checkout belt between her stuff and his.

The boy at the checkout was wide-eyed at McCoist's burst face, gave Mitch a nervous glance, then kept his eyes on the belt, mind on the beeps.

"Now here's your problem," McCoist said, back at the car, laden with goodies, screaming hot coffee in one hand—black and chopped with all those lines of sugar (way too much sugar, even for McCoist's boorish tastes in coffee) creating something like molten tar. "I can't squeeze back in my side holding all this stuff. Either you have to stand there and hold the gear while I get in and hope I don't drive off. Or, you get in first, I hand the stuff in to you, then go round—if I don't lock the door and run."

"Very funny. Ye said yersel, but, wit wid be the point in daein a runner?"

"Maybe I'm cracking under the pressure." McCoist smiled. "Maybe I don't care who your wummin puts a bullet in."

"Yer really annoyed aboot the door, eh? Dis it really matter if ye ding it aff the trolley hing? Yev goat a big dent in the bunnet wit needs hammered oot anyway. Wit wis it, a bollard?"

"A suspect."

Mitch whistled. "Fair dos. Right, ad rather be stuck oot the car than in it, so al hawd the treats an you get in first. But just mind, ye drive aff an those people are deed. Simple as that. An simple disnae mean quick—no if it's Hannah who's daein thum. Girrul's a fuckin psycho. Also, when we catch up wae ye, it'll be your turn. An if we cannae find ye at first, we'll work oor way wan be wan through yer friends an faimly until we dae."

McCoist's face throbbed, slithering tapeworm of fear in her guts. *Cunt will be begging to get sent to Sawney Bean's coastal retreat by the time I finish with him.* Bravado, yes, but with a hard seed of truth buried in it.

"A hink a can trust ye."

McCoist squashed herself back into the car and opened the door for Mitch. He handed the packets of crisps and biscuits over to her with a plastic tray of doughnuts and her cup of magma.

A silver Renault Clio reverse-parked into the space in front of McCoist—BMW-style, half over the line into the next space, so they, unlike McCoist, had plenty of room to get out the driver's side.

McCoist took the lid off her coffee, blowing at the release of steam, the surface of the liquid a burning, shiny black. "Give me a minute to have this before we set off, could you? Head's splitting." Not a lie.

Mitch made a big show of checking his watch—a chunky rubber thing with myriad buttons that a diver or soldier might wear, its face worn on the inside of his wrist. The kind of thing Cam loved when he was a wee boy. Press a button and the screen illuminates, electric blue. "Indiglo!" he'd say, enthralled. "It has a *timer*!"

A navy sedan pulled up in the space next to them.

McCoist had never been so happy to see Eddie Ralston's Sharpie-coloured dome.

Mitch caught the look, glanced out the window.

McCoist chucked her coffee into his lap.

A scream like James Brown having a good time.

McCoist slammed her door into the trolley shelter, dove down, dropping onto the tarmac and crawling through the gap before Mitch could react, grab at her.

Slam, slam, slam. Car doors. Footsteps thunking over the poor, battered bonnet of McCoist's car—the driver of the Clio in action.

McCoist got to her feet to see Mitch thrashing on the ground, trying to get his belt buckle undone, crotch soaked in prison napalm—albeit with a bit more flavour.

Ralston, his passenger (a man with a skin-fade haircut too young for the visible forty years on his coupon) and the woman from the Clio helped Mitch to free himself of his scalding scants.

McCoist grabbed the sodden jeans and ripped into the pockets. Wallet, keys, vape and—*bingo*—phone.

"*Fuck! Fuuuck!* Fuckin bitch!" Mitch's thighs were highlighter pink. He yanked at the already-threadbare elastic of his boxers and pulled them off too, showing a cooked prawn on a bed of grey pubes.

They got the cuffs on and wrestled him into the back of McCoist's motor.

"The fuck's going on?" Ralston was perturbed. She'd never seen him perturbed before. He didn't suit it. McCoist quite liked the ugly fit.

"Not here. Did you call Mal?"

"Picked him up." He pointed to the Clio. "Seriously—"

"We need to move. Now."

McCoist jumped back into her car. "There's a blanket back there for the dugs; cover yourself up."

Mitch glared, a look as fiery as his gonads currently were. But he didn't speak.

The stonewall continued all the way to Mad Hatter's and the apartment above. It continued when he sank into the cold bath they poured for him—only a gasp escaping clenched teeth, nothing more. Good, McCoist thought. If he was a genuine old-school type, it meant less trouble for her. No chance of him blabbing to anyone about crypto keys and hostages.

Ralston had his officers guard the tub while he debriefed McCoist and Mal: "What in the actual fucking name of Jesus Howard Christ is going on?"

"Thank you for the rescue," McCoist said.

"Nobody says 'car phone' any more, nobody has a fucking car phone. 'Dodgy microphone'? Very clever, well done you."

"I mean it."

"I don't. What the fuck have you got me involved in? What the fuck has happened to your face? Who is that guy?!" Thumb pointing to the bathroom door. "Is this to do with Devlin?"

"I have a life outside of your Devlin vendetta, you know."

"It's not a fucking vendetta," Ralston snapped. He really had lost his usual cool. He was pacing. "It's my job. I put away dodgy polis. Criminal polis. Ones who think they're above the law."

"And right now you're thinking that's me?"

"I *know* that's you. The only reason you're not already banged up is because you agreed to help take Devlin down."

Mal flinched. McCoist shot a look into his twitching eyes. *That's right. And you should have guessed already, Dexter's Lab.*

"Right now I'm wondering if you're becoming the bigger problem." Ralston finally stopped worrying the carpet, planted his hands on his hips, legs wide apart in power stance. The man in control.

McCoist waited a couple of beats, let his stare pore over her, into her. "Not at all, I promise you that. And I've not forgotten our agreement. I think I have something. Mal..."—the tech scratched his hair and it snowed onto his cardigan—"...I want you to search for any financial records or accounts, anything, for Roy Tomlinson." She turned back to Ralston. "This was Devlin's alias back when he was a UCO. This was way back, and he wasn't in that game for long, but what if he's managed to keep the false credentials and has used them to hide money?"

Ralston chewed his lip, then shook his head. "He's not a thief."

"You've bought into all his bullshit." And so had she, at first. All his pontificating, his power-playing and justifying, the projection of himself as something so far above such a base sin as greed, such a simple want as cash. "Find the money and we have him. He's not Moby Dick. Stop fucking about."

A big huff, a stroke of his tyre-shine hair. "Fine. I'll sort out the search but—"

"Mal will work on it too."

"I will?"

"He's the best in the business, and he knows the boss well."

Mal gulped, Adam's apple bobbing, gobbling in his turkey neck.

"What about your man cooling his goolies next door? You gonna tell me what that's about?"

"No, it's nothing for you to be concerned about. Keep your eyes on the baw."

"But—"

"Arrest him, take him to the hospital, charge him."

"For what?"

"Assaulting an officer and indecent exposure to start with. I'm sure his DNA and fingerprint samples will light up the PNC in all sorts of interesting ways."

"This was his work? Look like you could do with going to hospital yourself."

"I'm fine." She'd triple-dunted paracetamol, ibuprofen and aspirin but her face was still louping. The puffy bags swelling under her eyes were starting to mottle, a flush of greens and purples, tendrils of burst blood vessels spidering out from the bridge of her nose. Her lip was beginning to look like something from a lurid reality TV series: *When Plastic Surgery Goes Wrong—get a swatch ae these daft freaks! (They signed waivers to assure us they're not mentally ill so fill yer boots guilt-free.)* "Let's just get moving."

Ralston tried to give her the Paddington Bear stare again but Alison McCoist had taken that shite from all manner of psychos—dangerous, terrifying people who had hurt her and threatened her and tried to kill her and her loved ones and though she had been scared, always, tremendously, deeply scared right down to the lizardy core of her, none of them had stopped her yet. So fuck Eddie Ralston. And you know what? Fuck Paddington Bear too.

They hauled Mitch, still tight-lipped but skinning her with his eyes, out of the building, Ralston going with them after a final warning, chewing his nails.

She slapped Mitch's phone onto the small dining table where Mal had set himself up. "I need you to get into this."

"P-p-p…?"

"Pronto."

Mal rocked back in his chair, pulled his cardy sleeve up and scratched a freckly arm. "What the fuck are we doing? Going up against him, I-I—"

"It's time Mal. Time for change. He's going down. You can go down with him, or…"—she put a hand on his—"…you can be part of the new guard. New Labour, 1997. Cool Britannia. Mad fir it."

"You're fucking mental," he keened.

"I'm right, but. Deep breaths."

She gave him a minute to get a handle on it. "What am I doing?" he asked.

"Let's start at the top." She gave him the rundown: the missing crypto, Luce Branson's move against Callaghan and his Russian deal, Lottie McGuinn and the Forbes boys being held to ransom.

"Now, Mitch is off for an ice pack and a stretch inside, but we can't let his handlers know anything is wrong. He's been in regular contact with Branson and that appearance has to be kept up."

Mal twiddled, thumb tapping off each of his fingers in turn like a concert pianist's exercise. "OK. I can feed the texts between them into a programme so we can send messages in his style.

Won't be perfect but probably better than me trying to imitate him myself. But if someone calls...?"

"Let it ring out, reply later saying he can't speak right now. The deadline"—(painfully literal)—"is tomorrow night. Midnight. So it doesn't have to hold forever, just long enough for me to sort this shit out." She checked the time on her phone—long night and day ahead of her. "Once you've done that, I have a couple of other jobs for you."

"Just a couple?"

"Easy enough for you, I'm sure."

"Breaking into the MoD am I? Cracking the CIA? Want me to see if the Loch Ness Monster is being held in Area 51?"

"If you have some free time when you're done, go for it. But first I want you to start working on Tickly Tomlinson's financials. Give Ralston's lot a hand. But anything you find you report to me first."

"Sure. And second?"

"It's not quite Area 51 but I think you'll enjoy the challenge."

62

"A hink it actually looks quite cool," Fran said. "Honest."

"It's in the left yin, but. That means am gay, dis it no?"

"Wit?"

"If it's yer left ear that's pierced, yer gay; if it's the right, it means yer fae a cooncil estate. Or is it the other way roon?"

"Yev loast us."

"Dae folk no say that any mare?"

"If it bothers ye, ye could get the other wan done an aw. Ye wur a fitba player, they aw go in fir that. Get some tatts while yer at it."

"Fuck up." Neil smiled, and it made Fran smile too, despite everything.

"At least it wis just the ear an she didnae gee ye a Prince Albert."

Neil heaved a wheezy chuckle. "If she did, a couldae knocked her oot wae ma stawner while she wis doon there an made a break fir it."

"Och aye, that's how Jack Reacher dis it when he's in a jam."

"Big Jackie Boay!"

"The Reach-Aroony. The second series wis fuckin mint—"

"Can yous two shut the fuck up?"

They fell silent as if scolded by a schoolteacher, lips pinched tight together as if they couldn't trust them. Lottie McGuinn had been stewing in silence for most of the day since they'd been locked up in the warehouse cage together. A bitter brew. The set of her face looked like she was tasting it herself. Bottom jaw like an anglerfish's, eyes not blinking nearly enough. And those cherry-red talons of hers must have gouged right into her palms by now.

Fran would have felt sorry for her if he wasn't so shite-scared of her. Terror tended to block empathetic feelings. The fact his da hadn't made a move on her yet said he was feeling likewise.

She was bad people though. And bad things happened to bad people. Callaghan, for instance. Face turned inside out, bits of it transferred to Fran, wearing him. Weight of his body on him. Leaking on him, blood spreading like an oil slick. Was Fran a bad person then?

Bad things happened to good people too. Pontoon. Pontoon's maw. Never hurt a fly, as far as Fran knew. Just ordinary folk, the violence wrought on them an invader from another world. Fran was the connection, beaming the coordinates out to the vicious aliens.

"A never... a never meant any ae this tae happen." Tears brimmed, a burning at the back of his throat and nose. "Am sorry, Da. If a could..."

"A know, son." Neil put an arm around him, squeezed him in a half-cuddle, their second embrace in a long time. Fran tried to remember when they'd stopped hugging. When hugs had become a pat on the shoulder, a shaken hand, a matey nudge of the elbow.

"Should never huv..." Fran was leaking like a broken tap these days. None of the guys he followed online ever advocated a good cry. Did it never get lonely being the alpha? The leader of the pack? Maybe not, there seemed to be loads of them. Maybe they all hung out smoking cigars and taking ice baths together. Sustained by conference calls and product-placement deals. Fuck, maybe Fran was just losing it. Maybe the wheels were coming off. He'd lost his running legs, so why the fuck not? *The fuckin states ae ye, greetin like a wean, covered in snot*. At least his hangover had retreated to a niggling shadow at the base of his skull.

"It's ma fault." Neil's voice was a whisper, scratchy as his stubble rubbing on Fran's forehead as he spoke. "A shouldnae huv suggested… Shouldnae huv fuckin said anyhin. A shouldae telt ye tae, or… a dunno. A shouldae done somehin. Aw ma fuckin life a shouldae done somehin. Bin there fir ye. Maybe then—"

"If yous two don't fuckin button it am gonnae dae the joab fir Luce masel. A don't need tae hear yer fuckin whingein. Maybe this, maybe that. Maybe put a fuckin sock in it. Ma fit'll be inside it if ye keep oan like that."

"If am gonnae go oot, that's the way ad like it." Neil couldn't help himself after all.

"Da!" Fran cringed. Fuck it, let her kill him.

Lottie stood, all five and a half foot of her, and the cage shrunk around them. "Huv ye seen Hannah's work?" Close-ups of Pontoon's butchered digits rose in his mind like chunder up a gullet. "She likes tae play." Now to Neil: "Hows aboot a game ae nurse an patient? Ye like that wan, big man?"

Neil's face was a half-smiling picture of confusion and discomfort, like he was trying to work out the answer she wanted or even if he should say anything at all. Fran prayed he kept his mouth shut.

"Hannah's version's mare like surgeon an cadaver. The make-believe is that she's no qualified an *you* arnae deed. Ye ever wantet tae see wit the inside ae yer ain scrotum looks like?" Lottie was now standing so close to Neil their noses were almost touching. She skull-fucked him with her eyes. Not in an enjoyable way.

"A-av never hud much ae an interest in… anatomy." Neil's forehead was spritzing.

"You're in here an aw, but," Fran spoke up, forcing more mettle into his voice than he felt. "Ye hink yer exempt fae rough treatment?"

"Luce will dae me the courtesy ae no feedin me tae her pet."

"So wit's a courtesy then? Bullet in the back ae the heed? Lucky you."

Fran's turn to be penetrated, no grease.

"When the time comes, yel be sayin it waeoot the sarcasm."

"So that's it then? Yev geed up easy. A thoat ye were sittin there plottin."

Lottie moved away, dropped back into her seat. A whisper: "Hinkin aboot ma weans."

A look met and broke between Fran and his da.

Neil went to the bars. "Here, pal!" he called to the GI Joe guarding them.

In this case GI stood for Gimp Issue. The cunt was all black leathers and chains and belts and zips, facial piercings and fingerless gloves. Looked like he was moonlighting from his job as a bouncer at the Cathouse. Action Man going through a phase. Still, he was a big fucker carrying a big club and that was all that mattered. The handle of the knife poking out of its holster on the one practical, trouser-carrying belt had the kind of ergonomic shape and grippy texture which indicated it was attached to a serious bit of steel. He grunted to indicate he was listening.

"A need tae, eh, take a Lillian Gish, could ye, eh…"

"You've got your bucket." Voice thin for a man his size, and "proper" spoken for a man of his occupation. The middle classes were downwardly mobile these days. Fuckin Brexit.

"Aye, but—"

"It's not full, is it?"

"Naw, but—"

"Well then."

"Moan pal, it wis different when it wis just me but noo…" Neil's head nodded towards Lottie, his eyes trying to send a telepathic message to Biker Mouse from Mearns.

"Bucket."

"Look, pal, it's no just… ye know wit am sayin. A didnae want tae come right oot wae it in front ae compny, but, maybe it's no just a *Lillian*, eh?"

"For fuck—"

"It's a Jackie Burd an aw."

"—sake."

"Don't be like that, man, yev hud me loacked up here fir fuckin ages an av no bin fir a shite wance."

"The bucket is there. Have them turn their backs, cover their ears, and hold their noses."

"Moan tae fuck, man! There must be a proper bog in here."

Fran held his head in his hands. They didn't need that Hannah burd to do the torture, he was going through it already. Psychological. Chemical.

"Morgan." Lottie approached the gate, nails flashing like Freddy Krueger's.

"Everybody calls me Morgue," Trenchcoat Mafia said.

"Boss."

"Pardon?"

"Evrybdy caws me Boss. And a caw *you* Morgan."

"Not any more."

"Are ye hedgin yer bets here, Morgan, or are ye just a drone?"

The lad shifted, weight moving between his feet, Beefeater posture crumbling.

"Maybe yev hitched yer wagon tae the wrang pony. Ye hink ae that? Or did ye no hink at aw when Luce telt ye am the new enemy number wan? Wit kind are ye?"

He turned away from her, looked like he was fascinated by the serial numbers on the boxes piled up nearby.

"Ye just dae as yer telt, eh, Morgan? That's no way tae get

ahead. Yel be stawndin guerd fir a lang time wae an attitude like that. Yev no ambitions? Ye don't want tae climb the greasy pole?"

"He can climb ma greasy pole," Neil muttered. "Take a fuckin spin oan it while he's at it."

"Shut up, all of you." The Undertaker's voice pitched even higher.

"Look, Morgan, this is a tricky business wur in. Fortunes rise an faw. Witever happens, a promise ye if ye make this cunt take a shite in a bucket in front ae me, yel end up wearin that bucket oan yer heed. Sometime or another."

The lad's knuckles whitened on the club. "Right, everybody stand back from the door." He waved the club at Lottie and Fran—"The two of you right up against the back wall." Jabbed it at Neil—"I want to see your hands, keep them up in front the whole time. Try anything and I'll beat the shite out of you, literally."

"Fair dos," Neil said.

Fran shuffled back, pressing himself against the bare brick at the back of their pen, palms flat on the rough, flocking bats in his belly, muscles cold and tightening, tuning pegs turning brittle wire. About five metres to the gate. He was no sprinter, it wasn't his game, and with his knees... How fast could he launch himself off the blocks? And a false start would be the end of it.

"Stand back."

Neil obeyed. The gate swung open.

"Come out." Morgue gave Neil space to step through. "I'm going to close the gate. Try to run, fatty, and you'll feel this thing on the back of your knees before you've made it three steps."

"'Fatty' wis uncawed fir."

"Shut up." Morgue stepped to the gate, one hand on the metal bar.

"A am a bit oan the heavy side, right enough." Neil crashed into him, full weight piling into the lad, knocking him forwards, knocking him inside the cage.

Fran took off. Three long paces and he was across the cell, crashing into the Crow with knees and elbows, bundling him to the ground.

Bee-sting flash of pain as the pole caught Fran on the hand—wild swing, lucky contact. Morgue was screaming. Lottie was in the scrap, high heel in one hand, trying to stick the boy with it, like it was a meat thermometer.

Neil took a steel-toed boot to the gut, put him on his arse.

Fran had the club in both hands, hanging on, the lad's strength ferocious now he was cornered, trying to chew himself free of a trap.

Then the lad's backup arrived.

Lottie backed off. Neil panted on the deck. Fran let go of the club and stood, stepping away from Morgue, bleeding from grazes on his face and hands. Morgue dusted himself off, whipped the pipe into Fran's knee.

Explosion. Fran dropped like a high-rise demolition. His scream came from the very pits of him, the well that went all the way down to the dry bed of the soul.

"Use the bucket," Morgue said and spat on Neil.

As Master of Muppets turned to leave, he didn't notice the knife holster on his belt: empty.

DEADLINE DAY

63

It was a nice house in a nice neighbourhood. New-build estate out in Jackton. Competent builds, lots of grass for kids to play on, a school at its heart and nothing but other houses for miles around. It didn't scream embezzlement. But Devlin was smart, McCoist told her doubts, a long-game man. The money was a nest egg. Retire and up sticks, fuck off to France or Spain or halfway round the world where his stashed fortune and his recent acquisition of millions in binary doubloons could be spent without raising too many eyebrows. Live out the last years in luxury. *Sounds lush.* And there was no need for doubts, it was all there on the page, in black and white. Mal had shown her. Eddie Ralston's people corroborated. For decades he'd been squirrelling away money under the identity of a ghost, a man who had only really existed on paper.

Ralston had kept watch on the house himself. Mal tipped him when Devlin left the office, and Ralston, in turn, tipped McCoist when the super pulled up into his driveway.

"Is he alone?" McCoist asked, slipping into the passenger seat next to Ralston, parked a few houses down the street from Devlin's gaff. (McCoist, who had switched back to driving Acne-Greased Lightning with its demufflered, voice-breaking shriek, made sure to stop even further away.)

"Wife could be home, but there's no other car. Not seen her coming or going, not even at the window. Good chance she's out, I reckon. A cleaner left after he arrived home."

McCoist chewed a nail. She'd been a busy beaver that day, putting the plan in place, but it all hinged on this: did Devlin have the crypto key? "Fuck it, let's go. If the wife's in, she can stick the telly on in the other room." McCoist the eager beaver, palms slick. Ralston looked too keyed up himself to notice. It had been easy to convince him to come alone. No wonder, considering what she'd found out, once again thanks to Mal.

"Let's go."

Twin thumps of car doors slamming, breaking the settled, early autumnal evening bubble which sat over the estate, purposeful heels hitting the ground, *biz-ness, biz-ness, biz-ness*. Polisman's knock at the door from McCoist's knuckles.

He looked surprised. He really did, the fucker! But he recovered quickly, all smiles and a quick scratch at the sack. "Good evening, DCI McCoist. You look like you've been on one of your adventures again. And Superintendent Ralston, we've not had the pleasure of meeting in person." He held out his hand. Ralston clasped it like the ganglion of some monster; Devlin looked ready to pull him in and swallow him whole. "Come on in."

They stepped into the smell of too much air freshener with a heavy, bodily musk lurking underneath the Oust.

"Let's head upstairs to the office. One second." He poked his head into a half-open door to their right—living room, McCoist guessed, based on the view from the outside. "Sorry, petal, some colleagues need a word. I'll just be upstairs in the office, give me a buzz if you need anything." He closed it with a firm click, his back pressed against it. "This way." He led them down a hall—kitchen and dining space up ahead, French doors into a garden—the colour scheme new-build plain, untouched, and swung around into a carpeted staircase, a Stannah stairlift fitted to the wall.

McCoist caught Ralston's eye and his eyebrows hitched up in response—this was news to him too. It wasn't a cleaner leaving the house. A carer. The vision she'd had of Devlin on the beach sipping rum from a coconut crumbled. It had never been a good fit. The man wore his specs on a chain around his neck—not an accessory that went well with Hawaiian shirts and flip-flops. The idea of him as a petty thief had never sat well—Ralston had been right, almost. No, Devlin was saving his ill-gotten gains for another purpose. McCoist's stomach gave that lurch, that flaming lick of heartburn that she'd become accustomed to. After killing McGuinn. After vanishing Slater. After letting countless people down, the mutilated dead and the still living alike—her mum and dad, her weans. *What will they think when they find out?*

But they wouldn't. Because she had a plan, and she needed to stick to it. Not get derailed by guilt. Christ, it didn't matter what he'd been stealing the money for, he could have been using it to send orphans to school or rehome Romanian street dugs, it was blood money. And in this latest case, he was willing to let innocent people die over it. (Innocent-ish.)

The office was a modern affair with a minimalist, faux-Scandi feel. Or it would have been if there weren't books piled up everywhere, cluttering the floor and the few available surfaces and generally obscuring the faux-Scandi minimalism. The ANGÜS they sat down on either side of, which also held laptop, files and mugs, was buckling under the mix of crooked hardbacks, tobacco-hued paperbacks and Yellow Pages-sized textbooks it was expected to support outside its main function. McCoist could sympathise with its plight.

Devlin smiled at each of them in turn, gave his glasses a polish with a cloth and the warmth of his breath. "I think you should start. Say what you've come to say. Then I'll talk."

Ralston was holding himself back in his chair, knuckles snowy peaks thrusting up from under the skin. Sweat on his forehead, glistening in the stubble on his upper lip. Not the cool customer

McCoist had become familiar with. Certainly not Lionel Messi. "Courtesy is the only reason you're not already in handcuffs, Superintendent Devlin. You need to start acting like a man who is going to jail for a long time."

There was a meek nod in response, almost an attempt at contrition on his face. It had the effect of a catalyst on the already simmering Ralston, who slapped his hand on the desk, making books jump and the already overburdened legs of the desk creak. "We've found the paper trail. It's over. And when you start to sink, there will be plenty of people ready to talk to save themselves. It won't just be fraud or theft, corruption and misconduct bullshit. It'll be conspiracy to murder, Roy. Do you understand?"

Devlin looked to McCoist. "And are you managing to save yourself?"

McCoist wrangled the thundering blood in her veins, clamped down vice-tight on the twitching nerves that threatened to rip free through her body. "I'm here for the crypto key, sir."

Ralston's eyes hit her like spotlights. She ignored him.

Devlin smiled, and she could almost believe it was genuine. "I take it it's not for yourself?"

"Francesco and Neil Forbes are being held hostage by Luce Branson. I give her the money, they go free."

The smile broadened. Proud. Patronising. "Will they?"

"They will. I've made sure of it. I just need the money."

"And in return, you won't let him arrest me?"

Ralston's guppy-mouthed shock passed. "I don't know what DCI McCoist thinks she has authority to do here but—"

"She knows, Edward."

"What?"

"She's seen it all. Am I right?"

McCoist nodded.

"No, no, there's—"

"Yes. There is," McCoist said. "And I've seen the evidence. I've watched the video."

"No—" Eyes wide with panic, the oily varnish in his hair starting to sweat out onto his forehead.

"No wonder you were so keen to get the super put away," McCoist sneered. "'It's my job.' 'Not a fucking vendetta.'"

"That's true!" His eyes were like fists around her collar. "I don't know what you think you know—"

"You do, Eddie. You do." She bored into him.

Tears were leaking now, his breath began to catch. "It was one time."

"One time is enough." McCoist rose up, stood over them. "You both let me walk away with the crypto and none of this goes any further than this room. I'm holding all the evidence, so all you have against each other is your own say-so."

"Is that right?" Devlin's gentle, grandfather smiles had gone. That *thing* he hid behind them was naked to see.

"It is. Try logging in to the List and see what happens." Mal's second job had been to worm into the Vault and override everything, rewriting it so only McCoist had access. It was hers now. And everybody on it was hers, including Superintendent Eddie Ralston, campaigning anti-corruption officer.

Devlin didn't move to check anything; he read her. Saw the truth on her face, a vision of the future. "You think you can run this without me?"

McCoist's turn to smile. Sickly-sweet, showing off her burst, crusting lip and her ragged teeth. "I'm not planning to run anything. I'm *dismantling* it."

"Impossible," he scoffed.

"I'll do my worst."

"Playing to your strengths at least. And what about your own part in all this? Have you absolved yourself, Bear?"

Ralston came back to himself, roused by those words. "Aye, what about you? We know everything you've done too."

"I'm sure you have suspicions, Eddie," she said. "But I'm also sure you are missing vital bits of evidence. Not enough to build a case on, really. Maybe you were careless with your files. You know, you click the wrong link and..." She waved her hand, leaves blowing away on the wind. "Rest assured, I have everything under control. So as the old motto goes: 'Nobody talks, everybody walks.' Right?"

Two pairs of eyes butchered her but no cunt had anything to say, caught with their dicks in either end of a Chinese finger trap.

She held out her hand. "I'll take the crypto and be out of your hair now."

"This won't achieve anything, Alison," Devlin said. "All you're doing is putting this money back into circulation among criminals. It could be better used."

"Don't try to guilt me, you bastard."

"I'm not. I'm saying you need to look at the bigger picture. You can't just stumble from one situation to the next trying to solve problems as they come up. Think bigger; look further. What is ultimately gained by saving the Forbeses? What is it going to *cost*? If you're the one in charge now, you need to weigh these things up and—"

"Shut. Up. Give me the key."

Devlin unlocked a drawer in his desk then dropped the unassuming millions into her palm. "This is a mistake."

"In a long line of many."

64

There were guards waiting for her in the car park outside the warehouse, but McCoist had probably been on their radar since arriving in Ibrox. They'd have heard her coming at any rate, the engine of the plum street racer, Shite Rider, screaming out for attention all down the street.

Wit a fuckin motor! Bricky thinks. It's like something from *Pimp My Ride*—not the US version albeit, the UK one, which was like a Barras knock-off, a bit scaffier, a bit naffer, but still, the engine sounds like a proper wee goer as it rips past him, and the custom paint job is mint. He'd love to get a swatch inside it. Wasted on a polis—might be good in a car chase, but.

He's been told to look out for it, calls it in from his post at the bus shelter. His arse is numb from the anti-homeless half-seat he's been perching on. He relieved Jimbo from his shift a few hours ago now. Feels like longer.

Not much else in the way of traffic. It's nearly midnight and the street he's stationed on is an artery feeding an industrial hive, not much going on after business hours, though he can hear the sounds of the smoking crowd outside the Louden Tavern carrying on the wind.

Headlights approach. Red Toyota, electric engine from the soft, retro-futuristic hovercar hum it makes as it approaches and Dopplers past. So soft he doesn't hear it stop.

First he knows of the bloke is when he speaks: "Last bus must've gone by now, son." Older gent—beige coat and bunnet, grey stubble on loose skin. He has a longtime smoker's lips—a pursed ringpiece—and carries the fug of tobacco about him like a shroud. He's sat on the seat next to him. Too close. Bricky can feel the man's thigh brushing his, the oil and water contact of the geezer's scratchy, formal trousers against his own velour joggers.

Bricky is about to give his standard reply about waiting for a lift when he feels the needle pinch the side of his arse cheek. "Wi—" He jumps up, or tries to, but his leg is already filling with static, radiating out from the puncture point, and he lurches against the plastic side of the shelter instead. His heart thunders, whooshing in his head, making him nauseous, faint. Cold sweat prickles his back. He tries to push off the wall but it's like punching someone in a dream, his movements inexplicably lacking in any force. He can't speak. The old boy holds him up. Cunt's stronger than he looks.

Then there's another guy, and they've each got one of Bricky's arms over a shoulder and they're carrying him between them—toes of new Dunks dragging on the pavement—towards the red Toyota. The back door's already open and they bundle him inside. It smells like his granda's motor does. Stuffy, too hot.

Bricky can't move anything at all now. He can't even swallow the saliva sitting thick on his numb tongue. He can't breathe.

The boys at least let her inside the door before giving her the pat-down, sparing her the whole up-against-the-motor-with-creepy-overtones scene. One of them was dressed like a grunger (as they were called when McCoist was at school), with a face full of ironwork and clothes like Marilyn Manson on a dress-down Friday. The other looked like a picture on the wall of a Turkish barber's—style no. 3. "I don't have back pockets," she said, as someone's hand ran over her arse.

No. 3 took her inside while Manson went back outside to his post.

She reminds Morgue of his mummy. The harassed scowl, lecturing face. Her figure is slender and she's a full head smaller than him—he can see the grey roots of her hairline cutting sharp and clear across the top of her skull—yet she looms large. He has to quash a little niggle of guilt as he watches her disappear inside the unit and he heads back out to his patrol around the perimeter.

Doesn't feel right, but one thing he learnt quickly in this business was not to judge based on looks—it wasn't like on TV. People just looked like people, dangerous or not. He's seen guys who, like him, were bulked up and covered in tattoos and piercings, seemingly experts at enduring pain, made to cry by scrawny-looking, baldy middle-aged mutants who knew how to scrap and weren't afraid to use their nails and teeth.

Likewise, Morgue takes a load of shite from the lads about the guy-liner, but he is more than capable of—

The knife goes in under his jaw, soft gap between the mandibles, through his tongue and into the roof of his mouth. Second one goes into his thigh, a pro shot, severing the femoral artery as easy as a sparky snipping a wire.

He is hefted up by his new handholds onto a masked man's shoulders, carried into a dark spot between two vans and deposited. You can't see the blood because of the double-dark of night and shadow, but there is a lot of it.

She was escorted through shelves of beauty products stacked up near to the ceiling on pallets and over to the back corner, behind the false wall where the cage was kept.

"Bang oan time." Luce was waiting with Hannah—the girl with a gun already in hand—and another couple of geezers too dodgy-looking to be simple stock boys. The captives were cable-tied to the bars of the pen. Francesco and his da looked at her with something like relief on their faces. Hope, maybe. Certainly the strain of fear was evident there too, in the manic glint of the eye, the tight set of the lips. Lottie scowled, and even with the Botox fighting back against the muscles, it was a formidable thing.

"Where's Mitch?" Luce asked.

Hannah's gun moved towards Neil.

"Nipped to the toilet," McCoist said.

"Where?"

Hannah pressed the barrel of her pistol up against Neil's forehead. He tried to pull back but Hannah moved with him, pressing the gun further into the cage, deeper into the soft spot of his temple.

"You couldn't expect me to do what I needed to with him tagging along." McCoist's heart was going happy hardcore. This was devolving faster than she thought it would.

"Where is he? How lang's he bin goan?"

"I needed to get this thing out of a police station, I could hardly walk in there with fucking Ray Winstone—"

"Wit ye tryin tae dae?"

"Nothing."

Neil whimpered.

"Nothing! Look! LOOK!" She held out the USB stick, let it dangle from her fingers by its key ring. "I have it. Let them go and it's yours. That's all that matters."

"A need tae check it first."

"Once they're all out of harm's way." McCoist's words came out sticky. Her mouth was dry, adrenaline going to her head, limiting her thoughts to the seconds in front of her and nothing else, making her limbs gooey. Hannah still had the pistol at Neil's head. Needed her away from him. All of them. She was too unpredictable. Could go off firing. And the other lackies—one with another pistol, the other one packing a taser like Mitch and some choice hand-to-hand silverware.

"Yer no callin the shoats here, hen. This isnae yer beat. Ye gee us that hing, a check the wedge is aw there, then ye get yer sausages."

"It's all here, I promise you it's all here." She jangled the memory stick like a set of keys, the way her maw used to when the twins were babies. "Just put the guns away. How about that?"

"Hows aboot this?" Luce took the gun from Hannah and pointed it at McCoist instead. She felt the unblinking eye of its muzzle search out her heart. "Geez it here."

Stockholm—a nickname that refers to both his pulling technique and the reason his missus has stayed with him for twenty-odd years now—is supposed to be watching from the vantage point on the roof, tucked out of sight behind a vent. And he is watching. Sort of. But he keeps getting distracted by his phone. In particular, the messages on his phone from his latest wee burd who has just told him she's about twelve weeks pregnant.

It's his.

(What kind of fucking pig would even ask that? Of course it's his!)

Fuck. He's properly made a cunt of it this time. Jesus, what's Kat going to say? She's found out about his affairs in the past, and that was… She's still with him. But this? Surely it's the limit.

Stockholm and Kat have two weans, both in their late teens. And despite his… *philandering*… he's a good da to them. Or he thinks he is. He cares about whether he is and surely that means something. There isn't a show or event or parents evening he's ever missed. He's encouraged their interests at every turn, bought the gear, driven the car. And while this news fills him with dread about the potential confrontation with Kat, and the weans, there is a spark of excitement in him at the thought of a new baby. What if…?

Others have done it. Raised multiple families.

No, that's fucking madness. How?

But maybe—

Then the problem isn't Stockholm's any more.

The loop of reinforced wire is round his neck and he's tumbling, stomach miles away, over the edge of the roof. His phone falls from his hand, spinning all the way to the ground where it smashes. But he stays up in the air, legs kicking.

"That's fine," McCoist said. It really fucking wasn't, but. Should have picked up some Tena Lady when she was back at the shop. "We can do that." McCoist moved towards them, holding the drive out, away from her body, as if it might stop a bullet if it came to it. Hannah intercepted, snatching the drive from her fingers.

A laptop had been set up on a small stack of boxes. Hannah flipped it open. Interminable wait for the password to be entered, the machine to heat up. She plugged the drive in. *Tap, tap, tappity, tap, tap,* spider in clogs dancing, *tap, tap.* A smile flushed across the girl's face, making her cheeks rosy. "It's here."

Only then did Luce look away from McCoist. To see that long line of digits. All those zeroes.

When she looked back, he was there, standing behind McCoist. And the rest of them.

65

Mr Callaghan, DCI McCoist here.

Ye goat news?

I do indeed.

So?

I know who killed your brother.

...Good. Fuckin finally. Ye caught thum?

Not yet. I was wondering if there was somebody who might be interested in a word with them first.

How?

I think you know what I mean.

Av no fuckin clue wit yer oan aboot.

There are other interested parties. Ones who would maybe rather punish the perpetrators themselves.

...

I just need to know who to speak to.

Mr Belov, DCI McCoist here.

Again.

Again, aye. Because the last time we spoke you gave me a lot of horse shite and now it's time for you to shovel it up.

I'm sorry, Inspector—

Chief Inspector.

Chief Inspector, yes. Of course. But I don't know what you're talking about.

I'm talking about you and Euan Callaghan and his brother.

I don't know who—

His dead brother. You helped arrange a deal with a Russian criminal organisation. It went badly, and I'll bet they weren't happy about that. Fortunately, I can set everything right.

...

I just need to know who to speak to.

. . .

"You're not the first polis to set foot on this auld tub, but you are the first one of them I've been keen to actually talk to." If McCoist had to guess where the man came from based on his voice alone, she would have said Riddrie rather than Russia. Only the name, Demyan Sigarev, gave the game away.

(A name Callaghan the younger and Belov had both supplied independently—each of them conduits, willing or otherwise, between Ruaridh Callaghan's firm and the Russian mafia, crypto going one way, who-the-fuck-knew coming the other.)

Sigarev's narrowboat, for instance, was not the diamond-encrusted, platinum-plated, vodka-luge-and-cocaine-blizzard kind of place she associated with Russian oligarchs and mobsters. There was a monied elegance to it, sure, even a certain decadence, but not in a brash way. His suit was old-fashioned tailoring, well made for the shape of his body, surely extortionate but would last a lifetime if looked after. The assistant/butler who offered her a beverage was a well-heeled killer. Handsome too. All a bit genteel, kind of made McCoist want to throw up. That could also just be the vertigo from the tightrope she was walking though, the crocodiles in the paddling pool thirty feet below. There was nobody—bent polis, Glesga gangsters, Russian mafia—she was not about to fuck over. Things needed to go right.

"I'm honoured, Mr Sigarev."

"You don't have the right face for polite lies, missus. Doesn't hide sarcasm very well at all."

"Detective Chief Inspector."

"That's more like it."

"So say it then."

He grinned and said the words like they were dirty: "Detective Chief Inspector. I'm all yours. I'm listening."

"I'm gonna run through a scenario—I know it's true so don't give me any 'I don't know/it wasn't me' bullshit. I'm not here to arrest you."

"Wise."

McCoist felt the closeness of the walls, the low roof pressing down, the glass of ice water being offered to her by a man with hands big enough to snap her neck like the stalk of a dandelion. A steadying breath, then she told him what she knew about the deal with the crypto, and the hit against Callaghan that botched said deal, and finished with: "I know who did it."

Sigarev's face remained placid throughout. "Go and lock them up then. You're the polis, no?"

Heat needled her back, blushed on her face. She prayed he couldn't see it. The silence spooled out; she resisted the temptation to take a swally from her glass.

"…OK, so I guess my next question is: what are you wanting from me? What do you think I could, or would, give you?"

"You can Brando this out all you want but I know you've got other people trying to find out, trying to get hold of that money. I'm not the first coming to you making promises, am I?"

A slight shift in his posture, indicated by the scuffing movement of his jacket collar against his neck—a reaction. "I'll ask you again, Detective Chief Inspector: what do you want?"

"The people who took the money are holding friends of mine to ransom. You help me free my friends, you get your crypto and all the retribution you see fit to give."

"Retribution? For me or for you? I don't know these people. It's your friends they're threatening."

"But you do. It's your face they lied to. And it's your bosses they ripped off…"

He sniffed. "…McGuinn and Branson. The Burds ae Prey, eh?"

A smile appeared and vanished like a snake's flicking tongue. "I've been in Scotland a long time now. I love this country. I really do. It's my home. My true home. But you people, you have this funny idea of yourselves. This image: 'We are the underdogs.' We fight but the odds are insurmountable. It's convenient. It stops you from having to properly try, saves you from the disappointment of failure. That's the true nature of the Scots. You are ashamed of your own voices. I don't think I know of any other peoples who are so embarrassed by seeing themselves." He huffed. "It's nice to see a crew with a bit of vision, ambition, but if they want to play with the big boys..."

66

"Evrycunt, weapons at your feet," Sigarev said. His bally-clad lackies backed him up, gunsights on Luce, Hannah and their own lackies. "Miss Branson, did you manage to sniff out the guilty party yet? I was so looking forward to hearing from you again."

Luce's face was chalk, muscles spasming in a confused, stricken gurn.

"You fuckin—" Hannah was cut off by the gun barrel pressing against her cheek. She swatted it away, twisting round to throw a punch—

"NO!"

Lightning struck, thunder clapped, Hannah shrieked and the spendy-looking revolver in Sigarev's hand smoked.

"Hannah!"

"Don't move!" He had to shout now to be heard above all the damaged eardrums in the room. The cotton-wool effect took the edge off Hannah's bleating. Her knee was in bits, blood weeping from a hole in her jeans.

One of Sigarev's men had the key to the cage and was cutting Fran, Neil and Lottie free from their bonds. The lads had the look of a discarded fish supper that had been panned against a shop window on a Saturday night. "My car's outside," McCoist said. "Let's go."

They didn't have to be told again—Neil holding Fran up as he limped as quick as he could for the door.

"McCoist!" Lottie's voice, high, whining. "McCoist! Tell thum it wisnae me! A didnae know! A didnae know! Tell thum!"

McCoist turned to face her. Lottie's eyes were a poison mixture of pleading and pure hate. McCoist shook her head.

A masked man reached for Lottie—

She whipped a knife out, slicing it through the soldier's forearm. He yelped and dropped his weapon. Before anyone else could get a clean shot on her she had charged McCoist, had the scruff of her shirt in one hand, knife in the other, its point a baw-hair from McCoist's throat. "Tell thum. TELL THUM! A hud nothin tae dae wae it!"

The guns had found Lottie now, but McCoist was in the splash zone, the collateral damage zone, the oops-I-missed-and-hit-the-other-one-by-accident zone. Fury and fear made her high, made her nauseous. Her words squeezed out like dregs from a rolled-up toothpaste tube: "I don't care. I made this mistake before. I want you gone now."

Lottie's puffy lips pulled back from her teeth, helpless terror fighting with her anger.

"I know it's you who's been sending the messages, threatening me, threatening my family. And after what I did for you—"

"Ye killt ma husband!"

Desperate hurt in her eyes, but McCoist was numb. The usual guilt didn't surface, nor was she shocked by Lottie's words. So she knew. It made sense, why she was sending the messages, a pathetic kind of revenge though it was. McCoist had suspected as much when Tess sent the picture… "He was a fucking monster. He needed put down."

"Fuck you!"

"No, fuck you. Get her off me, Sigarev."

"Ye cannae!" she cried. "Ye cannae. Waeoot me…" Tears ran into her lips which contorted in a shoogly smile. "Somebdy get ma phone! A need tae show ye somehin, Ally."

"Is it a dick pic from my ex-husband, by any chance? I know you've been seeing him." The picture Tess had sent her the night Neil went missing was of her dad having a coffee with the new woman in his life, the one he was still keeping a secret from his kids. The one he must have met at the gym, with the gymnast's muscles and the crop tops and the leggings so tight you could take a print of her fanny through them. Lottie McGuinn. "Trying to worm your way in..."

She choked out a laugh. Why was the bitch laughing?

"Sadly no—a bet it's a lovely wee hing an aw." She let go of McCoist's collar to take her phone. The goon squad closed in but McCoist held up her hand to stay them. Her guts were slithering like eels in Vaseline. Something wrong, very wrong.

Lottie held her phone out for her to see. It was a video. Purple car in an anonymous car park. A Golf with a shitey, plastic-looking body-kit modification and spoiler. A lad in a hood approached the car.

McCoist's heart throbbed in her neck, close to the tip of the knife still held there.

The driver's side window slid down—

Cam.

Cam stuck his hand out the window to greet the hoody. There was a handshake to hide the first exchange, then the money was dropped in the window.

67

It was an old memory, because his maw and da were still together. They'd been to the beach at Troon. They had a kite with them, and coins for the arcades, and they'd eaten ice cream. But something had gone wrong. Fran remembered the stiff wind whipping in off the sea—maybe it had something to do with that but he couldn't remember. But something had gone wrong and they travelled back to the flat in silence. He sat in his booster seat behind his da, who was driving, and his maw stared out her window the whole time. The air was heavy, even Fran had to be silent, because it was suffocating him, words wouldn't have come out even if he'd tried.

He was reliving it now, McCoist and McGuinn in the front seats, words unspoken crackling between them, a heavier-than-air vapour of resentment squeezing all the oxygen out.

Fucking hell, Neil was about to say something. Fran jabbed his da in the arm, vigorously shook his head and pulled his lips tight—*zip it*. McCoist's eyes flashed at Fran in the rear-view and he made himself as small as possible in his seat, a chastised schoolboy. And he was content to be the brown-nose for now. The nightmare was finally fucking over. Fuck it, who cared what he did next? If he couldn't run he could clean toilets. Who gave a fuck? He'd be alive! Nothing was worth what he'd been through in the last week. Surely to fuck not.

McCoist pulled up at the BP garage on Pollokshaws Road. "Can you walk from here?"

Neil heard it as a question. "Actually, the boay's goat a sare knee an—"

"Here's fine, cheers." Fran tugged at the door handle.

"Wait." The poliswummin turned in her seat to face them both. "I don't want yous in my car again. Ever. All right?"

"Fine by us; cheers fir evryhin!"

The Golf tore off, its wee-sack engine splitting the night air, pissing off every cunt all down the street trying to sleep.

"Am starvin," Neil said. "A need somehin proper tae eat."

"Yer pumpin the table leg at this oor, could see if the garage has any sannies."

"As lang it's no fuckin crisps."

They managed to swag themselves a couple of yellow-sticker wraps and a twin packet of pork pies—things were looking up already—and washed them down with swigs of Irn-Bru as they shambled towards Neil's flat in Govanhill, a short walk severely lengthened by Fran's fuckt knees and double-fuckt left knee which the Goth lad had nailed him in with the club.

"Am hinkin it's oer," Fran said.

"A fuckin hope so, son. Am gonnae huv a fuckin heart attack, any mare ae this cops-an-robbers shite."

"A meant the runnin." Fran sniffed, took a big skoof of tingly Bru. "Ma career."

"Wull get ye tae the hoaspital in the mornin, get a look at it. Wull say ye fell or somehin."

"It's no just that…" They stopped, Fran holding himself up against the black railing which ran around the perimeter of Queen's Park. "A don't know if a can keep oan daein it. The physio's gonnae take fuckin firever, an it's excruciatin, man, frustratin, a don't… An a don't want tae take anyhin any mare, that…" He couldn't look at Neil, shame feeling a lot like indigestion caused by eating a pork pie in two bites and washing it down with a can of Bru. "A cannae dae it."

Neil lifted his son's arm around his neck, took his weight and they continued on down the street.

"That's fine, son. Witever ye want, yel make it work, a know ye will."

Fran remembered his recent dedication to toilet cleaning and this time felt miserable. It wouldn't do. "At least I'm alive" doesn't keep someone sustained for long. Running was his whole world, his pride, his identity, his source of confidence, his peace. He'd ruined it. Even before reaching out to Callaghan he'd ruined it with the doping. He'd let Neil talk him into that, when he was desperate, when what he really needed from someone was strength. Part of Fran felt bad thinking it, because Neil had certainly been trying hard these past few days, had went through hell for him, but for most of Fran's life he'd been flaky at best. His maw wasn't wrong about everything.

An idea struck him. "Wit aboot, like, coachin? Fir weans in the scheme. Gee them somehin tae dae, a bit ae guidance, a bit ae discipline." Running had got Fran out of a criminal life once (and briefly back into it, but you needed to focus on the positives—*a negative mindset won't get you anywhere*), maybe it could work for others.

"Aw aye, ye could stert a charity. Nice wee tax write-aff that."

"*Da.*"

68

McCoist headed for the river, crossed the Kingston Bridge, aiming for the West End. The video played on repeat in her head—the window sliding down, Cam behind it, the handshake badly concealing the transfer. "What have you got him selling?" The first words said between them since McCoist had taken Lottie from the warehouse, leaving the rest of the Burds ae Prey to their fate. McCoist doubted any parts of them would turn up—a nauseating thought that would surely haunt her as much as Paulo's exploding head or Si's muffled screams as he was dragged away.

"Ye want tae know wit a possession charge wid get him?"

McCoist kept her eyes fixed on the road, knowing if she looked at that woman's face she might just yank the steering wheel left and force the car into a wall. The fucking conniving bitch. Recruiting her son. Her fucking son! He was just a wee boy. How could he be so fucking stupid? Just a boy. How had she not noticed? The "Saturday" job, the hours in the cafe that surely didn't add up to the trainers and clothes he was wearing, the car he'd bought in cash that was supposed to be sitting in the driveway waiting for him to pass his test. *You're a fucking eejit, a fucking moron. And you didn't notice because you were barely paying attention, because you barely see them, because you thought you could keep them safe by staying away.*

BUT HOW COULD HE BE SO FUCKING STUPID?! She'd kill him, she'd wring his neck until it was a strand of spaghetti. She'd squeeze him in a hug until they couldn't be separated. Dealing. Her own son. Her wee boy. Cam had always been so shy compared to Tess. Never any trouble. He cried every day for a month when he started primary school. He cried when he started secondary too. That was only, what, five years ago? He couldn't have changed so fast. This woman had tricked him. Obviously. She was a fucking witch.

McCoist rapid-replayed her recent times with her son—there weren't many. What did they talk about? He communicated in a series of grunts, but that was teenage boys, wasn't it? They were all like that. *Did Tess know?*

She recalled reading through Francesco Forbes's files, imagining his mother's horror at finding out her teenage son was punting gear and running with gangsters, and judging her too—*What a terrible, Jeremy Kyle-class of parent.* McCoist had watched helpless tears fall down Corrina's face and felt sorry for her, but at the same time a weaselly part of her was thinking, *This is your fault.*

Mark had to take his fair share of the derry here, didn't he? The boy was under his roof most of the time. How had he missed this? Too busy running about with his new burd—the gangster wummin who'd turned their son into a drug mule.

She pictured the confrontation with Cam, the words she would scream at him, the ones he would scream back, righteous, and justified.

The engine thumped, car shuddering, as McCoist braked hard for a turn and shifted down carelessly. "You're going to fix this," she said. "I've let you live and you will get him out of your operation. And then you will shut it down forever."

"Yer no in the position tae make demands." Lottie's voice was haughty for someone whose face was streaked in mascara, dried snot on her upper lip. "Wit dye hink the folk Cammy works wae wid dae if they foond oot his maw wis a polis?"

Cammy—how long had he been working for her? How could he be so fucking stupid?! Knives twisted in her gut—how could he do this to *me*?

"You think you're safe now?" McCoist hissed. Her voice rose up from deep in her belly. "You are not safe. You do as I say or I will make your children orphans. It's true, I killed Paulo. I did it to save someone's life. I had to. And the world is a better place for it."

Tough talk, but McCoist was too strung out to question whether she really believed that or not. Certainly her failing body, collapsing and hallucinating at odd times, still felt guilty, even if her mind could rationalise it. And there were several fresh bodies tonight to add to the list. Bad guys, though. Criminals. Probably had families, some of them. Worth the cost. Right? Did it balance out? Impossible to say, but she knew she'd do anything to protect her kids. Anything.

"Don't threaten me. Yer askin favours, no makin demands."

"Stupid cow," McCoist snarled. "Luce was right. You're not cut out for this. Keep your salons and your Avon ladies, have a normal life. A long life."

"Ye don't know me."

"And I don't want to get to know you. You get Cam out of whatever it is you've involved him in, and as long as you go back to being a civvie, we'll have no reason to keep company. Never have to cross paths again. I forget your face and you forget mine."

Christ, she was tired. Her adrenal glands were pumping out dust. The full pain of her face was coming back into focus. The need to get hold of Cam, hear his voice, seized her. But he'd be in his bed. What use was waking him up in the night to talk about this? She couldn't trust herself not to scream at him and history said that would not help. This wasn't "tidy your room"/"do your homework". What would she say? How to even begin? Her heart ached—her wee boy. All her efforts to separate work from personal, keep her home life, her family from being tainted by this other world she inhabited, useless. She'd pushed her children away, kept her distance, and for what?

"Naw."

"What?"

"Naw. Fair dos, ye came through fir us the night. So al back aff yer boay, yer faimly, we can sort that aw oot, but this isnae the end. Wur linked, the two ae us. Huv bin er since ye pullt the trigger oan Paul."

"Get fucked. You're a mad boot."

Lottie burst into a drunken laugh. It was a nasty thing, the kind of laughter that is only ever directed *at* someone. School corridors rang with it. Apprentices cowered under its onslaught. "A know ye are but wit am a?"

McCoist gripped the wheel like it was Lottie's neck. No, she couldn't wait. It was like worms in her belly. They didn't need to talk about it now, but she needed to hear his voice. She slammed the brake and bumped up on the kerb—making Lottie squeal. *Ha!*

Called Cam.

Ringing.

Ringing.

Ringing.

"You have reached Vodafone voicemail—"

Again.

"You have reached—"

Didn't mean anything. It was like she thought. He was asleep. Had his phone switched off. Teenagers switch their phones off, right? Or maybe it was on silent. McCoist never put her phone on silent when she slept because of work. But normal people did, she was sure.

"Ye know, sometimes a hink ma girruls see ma name poap up oan their phones an just don't hit answer."

"Shut your flap."

Maybe she could text him. Would that do any good? Maybe that bint was right, he just didn't want to speak to her. But she could leave him a message—*Reply and let me know you're OK*. Then sit and stare at the ticks, willing them to turn blue. She rang again and again got the answer machine—leaving a voicemail would be even more useless than the text. Because he was asleep, that was all. Asleep in his bed, where he should be. Not in some shady car park handing out baggies of snap, crackle and pop. That sick, dirty ache in her heart again—her wee boy doing this, knowing these things. No, she even had his car. He must be home. Sleeping. She was being irrational, amped up from everything that had happened at the warehouse and the days before, nerves like burning white filaments.

She needed to hear his voice.

"Let me try." There was a hint of a smile on Lottie's face and every fibre of McCoist's being wanted to paste her one. She could almost feel the woman's teeth against the palm of her hand. "A could ring roon an see." Lottie held her own phone out. She was waiting for McCoist to say yes, to give her the go-ahead. *Yes, do me this favour.*

McCoist managed a nod, and it took all her strength, a fight against rigid muscles to do it. No chance she'd be getting a "please".

Lottie tapped away at the screen. "A few contacts tae clear oot noo hanks tae yersel," she murmured. McCoist imagined grabbing Lottie by her hair—two fistfuls—and slamming her face into the dash, over and over, decorating the glovebox with her nose and teeth. "Who's deed an who can a still trust, eh?" McCoist made do with strangling the steering wheel again.

Lottie's phone rang and McCoist jumped as if she'd had another jolt from the taser.

"Awright?"

McCoist couldn't make out what the voice on the other end was saying.

"Aye, a fuckin shitshow... No yet... Caw Rambo an Maxwell, we need tae get thegether, it's a fuckin... aye. Aye. Listen, fore ye go, dye know if that boay Cammy's aboot somewhere the night?"

Cammy. They never called him Cammy. Always Cam. It's like there was this whole other person she knew nothing about.

"Aye, right, cheers, will do. See ye soon." Lottie hung up, went straight back to tapping on her phone. Didn't look round. Didn't say a word. She wanted McCoist to ask, to plead—*What did they say?*—but McCoist wouldn't give the twisted cow the satisfaction.

"What did they say?"

Lottie just smiled, held the phone up to her ear again, faint sound of ringing. "Lorna, hen... Am awright, cheers, wis just wantin tae know if the new boay is oot somewhere fir us the night..."

McCoist could feel the pulse in her neck, a big fat artery thumping, choking her.

The girl's voice—Lorna—squeaked from the other end of the line, going on and on interminably. Lottie caught McCoist's eye and made a yapping motion with her hand. Finally: "Awright, cheers hen, speak soon."

"Well?"

"She says tae ask Wee Minty—but he's often up at the warehoose, so... Al try anyway." She was enjoying this, McCoist could see it on her rancid face. She scrolled to another contact and rang. The tinny artificial bells trilled, McCoist's heart getting faster with every peal...

"Minty, son! Ye made it oot then...?" Something changed in Lottie's expression. A slight clench of the jaw. "A see... Aye... Well, chicken soup will dae ye some good... Uh huh..." She switched the phone to her right ear, turned towards the passenger window, giving McCoist her back. Voice dropped: "Huv ye heard fae him, but?"

McCoist's guts were a river of ice water; her throat a dry bed. Her heart rattled so fast and hard she could see it beating through her top. Static fizzed at the edges of her vision. Adrenaline vertigo seized her.

Lottie took a millennium to turn back, to face her. And when she did, the bitchy, cat-torturing-a-mouse glee was gone.

"What?" McCoist's voice crackled like crispy, dead leaves.

Lottie's eyes darted around the car before coming back to McCoist, a hardness forced back into them.

"WHAT?!"

"Minty wis, wis sposed tae be up... up there, ye know. Luce hud telt him he wis oan lookout duty but..." There was a big, yawning void after the "but" and McCoist tumbled in. *But*... "But he wisnae feelin well so..." *So*... "He asked yer boay tae cover fir him."

69

"GET! OUT!"

Lottie did as she was told, meek at first, eyes betraying panic, horror, then straightened herself out, jutted her jaw and sneered: "Let us know where tae send the flowers." Slammed the door.

McCoist stomped the accelerator. The engine roared. The tyres spun, stinking black smoke—handbrake still on. McCoist slammed the lever down and the car lunged forward, the droopy body mods hanging off the chassis scraping down the kerb as the car careened into the middle of the road.

McCoist spun the wheel like a ship's captain, throwing the car round in a wild burly, the back end dunting a parked motor. Then she screamed forwards.

Lottie had no time to move. Caught in the headlights. She folded onto the bonnet, head cracking the windscreen, then tumbled off to the side.

McCoist felt the rear tyre hump over something small.

A jet of screenwash and swish of the wiper blade took the blood off the window but the small spider's web of shattered glass remained in the corner. McCoist did this with the attention she'd give to a fly smear or bird keech. Her mind was entirely on the House of Blusher. It rose from the ground in front of her as she flew south towards it in Cam's hideous boy-racer-mobile.

The guns were on her as soon as she stepped from the motor. She didn't feel the probing glare of the muzzles this time. Didn't feel anything except the nausea.

She had done this. She had gone to Sigarev, she had brought him here. She knew there would be violence. She knew there would be death.

But she didn't know Cam was here—couldn't know. Couldn't know what Lottie had done. No way. Unless she had—what? Paid more attention? Been in the same room as her kids for longer than ten minutes this month? And the two weekends the month before. And was it one or two weekends the month before that? Or had she been caught up in work? But caught up wasn't right. It had been deliberate. To keep them away. To keep them safe. From what her life had become, from her. *What will they think when they find out? Will they still love you?*

Oh, Cam. Cam, Cam, Cam, no.

The guard didn't stand in her way as she pushed through the door but stayed close at her back. The smell—it was like at the shopping centre, the Callaghan hit. Blood and waste. McCoist tasted whitey in the back of her throat. All the fluids in her body had been turned to frothing acid.

Masks and armour were off now. The men had changed into plastic coveralls and overshoes. They looked like SOCOs—again, echoes of the shopping centre. Hit squad-turned-clean-up crew. Two of them were dragging a corpse, a foot each, the thing moving across the concrete floor too easily, sliding on something. *Too big, that one was too big to be… right?* She recalled the last time she saw Cam, as he passed by his da in the doorway and she'd been struck by how tall and broad he suddenly seemed.

"Detective McCoist!" Even Sigarev had stripped down—presumably, his clothes would need torched too. They weren't fucking about. "Didn't think I'd be seeing you again so soon."

She had to drag the words up from under the bile simmering inside her. "I need to see."

"Sorry?"

"Them."

The two dragging the corpse came to a stop, the body lined up with others on a blue tarp which was folded over them, only their trainers visible. Scabby gutties on this one, a pair of Timbies on that one. *What was Cam wearing these days? You should know.*

"I need to see the bodies." She kept her voice steady, business, though her legs trembled and threatened to disintegrate.

"I think, detective, the less you know the b—"

"Is this all of them?" She moved closer though every muscle protested. Like the last mile of a marathon, everything was shutting down but she pushed forward to the end, something more than physical moving her on.

One of the paper suits who she now recognised as Sigarev's butler/bodyguard nodded to his boss. He posed the question with his eyes and Sigarev shrugged, made a jerking motion with his thumb—whatever, why not.

The bodyguard took a corner of the tarp…

Fuck, what if he's there? What if—what if he's one of those? What if he's lying there among them? Ready to be cleaned away. Ready to be chopped and torched or melted down to his oils, the bones pulverised, ground to dust. Not my boy, not—

…and pulled it back with a whooshing rustle.

The smell unfurled in a wave, even more intense than before. McCoist cowkt, bile rising in her throat, her eyes blurring with stinging tears. She closed them. Forced them open, everything unclear.

A row of people. Pale faces, veiny hands. Blood congealed on some of them like the crust on a ketchup bottle.

"Everything OK, Chief Inspector?" A voice, someone's voice, far away beyond the rushing of her own blood, the drumming of her heart. Sweat prickled under her clothes, heat steamed from under her collar, making her cheeks pink. Then it was like she wasn't inside her body any more at all, that she had risen above it, left it beneath to fall with the others. *Please to fuck, God, no…* She forced herself to look.

And her prayer was answered.

70

She found him—tracing her way to Mark's—his hood up, shoulders hunched, bent a little forward as if battling the wind, powering up the street quick march. Even from the back, something about the way he held himself told her, then his head turned at the sound of the purple motor, a half-moon of his face visible from under the hood.

She pulled over and for a second she thought he might run from her—the fear was on his face, the kind she'd seen on many young lads caught up in something way over their heads. And that was most of them—the meat and potatoes of this world, her job. Instead, he ran towards her.

The door was only just shut when the crying started. Him first. Just a shine in the eye, a trickle, then the big, shaky, wheezy sobs. She held him, her arms not going as far round as they used to. McCoist's head was buried in his shoulder, he was that much taller now. He smelt of sweat and Right Guard—he used that spray-snowy stuff like fire retardant from those big tins that looked like air freshener. Lines of it were always stained all over his clothes. Especially the all-black gym gear he favoured these days, whether he was at the gym or not.

Words formed and didn't come out—*Don't you ever do that to me again.* Words she'd said before, to a toddler wandered off at the shop. *I was scared. So scared. What if I lost you for good?*

"I'm sorry," he keened.

"Me too." She tousled his hair with a rough hand. The lecture could wait—and she knew she'd have to give up something of her own mistakes to make it stick (*What will they think when they find out? Will they still love you?*), but first, she needed to get rid of this car.

EPILOGUE

1

It was a good drive, spray of dew following the ball up into the blinding morning sun, *thwip* through the crisp air. His back twinged something awful but, and he had to make an effort not to make a noise or press his hand to the offending vertebrae.

"Nice one."

"Wasn't bad."

"You've been getting in some practice."

Devlin ignored the barb. *Fat prick.* Devlin was indeed tending the garden for good now—early retirement due to personal reasons—but the chief constable would soon be under it, the man a blubbery ventricle that could explode at any minute. His cheeks were already red, forehead slicked with sweat, and they were only on the third hole. "I get out when I can."

"How's Linda doing?"

"Good days and bad days." Stock answer. She was suffering. Every day was the same and would be until she eventually passed. There would be no big move now, but she was as comfortable as she could be in their current situation, Devlin had seen to that over the years, and his pension was very decent despite stopping short of full service, which helped too.

"Ach, I guess that's…" He trailed off, teeing up with a big huff as he bent over to the ground, hydraulic hiss as he raised himself back up.

"Best we can hope for, aye."

The chief lined up his shot, drawing his club backwards and forwards a few times, shifting his weight between his feet, shuffling, readying himself; Devlin imagined his own club swinging down onto the bulge of pink skin bursting out between the bottom of the chief's cap and the top of his collar.

Crack! The drive sliced towards the trees. "Fucksake!" Sound of the ball chipping tree bark. The chief turned his club upside down and examined its head. "I could do with spending more time on the course myself. Barely out the office at the moment."

"Aye?"

"One bloody headache after the other. And your protégée isn't exactly helping, Roy."

"She causing trouble again?"

"Always."

"She's a bit like that, unfortunately."

"Too fucking right she is. Like a fucking haemorrhoid with an angry face drawn on it." The chief re-socked his driver and slid it back into his bag, slung it over his shoulder.

"Give her time."

"I don't know why you, of all people, are defending her."

"I'm not. I'm just… interested, I guess."

"You want to shag her?"

Devlin didn't dignify that with a no, let his face tell the chief constable he'd gone too far, he wasn't his fucking boss any more and he knew enough that the man should show him some deference now. "I want to see how she handles it."

"What?"

"What's coming to her."

The chief put his bag back down with a clink. "You know something you want to tell me about?"

Devlin shrugged. "There's always something; nature of the job."

"Scuse me, boays! Startin early the day eh?" A lad in a bright-red jacket, walkie-talkie in his belt, approached. "It's just tae collect yer fees—"

The chief had a twenty ready, stuffed it into the boy's hand. "You didn't see us, son."

2

There would be a holiday. She'd decided. Her and the twins. Somewhere in the Canaries, maybe. Or Turkey. A place where it was still warm in the winter. She'd never taken them abroad by herself before. It was always Mark and the grandparents who did that sort of thing. The last trip McCoist had taken them on had been to Blackpool and, when she counted it up, that was five years ago. Oh, how the sand escapes the egg timer. Fucking hell. She pictured loungers by the pool, books and sunnies, a nice dinner outside the resort at some local place, a bit of wine, even a glass for Tess and Cam.

Things had gone better with Cam than she'd hoped they would. She put that down to her own monumental efforts not to go in like a bulldozer. Good job, drug dealer's maw! It had started with selling roids to classmates, moved up to a bit of weed and even some coke. But with Lottie McGuinn out of action, her Burds ae Prey hacked down at the knees by the Russians, the spoils of their carcasses divided, it wasn't too hard to extricate him. Luckily, in all the chaos of that time, McCoist hadn't bothered sorting the insurance or tax on his car as she'd said she would, so they just dumped it under the Kingston Bridge and reported it stolen. By the time it was discovered, it had been used as shelter and toilet and partially burnt out. A little blood on the windscreen wouldn't mean much.

There was no CCTV of Lottie's hit-and-run, and door-to-door came up with nothing useful. Oh, Lottie. McCoist had been to see her. One of her girls—the younger one—was asleep, crooked and stiff in an armchair by the bed. This, more than the sight of all the tubes and wires, the thick gauze cap, had stirred the tendrils of guilt inside McCoist. *I will make your children orphans*, she'd said. But she hadn't done the full job in the end. Instead, she'd left them in this limbo. Then she recalled her return to the warehouse and the corpse identification parade, wishing and praying and promising her life away if only one of them was not her son. No, this is what you get, she thought. This is the Life. This is Justice. Devlin had been right about that. Or "correct", even. "Right" was something harder to define.

McCoist sat in his chair, in his office, now her chair, her office. When it was back from the engraver's, her nameplate—Detective Superintendent Alison McCoist—would sit on his desk. Her desk. Inbox piled high. She'd started making cappuccinos with the coffee machine he'd left to her. Real beans, real milk, no sugar. It was good. She was getting a taste for it, detecting the notes of chocolate and caramel on her tongue. Decent stuff, actually.

Beyond the door, her squad, The Grey-Team, tapped away at computers, made calls, sifted and searched and ground through cases. She'd had a word with Mal about his manky cardigans; he now had a five-day cycle of Next packaged shirts but stopped short of wearing a tie. As planned, before handing it over, she'd also had him load that crypto key USB with more spyware than a song downloaded from LimeWire and the results had been passed up the chain to the NCA, among others. If Demyan Sigarev was smart, he'd be leaving his precious Scotland behind. And soon. She imagined him escaping down the canal in his narrowboat, a couple of uniforms giving chase in a pedalo.

On her computer, the Expedia and TripAdvisor tabs on the browser were a few squashed among twenty or so others. Plenty to get on with, but the holiday would happen. It had to happen. She couldn't deal with another shock like seeing Cam in that video. She needed to know her children.

It was time to fix the broken promises.

The mechanic wedged the tyre into the rim, sweat and grease making his palms slick on the handle of the tyre lever, grazed knuckles against rubber.

"You're a hard man to find."

"Fuck!" His hands slipped; the lever pinged up into the air, missed his face by an inch. *That voice*. He turned, heart bungee-jumping up and down. His mouth fell open, as if some divine being had appeared in front of him, engulfing the dingy, oil-stained garage in its fire, rather than a misery-faced woman in a bobbled duffel coat with a missing toggle. His brain reeled through shock, fear, anger and, finally, hope.

"Time to go home, Davey. Your family are waiting for you."

ACKNOWLEDGEMENTS

First and foremost, I want to thank my wife, Lisa McSorley, and our two wonderful children, to whom this book is dedicated: Elliot and Nina. Because of the three of you, I get to live the dream.

Thank you to my mum, Marion McDougall, for everything she's done for me and continues to do (but if you keep moving the books around in the shop they *are* going to ban you). And my brother, Stephen McSorley, and twin sister, Lyndsey McSorley—the ultra-marathon runner in the family—for their love and support. My family and friends have all, in some way, contributed their voices to these stories. Thank you.

I met my agent, Emily MacDonald, in 2020 through a tweet pitch event. I almost didn't bother tweeting, and that's a *Sliding Doors* moment I do not like to contemplate. None of this would have happened without Emily, her vision and her tireless support. I'm forever grateful!

They say it takes a village, and the village in this case is the wonderful Pushkin Vertigo: Daniel "Fancy Dan" Seton, Steven Cooper, Rima Rashid, Tom Martland, India Edwards, Alex Middleton and all who have worked on Ally McCoist over the past five years. You are all amazing!

(Which reminds me, special thanks to the real Ally McCoist for being cool about this, could have been a bit awkward otherwise.)

Mark Swan has created not only a great cover for this book but an amazing, eye-catching theme for the whole series. They look great on my shelf and will on yours too.

In 2024 I was awarded the Loch Long Crime Writing Residency at Cove Park. This is where I began writing the first draft of *Rat*

Race—in its beautiful, blissful surroundings—and without those two weeks to get stuck in, I would probably still be writing it.

Steven Cahill, Stuart Gillies, Neil Lancaster, Craig Thomson and Sarah Thomson all helped with matters of police procedure—any mistakes are, as always, my own, and this book is probably the wackiest, I'm sorry.

Since my first book was published in 2023, I've had the pleasure of meeting lots of fantastic authors, far too many to name here, but I want to give a special shout-out to my writing pals Cailean Steed, Chris Kelso, Frances Moloney, Mirri Glasson-Darling, Scott McNee and Martin Stewart.

And finally, you, the reader. Thank you for taking a chance on these books, giving them your time, and coming on this journey with me.

AVAILABLE AND COMING SOON FROM PUSHKIN VERTIGO

Jonathan Ames

You Were Never Really Here
A Man Named Doll
The Wheel of Doll

Simone Campos

Nothing Can Hurt You Now

Zijin Chen

Bad Kids

Maxine Mei-Fung Chung

The Eighth Girl

Candas Jane Dorsey

The Adventures of Isabel
What's the Matter with Mary Jane?

Margot Douaihy

Scorched Grace

Joey Hartstone

The Local

Seraina Kobler

Deep Dark Blue

Elizabeth Little

Pretty as a Picture

Jack Lutz

London in Black

Steven Maxwell

All Was Lost

Callum McSorley

Squeaky Clean
Paperboy

John Kåre Raake

The Ice

RV Raman

A Will to Kill
Grave Intentions
Praying Mantis

Paula Rodríguez

Urgent Matters

Nilanjana Roy

Black River

John Vercher

Three-Fifths
After the Lights Go Out

Emma Viskic

Resurrection Bay
And Fire Came Down
Darkness for Light
Those Who Perish

Yulia Yakovleva

Punishment of a Hunter
Death of the Red Rider